The Black Stranger
and Other
American Tales

The Works of Robert E. Howard

The Black Stranger and Other American Tales

Robert E. Howard

Edited and
with an introduction by
Steven Tompkins

University of Nebraska Press

LINCOLN

© 2005 by Robert E. Howard Properties, LLC.
Introduction © 2005 by the Board of Regents
of the University of Nebraska.
"The Black Stranger" © 1987 by Conan Properties International, LLC

Reprinted by permission of Del Rey /Ballantine
Books. Conan is a registered trademark of
Conan Properties International, LLC.

All rights reserved. Manufactured in the United
States of America.

Set in Fred Smeijers' Quadraat by Bob Reitz.
Designed by Richard Eckersley.

Printed and bound by Edwards Brothers, Inc.

♾

Library of Congress Cataloging-in-Publication Data
Howard, Robert Ervin, 1906–1936
The black stranger and other American tales /
Robert E. Howard ; edited and with an intro-
duction by Steven Tompkins.

p. cm. – (The works of Robert E. Howard)
ISBN 0-8032-2421-4 (hardcover : alk. paper) –
ISBN 0-8032-7353-3 (pbk.: alk. paper)
1. Horror tales, American. 2. Fantasy fiction,
American. I. Tompkins, Steven. II. Title.
PS3515.O842A6 2005 813'.52–dc22
2004019545

CONTENTS

STEVEN TOMPKINS

Introduction

America . . . has a powerful disintegrative effect on the white psyche. It is full of grinning, unappeased aboriginal demons, too, ghosts, and it persecutes the white men, like some Eumenides, until the white men give up their absolute whiteness. America is tense with latent violence and resistance.

— D. H. Lawrence, *Studies in Classic American Literature*

Welcome to the New World: the prehistory and history of North America as dreamed by Robert E. Howard (1906–36), whose characters brawled and brooded their way through the pages of *Weird Tales* and a variety of other 1920s and 1930s pulp magazines. Howard's gifts enabled him to lengthen perspective even as he heightened intensity, and this collection features stories that are linked not by a protagonist or a genre but by New World settings. The identification or idealization of America as Eden persists from Emerson's "Here is man in the Garden of Eden" through Fitzgerald's "fresh, green breast of the new world" in *The Great Gatsby*, but for Howard such dreams deepen and darken into nightmares commensurate with a continent as "lonely and gigantic and desolate as Eden, after man was cast forth." The Eden of these stories is trampled by invasion after invasion; its Adam is also Cain, and its serpents tempt with crimson fruit from which only the knowledge of evil and worse evil can be had. All that interrupts man's inhumanity to man is inhumanity's inhumanity to man.

Leslie Fiedler has noted that "the Celts, the Irish in particular, . . . from their home on the very verge of the West, have dreamed most variously and convincingly of that other place," a tradition that Howard, famously described as the "Last Celt," did his part to continue. As a Texan, he was predisposed to think in terms of empires; as a Celt, he could also discern, as does Turlogh Dubh O'Brien in "The Gods of Bal-Sagoth," that all empires were ultimately "dreams and ghosts and smoke." The dreams and ghosts and smoke waft from the pages Howard devoted to Conan's Hyborian

Age, Kull's Valusia, Solomon Kane's Africa, and Bran Mak Morn's Rome-resisting Caledonia. He resembles in this respect other American writers who made a place for themselves in fantasy by making up places: Poe's Ulalume, Baum's Oz, Burroughs's Barsoom, Cabell's Poictesme, Leiber's Nehwon, Anderson's Alfheim, LeGuin's Earthsea, and the Elder Earth through whose ruins Karl Edward Wagner's Kane stalks. But Howard also gradually wrote his way back to his own doorstep; by April of 1932 we find him informing H. P. Lovecraft that he was "trying to invest my native regions with spectral atmosphere," and being much too hard on one of the stories in this collection, "The Horror from the Mound," as "a feeble effort of the sort."

America had loomed as the Uttermost West of Howard's fantasy from the start. God's angry swordsman, Solomon Kane, learns "somewhat of stealth and woodcraft and strategy" from "the red Indians of the new lands." A farsighted wizard in the Bran Mak Morn story "Men of the Shadows" espies "red-skinned savages" who "roam the western lands, wandering o'er the valley of the Western River, befouling the entempled ramparts which the men of Lemuria reared in worship of the God of the Sea." And if we remind ourselves that America has been conflated with Atlantis almost as often as with Eden in the Western imagination, the Atlantean Kull begins to seem like a New World naïf constricted by the coils of the oldest of Old Worlds.

But what about Conan? Howard's best-known and often least-understood character is described by the heroic fantasy writer David C. Smith as "the archetypal American, full of gumption, restless, wandering, as cynical and knowledgeable, as predatory and deadly as an Indian fighter or gunslinger." Such a character logically deserved an American backdrop, and in the spring of 1936, when Howard was bringing it all back home with the unfinished but unforgettable American heroic fantasies "The Thunder-Rider" and "Nekht Semerkeht," Conan was no exception to the westering impulse. Replying to a fannish overture from P. Schuyler Miller on March 10, 1936, Howard confided that the Cimmerian had "even visited a nameless continent in the western hemisphere, and roamed among the islands adjacent to it."

Unfortunately, that adventure was never committed to paper, but we do have "The Black Stranger," the last and longest of the Pictish Wilderness stories in the Conan series. As the title of this collection implies, we hold the American-ness of "The Black Stranger" to be self-evident; the western edge of Pictland scarcely camouflages the eastern shore of North America. As we venture inland from Count Valenso's beachhead, we meet D. H. Lawrence's demons at their most grinning, unappeased, and aboriginal in a grandfather of all the old-growth forests that weighed and preyed on the minds of the European colonists in those first footholds of Plymouth, Jamestown, and St. Augustine.

The critic Alfred Kazin once described the Puritan enterprise as America's Middle Ages, and, indeed, the Puritans were the only Americans ever to dwell in a sword-and-sorcery universe. Later frontiersmen called Indians savages, primitives, or even vermin, but only the Puritans could employ an apocalyptic terminology – devils, demons, fiends – and believe every word. "The Black Stranger" (and its more acclaimed and anthologized predecessor "Beyond the Black River") are key texts in modern American fantasy because they recreate the literally be-wildered colonists' mindset described by Richard Slotkin in *Regeneration Through Violence*: "The eternal presence of the native people of the woods, dark of skin and seemingly dark of mind, mysterious, bloody, cruel, 'devil-worshipping:' to these must be added the sense of exile – the psychological anxieties attendant upon the tearing up of home roots for wide wandering outward in space and, apparently, backward in time."

For Belesa, the heroine of "The Black Stranger," "the world of cities and courts and gaiety [seem] not only thousands of miles but long ages away," and she is certain that the forests are "the logical hiding place for any evil thing, man or devil." The story's "black man" is on loan from classic American literature: "Art thou like the black man that haunts the forest round about us?" Hester Prynne asks Roger Chillingworth in *The Scarlet Letter*. Howard's story is full of hints that he had recently encountered Hawthorne's novel, whose crowd scenes are populated by "painted barbarians" and "rough-looking desperados from the Spanish Main." In many ways "The Black Stranger" is *The Scarlet Letter* after a sex change, a blood transfusion, and some cutlass lessons. Howard's fey girl child is all but cloned from Hawthorne's: Tina appears "with the light patter of small bare feet across the sand," while Pearl plays after "making bare her small white feet, pattering along the moist margin of the sea." Howard's "wild men of the sea" recall Hawthorne's "swarthy-cheeked wild men of the ocean," any of whom "might relinquish his calling, and become at once, if he chose, a man of probity and piety" – exactly the agenda of Howard's Zarono, with his elegant bows and a "tread as stately as if he trod the polished crystal floor of the Kordava royal court."

Conan, as Lawrence said of James Fenimore Cooper's Deerslayer, "seems to have been born under a hemlock tree out of a pine-cone." The early colonists triangulated themselves against both Europeans and Indians and became Americans by taking to the woods and taking them away from their previous owners. Mastery of woodcraft has served as shorthand for Americanization from the Leatherstocking Tales through movies like *Deliverance, Southern Comfort, First Blood, Red Dawn,* and, as an example of how not to survive, *The Blair Witch Project.* Conan, who is at home even on the hunting grounds of his age-old enemies, the Picts, is self-authenticating, and his cultural credentials as a Cimmerian, a white barbarian, are a way around what for so long was perceived as the problem of renegades and runaways who wanted to join Indians rather than beat them.

Rejected by *Weird Tales* in May of 1932, "Marchers of Valhalla" did not see print until 1972. Craig Edward Clifford has written that "Europeans trace themselves back into layer after layer after layer of previous civilizations; Texans go back into a vast unforgiving land, a timeless sun, a silence." Howard's "Marchers" goes back into that land, sun, and silence and recovers unsuspected layers by way of James Allison's yester-self, Hialmar, as when he and the other Æsir behold a heat-shimmery, chimerical anticipation of Cibola or Quivira: "Lurking in our minds had been the thought that it was a ghost city – one of the phantoms which had haunted us on our long march across the bitter dusty deserts to the west, where, in the burning skies we had seen mirrored, still lakes, bordered by palms, and winding rivers, and spacious cities, all of which vanished as we approached."

Discussing what he terms "Southwestern Gothic," Scott P. Sanders reminds us that "nowhere else in America do the crumbling walls of immense ruins look out from the deep shadows of caves. Nowhere else in America do stone towers mark the past tenure of an ancient civilization that has left those of us who remain uneasy successors to the land." One way to assuage that unease is to postulate even more ancient civilizations, and "Marchers" would have us believe that it is not a pre-Columbian but a pre-pre-Columbian episode. With its premature proto-Norsemen pitted against citified Skraelings, "Marchers" transplants the Vinland Saga from the Northeast to the Southwest. For want of longships, the Æsir endure a long walk, their trek brazenly appropriating the trans-Beringian epic of the peopling of the Americas from Siberian originals. The only "actual" Indians in the story appear from an unexpected direction: "the wayward, painted people of the islands," possibly the ancestors of the Caribs, who blacken the southern sea in their fleet of "skull-bedecked" war canoes.

Some readers have found it difficult to turn a blind eye to the emphatically blue eyes in "Marchers," and on the surface the story is as much of a Thirties keepsake as would be a menu from the *Hindenburg*. But the golden hair and azure gazes disguise an inner darkness: Howard's Æsir are peculiar wish-fulfillment figures at best, stunted and stinted as Conan never is, and at their frequent worst they become a meditation on the oldest and most terrible blue-eyed soul: "As we strode we clashed sword and shield in a crude thundering rhythm, and sang the slaying-song of Niord who ate the red smoking heart of Heimdul." "Aryans were not made to coop themselves in walls," Howard maintained to H. P. Lovecraft, and "Marchers" is a study of what befalls his fanciful Aryans within the walls of Khemu, with its necromancers, devil-worshippers, and "evil-eyed naked women" gliding "like dusky shadows among the purple gloom." The Khemuri, "a subject race, speaking a mongrel tongue," are pretenders to the throne of storied Lemuria, as were the Aztecs to that of the Toltecs, and the extent to which they are an echo-in-advance of the Aztecs (so often assigned the role of feathered serpent in the New World paradise) is clear if we consult Richard Slotkin: "At the end of the unslaked and savage desert, so like the wasteland of the Grail legends, they behold Mexico – great, white, castellated cities, heaped with greenery, floating in the midst of vast blue lakes. Within the enclosed luxuriant gardens of these enchanted cities live an exotic people, dressed in a fantastic garb of woven and many-colored feathers, intricately wrought gold, turquoise ornaments, and printed cotton. Yet these fair islands are rotten at the heart: within each towering white temple are chambers reeking of human blood from human sacrifice and human filth."

The Æsir chieftain Asgrimm is a Cortez with no gunpowder, warhounds, horses, pandemics, or cultic masquerades up his sleeve, and "Marchers" hurtles toward a premonition of the *noche triste* of July 1, 1520, when the people of Tenochtitlan became a nation-in-arms and nearly ended New Spain before it began. Resonances of another conquest are also at work in the story. The Texas writer closest in outlook to Howard is historian T. R. Fehrenbach, who has explored the "vast residue of violence left over from the making of Texas," and likened the Texans to "the Alemanni or the peoples who called themselves *Englisc*," who "in the process of entering, taking, and holding a territory . . . made themselves into a distinct tribe." If we read the Æsir as a sword-and-sorcery simplification of Texans at their deadliest and most driven, and the treacherous Khemuri as a combination of Aztec trappings and Mexican failings as seen unfairly through Texan eyes, we begin to realize that "Marchers of Valhalla" is a creation myth fit for a state that has spawned more mythology than some entire continents, a creation myth that, as is only to be expected with Howard, culminates in cataclysmic destruction.

"The Gods of Bal-Sagoth" provides a sanguinary twist on the Old World legends of the Isles of the Blest, the Hesperides, and Tir-nan-Og as Turlogh Dubh O'Brien, an outcast Gael who never loses sight of the skull beneath the skin, makes an unplanned landfall on Bal-Sagoth, an island-empire that has lingered too long. The premonitions of the conquistadorial epic to come are unmistakable, whether Quetzalcoatlan lore – "There is an old legend among this people – that men of iron will come out of the sea and the city of Bal-Sagoth will fall!" – or the vision vouchsafed to Turlogh and Athelstane, a reverie that can be glimpsed but never grasped: "Through the trees the warriors caught a glimmer, white and shimmery and apparently far away. There was an illusory impression of towering battlements, high in the air, with fleecy clouds hovering about them." The Irish axeman will not be the last European, stranded in "a strange land in a strange sea," to speculate that "mayhap Satan himself reigns here and it is the gate to Hell."

Howard wrote to August Derleth, May 9, 1936, that "I haven't written a weird story for nearly a year, though I've been contemplating one dealing with Coronado's expedition to the Staked Plains in 1541. A good theme if I can develop it." On the evidence of the two drafts of "Nekht Semerkeht" that survive, it was a very good theme, albeit one Howard denied himself the chance to develop fully. The errant conquistador Hernando de

Guzman, quixotic in appearance if otherwise grimly pragmatic, is much traveled in the realms of gold as a veteran of Pizarro's Peruvian depredations and Cortez's Mexican exploits but rich in experience rather than in retained loot. For de Guzman, Spain is "far away, a dream-like memory, a land of Cockaigne that had once been real, in the golden glow of youth and desire, but now had no more reality than a ghost-continent lost in a sea of mist," and he himself, for all his armored solidity, might as well be "a phantom, drifting futilely across a sleeping, indifferent land," his disorientation anticipating the comment of the historian Elliott West in his *The Contested Plains:* "When they looked at the land, the Spanish saw some trouble, but mostly they saw nothing at all."

It is to be regretted that "Nekht Semerkeht" as we have it dims and dwindles to a synopsis, but Howard's ability to telescope and streamline history is nowhere more dramatic than in the genuine war of the worlds with which the story opens. Nekht Semerkeht himself is an out-of-towner who does not quite manage to live up to his fantastic accessories, a silhouette that Howard would presumably have filled in and fleshed out in further drafts of the story. The richness here lies rather in the wealth of regional and historical detail (*tizwin*, Cajamarca, a *teocalla*, the Karankawas, a governing *tlacatecatl*), de Guzman's "blind black urge to live," and the enormities, equal parts Alexander of Macedon and Amadis of Gaul, that he has seen and committed: "the royal blood of Montezuma dripping from the parapets of Tenochtitlan – blood running ankle-deep in the plaza of Cajamarca, about the frantic feet of doomed Atahualpa."

Africans join Norsemen, Gaels, and conquistadors as intruders in the New World in "Black Vulmea's Vengeance," and it must be said not only of this story but also of "Black Canaan" and "Pigeons from Hell" that, although Howard's best work is timeless, he himself was not. He was a white Texan in a period when being one meant membership in a caste whose prerogatives and prejudices were unconstrained by the evolution of attitudes or the revolution in legal remedies achieved by the civil rights movement, which is to say that his vocabulary included what many of us might nominate as the ugliest word in American English. Fortunately for the sake of his fiction, Howard's worst outbursts were mostly confined to his letters, especially when he sought to out-nightrider the equally unenlightened H. P. Lovecraft. But there was another side to him, one that compulsively identified with underdogs (especially lupine underdogs) and for which all other color considerations were eclipsed by a detestation of the yellow streak that so often signifies cruelty. That part of Howard created his African-American heavyweight champion Ace Jessel and related Conan's axe-powered emancipation of black galley slaves in *The Hour of the Dragon*. In "Black Vulmea's Vengeance," Bigomba, the Cimarroon war-chief, is in the way but not necessarily in the wrong – he has reason for asserting that "the only devil is a white man" – nor should we overlook Howard's word choice when the Caucasians Vulmea and Wentyard lurk "like phantoms of murder."

In admiration or exasperation, the world continues to ponder the question that Hector St. John de Crevecouer first formulated in 1782: "What then is the American, this new man?" The answer, in "Black Vulmea's Vengeance," is Terence Vulmea, an Irish pirate who took over from Conan (to the extent that another character could) when Howard rewrote "The Black Stranger" as the semi-historical adventure "Swords of the Red Brotherhood," which also failed to sell. Vulmea comes into his own in "Vengeance," and his own is, like all revenger's tales, a kind of ghost story, in which he is haunted by having been hanged back in Galway by the Royal Navy's Wentyard. But as also occurred with Turlogh and Athelstane, the Old World quarrel of Gael and Saxon is overridden by the perils of the New World, not the least of which is the lordly snake, larger and hungrier than life, that lairs in the jungle-engulfed city. Has any other writer ever come close to Robert E. Howard's scrupulous compliance with the pronouncement, after the Fall in Eden, of ceaseless enmity between the seed of Eve and the seed of the serpent?

Other ghosts also threaten to appear in "Vengeance" but never quite do. Here the lost civilization is not dying, as are Khemu and Bal-Sagoth, but is already long dead; yet something new is being born too. The sea-thieves of piracy's Golden Age were amphibious frontiersmen on a waterworld that dissolved hierarchies, New World revolutionaries of sorts before there were New World revolutions. More roughhewn declarations of independence in the Americas preceded that which Thomas Jefferson authored by decades. "Your English king is no more to me than rotten driftwood," sneers Vulmea; could he but catch it afloat, he would sink the monarchy itself. On land Vulmea is a naturalized citizen of the wild, and having been schooled by North American Indians, he is better equipped to survive his South American predicament than Wentyard, who has much to learn and even more to unlearn.

The poet Kenneth Rexroth has argued that as literary devices Native Americans often play the parts of "nymphs and satyrs and dryads – the spirits of the places. They are our ecological link with our biota." In modern American fantasy, Indians serve the same function as do elves in northern European fantasies such as *The King of Elfland's Daughter* and *The Lord of the Rings*. They were here first and they were here *better*; Robert Frost's line from "The Gift Outright" – "The land was ours before we were the land's" – does not apply to them. "The Valley of the Lost" fascinates in this context because it opens another of Howard's temporal trapdoors, through which we plummet into an age of such unfathomable antiquity that even the Indians are not indigenes but invaders. Skeptical about how manifest Manifest Destiny actually was, Howard constantly poked and prodded the newness of the New World; in these stories there are always ruins beneath the ruins and ghosts before the ghosts.

"The Valley of the Lost" is an American cousin of "Worms of the Earth," and like the Roman occupiers of Britain in that masterpiece, the European conquerors of America are "a heavy-footed race," mercifully unaware for the most part that the ground beneath them shudders and seethes with secrets. The feud between the Reynolds clan and the McCrills is "a red obstacle in the way of progress and development, a savage retrogression" – in short, a Fall or a consequence of the primal Fall. Another downward journey, that of John Reynolds to the Inferno beneath Lost Valley, is foreshadowed by the "inferno of hate" raging in his heart. The collapse of what passes for civilization is paralleled by the descent into the deep places of the earth and even deeper potentialities for diabolism of the Old People. Howard's Southwest, like that of Cormac McCarthy in his harrowing *Blood Meridian*, is baked and blasted by hate as if by a second sun, and we learn with Reynolds that the elder race's "arsenal of death in strange and grisly forms" failed long ago to overcome "the blind ferocity" of their pre-Toltec dispossessors. The story is noteworthy for what we might borrow from Herman Melville's look at Hawthorne and call the "blackness ten times black" of its conclusion. The Old People need not be at the heels of "the last of the fighting Reynoldses," for they are now in his head: "The earth seemed hideously alive under his feet, the sun foul and blasphemous over his head. The light was sickly, yellowish and evil, and all things were polluted by the unholy knowledge locked in his skull, like hidden drums beating ceaselessly in the blackness beneath the hills."

In the same May 1936 letter in which he alluded to "Nekht Semerkeht," Howard sought to distance himself from a story that would appear in the next month's *Weird Tales*: "Ignore my forthcoming 'Black Canaan.' It started out as a good yarn, laid in the real Canaan, which lies between Tulip Creek and the Ouachita River in southwestern Arkansas, the homeland of the Howards, but I cut so much of the guts out of it, in response to editorial requirements, that in its published form it won't resemble the original theme, woven about the mysterious form of Kelly the Conjureman." Leading Howard experts now believe any evisceration that occurred was preemptive, that Howard cut in anticipation of, rather than in response to, editorial strictures. But the story remains what it intransigently is: a tour of what Richard Slotkin calls the South's "own unique internal frontiers, [beyond whose] borders lay a primitive world, peopled (for the white southerner) with nightmares of vengeful savagery and bloodlust or with fever dreams of forbidden eroticism." "Black Canaan" dispenses with the "or," combining the nightmare savagery and the fevered eroticism.

"Black Canaan" is almost as entitled to the title "Beyond the Black River" as is the Conan classic of that name, and riverine metaphors course through the story and the kernel from which it grew, "Kelly, the Conjure-Man": "In every community of whites and blacks, at least in the South, a deep, dark current flows forever, out of sight of the whites who but dimly suspect its existence. A dark current of colored folks' thoughts, deeds, ambitions and aspirations, like a river flowing unseen through the jungle." Howard was conflict-minded but also conflicted, and if the grandsires of Kirby Buckner and his compatriots were frontiersmen, they were also slaveholders whose rugged self-reliance relied upon coerced servitude. Buckner says of his "isolated, shut-mouthed breed" that they are "jealous of [their] seclusion and independence," but as we read on we see that the seclusion is also an incarceration. The whites are locked up in a private hell, whose demons are their families' former victims: "The fear of a black uprising lurked for ever in the depths of that forgotten back country; the very children absorbed it in their cradles." Is it possible that in some mysterious way the back country has been *remembered* as well as forgotten? Howard permits himself one reference to "antebellum days" and another to a blood-drenched revolt "back in '45," but the wider world, the outside authorities and the backdrop of Reconstruction are missing. Instead, the actors might almost be performing some time-lost dramatization of Lincoln's worst case scenario of retribution in his Second Inaugural: "until every drop of blood drawn by the lash shall be paid by another drawn with the sword, as was said three thousand years ago, so still it must be said, 'The judgments of the Lord are true and righteous altogether.'"

In this sense Saul Stark and the Bride of Damballah are debt collectors, avenging angels, and they dominate the story as they seek to dominate Canaan; in contrast, the white settlers merely react, at times with dismal predictability, as when the vigilantes are eager to loosen the tongue of the hapless Tope Sorely with the lash. Neither "Grimesville" as a town name nor Tope's surname requires much exegesis, but Saul Stark's monickers deserve our attention. Saul the warrior-king was Howard's favorite Old Testament figure, and the word "stark" and its variants mean "strong" in the Germanic languages. Stark is the "son of a Kongo witch-finder," but he hails from South Carolina, notorious as the state that was too small to be a country and too large to be an insane asylum, the epicenter of nullification and secession.

Sinuous and insinuating, the Bride of Damballah is both the result of, and an incitement to, miscegenation, the true forbidden fruit of the American Eden. Her "barbaric fascination" quickens Howard's already racing pulse, and her "heavy ornaments of crudely hammered gold," as "African as her loftily piled coiffure," provide clues to what kind of race war is being waged here, as does Stark's plan to make of the rivers and creeks moats to defend his domain: "No one can cross the waters to come against them. He will rule his tribe as his fathers ruled their tribes in the Ancient Land." This is a counter-secession, a separatism that will separate Canaan from America itself. Have the sins of the forefathers brought not just Africans but Africa itself to what should have been a New World? Buckner reflects that the essence of the Bride demands "a grimmer, more bestial background, a background of steaming jungle, reeking black swamps, flaring fires and cannibal feasts, and the bloody altars of abysmal tribal gods." Of course this has little to do with any Africa that ever was, except in the projections of Europeans and European-Americans whose access to Dark Continents came from closing their eyes, or their minds. But the worry that not Europe but "Africa" will reshape America in its own image – the jungle-grown marshes of Tularoosa Creek stretch "inlets southward like groping fingers" – is balanced by the tacit admission that the fallout from slavery disfigures and degrades the doers as well as the done-to. Long before Saul Stark arrives, everyone in Canaan has already been "put in the swamp."

Another view of the same process is on display in "Pigeons from Hell," one of the finest American horror stories, and one of the most American. Here the swamp has moved indoors and upstairs, but the "reek and rot of decay" are still pervasive. Miss Celia, "the proudest and the cruelest" of the haughty de Blassenvilles, is reduced to a *zuvembie* clad in "the rags of an old ballroom gown," like a hideous parody of Scarlett O'Hara. "Black Canaan" and "Pigeons from Hell" belong in any American library of burdened conscience and shadowed self-awareness, right next to *The Narrative of Arthur Gordon Pym*, Melville's "Benito Cereno," and *Absalom, Absalom!* These stories know more than they tell, and they fear even more than that: "– God, what frightful, ancient terrors there are on this continent fools call 'young'!"

The Garfield of "Old Garfield's Heart" was the first white settler in Howard's part of Texas (Lost Knob is a Cross Plains *Doppelganger*) when "hills no white man ever set foot in before" still "swarmed with Comanches." His elegy – that this was "good country before it filled up with cow-men and squatters" – echoes Howard's own lament to Lovecraft in 1933: "What I want is impossible, as I've told you before; I want, in a word, the frontier – which is compassed in the phrase new land, open land, free land, swarming with game and laden with fresh forests and sweet cold streams." Garfield owes his life to Ghost Man, "a witch doctor of the Lipans, who dwelt in this country before the Comanches came down from the Staked Plains and drove 'em south across the Rio Grande." Were his name not portentous enough, we learn that Ghost Man is a worshipper of "somethin' from away back and a long way off," and the significance of this story's fantastic heart transplant, from the perspective of a D. H. Lawrence or Leslie Fiedler, is fairly obvious.

Like "The Valley of the Lost," "The Horror from the Mound" rebukes the overconfidence of the Anglo-come-lately, and the story within the story is something of a companion tale to "Nekht Semerkeht." Here not all of the grinning, unappeased demons are aboriginal, for the caballero Hernando de Estrada and his armored pikemen have imported the epitome of Old World malevolence, an undead hidalgo in whom the doctrine of *limpieza de sangre*, pure-bloodedness, has become more sinister yet. As "black suspicion" eats at the heart of the expedition so also does suspicion of the only black among them, "a cannibal slave from Calabar." Far from being black, the pursuing evil turns out to be whiter-than-white, and at the moment of crisis the suspect from Calabar is no longer regarded as a black man but simply as a man who accompanies his fellow men to beard the leech in his makeshift den.

"The Thunder-Rider" is Howard at his most modern in his aversion to modernity; the assimilated Comanche John Garfield can only resist "the most highly artificialized civilization the world has ever known" by recovering the oxymoronic "all-seeing blindness" that made possible the "dreams and visions and prophesy" of his tribal forbears. Garfield evades psychosis by resorting to metempsychosis; his memories of warriors past and warrior pasts are a still-unconquered hinterland: "My mind began turning red. . . . The shadow of a dripping tomahawk began to take shape, to hover over me." The first, and more enthralling, half of "The Thunder-Rider" rewrites conventional American ethnography as Garfield in effect remembers too much: "I could tell you things that would shock you out of the amused tolerance with which you are reading this narrative of a race your ancestors crushed. I could tell you of long wanderings over a continent still teeming with prehuman terrors – but enough."

Howard was still in the early stages of mapping that continent and imagining those prehuman terrors in this story, and admittedly the swords could be sharper and the sorcery more spellbinding as the second half tapers off. Still, he is on native ground and in native guise; at last the founding father of American sword-and-sorcery is writing about authentic American warriors. "And the end of all our exploring / Will be to arrive where we started / And know the place for the first time," as T. S. Eliot puts it in "Little Gidding." And just as the blond berserkers of "Marchers" have been replaced by the Comanches, the barbarians at Howards's very own gate, the incongruous extra-continental nomenclature of the earlier story, with its Poseidon, Ishtar, and Ymir, has disappeared. Instead the master of the Darkening Land is addressed by his servants as Tezcatlipoca: "the name of one of the sun god's incarnations – taken, no doubt, in a spirit of blasphemy by the ruler of this evil castle." Howard's letter praising "Teotihuacan," a poem by one Alice l'Anson, had appeared in *Weird Tales* in January 1931 – "I believe that only one familiar with that ancient land could so reflect the slumbering soul of Aztec-land as she has done" – and the allusions in "The Thunder-Rider" to "mighty cities far in the serpent-haunted jungles of the dim South" and "the days of the Golden Kings" suggest that Howard had realized that the immensities of myth and memory symbolized in stone by Tenochtitlan, Tula, and Teotihuacan were available as a New World equivalent of Acheron and Stygia in the Conan series. Perhaps he would have gone on to give us a Mesoamerican fantasy to rank with *Montezuma's Daughter*, *Terra Nostra*, and *The Chalchiuhite Dragon*.

Even L. Sprague de Camp mustered enough depth perception to see that "a reason for the ferocity of Howard's barbarians is that the barbarians he knew the most about, the Comanche Indians of Texas, were one of the most warlike peoples on earth." The derivation of the noun "Comanche" from a Ute term for fractious cousins, *Koh-Mahts*, "those who are always against us," may remind those familiar with Howard of Khor-nah's boast in "Exile of Atlantis": "For Atlantis, thank Valka, is the foe of all men." Something of the incorrigibility that so intrigued Howard is captured in T. R. Fehrenbach's *Comanches: The Destruction of a People*: "The horse lifted them to riches as they understood riches and made them the most dangerous predators on the continent. These dark-eyed hunter-killers must be remembered as long as men remain men. For something in their lives – the hot thrill of the chase, the horses running in the wind, the lance and shield and war-whoop brandished against man's fate, their defiance to the bitter end – will always pull at powerful blood memories buried in all of us." Buried in all of us, but most easily unearthed by a Comanche like Garfield, who offers us a hint as to how Howard's own mind might have reddened even more had it not gone dark instead: *I see the dry grass waving under the southwest wind, and the tall white house of Quanah Parker looming against the steel-blue sky.*

If we wish to champion this writer, it must be on the basis of what he wrote, not what it is possible that he would have written; but the excerpts from Howard's correspondence presented at the end of this collection under the found title "The Classic Tale of the Southwest" can be regarded as appetizers from a withheld banquet. When Howard left the world in June of 1936, he surely left unwritten a Quanah Parker–centric Comanchiad in which nature and nurture, barbarism and civilization, would have circled each other before closing for the death-grapple. The result might have been more searching than *The Searchers*; to adapt Howard's own words, a new star might have flashed redly across the frontier of serious Western fiction. But at least we have "The Thunder-Rider," evidence that at the end of his life, in a state of mind bleaker than that of John Garfield in his skyscraping office, Howard came to much the same conclusion as Philip Deloria in his study *Playing Indian*: "In the end, Indian play was perhaps not so much about a desire to become Indian – or even to become American – as it was a longing for the utopian experience of being in between. . . . Americanness is perhaps not so much the product of a collision of European and Indian as it is a particular working out of a desire to preserve stability and truth while enjoying absolute, anarchic freedom." If the inner-directed outlets available to John Garfield and James Allison in their quests for "absolute, anarchic freedom" are denied to us, there is some consolation in our abiding ability to draw upon classic American artists like Hawthorne, Melville, and Faulkner, Sam Peckinpah and Cormac McCarthy, and at his best, Robert E. Howard – none of them much good at choking down pablum and placebos, all of them subversive in ways that no Congressional committee could ever weed out.

Working wherever possible from original typescripts, the goal of this Bison Books project has been to release Howard's imagination into its natural habitat, to stand back and let his Juggernauts of immediacy and momentum shake the purple mountains' majesty. We hope that his words will resound across the decades as if chanted to accompany his hammering on the keys of that long-suffering Underwood, transforming readers into rapt listeners. If you believe that *allusion* is just a misspelling of *illusion*, if you object to strip-mining text in search of subtext, no worries; enough blood to glut an Ares – or the real Tezcatlipoca – and several Ragnaroks worth of thunder await you within these pages. But if you suspect that classic is as classic does, if you're willing to grant a pulp prodigal the chance to crash the canon and penetrate the pantheon, we're pulling for these stories to move you to a proclamation like that the poet Hart Crane made on behalf of his magnum opus *The Bridge*: "Here one is on the pure mythical and smoky ground at last!" Maybe we can no longer be born into even a desolate Eden, but we can be borne there by Robert E. Howard's storytelling.

The Black Stranger
and Other
American Tales

The Black Stranger

CHAPTER I

The Painted Men

One moment the glade lay empty; the next, a man stood poised warily at the edge of the bushes. There had been no sound to warn the grey squirrels of his coming. But the gay-hued birds that flitted about in the sunshine of the open space took fright at his sudden appearance and rose in a clamoring cloud. The man scowled and glanced quickly back the way he had come, as if fearing their flight had betrayed his position to some one unseen. Then he stalked across the glade, placing his feet with care. For all his massive, muscular build he moved with the supple certitude of a panther. He was naked except for a rag twisted about his loins, and his limbs were criss-crossed with scratches from briars, and caked with dried mud. A brown-crusted bandage was knotted about his thickly-muscled left arm. Under his matted black mane his face was drawn and gaunt, and his eyes burned like the eyes of a wounded panther. He limped slightly as he followed the dim path that led across the open space.

Half-way across the glade he stopped short and whirled, catlike, facing back the way he had come, as a long-drawn call quavered out across the forest. To another man it would have seemed merely the howl of a wolf. But this man knew it was no wolf. He was a Cimmerian and understood the voices of the wilderness as a city-bred man understands the voices of his friends.

Rage burned redly in his bloodshot eyes as he turned once more and hurried along the path, which, as it left the glade, ran along the edge of a dense thicket that rose in a solid clump of greenery among the trees and bushes. A massive log, deeply embedded in the grassy earth, paralleled the fringe of the thicket, lying between it and the path. When the Cimmerian saw this log he halted and looked back across the glade. To the average eye there were no signs to show that he had passed; but there was evidence visible to his wilderness-sharpened eyes, and therefore to the equally keen eyes of those who pursued him. He snarled silently, the red rage growing in his eyes – the berserk fury of a hunted beast which is ready to turn at bay.

He walked down the trail with comparative carelessness, here and there crushing a grass-blade beneath his foot. Then, when he had reached the further end of the great log, he sprang upon it, turned and ran lightly back along it. The bark had long been worn away by the elements. He left no sign to show the keenest forest-eyes that he had doubled on his trail. When he reached the densest point of the thicket he faded into it like a shadow, with hardly the quiver of a leaf to mark his passing.

The minutes dragged. The grey squirrels chattered again on the branches – then flattened their bodies and were suddenly mute. Again the glade was invaded. As silently as the first man had appeared, three other men materialized out of the eastern edge of the clearing. They were dark-skinned men of short stature, with thickly-muscled chests and arms. They wore beaded buckskin loin-cloths, and an eagle's feather was thrust into each black mane. They were painted in hideous designs, and heavily armed.

They had scanned the glade carefully before showing themselves in the open, for they moved out of the bushes without hesitation, in close single-file, treading as softly as leopards, and bending down to stare at the path. They were following the trail of the Cimmerian, but it was no easy task even for these human bloodhounds. They moved slowly across the glade, and then one stiffened, grunted and pointed with his broad-bladed stabbing spear at a crushed grass-blade where the path entered the forest again. All halted instantly and their beady black eyes quested the forest wall. But their quarry was well hidden; they saw nothing to awake their suspicion, and presently they moved on, more rapidly, following the faint marks that seemed to indicate their prey was growing careless through weakness or desperation.

They had just passed the spot where the thicket crowded closest to the ancient trail when the Cimmerian bounded into the path behind them and plunged his knife between the shoulders of the last man. The attack was so quick and unexpected the Pict had no chance to save himself. The blade was in his heart before he knew he was in peril. The other two whirled with the instant, steel-trap quickness of savages, but even as his knife sank home, the Cimmerian struck a tremendous blow with the war-axe in his right hand. The second Pict was in the act of turning as the axe fell. It split his skull to the teeth.

The remaining Pict, a chief by the scarlet tip of his eagle-feather, came savagely to the attack. He was stabbing at the Cimmerian's breast even as the killer wrenched his axe from the dead man's head. The Cimmerian hurled the body against the chief and followed with an attack as furious and desperate as the charge of a wounded tiger. The Pict, staggering under the impact of the corpse against him, made no attempt to parry the dripping axe; the instinct to slay submerging even the instinct to live, he drove his spear ferociously at his enemy's broad breast. The Cimmerian had the advantage of a greater intelligence, and a weapon in each hand. The hatchet, checking its downward sweep, struck the spear aside, and the knife in the Cimmerian's left hand ripped upward into the painted belly.

An awful howl burst from the Pict's lips as he crumpled, disemboweled – a cry not of fear or of pain, but of baffled, bestial fury, the death-screech of a panther. It was answered by a wild chorus of yells some distance east of the glade. The Cimmerian started convulsively, wheeled, crouching like a wild thing at bay, lips asnarl, shaking the sweat from his face. Blood trickled down his forearm from under the bandage.

With a gasping, incoherent imprecation he turned and fled westward. He did not pick his way now, but ran with all the speed of his long legs, calling on the deep and all but inexhaustible reservoirs of endurance which are Nature's compensation for a barbaric existence. Behind him for a space the woods were silent, then a demoniacal howling burst out at the spot he had recently left, and he knew his pursuers had found the bodies of his victims. He had no breath for cursing the blood drops that kept spilling to the ground from his freshly opened wound, leaving a trail a child could follow. He had thought that perhaps these three Picts were all that still pursued him of the war-party which had followed him for over a hundred miles. But he might have known these human wolves never quit a blood-trail.

The woods were silent again, and that meant they were racing after him, marking his path by the betraying blood-drops he could not check. A wind out of the west blew against his face, laden with a salty dampness he recognized. Dully he was amazed. If he was that close to the sea the long chase had been even longer than he had realized. But it was nearly over. Even his wolfish vitality was ebbing under the terrible strain. He gasped for breath and there was a sharp pain in his side. His legs trembled with weariness and the lame one ached like the cut of a knife in the tendons each time he set the foot to earth. He had followed the instincts of the wilderness which bred him, straining every nerve and sinew, exhausting every subtlety and artifice to survive. Now in his extremity he was obeying another instinct, looking for a place to turn at bay and sell his life at a bloody price.

He did not leave the trail for the tangled depths on either hand. He knew that it was futile to hope to evade his pursuers now. He ran on down the trail while the blood pounded louder and louder in his ears and each breath he drew was a racking, dry-lipped gulp. Behind him a mad baying broke out, token that they were close on his heels and expected to overhaul their prey swiftly. They would come as fleet as starving wolves now, howling at every leap.

Abruptly he burst from the denseness of the trees and saw, ahead of him, the ground pitching upward, and the ancient trail winding up rocky ledges between jagged boulders. All swam before him in a dizzy red mist, but it was a hill he had come to, a rugged crag rising abruptly from the forest about its foot. And the dim trail wound up to a broad ledge near the summit.

That ledge would be as good a place to die as any. He limped up the trail, going on hands and knees in the steeper places, his knife between his teeth. He had not yet reached the jutting ledge when some forty painted savages broke from among the trees, howling like wolves. At the sight of their prey their screams rose to a devil's crescendo, and they raced toward the foot of the crag, loosing arrows as they came. The shafts showered about the man who doggedly climbed upward, and one stuck in the calf of his leg. Without pausing in his climb he tore it out and threw it aside, heedless of the less accurate missiles which splintered on the rocks about him. Grimly he hauled himself over the rim of the ledge and turned about, drawing his hatchet and shifting knife to hand. He lay glaring down at his pursuers over the rim, only his shock of hair and blazing eyes visible.

His chest heaved as he drank in the air in great shuddering gasps, and he clenched his teeth against a tendency toward nausea.

Only a few arrows whistled up at him. The horde knew its prey was cornered. The warriors came on howling, leaping agilely over the rocks at the foot of the hill, war-axes in their hand. The first to reach the crag was a brawny brave whose eagle feather was stained scarlet as a token of chieftainship. He halted briefly, one foot on the sloping trail, arrow notched and drawn half-way back, head thrown back and lips parted for an exultant yell. But the shaft was never loosed. He froze into motionlessness, and the blood-lust in his black eyes gave way to a look of startled recognition. With a whoop he gave back, throwing his arms wide to check the rush of his howling braves. The man crouching on the ledge above them understood the Pictish tongue, but he was too far away to catch the significance of the staccato phrases snapped at the warriors by the crimson-feathered chief.

But all ceased their yelping, and stood mutely staring up – not at the man on the ledge, it seemed to him, but at the hill itself. Then without further hesitation, they unstrung their bows and thrust them into buckskin cases at their girdles; turned their backs and trotted across the open space, to melt into the forest without a backward look.

The Cimmerian glared in amazement. He knew the Pictish nature too well not to recognize the finality expressed in the departure. He knew they would not come back. They were heading for their villages, a hundred miles to the east.

But he could not understand it. What was there about his refuge that would cause a Pictish war-party to abandon a chase it had followed so long with all the passion of hungry wolves? He knew there were sacred places, spots set aside as sanctuaries by the various clans, and that a fugitive, taking refuge in one of these sanctuaries, was safe from the clan which raised it. But the different tribes seldom respected sanctuaries of other tribes; and the men who had pursued him certainly had no sacred spots of their own in this region. They were the men of the Eagle, whose villages lay far to the east, adjoining the country of the Wolf-Picts.

It was the Wolves who had captured him, in a foray against the Aquilonian settlements along Thunder River, and they had given him to the Eagles in return for a captured Wolf chief. The Eagle-men had a red score against the giant Cimmerian, and now it was redder still, for his escape had cost the life of a noted war-chief. That was why they had followed him so relentlessly, over broad rivers and hills and through long leagues of gloomy forest, the hunting grounds of hostile tribes. And now the survivors of that long chase turned back when their enemy was run to earth and trapped. He shook his head, unable to understand it.

He rose gingerly, dizzy from the long grind, and scarcely able to realize that it was over. His limbs were stiff, his wounds ached. He spat dryly and cursed, rubbing his burning, bloodshot eyes with the back of his thick wrist. He blinked and took stock of his surroundings. Below him the green wilderness waved and billowed away and away in a solid mass, and above its western rim rose a steel-blue haze he knew hung over the ocean. The wind stirred his black mane, and the salt tang of the atmosphere revived him. He expanded his enormous chest and drank it in.

Then he turned stiffly and painfully about, growling at the twinge in his bleeding calf, and investigated the ledge whereon he stood. Behind it rose a sheer rocky cliff to the crest of the crag, some thirty feet above him. A narrow ladder-like stair of hand-holds had been niched into the rock. And a few feet from its foot there was a cleft in the wall, wide enough and tall enough for a man to enter.

He limped to the cleft, peered in, and grunted. The sun, hanging high above the western forest, slanted into the cleft, revealing a tunnel-like cavern beyond, and rested a revealing beam on the arch at which this tunnel ended. In that arch was set a heavy iron-bound oaken door!

This was amazing. This country was howling wilderness. The Cimmerian knew that for a thousand miles this western coast ran bare and uninhabited except by the villages of the ferocious sea-land tribes, who were even less civilized than their forest-dwelling brothers.

The nearest outposts of civilization were the frontier settlements along Thunder River, hundreds of miles to the east. The Cimmerian knew he was the only white man ever to cross the wilderness that lay between that river and the coast. Yet that door was no work of Picts.

Being unexplainable, it was an object of suspicion, and suspiciously he approached it, axe and knife ready. Then as his blood-shot eyes became more accustomed to the soft gloom that lurked on either side of the narrow shaft of sunlight, he noticed something else – thick iron-bound chests ranged along the walls. A blaze of comprehension came into his eyes. He bent over one, but the lid resisted his efforts. He lifted his hatchet to shatter the ancient lock, then changed his mind and limped toward the arched door. His bearing was more confident now, his weapons hung at his sides. He pushed against the ornately carven door and it swung inward without resistance.

Then his manner changed again, with lightning-like abruptness; he recoiled with a startled curse, knife and hatchet flashing as they leaped to positions of defense. An instant he poised there, like a statue of fierce menace, craning his massive neck to glare through the door. It was darker in the large natural chamber into which he was looking, but a dim glow emanated from the great jewel which stood on a tiny ivory pedestal in the center of the great ebony table about which sat those silent shapes whose appearance had so startled the intruder.

They did not move, they did not turn their heads toward him.

"Well," he said harshly; "are you all drunk?"

There was no reply. He was not a man easily abashed, yet now he felt disconcerted.

"You might offer me a glass of that wine you're swigging," he growled, his natural truculence roused by the awkwardness of the situation. "By Crom, you show damned poor courtesy to a man who's been one of your own brotherhood. Are you going to – " his voice trailed into silence, and in silence he stood and stared awhile at those bizarre figures sitting so silently about the great ebon table.

"They're not drunk," he muttered presently. "They're not even drinking. What devil's game is this?" He stepped across the threshold and was instantly fighting for his life against the murderous, unseen fingers that clutched his throat.

CHAPTER 2

Men From the Sea

Belesa idly stirred a sea-shell with a daintily slippered toe, mentally comparing its delicate pink edges to the first pink haze of dawn that rose over the misty beaches. It was not dawn now, but the sun was not long up, and the light, pearl-grey clouds which drifted over the waters had not yet been dispelled.

Belesa lifted her splendidly shaped head and stared out over a scene alien and repellent to her, yet drearily familiar in every detail. From her dainty feet the tawny sands ran to meet the softly lapping waves which stretched westward to be lost in the blue haze of the horizon. She was standing on the southern curve of the wide bay, and south of her the land sloped upward to the low ridge which formed one horn of that bay. From that ridge, she knew, one could look southward across the bare waters-into infinities of distance as absolute as the view to the westward and to the northward.

Glancing listlessly landward, she absently scanned the fortress which had been her home for the past year. Against a vague pearl and cerulean morning sky floated the golden and scarlet flag of her house-an ensign which awakened no enthusiasm in her youthful bosom, though it had flown triumphantly over many a bloody field in the far South. She made out the figures of men toiling in the gardens and fields that huddled near the fort, seeming to shrink from the gloomy rampart of the forest which fringed the open belt on the east, stretching north and south as far as she could see. She feared that forest, and that fear was shared by every one in that tiny settlement. Nor was it an idle fear – death lurked in those whispering depths, death swift and terrible, death slow and hideous, hidden, painted, tireless, unrelenting.

She sighed and moved listlessly toward the water's edge, with no set purpose in mind. The dragging days were all of one color, and the world of cities and courts and gaiety seemed not only thousands of miles but long ages away. Again she sought in vain for the reason that had caused a Count of Zingara to flee with his retainers to this wild coast, a thousand miles from the land that bore him, exchanging the castle of his ancestors for a hut of logs.

Her eyes softened at the light patter of small bare feet across the sands. A young girl came running over the low sandy ridge, quite naked, her slight body dripping, and her flaxen hair plastered wetly on her small head. Her wistful eyes were wide with excitement.

"Lady Belesa!" she cried, rendering the Zingaran words with a soft Ophirean accent. "Oh, Lady Belesa!"

Breathless from her scamper, she stammered and made incoherent gestures with her hands. Belesa smiled and put an arm about the child, not

8

minding that her silken dress came in contact with the damp, warm body. In her lonely, isolated life Belesa bestowed the tenderness of a naturally affectionate nature on the pitiful waif she had taken away from a brutal master encountered on that long voyage up from the southern coasts.

"What are you trying to tell me, Tina? Get your breath, child."

"A ship!" cried the girl, pointing southward. "I was swimming in a pool that the sea-tide left in the sand, on the other side of the ridge, and I saw it! A ship sailing up out of the south!"

She tugged timidly at Belesa's hand, her slender body all a-quiver. And Belesa felt her own heart beat faster at the mere thought of an unknown visitor. They had seen no sail since coming to that barren shore.

Tina flitted ahead of her over the yellow sands, skirting the tiny pools the outgoing tide had left in shallow depressions. They mounted the low undulating ridge, and Tina poised there, a slender white figure against the clearing sky, her wet flaxen hair blowing about her thin face, a frail quivering arm outstretched.

"Look, my Lady!"

Belesa had already seen it – a billowing white sail, filled with the freshening south wind, beating up along the coast, a few miles from the point. Her heart skipped a beat. A small thing can loom large in colorless and isolated lives; but Belesa felt a premonition of strange and violent events. She felt that it was not by chance that this sail was beating up this lonely coast. There was no harbor town to the north, though one sailed to the ultimate shores of ice; and the nearest port to the south was a thousand miles away. What brought this stranger to lonely Korvela Bay?

Tina pressed close to her mistress, apprehension pinching her thin features.

"Who can it be, my Lady?" she stammered, the wind whipping color to her pale cheeks. "Is it the man the Count fears?"

Belesa looked down at her, her brow shadowed. "Why do you say that, child? How do you know my uncle fears anyone?"

"He must," returned Tina naively, "or he would never have come to hide in this lonely spot. Look, my Lady, how fast it comes!"

"We must go and inform my uncle," murmured Belesa. "The fishing boats have not yet gone out, and none of the men have seen that sail. Get your clothes, Tina. Hurry!"

The child scampered down the low slope to the pool where she had been bathing when she sighted the craft, and snatched up the slippers, tunic and girdle she had left lying on the sand. She skipped back up the ridge, hopping grotesquely as she donned her scanty garments in mid-flight.

Belesa, anxiously watching the approaching sail, caught her hand, and they hurried toward the fort. A few moments after they had entered the gate of the log palisade which enclosed the building, the strident blare of a trumpet startled the workers in the gardens, and the men just opening the boat-house doors to push the fishing boats down their rollers to the water's edge.

Every man outside the fort dropped his tool or abandoned whatever he was doing and ran for the stockade without pausing to look about for the cause of the alarm. The straggling lines of fleeing men converged on the opened gate, and every head was twisted over its shoulder to gaze fearfully at the dark line of woodland to the east. Not one looked seaward.

They thronged through the gate, shouting questions at the sentries who patrolled the firing-ledges built below the up-jutting points of the upright palisade logs.

"What is it? Why are we called in? Are the Picts coming?"

For answer one taciturn man-at-arms in worn leather and rusty steel pointed southward. From his vantage-point the sail was now visible. Men began to climb up on the ledges, staring toward the sea.

On a small lookout tower on the roof of the manor house, which was built of logs like the other buildings, Count Valenso watched the on-sweeping sail as it rounded the point of the southern horn. The Count was a lean, wiry man of medium height and late middle age. He was dark, somber of expression. Trunk-hose and doublet were of black silk, the only color about his costume the jewels that twinkled on his sword hilt, and the wine-colored cloak thrown carelessly over his shoulder. He twisted his thin black mustache nervously, and turned his gloomy eyes on his seneschal – a leather-featured man in steel and satin.

"What do you make of it, Galbro?"

"A carack," answered the seneschal. "It is a carack trimmed and rigged like a craft of the Barachan pirates-look there!"

A chorus of cries below them echoed his ejaculation; the ship had cleared the point and was slanting inward across the bay. And all saw the flag that suddenly broke forth from the masthead – a black flag, with a scarlet skull gleaming in the sun.

The people within the stockade stared wildly at that dread emblem; then all eyes turned up toward the tower, where the master of the fort stood somberly, his cloak whipping about him in the wind.

"It's a Barachan, all right," grunted Galbro. "And unless I am mad, it's Strom's *Red Hand*. What is he doing on this naked coast?"

"He can mean no good for us," growled the Count. A glance below showed him that the massive gates had been closed, and that the captain of his men-at-arms, gleaming in steel, was directing his men to their stations, some to the ledges, some to the lower loop-boles. He was massing his main strength along the western wall, in the midst of which was the gate.

Valenso had been followed into exile by a hundred men: soldiers, vassals and serfs. Of these some forty were men-at-arms, wearing helmets and suits of mail, armed with swords, axes and crossbows. The rest were toilers, without armor save for shirts of toughened leather, but they were brawny stalwarts, and skilled in the use of their hunting bows, woodsmen's axes, and boar-spears. They took their places, scowling at their hereditary enemies. The pirates of the Barachan Isles, a tiny archipelago off the southeastern coast of Zingara, had preyed on the people of the mainland for more than a century.

The men on the stockade gripped their bows or boar-spears and stared somberly at the carack which swung inshore, its brass work flashing in the sun. They could see the figures swarming on the deck, and hear the lusty yells of the seamen. Steel twinkled along the rail.

The Count had retired from the tower, shooing his niece and her eager protege before him, and having donned helmet and cuirass, he betook himself to the palisade to direct the defense. His subjects watched him with moody fatalism. They intended to sell their lives as dearly as they could, but they had scant hope of victory, in spite of their strong position. They were oppressed by a conviction of doom. A year on that naked coast, with the brooding threat of that devil-haunted forest looming forever at their backs, had shadowed their souls with gloomy forebodings. Their women stood silently in the doorways of their huts, built inside the stockade, and quieted the clamor of their children.

Belesa and Tina watched eagerly from an upper window in the manor house, and Belesa felt the child's tense little body all aquiver within the crook of her protecting arm.

"They will cast anchor near the boat-house," murmured Belesa. "Yes! There goes their anchor, a hundred yards off-shore. Do not tremble so, child! They can not take the fort. Perhaps they wish only fresh water and supplies. Perhaps a storm blew them into these seas."

"They are coming ashore in long boats!" exclaimed the child. "Oh, my Lady, I am afraid! They are big men in armor! Look how the sun strikes fire from their pikes and burgenets! Will they eat us?"

Belesa burst into laughter in spite of her apprehension.

"Of course not! Who put that idea into your head?"

"Zingelito told me the Barachans eat women."

"He was teasing you. The Barachans are cruel, but they are no worse than the Zingaran renegades who call themselves buccaneers. Zingelito was a buccaneer once."

"He was cruel," muttered the child. "I'm glad the Picts cut his head off."

"Hush, child." Belesa shuddered slightly. "You must not speak that way. Look, the pirates have reached the shore. They line the beach, and one of them is coming toward the fort. That must be Strom."

"Ahoy, the fort there!" came a hail in a voice gusty as the wind. "I come under a flag of truce!"

The Count's helmeted head appeared over the points of the palisade; his stern face, framed in steel, surveyed the pirate somberly. Strom had halted just within good ear-shot. He was a big man, bare-headed, his tawny hair blowing in the wind. Of all the sea-rovers who haunted the Barachans, none was more famed for deviltry than he.

"Speak!" commanded Valenso. "I have scant desire to converse with one of your breed."

Strom laughed with his lips, not with his eyes.

"When your galleon escaped me in that squall off the Trallibes last year I never thought to meet you again on the Pictish Coast, Valenso!" said he. "Although at the time I wondered what your destination might be. By Mitra, had I known, I would have followed you then! I got the start of my life a little while ago when I saw your scarlet falcon floating over a fortress where I had thought to see naught but bare beach. You have found it, of course?"

"Found what?" snapped the Count impatiently.

"Don't try to dissemble with me!" The pirate's stormy nature showed itself momentarily in a flash of impatience. "I know why you came here – and I have come for the same reason. I don't intend to be balked. Where is your ship?"

"That is none of your affair."

"You have none," confidently asserted the pirate. "I see pieces of a galleon's masts in that stockade. It must have been wrecked, somehow, after you landed here. If you'd had a ship you'd have sailed away with your plunder long ago."

"What are you talking about, damn you?" yelled the Count. "My plunder? Am I a Barachan to burn and loot? Even so, what would I loot on this naked coast?"

"That which you came to find," answered the pirate coolly. "The same thing I'm after – and mean to have. But I'll be easy to deal with – just give me the loot and I'll go my way and leave you in peace."

"You must be mad," snarled Valenso. "I came here to find solitude and seclusion, which I enjoyed until you crawled out of the sea, you yellow-headed dog. Begone! I did not ask for a parley, and I weary of this empty talk. Take your rogues and go your ways."

"When I go I'll leave that hovel in ashes!" roared the pirate in a transport of rage. "For the last time – will you give me the loot in return for your lives? I have you hemmed in here, and a hundred and fifty men ready to cut your throats at my word."

For answer the Count made a quick gesture with his hand below the points of the palisade. Almost instantly a shaft hummed venomously through a loophole and splintered on Strom's breastplate. The pirate yelled ferociously, bounded back and ran toward the beach, with arrows whistling all about him. His men roared and came on like a wave, blades gleaming in the sun.

"Curse you, dog!" raved the Count, felling the offending archer with his iron-clad fist. "Why did you not strike his throat above the gorget? Ready with your bows, men – here they come!"

But Strom had reached his men, checked their headlong rush. The pirates spread out in a long line that overlapped the extremities of the western wall, and advanced warily, loosing their shafts as they came. Their weapon was the longbow, and their archery was superior to that of the Zingarans. But the latter were protected by their barrier. The long arrows arched over the stockade and quivered upright in the earth. One struck the window-sill over which Belesa watched, wringing a cry of fear from Tina, who cringed back, her wide eyes fixed on the venomous vibrating shaft.

The Zingarans sent their bolts and hunting arrows in return, aiming and loosing without undue haste. The women had herded the children into their huts and now stoically awaited whatever fate the gods had in store for them.

The Barachans were famed for their furious and headlong style of battling, but they were wary as they were ferocious, and did not intend to waste their strength vainly in direct charges against the ramparts. They maintained their wide-spread formation, creeping along and taking advantage of every natural depression and bit of vegetation – which was not much, for the ground had been cleared on all sides of the fort against the threat of Pictish raids.

A few bodies lay prone on the sandy earth, back-pieces glinting in the sun, quarrel shafts standing up from arm-pit or neck. But the pirates were quick as cats, always shifting their position, and were protected by their light armor. Their constant raking fire was a continual menace to the men In the stockade. Still, it was evident that as long as the battle remained an exchange of archery, the advantage must remain with the sheltered Zingarans.

But down at the boat-house on the beach, men were at work with axes. The Count cursed sulphurously when he saw the havoc they were making among his boats, which had been built laboriously of planks sawn out of solid logs.

"They're making a mantlet, curse them!" he raged. "A sally now, before they complete it – while they're scattered – "

Galbro shook his head, glancing at the bare-armed henchmen with their clumsy pikes.

"Their arrows would riddle us, and we'd be no match for them in hand-to-hand fighting. We must keep behind our walls and trust to our archers."

"Well enough," growled Valenso. "If we can keep them outside our walls."

Presently the intention of the pirates became apparent to all, as a group of some thirty men advanced, pushing before them a great shield made out of the planks from the boats, and the timbers of the boat-house itself. They had found an ox-cart, and mounted the mantlet on the wheels, great solid disks of oak. As they rolled it ponderously before them it hid them from the sight of the defenders except for glimpses of their moving feet.

It rolled toward the gate, and the straggling line of archers converged toward it, shooting as they ran.

"Shoot!" yelled Valenso, going livid. "Stop them before they reach the gate!"

A storm of arrows whistled across the palisade, and feathered themselves harmlessly in the thick wood. A derisive yell answered the volley. Shafts were finding loop-holes now, as the rest of the pirates drew nearer, and a soldier reeled and fell from the ledge, gasping and choking, with a clothyard shaft through his throat.

"Shoot at their feet!" screamed Valenso; and then – "Forty men at the gate with pikes and axes! The rest hold the wall!"

Bolts ripped into the sand before the moving shield. A blood-thirsty howl announced that one had found its target beneath the edge, and a man staggered into view, cursing and hopping as he strove to withdraw the quarrel that skewered his foot. In an instant he was feathered by a dozen hunting arrows.

But, with a deep-throated shout, the mantlet was pushed to the wall, and a heavy, iron-tipped boom, thrust through an aperture in the center of the shield, began to thunder on the gate, driven by arms knotted with brawny muscles and backed with blood-thirsty fury. The massive gate groaned and staggered, while from the stockade bolts poured in a steady hail and some struck home. But the wild men of the sea were afire with the fighting-lust.

With deep shouts they swung the ram, and from all sides the others closed in, braving the weakened fire from the walls, and shooting fast and hard.

Cursing like a madman the Count sprang from the wall and ran to the gate, drawing his sword. A clump of desperate men-at-arms closed in behind him, gripping their spears. In another moment the gate would cave in and they must stop the gap with their living bodies.

Then a new note entered the clamor of the melee. It was a trumpet, blaring stridently from the ship. On the cross-trees a figure waved his arms and gesticulated wildly.

That sound registered on Storm's ears, even as he lent his strength to the swinging ram. Exerting his mighty thews he resisted the surge of the other arms, bracing his legs to halt the ram on its backward swing. He turned his head, sweat dripping from his face.

"Wait!" he roared. "Wait, damn you! *Listen!*"

In the silence that followed that bull's bellow, the blare of the trumpet was plainly heard, and a voice that shouted something unintelligible to the people inside the stockade.

But Strom understood, for his voice was lifted again in profane command. The ram was released, and the mantlet began to recede from the gate as swiftly as it had advanced.

"Look!" cried Tina at her window, jumping up and down in her wild excitement. "They are running! All of them! They are running to the beach! Look! They have abandoned the shield just out of range! They are leaping into the boats and rowing for the ship! Oh, my Lady, have we won?"

"I think not!" Belesa was staring sea-ward. "Look!"

She threw the curtains aside and leaned from the window. Her clear young voice rose above the amazed shouts of the defenders, turned their heads in the direction she pointed. They sent up a deep yell as they saw another ship swinging majestically around the southern point. Even as they looked she broke out the royal golden flag of Zingara.

Strom's pirates were swarming up the sides of their carack, heaving up the anchor. Before the stranger had progressed half-way across the bay, the *Red Hand* was vanishing around the point of the northern horn.

CHAPTER 3

The Coming of the Black Man

"Out, quick!" snapped the Count, tearing at the bars of the gate. "Destroy that mantlet before these strangers can land!"

"But Strom has fled," expostulated Galbro, "and yonder ship is Zingaran."

"Do as I order!" roared Valenso. "My enemies are not all foreigners! Out,

dogs! Thirty of you, with axes, and make kindling wood of that mantlet.
Bring the wheels into the stockade."

Thirty axemen raced down toward the beach, brawny men in sleeveless
tunics, their axes gleaming in the sun. The manner of their lord had suggested a possibility of peril in that oncoming ship, and there was panic
in their haste. The splintering of the timbers under their flying axes came
plainly to the people inside the fort, and the axemen were racing back
scross the sands, trundling the great oaken wheels with them, before the
Zingaran ship had dropped anchor where the pirate ship had stood.

"Why does not the Count open the gate and go down to meet them?"
wondered Tina. "Is he afraid that the man he fears might be on that ship?"

"What do you mean, Tina?" Belesa demanded uneasily. The Count had
never vouchsafed a reason for this self-exile. He was not the sort of a man
to run from an enemy, though he had many. But this conviction of Tina's
was disquieting; almost uncanny.

Tina seemed not to have heard her question.

"The axemen are back in the stockade," she said. "The gate is closed
again and barred. The men still keep their places along the wall. If that
ship was chasing Strom, why did it not pursue him? But it is not a war-
ship. It is a carack, like the other. Look, a boat is coming ashore. I see a
man in the bow, wrapped in a dark cloak."

The boat having grounded, this man came pacing leisurely up the sands,
followed by three others. He was a tall, wiry man, clad in black silk and
polished steel.

"Halt!" roared the Count. "I will parley with your leader, alone!"

The tall stranger removed his morion and made a sweeping bow. His
companions halted, drawing their wide cloaks about them, and behind
them the sailors leaned on their oars and stared at the flag floating over
the palisade.

When he came within easy call of the gate: "Why, surely," said he, "there
should be no suspicion between gentlemen in these naked seas!"

Valenso stared at him suspiciously. The stranger was dark, with a lean,
predatory face, and a thin black mustache. A bunch of lace was gathered
at his throat, and there was lace on his wrists.

"I know you," said Valenso slowly. "You are Black Zarono, the buccaneer."

Again the stranger bowed with stately elegance.

"And none could fail to recognize the red falcon of the Korzettas!"

"It seems this coast has become the rendezvous of all the rogues of the southern seas," growled Valenso. "What do you wish?"

"Come, come, sir!" remonstrated Zarono. "This is a churlish greeting to one who has just rendered you a service. Was not that Argossean dog, Strom, just thundering at your gate? And did he not take to his sea-heels when he saw me round the point?"

"True," grunted the Count grudgingly. "Though there is little to choose between a pirate and a renegade."

Zarono laughed without resentment and twirled his mustache.

"You are blunt in speech, my lord. But I desire only leave to anchor in your bay, to let my men hunt for meat and water in your woods, and perhaps, to drink a glass of myself at your board."

"I see not how I can stop you," growled Valenso. "But understand this, Zarono: no man of your crew comes within this palisade. If one approaches closer than a hundred feet, he will presently find an arrow through his gizzard. And I charge you do no harm to my gardens or the cattle in the pens. Three steers you may have for fresh meat, but no more. And we can hold this fort against your ruffians, in case you think otherwise."

"You were not holding it very successfully against Strom," the buccaneer pointed out with a mocking smile.

"You'll find no wood to build mantlets unless you chop down trees, or strip it from your own ship," assured the Count grimly. "And your men are not Barachan archers; they're no better bowmen than mine. Besides, what little loot you'd find in this castle would not be worth the price."

"Who speaks of loot and warfare?" protested Zarono. "Nay, my men are sick to stretch their legs ashore, and nigh to scurvy from chewing salt pork. I guarantee their good conduct. May they come ashore?"

Valenso grudgingly signified his consent, and Zarono bowed, a thought sardonically, and retired with a tread as measured and stately as if he trod the polished crystal floor of the Kordavan royal court, where indeed, unless rumor lied, he had once been a familiar figure.

"Let no man leave the stockade," Valenso ordered Galbro." I do not trust that renegade dog. Because he drove Strom from our gate is no guarantee that he would not cut our throats."

Galbro nodded. He was well aware of the enmity which existed between the pirates and the Zingaran buccaneers. The pirates were mainly Argossean sailors, turned outlaw; to the ancient feud between Argos and Zingara was added, in the case of the freebooters, the rivalry of opposing interests. Both breeds preyed on the shipping and the coastal towns and they preyed on one another with equal rapacity.

So no one stirred from the palisade while the buccaneers came ashore, dark-faced men in flaming silk and polished steel, with scarfs bound about their heads and gold hoops in their ears. They camped on the beach, a hundred and seventy-odd of them, and Valenso noticed that Zarono posted lookouts on both points. They did not molest the gardens, and only the three beeves designated by Valenso, shouting from the palisade, were driven forth and slaughtered. Fires were kindled on the strand, and a wattled cask of ale was brought ashore and broached.

Other kegs were filled with water from the spring that rose a short distance south of the fort, and men began to straggle toward the woods, crossbows in their hands. Seeing this, Valenso was moved to shout to Zarono, striding back and forth through the camp: "Don't let your men go into the forest. Take another steer from the pens if you haven't enough meat. If they go trampling into the woods they may fall foul of the Picts.

"Whole tribes of the painted devils live back in the forest. We beat off an attack shortly after we landed, and since then six of my men have been murdered in the forest, at one time or another. There's peace between us just now, but it hangs by a thread. Don't risk stirring them up."

Zarono shot a startled glance at the lowering woods, as if he expected to see hordes of savage figures lurking there. Then he bowed and said: "I thank you for the warning, my lord." And he shouted for his men to come back, in a rasping voice that contrasted strangely with his courtly accents when addressing the Count.

If Zarono could have penetrated the leafy mask he would have been more apprehensive, if he could have seen the sinister figure that lurked there, watching the strangers with inscrutable black eyes – a hideously painted warrior, naked but for a doe-skin breech-clout, with a toucan feather drooping over his left ear.

As evening drew on, a thin skim of grey crawled up from the sea-rim and overcast the sky. The sun sank in a wallow of crimson, touching the tips of the black waves with blood. Fog crawled out of the sea and lapped at the feet of the forest, curling about the stockade in smoky wisps. The fires on the beach shone dull crimson through the mist, and the singing of the buccaneers seemed deadened and far away. They had brought old sail-canvas from the carack and made them shelters along the strand, where beef was still roasting, and the ale granted them by their captain was doled out sparingly.

The great gate was shut and barred. Soldiers stolidly tramped the ledges of the palisade, pike on shoulder, beads of moisture glistening on their steel caps. They glanced uneasily at the fires on the beach, stared with greater fixity toward the forest, now a vague dark line in the crawling fog. The compound lay empty of life, a bare, darkened space. Candles gleamed feebly through the cracks of the huts, and light streamed from the windows of the manor. There was silence except for the tread of the sentries, the drip of water from the eaves, and the distant singing of the buccaneers.

Some faint echo of this singing penetrated into the great hall where Valenso sat at wine with his unsolicited guest.

"Your men make merry, sir," grunted the Count.

"They are glad to feel the sand under their feet again," answered Zarono. "It has been a wearisome voyage – yes, a long, stern chase." He lifted his goblet gallantly to the unresponsive girl who sat on his host's right, and drank ceremoniously.

Impassive attendants ranged the walls, soldiers with pikes and helmets, servants in satin coats. Valenso's household in this wild land was a shadowy reflection of the court he had kept in Kordava.

The manor house, as he insisted on calling it, was a marvel for that coast. A hundred men had worked night and day for months building it. Its log-walled exterior was devoid of ornamentation, but within it was as nearly a copy of Korzetta Castle as was possible. The logs that composed the walls of the hall were hidden with heavy silk tapestries, worked in gold. Ship beams, stained and polished, formed the beams of the lofty ceiling. The floor was covered with rich carpets. The broad stair that led up from the hall was likewise carpeted, and its massive balustrade had once been a galleon's rail.

A fire in the wide stone fireplace dispelled the dampness of the night. Candles in the great silver candelabrum in the center of the broad mahogany board lit the hall, throwing long shadows on the stair. Count Valenso sat at the head of that table, presiding over a company composed of his niece, his piratical guest, Galbro, and the captain of the guard. The smallness of the company emphasized the proportions of the vast board, where fifty guests might have sat at ease.

"You followed Strom?" asked Valenso. "You drove him this far afield?"

"I followed Strom," laughed Zarono, "but he was not fleeing from me. Strom is not the man to flee from anyone. No; he came seeking for something; something I too desire."

"What could tempt a pirate or a buccaneer to this naked land?" muttered Valenso, staring into the sparkling contents of his goblet.

"What could tempt a count of Kordava?" retorted Zarono, and an avid light burned an instant in his eyes.

"The rottenness of a royal court might sicken a man of honor," remarked Valenso.

"Korzettas of honor have endured its rottenness with tranquility for several generations," said Zarono bluntly. "My lord, indulge my curiosity – why did you sell your lands, load your galleon with the furnishings of your castle and sail over the horizon out of the knowledge of the king and the nobles of Zingara? And why settle here, when your sword and your name might carve out a place for you in any civilized land?"

Valenso toyed with the golden seal-chain about his neck.

"As to why I left Zingara," he said, "that is my own affair. But it was chance that left me stranded here. I had brought all my people ashore, and much of the furnishings you mentioned, intending to build a temporary habitation. But my ship, anchored out there in the bay, was driven against the cliffs of the north point and wrecked by a sudden storm out of the west. Such storms are common enough at certain times of the year. After that there was naught to do but remain and make the best of it."

"Then you would return to civilization, if you could?"

"Not to Kordava. But perhaps to some far clime – to Vendhya, or Khitai – "

"Do you not find it tedious here, my Lady?" asked Zarono, for the first time addressing himself directly to Belesa.

Hunger to see a new face and hear a new voice had brought the girl to the great hall that night. But now she wished she had remained in her chamber with Tina. There was no mistaking the meaning in the glance Zarono turned on her. His speech was decorous and formal, his expression sober and respectful but it was but a mask through which gleamed the violent and sinister spirit of the man. He could not keep the burning desire out of his eyes when he looked at the aristocratic young beauty in her low-necked satin gown and jeweled girdle.

"There is little diversity here," she answered in a low voice.

"If you had a ship," Zarono bluntly asked his host, "you would abandon this settlement?"

"Perhaps," admitted the Count.

"I have a ship," said Zarono. "If we could reach an agreement – "

"What sort of an agreement?" Valenso lifted his head to stare suspiciously at his guest.

"Share and share alike," said Zarono, laying his hand on the board with the fingers spread wide. The gesture was curiously reminiscent of a great spider. But the fingers quivered with curious tension, and the buccaneer's eyes burned with a new light.

"Share what?" Valenso stared at him in evident bewilderment. "The gold I brought with me went down in my ship, and unlike the broken timbers, it did not wash ashore."

"Not that!" Zarono made an impatient gesture. "Let us be frank, my lord. Can you pretend it was chance which caused you to land at this particular spot, with a thousand miles of coast from which to choose?"

"There is no need for me to pretend," answered Valenso coldly. "My ship's master was one Zingelito, formerly a buccaneer. He had sailed this coast, and persuaded me to land here, telling me he had a reason he would later disclose. But this reason he never divulged, because the day after we landed he disappeared into the woods, and his headless body was found later by a hunting party. Obviously he was ambushed and slain by the Picts."

Zarono stared fixedly at Valenso for a space.

"Sink me," quoth he at last, "I believe you, my lord. A Korzetta has no skill at lying, regardless of his other accomplishments. And I will make you a proposal. I will admit when I anchored out there in the bay I had other plans in mind. Supposing you to have already secured the treasure, I meant to take this fort by strategy and cut all your throats. But circumstances have caused me to change my mind – " He cast a glance at Belesa that brought the color into her face, and made her lift her head indignantly.

"I have a ship to carry you out of exile," said the buccaneer, "with your household and such of your retainers as you shall choose. The rest can fend for themselves."

The attendants along the walls shot uneasy glances side-long at each other. Zarono went on, too brutally cynical to conceal his intentions

"But first you must help me secure the treasure for which I've sailed a thousand miles."

"What treasure, in Mitra's name?" demanded the Count angrily. "You are yammering like that dog Strom, now."

"Did you ever hear of Bloody Tranicos, the greatest of the Barachan pirates?" asked Zarono.

"Who has not? It was he who stormed the island castle of the exiled prince Tothmekri of Stygia, put the people to the sword and bore off the treasure the prince had brought with him when he fled from Khemi."

"Aye! And the tale of that treasure brought the men of the Red Brotherhood swarming like vultures after a carrion – pirates, buccaneers, even the black corsairs from the South. Fearing betrayal by his captains, he fled northward with one ship, and vanished from the knowledge of men. That was nearly a hundred years ago.

"But the tale persists that one man survived that last voyage, and returned to the Barachans, only to be captured by a Zingaran war-ship. Before he was hanged he told his story and drew a map in his own blood, on parchment, which he smuggled somehow out of his captor's reach. This was the tale he told: Tranicos had sailed far beyond the paths of shipping, until he came to a bay on a lonely coast, and there he anchored. He went ashore, taking his treasure and eleven of his most trusted captains who had accompanied him on his ship. Following his orders, the ship sailed away, to return in a week's time, and pick up their admiral and his captains. In the meantime Tranicos meant to hide the treasure somewhere in the vicinity of the bay. The ship returned at the appointed time, but there was no trace of Tranicos and his eleven captains, except the rude dwelling they had built on the beach.

"This had been demolished, and there were tracks of naked feet about it, but no sign to show there had been any fighting. Nor was there any trace of the treasure, or any sign to show where it was hidden. The pirates plunged into the forest to search for their chief and his captains, but were attacked by wild Picts and driven back to their ship. In despair they heaved anchor and sailed away, but before they raised the Barachans, a terrific storm wrecked the ship and only that one man survived.

"That is the tale of the Treasure of Tranicos, which men have sought in vain for nearly a century. That the map exists is known, but its whereabouts have remained a mystery.

"I have had one glimpse of that map. Strom and Zingelito were with me, and a Nemedian who sailed with the Barachans. We looked upon it in a hovel in a certain Zingaran sea-port town, where we were skulking in disguise. Somebody knocked over the lamp, and somebody howled in the dark, and when we got the light on again, the old miser who owned the map was dead with a dirk in his heart, and the map was gone, and the night-watch was clattering down the street with their pikes to investigate the clamor. We scattered, and each went his own way.

"For years thereafter Strom and I watched one another, each supposing the other had the map. Well, as it turned out, neither had it, but recently word came to me that Strom had departed northward, so I followed him. You saw the end of that chase.

"I had but a glimpse at the map as it lay on the old miser's table, and could tell nothing about it. But Strom's actions show that he knows this is the bay where Tranicos anchored. I believe that they hid the treasure somewhere in that forest and returning, were attacked and slain by the Picts. The Picts did not get the treasure. Men have traded up and down this coast a little, knowing nothing of the treasure, and no gold ornament or rare jewel has ever been seen in the possession of the coastal tribes.

"This is my proposal: let us combine our forces. Strom is somewhere within striking distance. He fled because he feared to be pinned between us, but he will return. But allied, we can laugh at him. We can work out from the fort, leaving enough men here to hold it if he attacks. I believe the treasure is hidden near by. Twelve men could not have conveyed it far. We will find it, load it in my ship, and sail for some foreign port where I can cover my past with gold. I am sick of this life. I want to go back to a civilized land, and live like a noble, with riches, and slaves, and a castle – and a wife of noble blood."

"Well?" demanded the Count, slit-eyed with suspicion.

"Give me your niece for my wife," demanded the buccaneer bluntly.

Belesa cried out sharply and started to her feet. Valenso likewise rose, livid, his fingers knotting convulsively about his goblet as it he contemplated hurling it at his guest. Zarono did not move; he sat still, one arm on the table and the fingers hooked like talons. His eyes smoldered with passion, and a deep menace.

"You dare!" ejaculated Valenso.

"You seem to forget you have fallen from your high estate, Count Valenso," growled Zarono. "We are not at the Kordavan court, my lord. On this naked coast nobility is measured by the power of men and arms. And there I rank you. Strangers tread Korzetta Castle, and the Korzetta fortune is at the bottom of the sea. You will die here, an exile, unless I give you the use of my ship.

"You will have no cause to regret the union of our houses. With a new name and a new fortune you will find that Black Zarono can take his place among the aristocrats of the world and make a son-in-law of which not even a Korzetta need be ashamed."

"You are mad to think of it!" exclaimed the Count violently. "You – who is that?"

A patter of soft-slippered feet distracted his attention. Tina came hurriedly into the hall, hesitated when she saw the Count's eyes fixed angrily on her, curtsied deeply, and sidled around the table to thrust her small hands into Belesa's fingers. She was panting slightly, her slippers were damp, and her flaxen hair was plastered down on her head.

"Tina!" exclaimed Belesa anxiously. "Where have you been? I thought you were in your chamber, hours ago."

"I was," answered the child breathlessly, "but I missed my coral necklace you gave me – " She held it up, a trivial trinket, but prized beyond all her other possessions because it had been Belesa's first gift to her. "I was afraid you wouldn't let me go if you knew – a soldier's wife helped me out of the stockade and back again – please, my Lady, don't make me tell who she was, because I promised not to. I found my necklace by the pool where I bathed this morning. Please punish me if I have done wrong."

"Tina!" groaned Belesa, clasping the child to her. "I'm not going to punish you. But you should not have gone outside the palisade, with these buccaneers camped on the beach, and always a chance of Picts skulking about. Let me take you to your chamber and change these damp clothes – "

"Yes, my Lady," murmured Tina, "but first let me tell you about the black man – "

"What?" The startling interruption was a cry that burst from Valenso's lips. His goblet clattered to the floor as he caught the table with both hands. If a thunderbolt had struck him, the lord of the castle's bearing could not have been more subtly or horrifyingly altered. His face was livid, his eyes almost starting from his head.

"What did you say?" he panted, glaring wildly at the child who shrank back against Belesa in bewilderment. "What did you say, wench?"

"A black man, my lord," she stammered, while Belesa, Zarono, and the attendants stared at him in amazement. "When I went down to the pool to get my necklace, I saw him. There was a strange moaning in the wind, and the sea whimpered like a thing in fear, and then he came. I was afraid, and hid behind a little ridge of sand. He came from the sea in a strange black boat with blue fire playing all about it, but there was no torch. He drew his boat up on the sands below the south point, and strode toward the forest, looking like a giant in the fog – a great, tall man, black like a Kushite – "

Valenso reeled as if he had received a mortal blow. He clutched at his throat, snapping the golden chain in his violence. With the face of a madman he lurched about the table and tore the child screaming from Belesa's arms.

"You little slut," he panted. "You lie! You have heard me mumbling in my sleep and have told this lie to torment me! Say that you lie before I tear the skin from your back!"

"Uncle!" cried Belesa in outraged bewilderment, trying to free Tina from his grasp. "Are you mad? What are you about?"

With a snarl he tore her hand from his arm and spun her staggering into the arms of Galbro who received her with a leer he made little effort to disguise.

"Mercy, my Lord!" sobbed Tina. "I did not lie!"

"I said you lied!" roared Valenso. "Gebbrelo!"

The stolid serving man seized the trembling youngster and stripped her with one brutal wrench that tore her scanty garments from her body.

Wheeling, he drew her slender arms over his shoulders, lifting her writhing feet clear of the floor.

"Uncle!" shrieked Belesa, writhing vainly in Galbro's lustful grasp. "You are mad! You can not – oh, you can not! – " The voice choked in her throat as Valenso caught up a jewel-hilted riding whip and brought it down across the child's frail body with a savage force that left a red weal across her naked shoulders.

Belesa moaned, sick with the anguish in Tina's shriek. The world had suddenly gone mad. As in a nightmare she saw the stolid faces of the soldiers and servants, beast-faces, the faces of oxen, reflecting neither pity nor sympathy. Zarono's faintly sneering face was part of the nightmare. Nothing in that crimson haze was real except Tina's naked white body, criss-crossed with red welts from shoulders to knees; no sound real except the child's sharp cries of agony, and the panting gasps of Valenso as he lashed away with the staring eyes of a madman, shrieking: "You lie! You lie! Curse you, you lie! Admit your guilt, or I will flay your stubborn body! *He* could not have followed me here – "

"Oh, have mercy, my Lord!" screamed the child, writhing vainly on the brawny servant's back, too frantic with fear and pain to have the wit to save herself by a lie. Blood trickled in crimson beads down her quivering thighs. "I saw him! I do not lie! Mercy! Please! Ahhhh!"

"You fool! *You fool!*" screamed Belesa, almost beside herself. "Do you not see she is telling the truth? Oh, you beast! Beast! Beast!"

Suddenly some shred of sanity seemed to return to the brain of Count Valenso Korzetta. Dropping the whip he reeled back and fell up against the table, clutching blindly at its edge. He shook as with an ague. His hair was plastered across his brow in dank strands, and sweat dripped from his livid countenance which was like a carven mask of Fear. Tina, released by Gebbrelo, slipped to the floor in a whimpering heap. Belesa tore free from Galbro, rushed to her, sobbing, and fell on her knees, gathering the pitiful waif into her arms. She lifted a terrible face to her uncle, to pour upon him the full vials of her wrath – but he was not looking at her. He seemed to have forgotten both her and his victim. In a daze of incredulity, she heard him say to the buccaneer: "I accept your offer, Zarono; in Mitra's name, let us find this accursed treasure and begone from this damned coast!"

At this the fire of her fury sank to sick ashes. In stunned silence she lifted the sobbing child in her arms and carried her up the stair. A glance backward showed Valenso crouching rather than sitting at the table, gulping wine from a huge goblet he gripped in both shaking hands, while Zarono towered over him like a somber predatory bird – puzzled at the turn of events, but quick to take advantage of the shocking change that had come over the Count. He was talking in a low, decisive voice, and Valenso nodded mute agreement, like one who scarcely heeds what is being said. Galbro stood back in the shadows, chin pinched between forefinger and thumb, and the attendants along the walls glanced furtively at each other, bewildered by their lord's collapse.

Up in her chamber Belesa laid the half-fainting girl on the bed and set herself to wash and apply soothing ointments to the weals and cuts on her tender skin. Tina gave herself up in complete submission to her mistress's hands, moaning faintly. Belesa felt as if her world had fallen about her ears. She was sick and bewildered, overwrought, her nerves quivering from the brutal shock of what she had witnessed. Fear of and hatred for her uncle grew in her soul. She had never loved him; he was harsh and apparently without natural affection, grasping and avid. But she had considered him just, and fearless. Revulsion shook her at the memory of his staring eyes and bloodless face. It was some terrible fear which had roused this frenzy: and because of this fear Valenso had brutalized the only creature she had to love and cherish; because of that fear he was selling her, his niece, to an infamous outlaw. What was behind this madness? Who was the black man Tina had seen?

The child muttered in semi-delirium.

"I did not lie, my Lady! Indeed I did not! It was a black man, in a black boat that burned like blue fire on the water! A tall man, black as a negro, and wrapped in a black cloak! I was afraid when I saw him, and my blood ran cold. He left his boat on the sands and went into the forest. Why did the Count whip me for seeing him?"

"Hush, Tina," soothed Belesa. "Lie quiet. The smarting will soon pass."

The door opened behind her and she whirled, snatching up a jeweled dagger. The Count stood in the door, and her flesh crawled at the sight. He looked years older; his face was grey and drawn, and his eyes stared in a way that roused fear in her bosom. She had never been close to him; now she felt as though a gulf separated them. He was not her uncle who stood there, but a stranger come to menace her.

She lifted the dagger.

"If you touch her again," she whispered from dry lips, "I swear before Mitra I will sink this blade in your breast."

He did not heed her.

"I have posted a strong guard about the manor," he said. "Zarono brings his men into the stockade tomorrow. He will not sail until he has found the treasure. When he finds it we shall sail at once for some port not yet decided upon."

"And you will sell me to him?" she whispered. "In Mitra's name – "

He fixed upon her a gloomy gaze in which all considerations but his own self-interest had been crowded out. She shrank before it, seeing in it the frantic cruelty that possessed the man in his mysterious fear.

"You will do as I command," he said presently, with no more human feeling in his voice than there is in the ring of flint on steel. And turning, he left the chamber. Blinded by a sudden rush of horror, Belesa fell fainting beside the couch where Tina lay.

CHAPTER 4

A Black Drum Droning

Belesa never knew how long she lay crushed and senseless. She was first aware of Tina's arms about her and the sobbing of the child in her ear. Mechanically she straightened herself and drew the girl into her arms; and she sat there, dry-eyed, staring unseeingly at the flickering candle. There was no sound in the castle. The singing of the buccaneers on the strand had ceased. Dully, almost impersonally, she reviewed her problem.

Valenso was mad, driven frantic by the story of the mysterious black man. It was to escape this stranger that he wished to abandon the settlement and flee with Zarono. That much was obvious. Equally obvious was the fact that he was ready to sacrifice her in exchange for that opportunity to escape. In the blackness of spirit which surrounded her she saw no glint of light. The serving men were dull or callous brutes, their women stupid and apathetic. They would neither dare nor care to help her. She was utterly helpless.

29

Tina lifted her tear-stained face as if she were listening to the prompting of some inner voice. The child's understanding of Belesa's inmost thoughts was almost uncanny, as was her recognition of the inexorable drive of Fate and the only alternative left to the weak.

"We must go, my Lady!" she whispered. "Zarono shall not have you. Let us go far away into the forest. We shall go until we can go no further, and then we shall lie down and die together."

The tragic strength that is the last refuge of the weak entered Belesa's soul. It was the only escape from the shadows that had been closing in upon her since that day when they fled from Zingara.

"We shall go, child."

She rose and was fumbling for a cloak, when an exclamation from Tina brought her about. The girl was on her feet, a finger pressed to her lips, her eyes wide and bright with terror.

"What is it, Tina?" The child's expression of fright induced Belesa to pitch her voice to a whisper, and a nameless apprehension crawled over her.

"Someone outside in the hall," whispered Tina, clutching her arm convulsively. "He stopped at our door, and then went on, toward the Count's chamber at the other end."

"Your ears are keener than mine," murmured Belesa. "But there is nothing strange in that. It was the Count himself, perchance, or Galbro." She moved to open the door, but Tina threw her arms frantically about her neck, and Belesa felt the wild beating of her heart.

"No, no, my Lady! Do not open the door! I am afraid! I do not know why, but I feel that some evil thing is skulking near us!"

Impressed, Belesa patted her reassuringly, and reached a hand toward the gold disk that masked the tiny peep-hole in the center of the door.

"He is coming back!" shivered the girl. "I hear him!"

Belesa heard something too – a curious stealthy pad which she knew, with a chill of nameless fear, was not the step of anyone she knew. Nor was it the step of Zarono, or any booted man. Could it be the buccaneer gliding along the hallway on bare, stealthy feet, to slay his host while he slept? She remembered the soldiers who would be on guard below. If the buccaneer had remained in the manor for the night, a man-at-arms would be posted before his chamber door. But who was that sneaking along the corridor? None slept upstairs besides herself, Tina and the Count, except Galbro.

With a quick motion she extinguished the candle so it would not shine through the hole in the door, and pushed aside the gold disk. All the lights were out in the hall, which was ordinarily lighted by candles. Someone was moving along the darkened corridor. She sensed rather than saw a dim bulk moving past her doorway, but she could make nothing of its shape except that it was manlike. But a chill wave of terror swept over her; so she crouched dumb, incapable of the scream that froze behind her lips. It was not such terror as her uncle now inspired in her, or fear like her fear of Zarono, or even of the brooding forest. It was blind unreasoning terror that laid an icy hand on her soul and froze her tongue to her palate.

The figure passed on to the stairhead, where it was limned momentarily against the faint glow that came up from below, and at the glimpse of that vague black image against the red, she almost fainted.

She crouched there in the darkness awaiting the outcry that would announce that the soldiers in the great hall had seen the intruder. But the manor remained silent; somewhere a wind wailed shrilly. That was all.

Belesa's hands were moist with perspiration as she groped to relight the candle. She was still shaken with horror, though she could not decide just what there had been about that black figure etched against the red glow that had roused this frantic loathing in her soul. It was manlike in shape, but the outline was strangely alien – abnormal – though she could not clearly define that abnormality. But she knew that it was no human being that she had seen, and she knew that the sight had robbed her of all her new-found resolution. She was demoralized, incapable of action.

The candle flared up, limning Tina's white face in the yellow glow.

"It was the black man!" whispered Tina. "I know! My blood turned cold, just as it did when I saw him on the beach. There are soldiers downstairs; why did they not see him? Shall we go and inform the Count?"

Belesa shook her head. She did not care to repeat the scene that had ensued upon Tina's first mention of the black man. At any event, she dared not venture out into that darkened hallway.

"We dare not go into the forest!" shuddered Tina. "He will be lurking there – "

Belesa did not ask the girl how she knew the black man would be in the forest; it was the logical hiding-place for any evil thing, man or devil. And she knew Tina was right; they dared not leave the fort now. Her determination, which had not faltered at the prospect of certain death, gave way at the thought of traversing those gloomy woods with that black shambling creature at large among them. Helplessly she sat down and sank her face in her hands.

Tina slept, presently, on the couch, whimpering occasionally in her sleep. Tears sparkled on her long lashes. She moved her smarting body uneasily in her restless slumber. Toward dawn Belesa was aware of a stifling quality in the atmosphere. She heard a low rumble of thunder somewhere off to sea-ward. Extinguishing the candle, which had burned to its socket, she went to a window whence she could see both the ocean and a belt of the forest behind the fort.

The fog had disappeared, but out to sea a dusky mass was rising from the horizon. From it lightning flickered and the low thunder growled. An answering rumble came from the black woods. Startled, she turned and stared at the forest, a brooding black rampart. A strange rhythmic pulsing came to her ears – a droning reverberation that was not the roll of a Pictish drum.

"The drum!" sobbed Tina, spasmodically opening and closing her fingers in her sleep. "The black man – beating on a black drum – in the black woods! Oh, save us – !"

Belesa shuddered. Along the eastern horizon ran a thin white line that presaged dawn. But that black cloud on the western rim writhed and billowed, swelling and expanding. She stared in amazement, for storms were practically unknown on that coast at that time of the year, and she had never seen a cloud like that one.

It came pouring up over the world-rim in great boiling masses of blackness, veined with fire. It rolled and billowed with the wind in its belly. Its thundering made the air vibrate. And another sound mingled awesomely with the reverberations of the thunder – the voice of the wind, that raced before its coming. The inky horizon was torn and convulsed in the lightning flashes; afar to sea she saw the white-capped waves racing before the wind. She heard its droning roar, increasing in volume as it swept shoreward. But as yet no wind stirred on the land. The air was hot, breathless. There was a sensation of unreality about the contrast; out there wind and thunder and chaos sweeping inland; but here stifling stillness. Somewhere below her a shutter slammed, startling in the tense silence, and a woman's voice was lifted, shrill with alarm. But most of the people of the fort seemed sleeping, unaware of the on-coming hurricane.

She realized that she still heard that mysterious droning drum-beat and she stared toward the black forest, her flesh crawling. She could see nothing, but some obscure instinct or intuition prompted her to visualize a black hideous figure squatting under black branches and enacting a nameless incantation on something that sounded like a drum –

Desperately she shook off the ghoulish conviction, and looked seaward, as a blaze of lightning fairly split the sky. Outlined against its glare she saw the masts of Zarono's ship; she saw the tents of the buccaneers on the beach, the sandy ridges of the south point and the rock cliffs of the north point as plainly as by midday sun. Louder and louder rose the roar of the wind, and now the manor was awake. Feet came pounding up the stair, and Zarono's voice yelled, edged with fright.

Doors slammed and Valenso answered him, shouting to be heard above the roar of the elements.

"Why didn't you warn me of a storm from the west?" howled the buccaneer. "If the anchors don't hold – "

"A storm never came from the west before, at this time of year!" shrieked Valenso, rushing from his chamber in his night-shirt, his face livid and his hair standing stiffly on end. "This is the work of – " His words were drowned as he raced madly up the ladder that led to the lookout tower, followed by the swearing buccaneer.

Belesa crouched at her window, awed and deafened. Louder and louder rose the wind, until it drowned all other sound – all except that maddening droning that now rose like an inhuman chant of triumph. It roared inshore, driving before it a foaming league-long crest of white – and then all hell and destruction was loosed on that coast. Rain fell in driving torrents, sweeping the beaches with blind frenzy. The wind hit like a thunderclap, making the timbers of the fort quiver. The surf roared over the sands, drowning the coals of the fires the seamen had built. In the glare of lightning Belesa saw, through the curtain of the slashing rain, the tents of the buccaneers whipped to ribbons and washed away, saw the men themselves staggering toward the fort, beaten almost to the sands by the fury of torrent and blast.

And limned against the blue glare she saw Zarono's ship, ripped loose from her moorings, driven headlong against the jagged cliffs that jutted up to receive her . . .

CHAPTER 5

A Man From the Wilderness

The storm had spent its fury. Full dawn rose in a clear blue rain-washed sky. As the sun rose in a blaze of fresh gold, bright-hued birds lifted a swelling chorus from the trees on whose broad leaves beads of water sparkled like diamonds, quivering in the gentle morning breeze.

At a small stream which wound over the sands to join the sea, hidden beyond a fringe of trees and bushes, a man bent to lave his hands and face. He performed his ablutions after the manner of his race, grunting lustily and splashing like a buffalo. But in the midst of these splashings he lifted his head suddenly, his tawny hair dripping and water running in rivulets over his brawny shoulders. He crouched in a listening attitude for a split second, then was on his feet and facing inland, sword in hand, all in one motion. And then he froze, glaring wide-mouthed.

A man as big as himself was striding toward him over the sands, making no attempt at stealth, and the pirate's eyes widened as he stared at the close-fitting silk breeches, high flaring-topped boots, wide-skirted coat and headgear of a hundred years ago. There was a broad cutlass in the stranger's hand and unmistakable purpose in his approach.

The pirate went pale, as recognition blazed in his eyes.

"You!" he ejaculated unbelievingly. "By Mitra! You!"

Oaths streamed from his lips as he heaved up his cutlass. The birds rose in flaming showers from the trees as the clang of steel interrupted their song. Blue sparks flew from the hacking blades, and the sand grated and ground under the stamping boot heels. Then the clash of steel ended in a chopping crunch, and one man went to his knees with a choking gasp. The hilt escaped his nerveless hand and he slid full-length on the sand which reddened with his blood. With a dying effort he fumbled at his girdle and drew something from it, tried to lift it to his mouth, and then stiffened convulsively and went limp.

The conqueror bent and ruthlessly tore the stiffening fingers from the object they crumpled in their desperate grasp.

Zarono and Valenso stood on the beach, staring at the driftwood their men were gathering – spars, pieces of masts, broken timbers. So savagely had the storm hammered Zarono's ship against the low cliffs that most of the salvage was match-wood. A short distance behind them stood Belesa, listening to their conversation, one arm about Tina. The girl was pale and listless, apathetic to whatever Fate held in store for her. She heard what the men said, but with little interest. She was crushed by the realization that she was but a pawn in the game, however it was to be played out – whether it was to be a wretched life dragged out on that desolate coast, or a return, effected somehow, to some civilized land.

Zarono cursed venomously, but Valenso seemed dazed.

"This is not the time of year for storms from the west," he muttered, staring with haggard eyes at the men dragging the wreckage up on the beach. "It was not chance that brought that storm out of the deep to splinter the ship in which I meant to escape. Escape? I am caught like a rat in a trap, as it was meant. Nay, we are all trapped rats – "

"I don't know what you're talking about," snarled Zarono, giving a vicious yank at his mustache. "I've been unable to get any sense out of you since that flaxen-haired slut upset you so last night with her wild tale of black men coming out of the sea. But I do know that I'm not going to spend my life on this cursed coast. Ten of my men went to hell in the ship, but I've got a hundred and sixty more. You've got a hundred. There are tools in your fort, and plenty of trees in yonder forest. We'll build a ship. I'll set men to cutting trees as soon as they get this drift dragged up out of the reach of the waves."

"It will take months," muttered Valenso.

"Well, is there any better way in which we could employ our time? We're here – and unless we build a ship we'll never get away. We'll have to rig up some kind of a sawmill, but I've never encountered anything yet that balked me long. I hope that storm smashed Strom to bits – the Argossean dog! While we're building the ship we'll hunt for old Tranicos's loot."

"We will never complete your ship," said Valenso somberly.

"You fear the Picts? We have enough men to defy them."

"I do not speak of the Picts. I speak of a black man."

Zarono turned on him angrily. "Will you talk sense? Who is this accursed black man?"

"Accursed indeed," said Valenso, staring sea-ward. "A shadow of mine own red-stained past risen up to hound me to hell. Because of him I fled Zingara, hoping to lose my trail in the great ocean. But I should have known he would smell me out at last."

"If such a man came ashore he must be hiding in the woods," growled Zarono. "We'll rake the forest and hunt him out."

Valenso laughed harshly.

"Seek for a shadow that drifts before a cloud that hides the moon; grope in the dark for a cobra; follow a mist that steals out of the swamp at midnight."

Zarono cast him an uncertain look, obviously doubting his sanity.

"Who is this man? Have done with ambiguity."

"The shadow of my own mad cruelty and ambition; a horror come out of the lost ages; no man of mortal flesh and blood, but a – "

"Sail ho!" bawled the lookout on the north point.

Zarono wheeled and his voice slashed the wind.

"Do you know her?"

"Aye!" the reply came back faintly. "It's *The Red Hand*!"

Zarono cursed like a wild man.

"Strom! The devil takes care of his own! How could he ride out that blow?" The buccaneer's voice rose to a yell that carried up and down the strand. "Back to the fort, you dogs!"

Before *The Red Hand*, somewhat battered in appearance, nosed around the point, the beach was bare of human life, the palisade bristling with helmets and scarf-bound heads. The buccaneers accepted the alliance with the easy adaptability of adventurers, the henchmen with the apathy of serfs.

Zarono ground his teeth as a longboat swung leisurely in to the beach, and he sighted the tawny head of his rival in the bow. The boat grounded, and Strom strode toward the fort alone.

36

Some distance away he halted and shouted in a bull's bellow that carried clearly in the still morning. "Ahoy, the fort! I want to parley!"

"Well, why in hell don't you?" snarled Zarono.

"The last time I approached under a flag of truce an arrow broke on my brisket!" roared the pirate. "I want a promise it won't happen again!"

"You have my promise!" called Zarono sardonically.

"Damn your promise, you Zingaran dog! I want Valenso's word."

A measure of dignity remained to the Count. There was an edge of authority to his voice as he answered: "Advance, but keep your men back. You will not be fired upon."

"That's enough for me," said Strom instantly. "Whatever a Korzetta's sins, once his word is given, you can trust him."

He strode forward and halted under the gate, laughing at the hate-darkened visage Zarono thrust over at him.

"How did you save your ship, you Messantian gutter-scum?" snarled the buccaneer.

"There's a cove some miles to the north protected by a high-ridged arm of land that broke the force of the gale," answered Strom. "I was anchored behind it. My anchors dragged, but they held me off the shore."

Zarono scowled blackly. Valenso said nothing. He had not known of that cove. He had done scant exploring of his domain. Fear of the Picts and lack of curiosity had kept him and his men near the fort. The Zingarans were by nature neither explorers nor colonists.

"I come to make a trade," said Strom, easily.

"We've naught to trade with you save sword-strokes," growled Zarono.

"I think otherwise," grinned Strom, thin-lipped. "You tipped your hand when you murdered Galacus, my first mate, and robbed him. Until this morning I supposed that Valenso had Tranicos's treasure. But if either of you had it, you wouldn't have gone to the trouble of following me and killing my mate to get the map."

"The map?" Zarono ejaculated, stiffening.

"Oh, don't disssemble," laughed Strom, but anger blazed blue in his eyes. "I know you have it. Picts don't wear boots!"

"But – " began the Count, nonplussed, but fell silent as Zarono nudged him.

"And if we have the map," said Zarono, "what have you to trade that we might require?"

"Let me come into the fort," suggested Strom. "There we can talk."

He was not so obvious as to glance at the men peering at them from along the wall, but his two listeners understood. And so did the men. Strom had a ship. That fact would figure in any bargaining, or battle. But it would carry just so many, regardless of who commanded; whoever sailed away in it, there would be some left behind. A wave of tense speculation ran along the silent throng at the palisade.

"Your men will stay where they are," warned Zarono, indicating both the boat drawn up on the beach, and the ship anchored out in the bay.

"Aye. But don't get the idea that you can seize me and hold me for a hostage!" He laughed grimly. "I want Valenso's word that I'll be allowed to leave the fort alive and unhurt within the hour, whether we come to terms or not."

"You have my pledge," answered the Count.

"All right, then. Open that gate and let's talk plainly."

The gate opened and closed, the leaders vanished from sight, and the common men of both parties resumed their silent surveillance of each other: the men on the palisade, and the men squatting beside their boat, with a broad stretch of sand between, and beyond a strip of blue water, the carack, with steel caps glinting all along her rail.

On the broad stair, above the great hall, Belesa and Tina crouched, ignored by the men below. These sat about the broad table: Valenso, Galbro, Zarono, and Strom. But for them the hall was empty.

Strom gulped wine and set the empty goblet on the table. The frankness suggested by his bluff countenance was belied by the dancing lights of cruelty and treachery in his wide eyes. But he spoke bluntly enough.

"We all want the treasure old Tranicos hid somewhere near this bay," he said abruptly. "Each has something the others need. Valenso has laborers, supplies, and a stockade to shelter us from the Picts. You, Zarono, have my map. I have a ship."

"What I'd like to know," remarked Zarono, "is this: if you've had that map all these years, why haven't you come after the loot sooner?"

"I didn't have it. It was that dog, Zingelito, who knifed the old miser in the dark and stole the map. But he had neither ship nor crew, and it took him more than a year to get them. When he did come after the treasure, the Picts prevented his landing, and his men mutinied and made him sail back to Zingara. One of them stole the map from him, and recently sold it to me."

"That was why Zingelito recognized the bay," muttered Valenso.

"Did that dog lead you here, Count? I might have guessed it. Where is he?"

"Doubtless in hell, since he was once a buccaneer. The Picts slew him, evidently while he was searching in the woods for the treasure."

"Good!" approved Strom heartily. "Well, I don't know how you knew my mate was carrying the map. I trusted him, and the men trusted him more than they did me, so I let him keep it. But this morning he wandered inland with some of the others, got separated from them, and we found him sworded to death near the beach, and the map gone. The men were ready to accuse me of killing him, but I showed the fools the tracks left by the slayer, and proved to them that my feet wouldn't fit them. And I knew it wasn't any one of the crew, because none of them wear boots that make that sort of track. And Picts don't wear boots at all. So it had to be a Zingaran.

"Well, you've got the map, but you haven't got the treasure. If you had it, you wouldn't have let me inside the stockade. I've got you penned up in this fort. You can't get out to look for the loot, and even if you did get it, you have no ship to get away in.

"Now here's my proposal: Zarono, give me the map. And you, Valenso, give me fresh meat and other supplies. My men are nigh to scurvy after the long voyage. In return I'll take you three men, the Lady Belesa and her girl, and set you ashore within reach of some Zingaran port – or I'll put Zarono ashore near some buccaneer rendezvous if he prefers, since doubtless a noose awaits him in Zingara. And to clinch the bargain I'll give each of you a handsome share in the treasure."

The buccaneer tugged his mustache meditatively. He knew that Strom would not keep any such pact, if made. Nor did Zarono even consider agreeing to his proposal. But to refuse bluntly would be to force the issue into a clash of arms. He sought his agile brain for a plan to outwit the pirate. He wanted Strom's ship as avidly as he desired the lost treasure.

"What's to prevent us from holding you captive and forcing your men to give us your ship in exchange for you?" he asked.

Strom laughed at him.

"Do you think I'm a fool? My men have orders to heave up the anchors and sail hence if I don't reappear within the hour, or if they suspect treachery. They wouldn't give you the ship, if you skinned me alive on the beach. Besides, I have the Count's word."

"My pledge is not straw," said Valenso somberly. "Have done with threats, Zarono."

Zarono did not reply, his mind wholly absorbed in the problem of getting possession of Strom's ship, of continuing the parley without betraying the fact that he did not have the map. He wondered who in Mitra's name did have the accursed map.

"Let me take my men away with me on your ship when we sail," he said. "I can not desert my faithful followers – "

Strom snorted.

"Why don't you ask for my cutlass to slit my gullet with? Desert your faithful – hah! You'd desert your brother to the devil if you could gain anything by it. No! You're not going to bring enough men aboard to give you a chance to mutiny and take my ship."

"Give us a day to think it over," urged Zarono, fighting for time.

Strom's heavy fist banged on the table, making the wine dance in the glasses.

"No, by Mitra! Give me my answer now!"

Zarono was on his feet, his black rage submerging his craftiness.

"You Barachan dog! I'll give you your answer – in your guts – "

He tore aside his cloak, caught at his sword-hilt. Strom heaved up with a roar, his chair crashing backward to the floor. Valenso sprang up, spreading his arms between them as they faced one another across the board, jutting jaws close together, blades half drawn, faces convulsed.

"Gentlemen, have done! Zarono, he has my pledge – "

"The foul fiends gnaw your pledge!" snarled Zarono.

"Stand from between us, my Lord," growled the pirate, his voice thick with the killing lust. "Your word was that I should not be treacherously entreated. It shall be considered no violation of your pledge for this dog and me to cross swords in equal play."

"Well spoken, Strom!" it was a deep, powerful voice behind them, vibrant with grim amusement. All wheeled and glared, open-mouthed. Up on the stair Belesa started up with an involuntary exclamation.

A man strode out from the hangings that masked a chamber door, and advanced toward the table without hesitation. Instantly he dominated the group, and all felt the situation subtly charged with a new, dynamic atmosphere.

The stranger was as tall as either of the freebooters, and more powerfully built than either, yet for all his size he moved with pantherish suppleness in his high, flaring-topped boots. His thighs were cased in close-fitting breeches of white silk, his wide-skirted sky-blue coat open to reveal an open-necked white silken shirt beneath, and the scarlet sash that girdled his waist. There were silver acorn-shaped buttons on his coat, and it was adorned with gilt-worked cuffs and pocket-flaps, and a satin collar. A lacquered hat completed a costume obsolete by nearly a hundred years. A heavy cutlass hung at the wearer's hip.

"Conan!" ejaculated both freebooters together, and Valenso and Galbro caught their breath at that name.

"Who else?" The giant strode up to the table, laughing sardonically at their amazement.

"What – what do you here?" stuttered the seneschal. "How come you here, uninvited and unannounced?"

"I climbed the palisade on the east side while you were fools were arguing at the gate," Conan answered. "Every man in the fort was craning his neck westward. I entered the manor while Strom was being let in at the gate. I've been in that chamber there ever since, eavesdropping."

"I thought you were dead," said Zarono slowly. "Three years ago the shattered hull of your ship was sighted off a reefy coast, and you were heard of on the Main no more."

"I didn't drown with my crew," answered Conan. "It'll take a bigger ocean than that one to drown me."

Up on the stair Tina was clutching Belesa in her excitement and staring through the balustrades with all her eyes.

"Conan! My Lady, it is Conan! Look! Oh, look!"

Belesa was looking; it was like encountering a legendary character in the flesh. Who of all the sea-folk had not heard the wild, bloody tales told of Conan, the wild rover who had once been a captain of the Barachan pirates, and one of the greatest scourges of the sea? A score of ballads celebrated his ferocious and audacious exploits. The man could not be ignored; irresistibly he had stalked into the scene, to form another, dominant element in the tangled plot. And in the midst of her frightened fascination, Belesa's feminine instinct prompted the speculation as to Conan's attitude toward her – would it be like Strom's brutal indifference, or Zarono's violent desire?

Valenso was recovering from the shock of finding a stranger within his very hall. He knew Conan was a Cimmerian, born and bred in the wastes of the far north, and therefore not amenable to the physical limitations which controlled civilized men. It was not so strange that he had been able to enter the fort undetected, but Valenso flinched at the reflection that other barbarians might duplicate that feat – the dark, silent Picts, for instance.

"What do you want here?" he demanded. "Did you come from the sea?"

"I came from the woods." The Cimmerian jerked his head toward the east.

"You have been living with the Picts?" Valenso asked coldly.

A momentary anger flickered bluely in the giant's eyes.

"Even a Zingaran ought to know there's never been peace between Picts and Cimmerians, and never will be," he retorted with an oath. "Our feud with them is older than the world. If you'd said that to one of my wilder brothers, you'd have found yourself with a split head. But I've lived among you civilized men long enough to understand your ignorance and lack of common courtesy – the churlishness that demands his business of a man who appears at your door out of a thousand-mile wilderness. Never mind that." He turned to the two freebooters who stood staring glumly at him.

"From what I overheard," quoth he, "I gather there is some dissension over a map!"

"That is none of your affair," growled Strom.

"Is this it?" Conan grinned wickedly and drew from his pocket a crumpled object – a square of parchment, marked with crimson lines.

Strom stared violently, paling.

"My map!" he ejaculated. "Where did you get it?"

"From your mate, Galacus, when I killed him," answered Conan with grim enjoyment.

"You dog!" raved Strom, turning on Zarono. "You never had the map! You lied – "

"I didn't say I had it," snarled Zarono. "You deceived yourself. Don't be a fool. Conan is alone. If he had a crew he'd have already cut our throats. We'll take the map from him – "

"You'll never touch it!" Conan laughed fiercely.

Both men sprang at him, cursing. Stepping back he crumpled the parchment and cast it into the glowing coals of the fireplace. With an incoherent bellow Strom lunged past him, to be met with a buffet under the ear that stretched him half senseless on the floor. Zarono whipped out his sword but before he could thrust, Conan's cutlass beat it out of his hand.

Zarono staggered against the table, with all hell in his eyes. Strom dragged himself erect, his eyes glazed, blood dripping from his bruised ear. Conan leaned slightly over the table, his outstretched cutlass just touched the breast of Count Valenso.

"Don't call for your soldiers, Count," said the Cimmerian softly. "Not a sound out of you – or from you either, dog-face!" His name for Galbro, who showed no intention of braving his wrath. "The map's burned to ashes, and it'll do no good to spill blood. Sit down, all of you."

Strom hesitated, made an abortive gesture toward his hilt, then shrugged his shoulders and sank sullenly into a chair. The others followed suit. Conan remained standing, towering over the table, while his enemies watched him with bitter eyes of hate.

"You were bargaining," he said. "That's all I've come to do."

"And what have you to trade?" sneered Zarono.

"The treasure of Tranicos!"

"What?" all four men were on their feet, leaning toward him.

"Sit down!" he roared, banging his broad blade on the table. They sank back, tense and white with excitement.

He grinned in huge enjoyment of the sensation his words had caused.

"Yes! I found it before I got the map. That's why I burned the map. I don't need it, and now nobody will ever find it, unless I show him where it is."

They stared at him with murder in their eyes,

"You're lying," said Zarono without conviction. "You've told us one lie already. You said you came from the woods, yet you say you haven't been

43

living with the Picts. All men know this country is a wilderness, inhabited only by savages. The nearest outposts of civilization are the Aquilonian settlements on Thunder River, hundreds of miles to eastward."

"That's where I came from," replied Conan imperturbably. "I believe I'm the first white man to cross the Pictish Wilderness. I crossed Thunder River to follow a raiding party that had been harrying the frontier. I followed them deep into the wilderness, and killed their chief, but was knocked senseless by a stone from a sling during the melee, and the dogs captured me alive. They were Wolfmen, but they traded me to the Eagle clan in return for a chief of theirs the Eagles had captured. The Eagles carried me nearly a hundred miles westward to burn me in their chief village, but I killed their war-chief and three or four others one night, and broke away.

"I couldn't turn back. They were behind me, and kept herding me westward. A few days ago I shook them off, and by Crom, the place where I took refuge turned out to be the treasure trove of old Tranicos! I found it all: heaps of coins and gems and gold ornaments, and in the midst of all, the jewels of Tothmekri gleaming like frozen starlight! And old Tranicos and his eleven captains sitting about an ebon table and staring at the hoard, as they've stared for a hundred years!"

"What?"

"Aye!" he laughed. "Tranicos died in the midst of his treasure, and all with him! Their bodies have not rotted nor shrivelled. They sit there in their high boots and skirted coats and lacquered hats, with their wineglasses in their stiff hands, just as they have sat for a century!"

"That's an unchancy thing!" muttered Strom uneasily, but Zarono snarled: "What boots it? It's the treasure we want. Go on, Conan."

Conan seated himself at the board, filled a goblet and quaffed it before he answered.

"The first wine I've drunk since I left Conawaga, by Crom! Those cursed Eagles hunted me so closely through the forest I had hardly time to munch the nuts and roots I found. Sometimes I caught frogs and ate them raw because I dared not light a fire."

His impatient hearers informed him profanely that they were not interested in his adventures prior to finding the treasure.

He grinned hardly and resumed: "Well, after I stumbled onto the trove I lay up and rested a few days, and made snares to catch rabbits, and let my wounds heal. I saw smoke against the western sky, but thought it some Pictish village on the beach. I lay close, but as it happens, the loot's hidden in a place the Picts shun. If any spied on me, they didn't show themselves.

"Last night I started westward, intending to strike the beach some miles north of the spot where I'd seen the smoke. I wasn't far from the shore when that storm hit. I took shelter under the lee of a rock and waited until it had blown itself out. Then I climbed a tree to look for Picts, and from it I saw your carack at anchor, Strom, and your men coming in to shore. I was making my way toward your camp on the beach when I met Galacus. I shoved a sword through him because there was an old feud between us. I wouldn't have known he had a map, if he hadn't tried to eat it before he died.

"I recognized it for what it was, of course, and was considering what use I could make of it, when the rest of you dogs came up and found the body. I was lying in a thicket not a dozen yards from you while you were arguing with your men over the matter. I judged the time wasn't ripe for me to show myself then!"

He laughed at the rage and chagrin displayed in Strom's face.

"Well, while I lay there, listening to your talk, I got a drift of the situation, and learned, from the things you let fall, that Zarono and Valenso were a few miles south on the beach. So when I heard you say that Zarono must have done the killing and taken the map, and that you meant to go and parley with him, seeking an opportunity to murder him and get it back – "

"Dog!" snarled Zarono. Strom was livid, but he laughed mirthlessly.

"Do you think I'd play fairly with a treacherous dog like you? – Go on, Conan."

The Cimmerian grinned. It was evident that he was deliberately fanning the fires of hate between the two men.

"Nothing much, then. I came straight through the woods while you tacked along the coast, and raised the fort before you did. Your guess that the storm had destroyed Zarono's ship was a good one – but then, you knew the configuration of this bay.

"Well, there's the story. I have the treasure, Strom has a ship, Valenso has supplies. By Crom, Zarono, I don't see where you fit into the scheme, but to avoid strife I'll include you. My proposal is simple enough.

"We'll split the treasure four ways. Strom and I will sail away with our shares aboard *The Red Hand*. You and Valenso takes yours and remain lords of the wilderness, or build a ship out of tree trunks, as you wish."

Valenso blenched and Zarono swore, while Strom grinned quietly.

"Are you fool enough to go aboard *The Red Hand* alone with Strom?" snarled Zarono. "He'll cut your throat before you're out of sight of land!"

Conan laughed with genuine enjoyment.

"This is like the problem of the sheep, the wolf, and the cabbage," he admitted. "How to get them across the river without their devouring each other!"

"And that appeals to your Cimmerian sense of humor," complained Zarono.

"I will not stay here!" cried Valenso, a wild gleam in his dark eyes. "Treasure or no treasure, I must go!"

Conan gave him a slit-eyed glance of speculation.

"Well, then," said he, "how about this plan: we divide the loot as I suggested. Then Strom sails away with Zarono, Valenso, and such members of the Count's household as he may select, leaving me in command of the fort and the rest of Valenso's men, and all of Zarono's. I'll build my own ship."

Zarono looked slightly sick.

"I have the choice of remaining here in exile, or abandoning my crew and going alone on *The Red Hand* to have my throat cut?"

Conan's laughter rang gustily through the hall, and he smote Zarono jovially on the back, ignoring the black murder in the buccaneer's glare.

"That's it, Zarono!" quoth he. "Stay here while Strom and I sail away, or sail away with Strom, leaving your men with me."

"I'd rather have Zarono," said Strom frankly. "You'd turn my own men against me, Conan, and cut my throat before I raised the Barachans."

Sweat dripped from Zarono's livid face.

"Neither I, the Count, nor his niece will ever reach the land alive if we ship with that devil," said he. "You are both in my power in this hall. My men surround it. What's to prevent me cutting you both down?"

"Not a thing," Conan admitted cheerfully. "Except the fact that if you do Strom's men will sail away and leave you stranded on the coast where the Picts will presently cut all your throats; and the fact that with me dead

46

you'll never find the treasure; and the fact that I'll split your skull down to your chin if you try to summon your men."

Conan laughed as he spoke, as if at some whimsical situation, but even Belesa sensed that he meant what he said. His naked cutlass lay across his knees, and Zarono's sword was under the table, out of the buccaneer's reach. Galbro was not a fighting man, and Valenso seemed incapable of decision or action.

"Aye!" said Strom with an oath. "You'd find the two of us no easy prey. I'm agreeable to Conan's proposal. What do you say, Valenso?"

"I must leave this coast!" whispered Valenso, staring blankly. "I must hasten – I must go – go far – quickly!"

Strom frowned, puzzled at the Count's strange manner, and turned to Zarono, grinning wickedly: "And you, Zarono?"

"What can I say?" snarled Zarono. "Let me take my three officers and forty men aboard *The Red Hand*, and the bargain's made."

"The officers and thirty men!"

"Very well."

"Done!"

There was no shaking of hands, or ceremonial drinking of wine to seal the pact. The two captains glared at each other like hungry wolves. The Count plucked his mustache with a trembling hand, rapt in his own somber thoughts. Conan stretched like a great cat, drank wine, and grinned on the assemblage, but it was the sinister grin of a stalking tiger. Belesa sensed the murderous purposes that reigned there, the treacherous intent that dominated each man's mind. Not one had any intention of keeping his part of the pact, Valenso possibly excluded. Each of the freebooters intended to possess both the ship and the entire treasure. Neither would be satisfied with less. But how? What was going on in each crafty mind? Belesa felt oppressed and stifled by the atmosphere of hatred and treachery. The Cimmerian, for all his ferocious frankness, was no less subtle than the others – and even fiercer. His domination of the situation was not physical alone, though his gigantic shoulders and massive limbs seemed too big even for the great hall. There was an iron vitality about the man that overshadowed even the hard vigor of the other buccaneers.

"Lead us to the treasure!" Zarono demanded.

"Wait a bit," answered Conan. "We must keep our power evenly balanced, so one can't take advantage of the others. We'll work it this way: Strom's men will come ashore, all but half a dozen or so, and camp on the beach. Zarono's men will come out of the fort, and likewise camp on the strand, within easy sight of them. Then each crew can keep a check on the other, to see that nobody slips after us who go after the treasure, to ambush either of us. Those left aboard *The Red Hand* will take her out into the bay out of reach of either party. Valenso's men will stay in the fort, but will leave the gate open. Will you come with us, Count?"

"Go into that forest?" Valenso shuddered, and drew his cloak about his shoulders. "Not for all the gold of Tranicos!"

"All right. It'll take about thirty men to carry the loot. We'll take fifteen men from each crew and start as soon as possible."

Belesa, keenly alert to every angle of the drama being played out beneath her, saw Zarono and Strom shoot furtive glances at one another, then lower their gaze quickly as they lifted their glasses to hide the murky intent in their eyes. Belesa saw the fatal weakness in Conan's plan, and wondered how he could have overlooked it. Perhaps he was too arrogantly confident in his personal prowess. But she knew that he would never come out of that forest alive. Once the treasure was in their grasp, the others would form a rogues' alliance long enough to rid themselves of the man both hated. She shuddered, staring morbidly at the man she knew was doomed; strange to see that powerful fighting man sitting there, laughing and swilling wine, in full prime and power, and to know that he was already doomed to a bloody death.

The whole situation was pregnant with dark and bloody portents. Zarono would trick and kill Strom if he could, and she knew that Strom had already marked Zarono for death, and doubtless, also, her uncle and herself. If Zarono won the final battle of cruel wits, their lives were safe – but looking at the buccaneer as he sat there chewing his mustache, with all the stark evil of his nature showing naked in his dark face, she could not decide which was more abhorrent – death or Zarono.

"How far is it?" demanded Strom.

"If we start within the hour we can be back before midnight," answered Conan. He emptied his glass, rose, adjusted his girdle, and glanced at the Count.

"Valenso," he said, "are you mad, to kill a Pict in his hunting paint?"

48

Valenso started.

"What do you mean?"

"Do you mean to say you don't know that your men killed a Pict hunter in the woods last night?"

The Count shook his head.

"None of my men was in the woods last night."

"Well, somebody was," grunted the Cimmerian, fumbling in a pocket. "I saw his head nailed to a tree near the edge of the forest. He wasn't painted for war. I didn't find any boot-tracks, from which I judged that it had been nailed up there before the storm. But there were plenty of other signs – moccasin tracks on the wet ground. Picts have been there and seen that head. They were men of some other clan, or they'd have taken it down. If they happen to be at peace with the clan the dead man belonged to, they'll make tracks to his village to tell his tribe."

"Perhaps they killed him," suggested Valenso.

"No, they didn't. But they know who did, for the same reason that I know. This chain was knotted about the stump of the severed neck. You must have been utterly mad, to identify your handiwork like that."

He drew forth something and tossed it on the table before the Count, who lurched up, choking, as his hand flew to his throat. It was the gold seal-chain he habitually wore about his neck.

"I recognized the Korzetta seal," said Conan. "The presence of that chain would tell any Pict it was the work of a foreigner."

Valenso did not reply. He sat staring at the chain as if at a venomous serpent.

Conan scowled at him, and glanced questioningly at the others. Zarono made a quick gesture to indicate the Count was not quite right in the head.

Conan sheathed his cutlass and donned his lacquered hat.

"All right, let's go."

The captains gulped down their wind and rose, hitching at their sword-belts. Zarono laid a hand on Valenso's arm and shook him slightly. The Count started and stared about him, then followed the others out, like a man in a daze, the chain dangling from his fingers. But not all left the hall.

Belesa and Tina, forgotten on the stair, peeping between the balusters, saw Galbro fall behind the others, loitering until the heavy door closed after them. Then he hurried to the fireplace and raked carefully at the smoldering coals. He sank to his knees and peered closely at something for a long space. Then he straightened, and with a furtive air stole out of the hall by another door.

"What did Galbro find in the fire?" whispered Tina. Belesa shook her head, then, obeying the promptings of her curiosity, rose and went down to the empty hall. An instant later she was kneeling where the seneschal had knelt, and she saw what he had seen.

It was the charred remnant of the map Conan had thrown into the fire. It was ready to crumble at a touch, but faint lines and bits of writing were still discernible upon it. She could not read the writing, but she could trace the outlines of what seemed to be the picture of a hill or crag, surrounded by marks evidently representing dense trees. She could make nothing of it, but from Galbro's actions, she believed he recognized it as portraying some scene or topographical feature familiar to him. She knew the seneschal had penetrated inland further than any other man of the settlement.

CHAPTER 6

The Plunder of the Dead

Belesa came down the stair and paused at the sight of Count Valenso seated at the table, turning the broken chain about in his hands. She looked at him without love, and with more than a little fear. The change that had come over him was appalling; he seemed to be locked up in a grim world all his own, with a fear that flogged all human characteristics out of him.

The fortress stood strangely quiet in the noonday heat that had followed the storm of the dawn. Voices of people within the stockade sounded subdued, muffled. The same drowsy stillness reigned on the beach outside where the rival crews lay in armed suspicion, separated by a few hundred yards of bare sand. Far out in the bay The Red Hand lay at anchor with a handful of men aboard her, ready to snatch her out of reach at the slightest indication of treachery. The carack was Strom's trump card, his best guarantee against the trickery of his associates.

Conan had plotted shrewdly to eliminate the chances of an ambush in the forest by either party. But as far as Belesa could see, he had failed utterly to safeguard himself against the treachery of his companions. He had disappeared into the woods, leading the two captains and their thirty men, and the Zingaran girl was positive that she would never see him alive again.

Presently she spoke, and her voice was strained and harsh to her own ear.

"The barbarian has led the captains into the forest. When they have the gold in their hands, they'll kill him. But when they return with the treasure, what then? Are we to go aboard the ship? Can we trust Strom?"

Valenso shook his head absently.

"Strom would murder us all for our shares of the loot. But Zarono whispered his intentions to me secretly. We will not go aboard The Red Hand save as her masters. Zarono will see that night overtakes the treasure-party, so they are forced to camp in the forest. He will find a way to kill Strom and his men in their sleep. Then the buccaneers will come on stealthily to the beach. Just before dawn I will send some of my fishermen secretly from the fort to swim out to the ship and seize her. Strom never thought of that, neither did Conan. Zarono and his men will come out of the forest and with the buccaneers encamped on the beach, fall upon the pirates in the dark, while I lead my men-at-arms from the fort to complete the rout. Without their captain they will be demoralized, and outnumbered, fall easy prey to Zarono and me. Then we will sail in Strom's ship with all the treasure."

"And what of me?" she asked with dry lips.

"I have promised you to Zarono," he answered harshly. "But for my promise he would not take us off."

"I will never marry him," she said helplessly.

"You will," he responded gloomily, and without the slightest touch of sympathy. He lifted the chain so it caught the gleam of the sun, slanting through a window. "I must have dropped it on the sand," he muttered. "He has been that near – on the beach – "

"You did not drop it on the strand," said Belesa, in a voice as devoid of mercy as his own; her soul seemed turned to stone. "You tore it from your throat, by accident, last night in this hall, when you flogged Tina. I saw it gleaming on the floor before I left the hall."

He looked up, his eyes grey with a terrible fear.

She laughed bitterly, sensing the mute question in his dilated eyes.

"Yes! The black man! He was here! In this hall! He must have found the chain on the floor. The guardsmen did not see him. But he was at your door last night. I saw him, padding along the upper hallway."

For an instant she thought he would drop dead of sheer terror. He sank back in his chair, the chain slipping from his nerveless fingers and clinking on the table.

"In the manor!" he whispered. "I thought bolts and bars and armed guards could keep him out, fool that I was! I can no more guard against him than I can escape him! At my door! At my door!" The thought overwhelmed him with horror. "Why did he not enter?" he shrieked, tearing at the lace upon his collar as though it strangled him. "Why did he not end it? I have dreamed of waking in my darkened chamber to see him squatting above me and the blue hell-fire playing about his horned head! Why – "

The paroxysm passed, leaving him faint and trembling.

"I understand!" he panted. "He is playing with me, as a cat with a mouse. To have slain me last night in my chamber were too easy, too merciful. So he destroyed the ship in which I might have escaped him, and he slew that wretched Pict and left my chain upon him, so that the savages might believe I had slain him – they have seen that chain upon my neck many a time.

"But why? What subtle deviltry has he in mind, what devious purpose no human mind can grasp or understand?"

"Who is this black man?" asked Belesa, chill fear crawling along her spine.

"A demon loosed by my greed and lust to plague me throughout eternity!" he whispered. He spread his long thin fingers on the table before him, and stared at her with hollow, weirdly luminous eyes that seemed to see her not at all, but to look through her and far beyond to some dim doom.

"In my youth I had an enemy at court," he said, as if speaking more to himself than to her. "A powerful man who stood between me and my ambition. In my lust for wealth and power I sought aid from the people of the black arts – a black magician, who, at my desire, raised up a fiend from the outer gulfs of existence and clothed it in the form of a man. It crushed and slew my enemy; I grew great and wealthy and none could stand before me. But I thought to cheat my fiend of the price a mortal must pay who calls the black folk to do his bidding.

"By his grim arts the magician tricked the soulless waif of darkness and bound him in hell where he howled in vain – I supposed for eternity. But because the sorcerer had given the fiend the form of a man, he could never break the link that bound it to the material world; never completely close the cosmic corridors by which it had gained access to this planet.

"A year ago in Kordava word came to me that the magician, now an ancient man, had been slain in his castle, with marks of demon fingers on his throat. Then I knew that the black one had escaped from the hell where the magician had bound him, and that he would seek vengeance upon me. One night I saw his demon face leering at me from the shadows in my castle hall –

"It was not his material body, but his spirit sent to plague me – his spirit which could not follow me over the windy waters. Before he could reach Kordava in the flesh, I sailed to put broad seas between me and him. He has his limitations. To follow me across the seas he must remain in his man-like body of flesh. But that flesh is not human flesh. He can be slain, I think, by fire, though the magician, having raised him up, was powerless to slay him – such are the limits set upon the powers of sorcerers.

"But the black one is too crafty to be trapped or slain. When he hides himself no man can find him. He steals like a shadow through the night, making naught of bolts and bars. He blinds the eyes of guardsmen with sleep. He can raise storms and command the serpents of the deep, and the fiends of the night. I hoped to drown my trail in the blue rolling wastes – but he has tracked me down to claim his grim forfeit."

The weird eyes lit palely as he gazed beyond the tapestried walls to far, invisible horizons.

"I'll trick him yet," he whispered. "Let him delay to strike this night – dawn will find me with a ship under my heels and again I will cast an ocean between me and his vengeance."

"Hell's fire!"

Conan stopped short, glaring upward. Behind him the seamen halted – two compact clumps of them, bows in their hands, and suspicion in their attitude. They were following an old path made by Pictish hunters which led due east, and though they had progressed only some thirty yards, the beach was no longer visible.

"What is it?" demanded Strom suspiciously. "What are you stopping for?"

"Are you blind? Look there!"

From the thick limb of a tree that overhung the trail a head grinned down at them – a dark painted face, framed in thick black hair, in which a toucan feather drooped over the left ear.

"I took that head down and hid it in the bushes," growled Conan, scanning the woods about them narrowly. "What fool could have stuck it back up there? It looks as if somebody was trying his damndest to bring the Picts down on the settlement."

Men glanced at each other darkly, a new element of suspicion added to the already seething cauldron.

Conan climbed the tree, secured the head and carried it into the bushes, where he tossed it into a stream and saw it sink.

"The Picts whose tracks are about this tree weren't Toucans," he growled, returning through the thicket. "I've sailed these coasts enough to know something about the sea-land tribes. If I read the prints of their moccasins right, they were Cormorants. I hope they're having a war with the Toucans. If they're at peace, they'll head straight for the Toucan village, and there'll be hell to pay. I don't know how far away that village is – but as soon as they learn of this murder, they'll come through the forest like starving wolves. That's the worst insult possible to a Pict – kill a man not in war-paint and stick his head up in a tree for the vultures to eat. Damn' peculiar things going on along this coast. But that's always the case when civilized men come into the wilderness. They're all crazy as hell. Come on."

Men loosened blades in their scabbards and shafts in their quivers as they strode deeper into the forest. Men of the sea, accustomed to the rolling expanses of grey water, they were ill at ease with the green mysterious walls of trees and vines hemming them in. The path wound and twisted until most of them quickly lost their sense of direction, and did not even know in which direction the beach lay.

Conan was uneasy for another reason. He kept scanning the trail, and finally grunted: "Somebody's passed along here recently – not more than an hour ahead of us. Somebody in boots, with no woods-craft. Was he the fool who found that Pict's head and stuck it back up in that tree? No, it couldn't have been him. I didn't find his tracks under the tree. But who was it? I didn't find any tracks there, except those of the Picts I'd seen already. And who's this fellow hurrying ahead of us? Did either of you bastards send a man ahead of us for any reason?"

Both Strom and Zarono loudly disclaimed any such act, glaring at each other with mutual disbelief. Neither man could see the signs Conan pointed out; the faint prints which he saw on the grassless, hard-beaten trail were invisible to their untrained eyes.

Conan quickened his pace and they hurried after him, fresh coals of suspicion added to the smoldering fire of distrust. Presently the path veered veered northward, and Conan left it, and began threading his way through the dense trees in a southeasterly direction. Strom stole an uneasy glance at Zarono. This might force a change in their plans. Within a few hundred feet from the trail both were hopelessly lost, and convinced of their inability to find their way back to the path. They were shaken by the fear that, after all, the Cimmerian had a force at his command, and was leading them into an ambush.

This suspicion grew as they advanced, and had almost reached panic-proportions when they emerged from the thick woods and saw just ahead of them a gaunt crag that jutted up from the forest floor. A dim path leading out of the woods from the east ran among a cluster of boulders and wound up the crag on a ladder of stony shelves to a flat ledge near the summit.

Conan halted, a bizarre figure in his piratical finery.

"That trail is the one I followed, running from the Eagle-Picts," he said. "It leads up to a cave behind that ledge. In that cave are the bodies of Tranicos and his captains, and the treasure he plundered from Tothmekri. But a word before we go up after it: if you kill me here, you'll never find your way back to the trail we followed from the beach. I know you seafaring men. You're helpless in the deep woods. Of course the beach lies due west, but if you have to make your way through the tangled woods, burdened with the plunder, it'll take you not hours, but days. And I don't think these woods will be very safe for white men, when the Toucans learn about their hunter." He laughed at the ghastly, mirthless smiles with which they greeted his recognition of their intentions regarding him. And he also comprehended the thought that sprang in the mind of each: let the barbarian secure the loot for them, and lead them back to the beach-trail before they killed him.

"All of you stay here except Strom and Zarono," said Conan. "We three are enough to pack the treasure down from the cave."

Strom grinned mirthlessly.

"Go up there alone with you and Zarono? Do you take me for a fool? One man at least comes with me!" And he designated his boatswain, a brawny, hard-faced giant, naked to his broad leather belt, with gold hoops in his ears, and a crimson scarf knotted about his head.

"And my executioner comes with me!" growled Zarono. He beckoned to a lean sea-thief with a face like a parchment-covered skull, who carried a two-handed scimitar naked over his bony shoulder.

Conan shrugged his shoulders. "Very well. Follow me."

They were close on his heels as he strode up the winding path and mounted the ledge. They crowded him close as he passed through the cleft in the wall behind it, and their breath sucked greedily between their teeth as he called their attention to the iron-bound chests on either side of the short tunnel-like cavern.

"A rich cargo there," he said carelessly. "Silks, laces, garments, ornaments, weapons – the loot of the southern seas. But the real treasure lies beyond that door."

The massive door stood partly open. Conan frowned. He remembered closing that door before he left the cavern. But he said nothing of the matter to his eager companions as he drew aside to let them look through.

They looked into a wide cavern, lit by a strange blue glow that glimmered through a smoky mist-like haze. A great ebon table stood in the midst of the cavern, and in a carved chair with a high back and broad arms, that might once have stood in the castle of some Zingaran baron, sat a giant figure, fabulous and fantastic – there sat Bloody Tranicos, his great head sunk on his bosom, one brawny hand still gripping a jeweled goblet in which wine still sparkled; Tranicos, in his lacquered hat, his gilt-embroidered coat with jeweled buttons that winked in the blue flame, his flaring boots and gold-worked baldric that upheld a jewel-hilted sword in a golden sheath.

And ranging the board, each with his chin resting on his lace-bedecked breast, sat the eleven captains. The blue fire played weirdly on them and on their giant admiral, as it flowed from the enormous jewel on the tiny ivory pedestal, striking glints of frozen fire from the heaps of fantastically cut gems which shone before the place of Tranicos – the plunder of Khemi, the jewels of Tothmekri! The stones whose value was greater than the value of all the rest of the known jewels in the world put together!

The faces of Zarono and Strom showed pallid in the blue glow; over their shoulders their men gaped stupidly.

"Go in and take them," invited Conan, drawing aside, and Zarono and Strom crowded avidly past him, jostling one another in their haste. Their followers were treading on their heels. Zarono kicked the door wide open – and halted with one foot on the threshold at the sight of a figure on the floor, previously hidden from view by the partly-closed door. It was a man, prone and contorted, head drawn back between his shoulders, white face twisted in a grin of mortal agony, gripping his own throat with clawed fingers.

"Galbro!" ejaculated Zarono. "Dead! What – " With sudden suspicion he thrust his head over the threshold, into the bluish mist that filled the inner cavern. And he screamed, chokingly: "There is death in the smoke!"

Even as he screamed, Conan hurled his weight against the four men bunched in the doorway, sending them staggering – but not headlong into the mist-filled cavern as he had planned. They were recoiling at the sight of the dead man and the realization of the trap, and his violent push, while it threw them off their feet, yet failed of the result he desired. Strom and Zarono sprawled half over the threshold on their knees, the boatswain tumbling over their legs, and the executioner caromed against the wall. Before Conan could follow up on his ruthless intention of kicking the fallen men into the cavern and holding the door against them until the poisonous mist did its deadly work, he had to turn and defend himself against the frothing onslaught of the executioner who was the first to regain his balance and his wits.

The buccaneer missed a tremendous swipe with his headsman's sword as the Cimmerian ducked, and the great blade banged against the stone wall, spattering blue sparks. The next instant his skull-faced head rolled on the cavern floor under the bite of Conan's cutlass.

In the split seconds this swift action consumed, the boatswain regained his feet and fell on the Cimmerian, raining blows with a cutlass that would have overwhelmed a lesser man. Cutlass met cutlass with a ring of steel that was deafening in the narrow cavern. The two captains rolled back across the threshold, gagging and gasping, purple in the face and too near strangled to shout, and Conan redoubled his efforts, in an endeavor to dispose of his antagonist and cut down his rivals before they could recover from the effects of the poison. The boatswain dripped blood at each step, as he was driven back before the ferocious onslaught, and he began desperately to bellow for his companions. But before Conan could deal the finishing stroke, the two chiefs, gasping but murderous, came at him with swords in their hands, croaking for their men.

The Cimmerian bounded back and leaped out onto the ledge. He felt himself a match for all three men, though each was a famed swordsman, but he did not wish to be trapped by the crews which would come charging up the path at the sound of the battle.

These were not coming with as much celerity as he expected, however. They were bewildered at the sounds and muffled shouts issuing from the cavern above them, but no man dared start up the path for fear of a sword in the back. Each band faced the other tensely, grasping their weapons but incapable of decision, and when they saw the Cimmerian bound out on the ledge, they still hesitated. While they stood with their arrows nocked he ran up the ladder of handholds niched in the rock near the cleft, and threw himself prone on the summit of the crag, out of their sight.

The captains stormed out on the ledge, raving and brandishing their swords, and their men, seeing their leaders were not at sword-strokes, ceased menacing each other, and gaped bewilderedly.

"Dog!" screamed Zarono. "You planned to poison us! Traitor!"

Conan mocked them from above.

"Well, what did you expect? You two were planning to cut my throat as soon as I got the plunder for you. If it hadn't been for that fool Galbro I'd have trapped the four of you, and explained to your men how you rushed in heedless to your doom."

"And with us both dead, you'd have taken my ship, and all the loot too!" frothed Strom.

"Aye! And the pick of each crew! I've been wanting to get back on the Main for months, and this was a good opportunity!

"It was Galbro's foot-prints I saw on the trail. I wonder how the fool learned of this cave, or how he expected to lug away the loot by himself."

"But for the sight of his body we'd have walked into that death-trap," muttered Zarono, his swarthy face still ashy. "That blue smoke was like unseen fingers crushing my throat."

"Well, what are you going to do?" their unseen tormentor yelled sardonically.

"What *are* we to do?" Zarono asked of Strom. "The treasure-cavern is filled with that poisonous mist, though for some reason it does not flow across the threshold."

"You can't get the treasure," Conan assured them with satisfaction from his aerie. "That smoke will strangle you. It nearly got me, when I stepped in there. Listen, and I'll tell you a tale the Picts tell in their huts when the fires burn low! Once, long ago, twelve strange men came out of the sea, and found a cave and heaped it with gold and jewels; but a Pictish shaman made magic and the earth shook, and smoke came out of the earth and strangled them where they sat at wine. The smoke, which was the smoke of hell's fire, was confined within the cavern by the magic of the wizard. The tale was told from tribe to tribe, and all the clans shun the accursed spot.

"When I crawled in there to escape the Eagle-Picts, I realized that the old legend was true, and referred to old Tranicos and his men. An earthquake cracked the rock floor of the cavern while he and his captains sat at wine, and let the mist out of the depths of the earth – doubtless out of hell, as the Picts say. Death guards old Tranicos's treasure!"

"Bring up the men!" frothed Strom. "We'll climb up and hew him down!"

"Don't be a fool," snarled Zarono. "Do you think any man on earth could climb those hand-holds in the teeth of his sword? We'll have the men up here, right enough, to feather him with shafts if he dares show himself. But we'll get those gems yet. He had some plan of obtaining the loot, or he wouldn't have brought thirty men to bear it back. If he could get it, so can we. We'll bend a cutlass-blade to make a hook, tie it to a rope and cast it about the leg of that table, then drag it to the door."

"Well thought, Zarono!" came down Conan's mocking voice. "Exactly what I had in mind. But how will you find your way back to the beach-path? It'll be dark long before you reach the beach, if you have to feel your way through the woods, and I'll follow you and kill you one by one in the dark."

"It's no empty boast," muttered Strom. "He can move and strike in the dark as subtly and silently as a ghost. If he hunts us back through the forest, few of us will live to see the beach."

"Then we'll kill him here," gritted Zarono. "Some of us will shoot at him while the rest climb the crag. If he is not struck by arrows, some of us will reach him with our swords. Listen! Why does he laugh?"

"To hear dead men making plots," came Conan's grimly amused voice.

"Heed him not," scowled Zarono, and lifting his voice, shouted for the men below to join him and Strom on the ledge.

The sailors started up the slanting trail, and one started to shout a question. Simultaneously there sounded a hum like that of an angry bee, ending in a sharp thud. The buccaneer gasped and blood gushed from his open mouth. He sank to his knees, clutching the black shaft that quivered in his breast. A yell of alarm went up from his companions.

"What's the matter?" shouted Strom.

"Picts!" bawled a pirate, lifting his bow and loosing blindly. At his side a man moaned and went down with an arrow through his throat.

"Take cover, you fools!" shrieked Zarono. From his vantage-point he glimpsed painted figures moving in the bushes. One of the men on the winding path fell back dying. The rest scrambled hastily back down among the rocks about the foot of the crag. They took cover clumsily, not used to this kind of fighting. Arrows flickered from the bushes, splintering on the boulders. The men on the ledge lay prone at full length.

"We're trapped!" Strom's face was pale. Bold enough with a deck under his feet, this silent, savage warfare shook his ruthless nerves.

"Conan said they feared this crag," said Zarono. "When night falls the men must climb up here. We'll hold the crag. The Picts won't rush us."

"Aye!" mocked Conan above them. "They won't climb the crag to get at you, that's true. They'll merely surround it and keep you here until you all die of thirst and starvation."

"He speaks truth," said Zarono helplessly. "What shall we do?"

"Make a truce with him," muttered Strom. "If any man can get us out of this jam, he can. Time enough to cut his throat later." Lifting his voice he called: "Conan, let's forget our feud for the time being. You're in this fix as much as we are. Come down and help us out of it."

"How do you figure that?" retorted the Cimmerian. "I have but to wait until dark, climb down the other side of this crag and melt into the forest.

I can crawl through the lines the Picts have thrown around this hill, and return to the fort to report you all slain by the savages – which will shortly be truth!"

Zarono and Strom stared at each other in pallid silence.

"But I'm not going to do that!" Conan roared. "Not because I have any love for you dogs, but because a white man doesn't leave white men, even his enemies, to be butchered by Picts."

The Cimmerian's tousled black head appeared over the crest of the crag.

"Now listen closely: that's only a small band down there. I saw them sneaking through the brush when I laughed, a while ago. Anyway, if there had been many of them, every man at the foot of the crag would be dead now. I think that's a band of fleet-footed young men sent ahead of the main war-party to cut us off from the beach. I'm certain a big war-band is heading in our direction from somewhere.

"They've thrown a cordon around the west side of the crag, but I don't think there are any on the east side. I'm going down on that side and get in the forest and work around behind them. Meanwhile, you crawl down the path and join your men among the rocks. Tell them to sling their bows and draw their swords. When you hear me yell, rush the trees on the west side of the clearing."

"What of the treasure?"

"To hell with the treasure! We'll be lucky if we get out of here with our heads on our shoulders."

The black-maned head vanished. They listened for sounds to indicate that Conan had crawled to the almost sheer eastern wall and was working his way down, but they heard nothing. Nor was there any sound in the forest. No more arrows broke against the rocks where the sailors were hidden. But all knew that fierce black eyes were watching with murderous patience. Gingerly Strom, Zarono, and the boatswain started down the winding path. They were halfway down when the black shafts began to whisper around them. The boatswain groaned and toppled limply down the slope, shot through the heart. Arrows shivered on the helmets and breastplates of the chiefs as they tumbled in frantic haste down the steep trail. They reached the foot in a scrambling rush and lay panting among the boulders, swearing breathlessly.

"Is this more of Conan's trickery?" wondered Zarono profanely.

"We can trust him in this matter," asserted Strom. "These barbarians live by their own particular code of honor, and Conan would never desert men of his own complexion to be slaughtered by people of another race. He'll help us against the Picts, even though he plans to murder us himself – hark!"

A blood-freezing yell knifed the silence. It came from the woods to the west, and simultaneously an object arched out of the trees, struck the ground and rolled bouncingly toward the rocks – a severed human head, the hideously painted face frozen in a snarl of death.

"Conan's signal!" roared Strom, and the desperate freebooters rose like a wave from the rocks and rushed headlong toward the woods.

Arrows whirred out of the bushes, but their flight was hurried and erratic, only three men fell. Then the wild men of the sea plunged through the fringe of foliage and fell on the naked painted figures that rose out of the gloom before them. There was a murderous instant of panting, ferocious effort, hand-to-hand, cutlasses beating down war-axes, booted feet trampling naked bodies, and then bare feet were rattling through the bushes in headlong flight as the survivors of that brief carnage quit the fray, leaving seven still, painted figures stretched on the blood-stained leaves that littered the earth. Further back in the thickets sounded a thrashing and heaving, and then it ceased and Conan strode into view, his lacquered hat gone, his coat torn, his cutlass dripping in his hand.

"What now?" panted Zarono. He knew the charge had succeeded only because Conan's unexpected attack on the rear of the Picts had demoralized the painted men, and prevented them from falling back before the rush. But he exploded into curses as Conan passed his cutlass through a buccaneer who writhed on the ground with a shattered hip.

"We can't carry him with us," grunted Conan. "It wouldn't be any kindness to leave him to be taken alive by the Picts. Come on!"

They crowded close at his heels as he trotted through the trees. Alone they would have sweated and blundered among the thickets for hours before they found the beach-trail – if they had ever found it. The Cimmerian led them as unerringly as if he had been following a blazed path, and the rovers shouted with hysterical relief as they burst suddenly upon the trail that ran westward.

"Fool!" Conan clapped a hand on the shoulder of a pirate who started to break into a run, and hurled him back among his companions. "You'll burst your heart and fall within a thousand yards. We're miles from the beach. Take an easy gait. We may have to sprint the last mile. Save some of your wind for it. Come on, now."

He set off down the trail at a steady jog-trot; the seamen followed him, setting their pace to his.

The sun was touching the waves of the western ocean. Tina stood at the window from which Belesa had watched the storm.

"The setting sun turns the ocean to blood," she said. "The carack's sail is a white fleck on the crimson waters. The woods are already darkened with clustering shadows."

"What of the seamen on the beach?" asked Belesa languidly. She reclined on a couch, her eyes closed, her hands clasped behind her head.

"Both camps are preparing their supper," said Tina. "They gather driftwood and build fires. I can hear them shouting to one another – *what is that?*"

The sudden tenseness in the girl's tone brought Belesa upright on the couch. Tina grasped the window-sill, her face white.

"Listen! A howling, far off, like many wolves!"

"Wolves?" Belesa sprang up, fear clutching her heart. "Wolves do not hunt in packs at this time of the year – "

"Oh, look!" shrilled the girl, pointing. "Men are running out of the forest!"

In an instant Belesa was beside her, staring wide-eyed at the figures, small in the distance, streaming out of the woods.

"The sailors!" she gasped. "Empty-handed! I see Zarono – Strom – "

"Where is Conan?" whispered the girl.

Belesa shook her head.

"Listen! Oh, listen!" whimpered the child, clinging to her. "The Picts!"

All in the fort could hear it now – a vast ululation of mad exultation and blood-lust, from the depths of the dark forest.

That sound spurred on the panting men reeling toward the stockade.

"Hasten!" gasped Strom, his face a drawn mask of exhausted effort. "They're almost at our heels. My ship – "

"She is too far out for us to reach," panted Zarono. "Make for the stockade. See, the men camped on the beach have seen us!" He waved his arms in breathless pantomime, but the men on the strand understood, and they recognized the significance of that wild howling, rising to a triumphant crescendo. The sailors abandoned their fires and cooking-pots and fled for the stockade gate. They were pouring through it as the fugitives from the forest rounded the south angle and reeled into the gate, a heaving, frantic mob, half-dead from exhaustion. The gate was slammed with frenzied haste, and sailors began to climb the firing-ledge, to join the men-at-arms already there.

Belesa confronted Zarono.

"Where is Conan?"

The buccaneer jerked a thumb toward the blackening woods; his chest heaved; sweat poured down his face. "Their scouts were at our heels before we gained the beach. He paused to slay a few and give us time to get away."

He staggered away to take his place on the firing-ledge, whither Strom had already mounted. Valenso stood there, a somber, cloak-wrapped figure, strangely silent and aloof. He was like a man bewitched.

"Look!" yelped a pirate, above the deafening howling of the yet unseen horde.

A man emerged from the forest and raced fleetly across the open belt.

"Conan!"

Zarono grinned wolfishly.

"We're safe in the stockade; we know where the treasure is. No reason why we shouldn't feather him with arrows now."

"Nay!" Strom caught his arm. "We'll need his sword! Look!"

Behind the fleet-footed Cimmerian a wild horde burst from the forest, howling as they ran – naked Picts, hundreds and hundreds of them. Their arrows rained about the Cimmerian. A few strides more and Conan reached the eastern wall of the stockade, bounded high, seized the points of the logs and heaved himself up and over, his cutlass in his teeth. Arrows thudded venomously into the logs where his body had just been. His resplendent coat was gone, his white silk shirt torn and blood-stained.

"Stop them!" he roared as his feet hit the ground inside. "If they get on the wall, we're done for!"

Pirates, buccaneers and men-at-arms responded instantly, and a storm of arrows and quarrels tore into the oncoming horde.

Conan saw Belesa, with Tina clinging to her hand, and his language was picturesque.

"Get into the manor," he commanded in conclusion. "Their shafts will arch over the wall – what did I tell you?" as a black shaft cut into the earth at Belesa's feet and quivered like a serpent-head, Conan caught up a longbow and leaped to the firing-ledge. "Some of you fellows prepare torches!" he roared, above the rising clamor of battle. "We can't fight them in the dark!"

The sun had sunk in a welter of blood; out in the bay the men aboard the carack had cut the anchor chain and *The Red Hand* was rapidly receding on the crimson horizon.

CHAPTER 7

Men of the Woods

Night had fallen, but torches streamed across the strand, casting the mad scene into lurid revealment. Naked men in paint swarmed the beach; like waves they came against the palisade, bared teeth and blazing eyes gleaming in the glare of the torches thrust over the wall. Toucan feathers waved in black manes, and the feathers of the cormorant and the sea-falcon. A few warriors, the wildest and most barbaric of them all, wore shark's teeth woven in their tangled locks. The sea-land tribes had gathered from up and down the coast in all directions to rid their country of the white-skinned invaders.

They surged against the palisade, driving a storm of arrows before them, fighting into the teeth of the shafts and bolts that tore into their masses from the stockade. Sometimes they came so close to the wall they were hewing at the gate with their war-axes and thrusting their spears through the loop-holes. But each time the tide ebbed back without flowing over the palisade, leaving its drift of dead. At this kind of fighting the freebooters of the sea were at their stoutest; their arrows and bolts tore holes in the charging horde, their cutlasses hewed the wild men from the palisades they strove to scale.

Yet again and again the men of the woods returned to the onslaught with all the stubborn ferocity that had been roused in their fierce hearts.

"They are like mad dogs!" gasped Zarono, hacking downward at the dark hands that grasped at the palisade points, the dark faces that snarled up at him.

"If we can hold the fort until dawn they'll lose heart," grunted Conan, splitting a feathered skull with professional precision. "They won't maintain a long siege. Look, they're falling back."

The charge rolled back and the men on the wall shook the sweat out of their eyes, counted their dead and took a fresh grasp on the blood-slippery hilts of their swords. Like blood-hungry wolves, grudgingly driven from a cornered prey, the Picts skulked back beyond the ring of torches. Only the bodies of the slain lay before the palisade.

"Have they gone?" Strom shook back his wet, tawny locks. The cutlass in his fist was notched and red, his brawny bare arm was splashed with blood.

"They're still out there," Conan nodded toward the outer darkness which ringed the circle of torches, made more intense by their light. He glimpsed movements in the shadows; glitter of eyes and the dull sheen of steel.

"They've drawn off for a bit, though," he said. "Put sentries on the wall, and let the rest drink and eat. It's past midnight. We've been fighting for hours without much interval."

The chiefs clambered down from the ledges, calling their men from the walls. A sentry was posted in the middle of each wall, east, west, north and south, and a clump of men-at-arms were left at the gate. The Picts, to reach the wall, would have to charge across a wide, torch-lit space, and the defenders could resume their places long before the attackers could reach the palisade.

"Where's Valenso?" demanded Conan, gnawing a huge beef-bone as he stood beside the fire the men had built in the center of the compound. Pirates, buccaneers, and henchmen mingled with each other, wolfing the meat and ale the women brought them, and allowing their wounds to be bandaged.

"He disappeared an hour ago," grunted Strom. "He was fighting on the wall beside me, when suddenly he stopped short and glared out into the darkness as if he saw a ghost. 'Look!' he croaked. 'The black devil! I see him! Out there in the night!' Well, I could swear I saw a figure moving among the shadows that was too tall for a Pict. But it was just a glimpse and it was gone. But Valenso jumped down from the firing-ledge and staggered into the manor like a man with a mortal wound. I haven't seen him since."

"He probably saw a forest-devil," said Conan tranquilly. "The Picts say this coast is lousy with them. What I'm more afraid of is fire-arrows. The Picts are likely to start shooting them at any time. What's that? It sounded like a cry for help!"

When the lull came in the fighting, Belesa and Tina had crept to their window, from which they had been driven by the danger of flying arrows. Silently they watched the men gather about the fire.

"There are not enough men on the stockade," said Tina.

In spite of her nausea at the sight of the corpses sprawled about the palisade, Belesa was forced to laugh.

"Do you think you know more about wars and siege than the freebooters?" she chided gently.

"There should be more men on the walls," insisted the child, shivering. "Suppose the black man came back?"

Belesa shuddered at the thought.

"I am afraid," murmured Tina. "I hope Strom and Zarono are killed."

"And not Conan?" asked Belesa curiously.

"Conan would not harm us," said the child, confidently. "He lives up to his barbaric code of honor, but they are men who have lost all honor."

"You are wise beyond your years, Tina," said Belesa, with the vague uneasiness the precocity of the girl frequently roused in her.

"Look!" Tina stiffened. "The sentry is gone from the south wall! I saw him on the ledge a moment ago; now he has vanished."

From their window the palisade points of the south wall were just visible over the slanting roofs of a row of huts which paralleled that wall almost its entire length. A sort of open-topped corridor, three or four yards wide, was formed by the stockade and the back of the huts, which were built in a solid row. These huts were occupied by the serfs.

"Where could the sentry have gone?" whispered Tina uneasily.

Belesa was watching one end of the hut-row which was not far from a side-door of the manor. She could have sworn she saw a shadowy figure glide from behind the huts and disappear at the door. Was that the vanished sentry? Why had he left the wall, and why should he steal so subtly into the manor? She did not believe it was the sentry she had seen, and a nameless fear congealed her blood.

"Where is the Count, Tina?" she asked.

"In the great hall, my Lady. He sits alone at the table, wrapped in his cloak and drinking wine, with a face grey as death."

"Go and tell him what we have seen. I will keep watch from this window, lest the Picts steal to the unguarded wall."

Tina scampered away. Belesa heard her slippered feet pattering along the corridor, receding down the stair. Then abruptly, terribly, there rang out a scream of such poignant fear that Belesa's heart almost stopped with the shock of it. She was out of the chamber and flying down the corridor before she was aware that her limbs were in motion. She ran down the stair – and halted as if turned to stone.

She did not scream as Tina had screamed. She was incapable of sound or motion. She saw Tina, was aware of the reality of small hands grasping her frantically. But these were the only sane realities in a scene of black nightmare and lunacy and death, dominated by the monstrous, anthropo-morphic shadow which spread awful arms against a lurid, hell-fire glare.

Out in the stockade Strom shook his head at Conan's question.

"I heard nothing."

"I did!" Conan's wild instincts were roused; he was tensed, his eyes blazing. "It came from the south wall, behind those huts!"

Drawing his cutlass he strode toward the palisade. From the compound the wall on the south and the sentry posted there were not visible, being hidden behind the huts. Strom followed, impressed by the Cimmerian's manner.

At the mouth of the open space between the huts and wall Conan halted, warily. The space was dimly lighted by torches flaring at either corner of the stockade. And about mid-way of that natural corridor a crumpled shape sprawled on the ground.

"Bracus!" swore Strom, running forward and dropping on one knee beside the figure. "By Mitra, his throat's been cut!"

Conan swept the space with a quick glance, finding it empty save for himself, Strom, and the dead man. He peered through a loop-hole. No living man moved within the ring of torch-light outside the fort.

"Who could have done this?" he wondered.

"Zarono!" Strom sprang up, spitting fury like a wildcat, his hair bristling, his face convulsed. "He has set his thieves to stabbing my men in the back! He plans to wipe me out by treachery! Devils! I am leagued within and without!"

"Wait!" Conan reached a restraining hand. "I don't believe Zarono – "

But the maddened pirate jerked away and rushed around the end of the hut-row, breathing blasphemies. Conan ran after him, swearing. Strom made straight toward the fire by which Zarono's tall lean form was visible as the buccaneer chief quaffed a jack of ale.

His amazement was supreme when the jack was dashed violently from his hand, spattering his breastplate with foam, and he was jerked around to confront the passion-distorted face of the pirate captain.

"You murdering dog!" roared Strom. "Will you slay my men behind my back while they fight for your filthy hide as well as for mine?"

Conan was hurrying toward them and on all sides men ceased eating and drinking to stare in amazement.

"What do you mean?" sputtered Zarono.

"You've set your men to stabbing mine at their posts!" screamed the maddened Barachan.

"You lie!" Smoldering hate burst into sudden flame.

With an incoherent howl Strom heaved up his cutlass and cut at the buccaneer's head. Zarono caught the blow on his armored left arm and sparks flew as he staggered back, ripping out his own sword.

In an instant the captains were fighting like madmen, their blades flaming and flashing in the firelight. Their crews reacted instantly and blindly. A deep roar went up as pirates and buccaneers drew their swords and fell upon each other. The men left on the walls abandoned their posts and leaped down into the stockade, blades in hand. In an instant the compound was a battle-ground, where knotting, writhing groups of men smote and slew in a blind frenzy. Some of the men-at-arms and serfs were drawn into the melee, and the soldiers at the gate turned and stared down in amazement, forgetting the enemy which lurked outside.

It had all happened so quickly – smoldering passions exploding into sudden battle – that men were fighting all over the compound before Conan could reach the maddened chiefs. Ignoring their swords he tore them apart with such violence that they staggered backward, and Zarono tripped and fell headlong.

"You cursed fools, will you throw away all our lives?"

Strom was frothing mad and Zarono was bawling for assistance. A buccaneer ran at Conan from behind and cut at his head. The Cimmerian half turned and caught his arm, checking the stroke in mid-air.

"Look, you fools!" he roared, pointing with his sword. Something in his tone caught the attention of the battle-crazed mob; men froze in their places, with lifted swords, Zarono on one knee, and twisted their heads to stare. Conan was pointing at a soldier on the firing-ledge. The man was reeling, arms clawing the air, choking as he tried to shout. Suddenly he pitched headlong to the ground and all saw the black arrow standing up between his shoulders.

A cry of alarm rose from the compound. On the heels of the shout came a clamor of blood-freezing screams, the shattering impact of axes on the gate. Flaming arrows arched over the wall and stuck in logs, and thin wisps of blue smoke curled upward. Then from behind the huts that ranged the south wall came swift and furtive figures racing across the compound.

"The Picts are in!" roared Conan.

Bedlam followed his shout. The freebooters ceased their feud, some turned to meet the savages, some to spring to wall. Savages were pouring from behind the huts and they streamed over the compound; their axes flashed against the cutlasses of the sailors.

Zarono was struggling to his feet when a painted savage rushed upon him from behind and brained him with a war-axe.

Conan with a clump of sailors behind him was battling with the Picts inside the stockade, and Strom, with most of his men, was climbing up on the firing-ledges, slashing at the dark figures already swarming over the wall. The Picts, who had crept up unobserved and surrounded the fort while the defenders were fighting among themselves, were attacking from all sides. Valenso's soldiers were clustered at the gate, trying to hold it against a howling swarm of exultant demons.

More and more savages streamed from behind the huts, having scaled the undefended south wall. Strom and his pirates were beaten back from the other sides of the palisade and in an instant the compound was swarming with naked warriors. They dragged down the defenders like wolves; the battle revolved into swirling whirlpools of painted figures surging about small groups of desperate white men. Picts, sailors, and henchmen littered the earth, stamped underfoot by the heedless feet. Blood-smeared braves dived howling into huts and the shrieks that rose from the interiors where women and children died beneath the red axes rose above the din of the battle. The men-at-arms abandoned the gate when they heard those pitiful cries, and in an instant the Picts had burst it and were pouring into the palisade at that point also. Huts began to go up in flames.

"Make for the manor!" roared Conan, and a dozen men surged in behind him as he hewed an inexorable way through the snarling pack.

Strom was at his side, wielding his red cutlass like a flail.

"We can't hold the manor," grunted the pirate.

"Why not?" Conan was too busy with his crimson work to spare a glance.

"Because – oh!" A knife in a dark hand sank deep in the Barachan's back. "Devil eat you, bastard!" Strom turned staggeringly and split the savage's head to the teeth. The pirate reeled and fell to his knees, blood starting from his lips.

"The manor's burning!" he croaked, and slumped over in the dust.

Conan cast a swift look about him. The men who had followed him were all down in their blood. The Pict gasping out his life under the Cimmerian's feet was the last of the group which had barred his way. All about him battle was swirling and surging, but for the moment he stood alone. He was not far from the south wall. A few strides and he could leap to the ledge, swing over and be gone through the night. But he remembered the helpless girls in the manor-from which, now, smoke was rolling in billowing masses. He ran toward the manor.

A feathered chief wheeled from the door, lifting a war-axe, and behind the racing Cimmerian lines of fleet-footed braves were converging upon him. He did not check his stride. His downward sweeping cutlass met and deflected the axe and split the skull of its wielder. An instant later Conan was through the door and had slammed and bolted it against the axes that splintered into the wood.

The great hall was full of drifting wisps of smoke through which he groped, half-blinded. Somewhere a woman was whimpering, little, catchy, hysterical sobs of nerve-shattering horror. He emerged from a whorl of smoke and stopped dead in his tracks, glaring down the hall.

The hall was dim and shadowy with drifting smoke; the silver candelabrum was overturned, the candles extinguished; the only illumination was a lurid glow from the great fireplace and the wall in which it was set, where the flames licked from burning floor to smoking roof-beams. And limned against that lurid glare Conan saw a human form swinging slowly at the end of a rope. The dead face turned toward him as the body swung, and it was distorted beyond recognition. But Conan knew it was Count Valenso, hanged to his own roof-beam.

But there was something else in the hall. Conan saw it through the drifting smoke – a monstrous black figure, outlined against the hell-fire glare. That outline was vaguely human; but the shadow thrown on the burning wall was not human at all.

"Crom!" muttered Conan aghast, paralyzed by the realization that he was confronted with a being against which his sword was helpless. He saw Belesa and Tina, clutched in each other's arms, crouching at the bottom of the stair.

The black monster reared up, looming gigantic against the flame, great arms spread wide; a dim face leered through the drifting smoke, semi-human, demonic, altogether terrible – Conan glimpsed the close-set horns, the gaping mouth, the peaked ears – it was lumbering toward him through the smoke, and an old memory woke with desperation.

Near the cimmerian stood a massive silver bench, ornately carven, once part of the splendor of Korzelta Castle. Conan grasped it, heaved it high above his head.

"Silver and fire!" he roared in a voice like a clap of wind, and hurled the bench with all the power of his iron muscles. Full on the great black breast it crashed, a hundred pounds of silver winged with terrific velocity. Not even the black one could stand before such a missile. He was carried off his feet – hurtled backward headlong into the open fireplace which was a roaring mouth of flame. A horrible scream shook the hall, the cry of an unearthly thing gripped suddenly by earthly death. The mantel cracked and stones fell from the great chimney, half-hiding the black writhing limbs at which the flames were eating in elemental fury. Burning beams crashed down from the roof and thundered on the stones, and the whole heap was enveloped by a roaring burst of fire.

Flames were racing down the stair when Conan reached it. He caught up the fainting child under one arm and dragged Belesa to her feet. Through the crackle and snap of the fire sounded the splintering of the door under the war-axes.

He glared about, sighted a door opposite the stair-landing, and hurried through it, carrying Tina and half-dragging Belesa, who seemed dazed. As they came into the chamber beyond, a reverberation behind them announced that the roof was falling in the hall. Through a strangling wall of smoke Conan saw an open, outer door on the other side of the chamber. As he lugged his charges through it, he saw it sagged on broken hinges, lock and bolt snapped and splintered as if by some terrific force.

"The black man came in by this door!" Belesa sobbed hysterically. "I saw him – but I did not know – "

They emerged into the fire-lit compound, a few feet from the hut-row that lined the south wall. A Pict was skulking toward the door, eyes red in the firelight, axe lifted. Turning the girl on his arm away from the blow, Conan drove his cutlass through the savage's breast, and then, sweeping Belesa off her feet, ran toward the south wall, carrying both girls.

The compound was full of billowing smoke clouds that hid half the red work going on there; but the fugitives had been seen. Naked figures, black against the dull glare, pranced out of the smoke, brandishing gleaming axes. They were still yards behind him when Conan ducked into the spaces between the huts and the wall. At the other end of the corridor he saw other howling shapes, running to cut him off. Halting short he tossed Belesa bodily to the firing-ledge and leaped after her. Swinging her over the palisade he dropped her into the sand outside, and dropped Tina after her. A thrown axe crashed into a log by his shoulder, and then he too was over the wall and gathering up his dazed and helpless charges. When the Picts reached the wall the space before the palisade was empty of all except the dead.

CHAPTER 8

A Pirate Returns to the Sea

Dawn was tinging the dim waters with an old rose hue. Far out across the tinted waters a fleck of white grew out of the mist – a sail that seemed to hang suspended in the pearly sky. On a bushy headland Conan the Cimmerian held a ragged cloak over a fire of green wood. As he manipulated the cloak, puffs of smoke rose upward, quivered against the dawn and vanished.

Belesa crouched near him, one arm about Tina.

"Do you think they'll see it and understand?"

"They'll see it, right enough," he assured her. "They've been hanging off and on this coast all night, hoping to sight some survivors. They're scared stiff. There's only half a dozen of them, and not one can navigate well enough to sail from here to the Barachan Isles. They'll understand my signals; it's the pirate code. I'm telling them that the captains are dead and all the sailors, and for them to come inshore and take us aboard. They know I can navigate, and they'll be glad to ship under me; they'll have to. I'm the only captain left."

"But suppose the Picts see the smoke?" She shuddered, glancing back over the misty sands and bushes to where, miles to the north, a column of smoke stood up in the still air.

"They're not likely to see it. After I hid you in the woods I crept back and saw them dragging barrels of wine and ale out of the storehouses. Already most of them were reeling. They'll all be lying around too drunk to move by this time. If I had a hundred men I could wipe out the whole horde. Look! There goes a rocket from *The Red Hand*! That means they're coming to take us off!"

Conan stamped out the fire, handed the cloak back to Belesa and stretched like a great lazy cat. Belesa watched him in wonder. His unperturbed manner was not assumed; the night of fire and blood and slaughter, and the flight through the black woods afterward, had left his nerves untouched. He was as calm as if he had spent the night in feast and revel. Belesa did not fear him; she felt safer than she had felt since she landed on that wild coast. He was not like the freebooters, civilized men who had

74

repudiated all standards of honor, and lived without any. Conan, on the other hand, lived according to the code of his people, which was barbaric and bloody, but at least upheld its own peculiar standards of honor.

"Do you think he is dead?" she asked, with seeming irrelevancy.

He did not ask her to whom she referred.

"I believe so. Silver and fire are both deadly to evil spirits, and he got a belly-full of both."

Neither spoke of that subject again; Belesa's mind shrank from the task of conjuring up the scene when a black figure skulked into the great hall and a long-delayed vengeance was horribly consummated.

"What will you do when you get back to Zingara?" Conan asked.

She shook her head helplessly. "I do not know. I have neither money nor friends. I am not trained to earn my living. Perhaps it would have been better had one of those arrows struck my heart."

"Do not say that, my Lady!" begged Tina. "I will work for us both!"

Conan drew a small leather bag from inside his girdle.

"I didn't get Tothmekri's jewels," he rumbled. "But here are some baubles I found in the chest where I got the clothes I'm wearing." He spilled a handful of flaming rubies into his palm. "They're worth a fortune, themselves." He dumped them back into the bag and handed it to her.

"But I can't take these – " she began.

"Of course you'll take them. I might as well leave you for the Picts to scalp as to take you back to Zingara to starve," said he. "I know what it is to be penniless in a Hyborian land. Now in my country sometimes there are famines; but people are hungry only when there's no food in the land at all. But in civilized countries I've seen people sick of gluttony while others were starving. Aye, I've seen men fall and die of hunger against the walls of shops and storehouses crammed with food.

"Sometimes I was hungry, too, but then I took what I wanted at sword's-point. But you can't do that. So you take these rubies. You can sell them and buy a castle, and slaves, and fine clothes, and with them it won't be hard to get a husband, because civilized men all desire wives with these possessions."

"But what of you?"

Conan grinned and indicated The Red Hand drawing swiftly inshore.

"A ship and a crew are all I want. As soon as I set foot on that deck, I'll have a ship, and as soon as I can raise the Barachans I'll have a crew. The lads of the Red Brotherhood are eager to ship with me, because I always lead them to rare loot. And as soon as I've set you and the girl ashore on the Zingaran coast, I'll show the dogs some looting! Nay, nay, no thanks! What are a handful of jewels to me, when all the loot of the southern seas will be mine for the grasping?"

Marchers of Valhalla

The sky was lurid, gloomy and repellent, of the blue of tarnished steel, streaked with dully crimson banners. Against the muddled red smear lowered the low hills that are the peaks of that barren upland which is a dreary expanse of sand drifts and post-oak thickets, checkered with sterile fields where tenant farmers toil out their hideously barren lives in fruitless labor and bitter want.

I had limped to a ridge which rose above the others, flanked on either hand by the dry post-oak thickets. The terrible dreariness of the grim desolation of the vistas spread before me turned my soul to dust and ashes. I sank down upon a half-rotted log, and the agonizing melancholy of that drab land lay hard upon me. The red sun, half veiled in blowing dust and filmy cloud, sank low; it hung a hand's breadth above the western rim. But its setting lent no glory to the sand drifts and shinnery. Its somber glow but accentuated the grisly desolation of the land.

Then suddenly I realized that I was not alone. A woman had come from the dense thicket, and stood looking down at me. I gazed at her in silent wonder. Beauty was so rare in my life I was hardly able to recognize it, yet I knew that this woman was unbelievably beautiful. She was neither short nor tall; slender and yet splendidly shaped. I do not remember her dress; I have a vague impression that she was richly but modestly clad. But I remember the strange beauty of her face, framed in the dark rippling glory of her hair. Her eyes held mine like a magnet; I can not tell you the color of those eyes. They were dark and luminous, lighted as no eyes I ever saw were lighted. She spoke and her voice, strangely accented, was alien to my ears, and golden as distant chimes.

"Why do you fret, Hialmar?"

"You mistake me, Miss," I answered. "My name is James Allison. Were you looking for someone?"

She shook her head slowly.

"I came to look at the land once more. I had not thought to find you here."

"I don't understand you," I said. "I never saw you before. Are you a native of this country? You don't talk like a Texan."

She shook her head.

"No. But I knew this land long ago – long, long ago."

"You don't look that old," I said bluntly. "You'll pardon me for not getting up. As you see, I have but one leg, and it was such a long walk up here that I'm forced to sit and rest."

"Life has dealt harshly with you," she said softly. "I had hardly recognized you. Your body is so changed – "

"You must have known me before I lost my leg," I said bitterly, "although I'll swear I can't remember you. I was only fourteen when a mustang fell on me and crushed my leg so badly it had to be amputated. I wish to God it had been my neck."

Thus cripples speak to utter strangers – not so much a bid for sympathy, but the despairing cry of a soul tortured beyond endurance.

"Do not fret," she said softly. "Life takes but it also gives – "

"Oh, don't give me a speech about resignation and cheerfulness!" I cried savagely. "If I had the power I'd strangle every damned blatant optimist in the world! What have I to be merry about? What have I to do except sit and wait for the death which is slowly creeping on me from an incurable malady? I have no memories to cheer me – no future to look forward to – except a few more years of pain and woe, and then the blackness of utter oblivion. There has not even been any beauty in my life, lying as it has in this forsaken and desolate wilderness."

The dams of my reticence were broken, and my bitter dreams, long pent up, burst forth; nor did it seem strange that I should pour out my soul to a strange woman I had never seen before.

"The country has memories," she said.

"Yes, but I have not shared in them. I could have loved life and lived deeply as a cowboy, even here, before the squatters turned the country from an open range to a drift of struggling farms. I could have lived deep as a buffalo hunter, an Indian fighter, or an explorer, even here. But I was born out of my time, and even the exploits of this weary age were denied me.

"It's bitter beyond human telling to sit chained and helpless, and feel the hot blood drying in my veins, and the glittering dreams fading in my brain. I come of a restless, roving, fighting race. My great-grandfather died at the Alamo, shoulder to shoulder with David Crockett. My grandfather rode with Jack Hayes and Bigfoot Wallace, and fell with three-quarters of Hood's brigade. My oldest brother fell at Vimy Ridge, fighting with the Canadians, and the other died at the Argonne. My father is a cripple, too; he sits drowsing in his chair all day, but his dreams are full of brave memories, for the bullet that broke his leg struck him as he charged up San Juan Hill.

"But what have I to feel or dream or think?"

"You should remember," she said softly. "Even now dreams should come to you like the echoes of distant lutes. I remember! How I crawled to you on my knees, and you spared me – aye, and the crashing and the thundering as the land gave way – man, do you never dream of drowning?"

I started.

"How could you know that? Time and again I have felt the churning, seething waters rise like a green mountain over me, and have wakened, gasping and strangling – but how could you know?"

"The bodies change, the soul remains slumbering and untouched," she answered cryptically. "Even the world changes. This is a dreary land, you say, yet its memories are ancient and marvelous beyond the memories of Egypt."

I shook my head in wonder.

"Either you're insane, or I am. Texas has glorious memories of war and conquest and drama – but what are her few hundred years of history, compared to the antiquities of Egypt – in ancientness, I mean?"

"What is the peculiarity of the state as a whole?" she asked.

"I don't know exactly what you mean," I answered. "If you mean geologically, the peculiarity that has struck me is the fact that the land is but a succession of broad tablelands, or shelves, sloping upward from sea-level to over four thousand feet elevation, like the steps of a giant stair, with breaks of timbered hills between. The last break is the Caprock, and above that begins the Great Plains."

"Once the Great Plains stretched to the Gulf," she said. "Long, long ago what is now the state of Texas was a vast upland plateau, sloping gently to the coast, but without the breaks and shelvings of today. A mighty cataclysm broke off the land at the Caprock, the ocean roared over it, and the

Caprock became the new shoreline. Then, age-by-age, the waters slowly receded, leaving the steppes as they are today. But in receding they swept into the depths of the Gulf many curious things – man, do you not remember – the vast plains that ran from the sunset to the cliffs above the shining sea? And the great city that loomed above those cliffs?

I stared at her, bewildered. Suddenly she leaned toward me, and the glory of her alien beauty almost overpowered me. My senses reeled. She threw her hands before my eyes with a strange gesture.

"You shall see!" she cried sharply. "You see – what do you see?"

"I see the sand drifts and the shinnery thickets gloomy with sunset," I answered like a man speaking slowly, in a trance. "I see the sun resting on the western horizon."

"You see vast plains stretching to shining cliffs!" she cried. "You see the spires and the golden dome of the city, shimmering in the sunset! You see – "

As if night had shut down suddenly, darkness came upon me, and unreality, in which the only thing that had existence was her voice, urgent, commanding –

There was a sense of fading time and space – a sensation of being whirled over illimitable gulfs, with cosmic winds blowing against me – then I looked upon churning clouds, unreal and luminous, which crystallized into a strange landscape – familiar, and yet fantastically unfamiliar. Vast treeless plains swept away to merge with hazy horizons. In the distance, to the south, a great black cyclopean city reared its spires against the evening sky, and beyond it shone the blue waters of a placid sea. And in the near distance a line of figures moved through the still expanse. They were big men, with yellow hair and cold blue eyes, clad in scale-mail corselets and horned helmets, and they bore shields and swords.

One differed from the rest in that he was short, though strongly made, and dark. And the tall yellow-haired warrior that walked beside him – for a fleeting instant there was a distinct sense of duality. I, James Allison of the twentieth century, saw and recognized the man who was I in that dim age and that strange land. This sensation faded almost instantly, and I was Hialmar, a son of the Fair-haired, without cognizance of any other existence, past or future.

Yet as I tell the tale of Hialmar, I shall perforce interpret some of what he saw and did and was, not as Hialmar, but as the modern I. These interpretations you will recognize in their place. But remember Hialmar was Hialmar and not James Allison; that he knew no more and no less than was contained in his own experiences, bounded by the boundaries of his own voice. I am James Allison and I was Hialmar, but Hialmar was not James Allison; man may look back for ten thousand years; he can not look forward, even for an instant.

We were five hundred men and our gaze was fixed on the black towers which reared against the blue of sea and sky. All day we had guided our course by them, since the first red glow of dawn had disclosed them to our wondering eyes. A man could see far across those level, grassy plains; at first sight we had thought that city near, but we had trudged all day, and still we were miles away.

Lurking in our minds had been the thought that it was a ghost city-one of the phantoms which had haunted us on our long march across the bitter dusty deserts to the west, where, in the burning skies we had seen mirrored, still lakes, bordered by palms, and winding rivers, and spacious cities, all which vanished as we approached. But this was no mirage, born of sun and dust and silence. Etched in the clear evening sky we saw plainly the giant details of massive turret and grim abutment; of serrated tower and titanic wall.

In what dim age did I, Hialmar, march with my tribesmen across those plains toward a nameless city? I can not say. It was so long ago that the yellow-haired folk still dwelt in Nordheim, and were called, not Aryans, but red-haired Vanir and golden-haired Æsir. It was before the great drifts of my race had peopled the world, yet lesser, nameless drifts, had already begun. We were the travelling of years from our northern homeland. Lands and seas lay between. Oh, that long, long trek! No drift of people, not even of my own people, whose drifts have been epic, has ever equaled it. It had led us around the world – down from the snowy north into rolling plains, and mountain valleys tilled by peaceful brown folk – into hot breathless jungles, reeking with rot and teeming with spawning life – through eastern lands flaming with raw primitive colors under the waving palm-trees, where ancient races lived in cities of carven stone – up again into the ice and snow and across a frozen arm of the sea – then down through the snow-clad wastes, where squat blubber-eating men fled squalling from our swords; southward and eastward through gigantic mountains and titanic forest, lonely and gigantic and desolate as Eden, after man was cast forth – over searing desert sands and boundless plains, until at last, beyond the silent black city, we saw the sea once more.

Men had grown old on that trek. I, Hialmar, had come to manhood. When I had first set forth on the long trail, I had been a young boy; now I was a young man, a proven warrior, mighty limbed, with great broad shoulders, a corded throat, and an iron heart.

We were all mighty men – giants beyond the comprehension of moderns. There is not on earth today a man as strong as the weakest of our band, and our mighty thews were tuned to a blinding speed that would make the motions of finely-trained modern athletes seem stodgy and clumsy and slow. Our might was more than physical; born of a wolfish race, the years of our wandering and fighting man and beast and the elements in all forms, had instilled in our souls the very spirit of the wild – the intangible power that quivers in the long howl of the grey wolf, that roars in the north wind, that sleeps in the mighty unrest of turbulent rivers, that sounds in the slashing of icy sleet, the beat of the eagle's wings, and lurks in the brooding silence of the vast places.

I have said it was a strange trek. It was no drift of a whole tribe, men and yellow-haired women and naked children. We were all men, adventurers to whom even the ways of wandering, warlike folk were too tame. We had taken the trail alone, conquering, exploring, and wandering, driven only by our paranoidal drive to see beyond the horizon.

There had been more than a thousand at the beginning; now there were five hundred. The bones of the rest bleached along that world-circling trail. Many chiefs had led us and died. Now our chief was Asgrimm, grown old on that endless wandering – a gaunt, bitter fighter, one-eyed and wolfish, who forever gnawed his graying beard.

We came of many clans, but all of the golden-haired Æsir, except the man who strode beside me. He was Kelka, my blood brother, and a Pict. He had joined us among the jungle-clad hills of a far land that marked the eastern-most drift of his race, where the tom-toms of his people pulsed incessantly through the hot star-flecked night. He was short, thick-limbed, deadly as a jungle-cat. We of the Æsir were barbarians, but Kelka was a savage. Behind him lay the abysmal chaos of the squalling black jungle. The pad of the tiger was in his stealthy tread, the grip of the gorilla in his black-nailed hands; the fire that burns in a leopard's eyes burned in his.

Oh, we were a hard-bitten horde, and our tracks had been laid in blood and smoldering embers in many lands. I dare not repeat what slaughters, rapine, and massacres lay behind us, for you would recoil in horror. You are of a softer, milder age, and you can not understand those savage times when wolf pack tore wolf pack, and the morals and standards of life differed from those of this age as the thoughts of a grey killer wolf differ from those of a fat lap-dog dozing before the hearth.

This long explanation I have given in order that you may understand what sort of men marched across that plain toward the city, and by this understanding interpret what came after. Without this understanding the saga of Hialmar is howling chaos, without rhyme or meaning.

As we looked at the great city we were not awed. We had ravaged red-handed through cities in other lands beyond the sea. Many conflicts had taught us to avoid battle with superior forces when possible, but we had no fear. We were equally ready for war or the feast of friendship, as the people of the city might choose.

They had seen us. We were close enough to make out the lines of orchards, fields, and vineyards outside the walls, and the figures of the workers scurrying to the city. We saw the glitter of spears on the battlements, and heard the quick throb of war-drums.

"It will be war, brother," said Kelka gutturally, settling his buckler firmly on his left arm. We took up our girdles and gripped our weapons – not of copper and bronze as our people in far Nordheim still worked in, but of keen steel, fashioned by a conquered, cunning people in the land of palm-trees and elephants, whose steel-armed warriors had not been able to withstand us.

We drew up on the plain a moderate distance from the great black walls, which seemed to be built of gigantic blocks of basaltic stone. From our lines Asgrimm strode, weaponless, with his hands lifted, open palm outward, as a sign of parley. But an arrow cut into the sod near him, arching from the turrets, and he fell back to our lines.

"War, brother!" hissed Kelka, red fires glimmering in his black eyes. And at that instant the mighty gates swung open, and out filed lines of warriors, their war-plumes nodding above them in a glitter of lifted spears. The westering sun striking fire from their burnished copper helmets.

They were tall and leanly built, dark of skin, though neither brown nor black, with straight hawk-like features. Their harness was of copper and leather, their bucklers covered with glossy shagreen. Their spears and slender swords and long daggers were of bronze. They advanced in perfect formation, fifteen hundred strong, a surging tide of nodding plumes and gleaming spears. The battlements behind them were lined with watchers.

There was no parley. As they came, old Asgrimm gave tongue like a hunting wolf and we charged to meet the attack. We had no formation; we ran toward them like wolves, and we saw scorn on their hawk-features as we neared them. They had no bows, and not an arrow was winged from our racing lines, not a spear thrown. We wished only to come to hand-grips. When we were within javelin-cast they sent a shower of spears, most of which glanced from our shields and corselets, and then with a deep-throated roar, our charge crashed home.

Who said the ordered discipline of a degenerate civilization can match the sheer ferocity of barbarism? They strove to fight as a unit; we fought as individuals, rushing headlong against their spears, hacking like mad-men. Their entire first rank went down beneath our whistling swords, and the ranks behind crushed back and wavered as the warriors felt the brute impact of our incredible strength. If they had held, they might have flanked us, hemmed us in with their superior numbers, and slaughtered us. But they could not stand. In a storm of hammering swords we ploughed through, breaking their lines, treading their dead underfoot as we surged irresistibly onward. Their battle formation melted; they strove against us, man to man, and the battle became a slaughter. For in personal strength and ferocity, they were no match for us.

We hewed them down like corn; we reaped them like ripe grain! Oh, when I relive that battle, it seems that James Allison gives place to the mailed and mighty Hialmar, with the war-madness in his brain and the war-chant on his lips! And I am drunk again with the singing of the swords, the spattering of hot blood, and the roar of the slaying.

They broke and fled, casting away their spears. We were hard at their heels, cutting them down as they ran, to the very gates through which the foremost streamed and which they slammed in our faces, and in the faces of the wretches who were last in the flight. Shut off from safety these clawed and hammered at the unyielding portals until we hewed them down. Then we, in turn, battered at the gates until a shower of stones and beams cast from above brained three of our warriors, and we gave back to a safe distance. We heard the women howling in the streets, and the men lined the walls and shot arrows at us, with no great skill.

The bodies of the slain strewed the plain from the spot where the hosts clashed to the threshold of the gates, and where one Æsir had died, half a dozen plumed warriors had fallen. The sun had set. We pitched our rude camp before the gates, and all night we heard wailing and moaning within the walls, where the people howled for those whose still bodies we plundered and cast in a heap some distance away. At dawn we took the corpses of the thirty Æsir who had fallen in the fight, and leaving archers to watch the city, we bore them to the cliffs, which pitched sheer for fifteen hundred feet to the white sandy beach. We found sloping defiles which led down, and made our way to the water's edge with our burdens.

There, from fishing boats drawn up on the sands, we fashioned a great raft, and heaped it high with driftwood. On the pile we laid the dead warriors, clad in their mail, with their weapons by their sides, and we cut the throats of the dozen captives we had taken, and stained the weapons and the raft-sides with their blood. Then we set the torch to the wood, and shoved the raft off. It floated far out on the mirrored surface of the blue water, until it was but a red glare, fading into the rising dawn.

Then we went back up the defiles, and ranged ourselves before the city, chanting our war-songs. We unslung our bows, and man after man toppled from the turrets, pierced by our long shafts. From trees we found growing in the gardens outside the city, we built scaling ladders, and set them against the walls. We swarmed up them in the teeth of arrow and spear and falling beam. They poured molten lead down on us, and burnt four warriors like ants in a flame. Then once more we plied our shafts, until no plumed heads showed on the battlements.

Under cover of our archers, we again set up the ladders. As we tensed ourselves for the upward rush that would carry us over the walls, on one of the towers that rose above the gates appeared a figure which halted us in our tracks.

It was a woman, such as we had not seen for long years – golden hair blowing free in the wind, milky white skin gleaming in the sunlight. She called to us in our own tongue, stumblingly, as if she had not used the language in many years.

"Wait! My masters have a word for you."

"Masters!" Asgrimm spat the word. "Whom does a woman of the Æsir call masters, except the men of her own clan?"

She did not seem to understand, but she answered, "This is the city of Khemu, and the masters of Khemu are lords of this land. They bid me say to you that they can not stand before you in battle, but they say you shall have small profit if you scale the walls, because they will cut down their women and children with their own hands, and set fire to the palaces, so you will take only a mass of crumbling stones. But if you will spare the city, they will send out to you presents of gold and jewels, rich wines, and rare foods, and the fairest girls of the city."

Asgrimm tugged his beard, loath to forego the sacking and the bloodletting, but the younger men roared: "Spare the city, old grizzly! Otherwise they will kill the women – and we have wandered many a moon where no women came."

"Young fools!" snarled Asgrimm. "The kisses and love-cries of women fade and pall, but the sword sings a fresh song with each stroke. Is it the false lure of women, or the bright madness of slaughter?"

"Women!" roared the young warriors, clashing their swords. "Let them send out their girls, and we will spare their cursed city."

Old Asgrimm turned with a sneer of bitter scorn, and called to the golden-haired girl on the tower.

"I would raze your walls and spires into dust, and drench the dust with the blood of your masters," he said, "but my young men are fools! Send us forth food and women – and send us the sons of the chiefs for hostages."

"It shall be done, my lord," replied the girl, and we cast down the scaling ladders and retired to our camp.

Soon then the gates swung open again, and out filed a procession of naked slaves, laden with golden vessels containing foods and wines such as we had not known existed. They were directed by a hawk-faced man in a mantle of bright-hued feathers, bearing an ivory wand in his hand, and wearing on his temples a circlet of copper like a coiling serpent, the head reared up in front. It was evident from his bearing that he was a priest, and he spoke the name, Shakkaru, indicating himself. With him came half a dozen youths, clad in silken breeks, jeweled girdles, and gay feathers, and trembling with fear. The yellow-haired girl stood on the tower and called to us that these were the sons of princes, and Asgrimm made them taste the wine and food before we ate or drank.

For Asgrimm the slaves brought amber jars filled with gold dust, a cloak of flaming crimson silk, a shagreen belt with a jeweled golden buckle, and a burnished copper head-dress adorned with great black plumes.

He shook his head and muttered, "Gauds and bright trappings are dust of vanity and fade before the march of the years, but the edge of slaughter is not dulled, and the scent of fresh-spilled blood is good to an old man's nostrils."

But he donned the gleaming apparels, and then the girls came forth – slender young things, lithe and dark-eyed, scantily clad in shimmering silk – he chose the most beautiful, though morosely, as a man might pluck a bitter fruit.

Many a moon had passed since we had seen women, save the swart, smoke-stained creatures of the blubber-eaters. The warriors seized the terrified girls in fierce hunger – but my soul was dizzy with the sight of the golden-haired girl on the tower. In my mind there was room for no other thought. Asgrimm set me to guard the hostages, and to cut them down without mercy if the wine or food proved poisoned, or any woman stabbed a warrior with a hidden dagger, or the men of the city made a sudden sally on us.

But men came forth only to collect the bodies of their dead, which they burned, with many weird rituals, on a lofty promontory overlooking the sea.

Then there came to us another procession, longer and more elaborate than the first. Chiefs of the fighting men walked along unarmed, their harness exchanged for silken tunics and cloaks. Before them came Shakkaru, his ivory wand uplifted, and between the lines young slave youths, clad only in short mantles of parrot feathers, bore a canopied litter of polished mahogany, crusted with jewels.

Within sat a lean man with a curious crown on his high, narrow head and the eyes of a vulture. Beside the litter walked the white-skinned girl who had spoken from the tower. They came before us, and the slaves knelt, still supporting the litter, while the nobles gave back to each side, dropping to their knees. Only Shakkaru and the girl stood upright.

Old Asgrimm faced them, gaunt, fierce, wary, his deep-lined face shadowed by the black plume which waved above it. And I thought how much more the natural king he looked, standing on his feet among his giant fighting men, sword in hand, than the man who lolled supinely in the slave-borne litter.

But my eyes were all for the girl, whom I saw for the first time face to face. She was clad only in a short, sleeveless, and low-necked tunic of blue silk, which came to a hand's breadth above her knees, and soft green leather sandals were on her feet. Her eyes were wide and clear, her skin whiter than the purest milk, and her hair caught the sun in a sheen of rippling gold. There was a softness about her slender form that I had never seen in any woman of the Æsir. There was a fierce beauty about our flaxen-haired women, but this girl was equally beautiful without that fierceness. She had not grown up in a naked land, as they had, where life was a merciless battle for existence, for man and for woman. But these thoughts I did not pursue to their last analysis; I merely stood, dazzled by the blond radiance of her, as she translated the words of the king, and the deep-growled replies of Asgrimm.

"My lord says to you, 'Lo, I am Akkheba, priest of Ishtar, king of Khemu. Let there be friendship between us. We have need of each other, for ye be men wandering blindly in a naked land, as my sorcery tells me, and the city of Khemu has need of keen swords and mighty arms, for a foe comes up against us out of the sea whom we can not withstand alone. Abide in this land, and lend your swords to us, and take our gifts for your pleasure and our girls for your wives. Our slaves shall toil for you, and each day you shall sit ye down at boards groaning with meats, fishes, grains, white breads, fruits, and wines. Fine raiment shall you wear, and you shall dwell in marble palaces with silken couches, and tinkling fountains.' "

Now Asgrimm understood this speech, for we had seen the cities of the palm-tree lands; but it was at the talk of foes and sword-heaving that his cold blue eyes gleamed.

"We will bide," he answered, and we roared our assent. "We will bide and cut out the hearts of the foes who come against you. But we will camp outside the walls, and the hostages will abide with us, night and day."

"It is well," said Akkheba, with a stately inclination of his narrow head, and the nobles of Khemu knelt before Asgrimm and would have kissed his high-strapped sandals. But he swore at them and gave back in wrathful embarrassment, while his warriors roared with rough mirth. Then Akkheba went back in his litter, bobbing on the shoulders of the slaves, and we settled ourselves for a long rest from our wanderings. But my gaze hung on the golden-haired interpreter, until the gates of the city closed behind her.

So we dwelt outside the walls, and day by day the people brought us food and wine, and more girls were sent out to us. The workers came and toiled in the gardens, the fields, and the vineyards without fear of us, and the fishing boats went out – narrow crafts with curving bows and striped silken sails. And we accepted the king's invitation at last, and went in a compact body, the hostages in the center with naked swords at their throats, through the iron-grilled gates and into the city.

By Ymir, Khemu was mightily built! Surely the present masters of the city sprang from the loins of gods, for who else could have reared up those black basaltic walls, eighty feet in height, and forty feet at the base? Or erected that great golden dome which rose five hundred feet above the marble-paved streets?

As we strode down the broad column-flanked street, and into the broad market place, our swords in our fists, doors and windows were crowded by eager faces, fascinated and frightened. The chatter of the market place died suddenly as we swung into it, and the people crowded back from the shops and stalls to give us room. We were wary as tigers, and the slightest mishap would have sufficed to make us explode in a frenzied burst of slaughter. But the people of Khemu were wise, and the provocation did not come.

The priests came and bowed before us and led us to the great palace of the king, a colossal pile of black stone and marble. Beside the palace was a broad, open court, paved with marble flags, and from this court marble steps, broad enough for ten men to mount abreast, led up to a dais, where the king stood on occasion to harangue the multitude. One wing of the palace extended behind this court, and against this wing the steps were built. This wing was of older construction than the rest of the palace, and was furnished with a curiously carved slanting roof of stone, steep and high, towering above all other spires in the city except the golden dome.

The edge of this carven slope of masonry was but a few feet above the dais, and what was contained in that wing, none of the Æsir ever saw; folk said it was Akkheba's seraglio.

Beyond this open court were the mysterious column-fronted stone houses of the lesser priests, on both sides of a broad, marble-paved street, and beyond them again the lofty golden dome which crowned the great temple of Ishtar. On all sides rose sapphirean spires and gleaming towers, but the dome shone serenely above all, just as the bright glory of Ishtar, Shakkaru told us, shone above the heads of men. I say Shakkaru told us; in the few days they had spent among us, the young princes had learned much of our rugged, simple language, and by their interpretation and by the medium of signs, the priests of Khemu talked with us.

They led us to the lofty portals of the temple, but looking through the lines of tall marble columns, into the mysterious dim gloom of the interior, we balked, fearing a trap, and refused to go in. All the time I was looking eagerly for the golden-haired girl, but she was not in evidence. No longer needed as interpreter, the silence of the mysterious city had engulfed her.

After this first visit, we returned to our camp outside the walls, but we came again and again, at first in bands, and then, as our suspicions were lulled, in small groups or singly. However, we would not sleep within the city, though Akkheba urged us to pitch our tents in the great market place, if we disliked the marble palaces he offered us. No man of us had ever lived in a stone house, or within high walls. Our race dwelt in tents of tanned hides, or huts of mud and wattle, and we of the long trek as often as not slept like wolves on the naked earth. But by day we wandered through the city, marveling at the wonders of it, taking what we wished at the stalls, to the despair of the merchants, and entering palaces, warily, but at will, to be entertained by women who feared us, yet seemed to be fascinated by us. The people of Khemu were wondrous apt at learning; they soon spoke our language as well as we, though their speech came hard to our barbaric tongues.

But all this came in time. The day after we first visited the city, a number of us went again, and Shakkaru guided us to the palace of the higher priests which adjoined the temple of Ishtar. As we entered I saw the golden-haired girl, shining a pudgy copper idol with a handful of silk. Asgrimm laid a heavy hand on the shoulder of one of the young princes.

"Tell the priest that I would have that girl for my own," he growled, but before the priest could reply, red rage rose in my brain and I stepped toward Asgrimm as a tiger steps toward his rival.

"If any man of us takes that woman it shall be Hialmar," I growled, and Asgrimm wheeled cat-like at the thick killer's purr in my voice. We faced each other tensely, our hands on our hilts, and Kelka grinned wolfishly and began to edge toward Asgrimm's back, stealthily drawing his long knife, when Akkheba spoke through the hostage.

"Nay, my lords, Aluna is not for either of you, or for any other man. She is handmaiden to the goddess Ishtar. Ask for any other woman in the city, and she shall be yours, even to the favorite of the king; but this woman is sacred to the goddess."

Asgrimm grunted and did not press the matter. The incense-breathing mystery of the temple had impressed even his fierce soul, and though we of the Æsir had not overmuch regard for other people's gods, yet he had no desire to take a girl who had been in such close communion with deity. But my superstitions were less than my desire for the girl Aluna. I came again and again to the palace of the priests, and though they little liked my coming, they would not, or dared not, say me nay; and with small beginnings, I did my wooing.

What shall I say of my skill at courtship? Another woman I might have dragged to my tent by her long hair, but even without the priestly ban, there was something in my regard for Aluna that tied my hands from violence. I wooed her in the way we of the Æsir wooed our fierce lithe beauties – with boastings of prowess, and tales of slaughter and rapine. And in truth, without exaggeration, my tales of battle and massacre might have drawn to me the most wayward of the fierce beauties of Nordheim. But Aluna was soft and mild, and had grown up in temple and palace, instead of wattle hut and ice field! My ferocious boastings frightened her; she did not understand. And by the strange perversity of nature, it was this very lack of understanding which made her more enthralling to me. Even as the very savagery she feared in me made her look upon me with more interest than she looked on the soft-thewed men of Khemu.

But in my conversations with her, I learned of her coming to Khemu, and her saga was strange as that of Asgrimm and our band. Where she had dwelt in her childhood she could little say, having no geography, but it had been far away across the sea to the east. She remembered a bleak wave-lashed coast, and straggling huts of wattle and mud, and yellow-haired people like herself. So I believe she came of a branch of the Æsir which marked the westernmost drift of our race up to that time. She was perhaps nine or ten years old when she had been taken in a raid on the village by dark-skinned men in galleys – who they were she did not know, and my knowledge of ancient times does not tell me, for then the Phoenicians had not yet put to sea, nor the Egyptians. I can but guess that they were men of some ancient race, a survival of another age, like the people of Khemu – destroyed and forgotten before the rise of the younger races.

They took her, and a storm drove them westward and southward for many days, until their galley crashed on the reefs of a strange island where alien, painted men swarmed onto the beach and slaughtered the survivors for their cooking pots. The yellow-haired child they spared, for some whim, and placing her in a great canoe with skulls grinning along the gunwales, they rowed until they sighted the spires of Khemu on the high cliffs.

There they sold her to the priests of Khemu, to be a handmaiden for the goddess Ishtar. I had supposed her position to be holy and revered, but I found that it was otherwise. The worm of suspicion stirred in my soul against the Khemuri, as I realized, in her words, the cruel and bitter contempt in which they held folk of other, younger races.

Her position in the temple was neither honorable nor dignified, and though the servant of the goddess, she was without honor herself, save that no man except the priests was allowed to touch her. She was, in fact, no more than a menial, subject to the cold cruelty of the hawk-like priests. She was not beautiful to them; to them her fair skin and shimmering golden hair were but the marks of an inferior race. And even to me, who was not prone to tax my brain, came the vague thought that if a blond girl was so contemptible in their eyes, that treachery must lurk behind the honor they gave to men of the same race.

Of Khemu I learned a little from Aluna and more from the priests and the princes. As a people, they were very old. They claimed descent from the half-mythical Lemurians. Once their cities had girdled the gulf upon which Khemu overlooked. But some the sea had gulped down, some had fallen before the painted savages of the islands, and some had been destroyed by civil wars, so that now, for nearly a thousand years, Khemu had reigned alone in solitary majesty. Their only contact had been with the wayward, painted people of the islands, who, until a year or two before, had come regularly in their long, high-prowed canoes to trade ambergris, coconuts, whale's teeth, and coral gotten from among their islands; and mahogany, leopard-skins, virgin gold, elephant tusks, and copper ore, procured from some unknown tropical mainland far to the south.

The people of Khemu were a waning race. Although they still numbered thousands, many were slaves, descendants of a thousand generations of slaves. Their race was but a shadow of its former glory. A few more centuries would have seen the last of them, but on the sea to the south, out of sight over the horizon, was brooding a menace that threatened to sweep them all out of existence at one stroke.

The painted people had ceased to come in peaceful trade. They had come in war-canoes, with a clashing of spears on hide-covered shields, and a barbaric chant of war. A king had risen among them who had united the warring tribes, and now launched them against Khemu – not their former masters, for the old empire of which Khemu had been a part had crumbled before the drift of these people into the isles from that far-away continent which was the cradle of their race. This king was unlike them; he was a white-skinned giant like ourselves, with mad blue eyes and hair crimson as blood.

They had seen him, the people of Khemu. By night his war-canoes full of painted spearmen had stolen along the coast, and at sunrise the slayers had swept up the defiles of the cliff, slaying the fishermen who then slept in huts along the beach, cutting down the laborers just going to work in the fields, and storming at the gates. The great walls had held, however, and the attackers had despaired of the storming and drawn off. But the red-haired king had stood up before the gates, dangling the severed head of a woman by its long hair, and shouted his bloody vow to return with a fleet of war-canoes that should blacken the sea, and to raze the towers of Khemu to the red-stained dust. He and his slayers were the foes we had been hired to fight, and we awaited their coming with fierce impatience.

And while we waited we grew more and more used to the ways of civilization, insofar as barbarians can accustom themselves in such a short time. We still camped outside the walls, and kept our swords ready within, but it was more in instinctive caution than fear of treachery. Even Asgrimm seemed lulled to a sense of security, especially after Kelka, maddened by the wine they gave him, killed three Khemurians in the market-place, and no blood-vengeance or man-bote for the deed.

We overcame our superstitions and allowed the priests to guide us into the breathless dim cavern of a building that was the temple of Ishtar. We went even into the inner shrine, where sacred fires burned dimly in the scented gloom. There a screaming slave girl was sacrificed on the great black, red-veined altar at the foot of the marble stairs which mounted upward in the darkness until they were lost to view. These stairs led to the abode of Ishtar, we were told, and up them the spirit of the sacrifice mounted to serve the goddess. Which I decided was true, for after the corpse on the altar lay still, and the chants of worship died to a blood-freezing whisper, I heard the sound of weeping far above us, and knew that the naked soul of the victim stood whimpering in terror before her goddess.

I asked Aluna later if she had ever seen the goddess, and she shook with fright, and said only the spirit of the dead looked on Ishtar. She, Aluna, had never set foot on the marble stair that led up to the abode of the goddess. She was called the hand-maiden of Ishtar, but her duties were to do the biddings of the hawk-faced priests and the evil-eyed naked women who served them, and who glided like dusky shadows among the purple gloom amidst the columns.

But among the warriors grew discontent, and they wearied of ease and luxury, and even of the dark-skinned women. For in the strange soul of the Æsir, only the lust for red battle and far-wandering remain constant. Asgrimm daily conversed with Shakkaru and Akkheba on ancient times; I was chained by the lure of Aluna; Kelka guzzled each day in the wine shops until he feel senseless in the streets. But the rest clamored against the life we were leading and asked Akkheba what of the foe we were to slay?

"Be patient," said Akkheba. "They will come, and their red-haired king with them."

Dawn rose over the shimmering spires of Khemu. Warriors had begun to spend the nights as well as the days in the city. I had drunk with Kelka the night before and lain with him in the streets until the breeze of morn had blown the fumes of the wine from my brain. Seeking Aluna, I strode down the marble pave and entered the palace of Shakkaru, which adjoined the temple of Ishtar. I passed through the wide outer chambers, where priests and women still lolled in slumber, and heard on a sudden, beyond a closed door, the sound of sharp blows on soft naked flesh. Mingled with them was a piteous weeping and sobs for mercy in a voice I knew.

The door was bolted, and it was of silver-braced mahogany, but I burst it inwards as if it had been match-wood. Aluna grovelled on the floor with her scanty tunic tucked up, before a hatchet-faced priest who with cold venom was scourging her with a cruel, small-thonged whip which left crimson weals on her bare flesh. He turned as I entered, and his face went ashy. Before he could move I clenched my first and gave him a buffet that crushed his skull like an egg shell and broke his neck in the bargain.

The whole palace swam red to my maddened glare. Perhaps it was not so much the pain the priest had inflicted on Aluna – because pain was the most common thing in that fierce life – but the proprietorial way in which he inflicted it – the knowledge that the priests had possessed her – all of them, perhaps.

A man is no better and no worse than his feelings regarding the women of his blood, which is the true and only test of racial consciousness. A man will take to himself the stranger woman, and sit down at meat with the stranger man, and feel no twinges of race-consciousness. It is only when he sees the alien man in possession of, or intent upon, a woman of his blood, that he realizes the difference in race and strain. So I, who had held women of many races in my arms, who was blood-brother to a Pictish savage, was shaken by mad fury at the sight of an alien laying hands on a woman of the Æsir.

I believe it was the sight of her, a slave of an alien race, and the slow wrath it produced, which first stirred me toward her. For the roots of love are set in hate and fury. And her unfamiliar softness and gentleness crystallized the first vague sensation.

Now I stood scowling down at her as she whimpered at my feet. I did not lift her and wipe her tears as a civilized man would have done. Had such a thought occurred to me, I would have rejected it disgustedly as unmanly.

As I stood so, I heard my name shouted suddenly, and Kelka raced into the chamber, yelling: "They come, brother, just as the old one said! The watchers on the cliffs have run to the city, with a tale of the sea black with war-boats!"

With a glance at Aluna, and a dumb incoherence struggling for expression, I turned to go with the Pict, but the girl staggered up and ran toward me, tears streaming down her cheeks, her arms outstretched pleadingly.

"Hialmar!" she wailed. "Do not leave me! I am afraid! I am afraid!"

"I can not take you now," I growled. "War and slaughter are forward. But when I return I will take you, and not the priests of all the gods shall stay me!"

I took a quick step toward her, my hands yearning toward her – then smitten with the fear of bruising her tender flesh, my hands dropped empty to my side. An instant I stood, dumb, torn by fierce yearning, speech and action frozen by the strangeness of the emotion which tore my soul. Then tearing myself away, I followed the impatient Pict into the streets.

The sun was rising as we of the Æsir marched toward the crimson-etched cliffs, followed by the regiments of Khemu. We had thrown aside the gay garments and head-pieces we had worn in the city. The rising sun sparkled on our horned helmets, worn hauberks, and naked swords. Forgotten the months of idleness and debauchery. Our souls were riot with the wild exultation of coming strife. We went to slaughter as to a feast, and as we strode we clashed sword and shield in crude thundering rhythm, and sang the slaying-song of Niord who ate the red smoking heart of Heimdul. The warriors of Khemu looked at us in amazement, and the people who lined the walls of the city shook their heads in bewilderment and whispered among themselves.

So we came to the cliffs, and saw, as Kelka had said, the sea black with war-canoes, high prowed, and adorned with grinning skulls. Scores of these boats were already pulled up on the beach, and others were sweeping in on the crests of the waves. Warriors were dancing and shouting on the sands, and their clamor came up to us. There were many of them – three thousand, at the very least – probably many more. The men of Khemu blenched, but old Asgrimm laughed as we had not heard him laugh in many a moon, and his age fell from him like a cast-off mantle.

There were half a dozen runways leading down through the cliffs to the beach, and up these the invaders must come, for the precipices on all other sides were unclimbable. We ranged ourselves at the heads of these runways, and the men of Khemu were behind us. Little part they had in that battle, holding themselves in reserve for aid that we did not call for.

Up the passes swarmed the chanting, painted warriors, and at last we saw their king, towering above the huge figures. The morning sun caught his hair in a crimson blaze, and his laughter was like a gust of sea wind. Alone of that horde he wore mail and helmet, and in his hand his great sword shone like a sheen of silver. Aye, he was one of the wandering Vanir, our red-haired kin in Nordheim. Of his long trek, his wanderings, and his wild saga, I know not, but that saga must have been wilder and stranger than that of Aluna or of ours. By what madness in his soul he came to be king of these fierce savages, I can not even offer a guess. But when he saw what manner of men confronted him, new fury entered his yells, and at his bellow his warriors rolled up the runways like steel-crested waves.

We bent our bows and our arrows whistled in clouds down the defiles. The front ranks melted away, the hordes reeled backward, then stiffened and came on once more. Charge after charge we broke, and charge after charge hurtled up the passes in blind ferocity. The attackers wore no armor, and our long shafts tore through hide-covered shields like they were cloth. They had no skill at archery. When they came near enough they threw their spears in whistling showers, and some of us died. But few of them came within spear-cast and less won through to the heads of the passes. I remember one huge warrior who came crawling up out of the defile like a snake, crimson froth drooling from his lips, and the feathered ends of arrows standing out from his belly, ribs, neck and limbs. He howled like a mad dog, and his death-bite tore the heel of my sandal as I stamped his head into a red ruin.

Some few did break through the blinding hail and came to hand-grips, but there they fared little better. Man to man we of the Æsir were the stronger, and our armor turned their spears, while our swords and axes crashed through their wooden shields as though they were paper. Yet so many there were, but for our advantage in location, all the Æsir had died there on the cliffs, and the setting sun had lighted the smoking ruins of Khemu.

All through that long summer day we held the cliffs, until, when our quivers were empty and our bow-strings frayed through, and the defiles were choked with painted bodies, we threw aside our bows, and drawing our swords, went down into the defiles and met the invaders hand to hand and blade to blade. They had died like flies in the passes, yet there were many of them left, and the fire of their rage burned no less brightly because of the arrow-feathered corpses which lay beneath our feet.

They came on and up, roaring like a wave, stabbing with spear and lashing with war-club. We met them in a whirlwind of steel, cleaving skulls, smashing breasts, hewing limbs from their bodies and heads from their shoulders, till the defiles were shambles where men could scarcely keep their feet on the blood-washed, corpse-littered paths.

The westering sun cast long shadows across the cliff-shaded beaches when I came upon the king of the attackers. He was on a level expanse where the upward trending slope ran level for a short distance before it tipped up again at a steeper slant. Arrows had wounded him, and swords had gashed him, but the mad blaze in his eyes was undimmed, and his thundering voice still urged his gasping, weary, staggering warriors to the onset. Yet now, though the battle raged fiercely in the other defiles, he stood among a host of the dead, and only two huge warriors stood beside him, their spears clotted with blood and brains.

Kelka was at my heels as I rushed at the Vanir. The two painted warriors leaped to bar my path, but Kelka was upon them. From each side they leaped at him, their spears driving in with a hiss. Yet as a wolf avoids the stroke he writhed beyond the goring blades, and the three figures caromed together an instant; then one warrior fell away, disemboweled, and the other dropped across him, his head half severed from his body.

As I leaped toward the red-haired king, we struck simultaneously. My sword tore the helmet from his head, and at his terrible stroke, his sword and my shield shattered together, before I could strike again, he dropped the broken hilt and grappled with me as a grizzly grapples. I let go my sword, useless at such close quarters, and close-locked we reeled on the crest of the slope.

We were evenly matched in strength, but his might was ebbing from him with the blood of a score of wounds. Straining and gasping with the effort, we swayed, hard-braced, and I felt my pulse pound in my temples, saw the great veins swell in his. Then suddenly he gave way, and we pitched headlong, to roll down the slanting defile. In that grim strife neither dared try to draw a dagger. But as we rolled and tore at each other, I felt the iron ebbing from his mighty limbs, and by a volcanic burst of effort, heaved up on top, and sunk my fingers deep in his corded throat. Sweat and blood misted my vision, my breath came in whistling gasps, but I sank my fingers deeper and deeper. His tearing hands grew aimless and groping, until with a racking gasp of effort, I tore out my dagger and drove it home again and again, until the giant lay motionless beneath me.

Then as I reeled upright, half-blinded and shaking from the desperate strife, Kelka would have hewed off the king's head, but I prevented it.

A long wavering cry went up from the invaders and they flinched for the first time. Their king had been the fire which had held them like doom to their fate all day. Now they broke suddenly and fled down the defiles, and we cut them down as they ran. We followed them down onto the beach, still slaughtering them like cattle, and as they ran to their canoes and pushed off, we waded into the water until it flowed over our shoulders, glutting our mad fury. When the last survivors, rowing madly, had passed to safety, the beach was littered with still forms, and floating bodies sprawled to the wash of the surf.

Only painted bodies lay on the beach and in the shallow water, but in the defiles, where the fighting had been fiercest, seventy of the Æsir lay dead. Of the rest of us, few there were who bore not some mark or wound.

By Ymir, that was a slaying! The sun was dipping toward the horizon when we came back from the cliffs, weary, dusty and bloody, with little breath left for singing, but with our hearts glad because of the red deeds we had done. The people of Khemu did the singing for us. They swarmed out of the city in a vast shouting, cheering throng, and they laid carpets of silk, strewn with roses and gold dust, before our feet. We bore with us our wounded on litters. But first we took our dead to the beach, and broke up war-canoes to make a mighty raft, and lade it with the corpses and set it afire. And we took the red-haired king of the invaders, and laid him in his great war-canoe, with the corpses of his bravest chiefs about him to serve him in ghostland, and we gave to him the same honors we gave to our own men.

I looked eagerly for Aluna among the throng, but I did not see her. They had put up tents in the market place, and there we placed our wounded, and leeches of the Khemuri came among them, and they dressed the wounds of the rest of us. Akkheba had prepared a mighty victory feast for us in his great hall, and thither we went, dust-stained and blood-stained. Even old Asgrimm grinned like a hungry wolf as he wiped the clotted blood from his knotty hands and donned the garb they had given him.

I lingered for a space among the tents where lay those too desperately wounded to walk or even be carried to the feast, hoping that Aluna would come to me. But she did not come, and I went to the great hall of the king, without which the warriors of Khemu stood at attention – the more to do honor to their allies, Akkheba said.

That hall was three hundred feet in length, and half as many wide. It was floored with polished mahogany, half covered with thick rugs and leopard-skins. The walls were of carven stone, pierced by many arched, mahogany-paneled doors, and towering up to a lofty arching ceiling, and half covered with velvet tapestries. On a throne at the back of the hall, Akkheba sat, looking down at the revelry from a raised dais, with files of plumed spearmen on either side. At the great board which ran the full length of the hall, the Æsir in their battered, stained, dusty garments and corselets, many with bloody bandages, drank and roared and gorged, served by bowing slaves, both men and women.

Chiefs and nobles and warriors of the city in their burnished harnesses sat among their allies, and for each Æsir it seemed to me there were at least three or four girls, laughing, jesting, submitting to their rude caresses. Their laughter rose shrill and strident above the clamor. There was an unreality about the scene – a strained levity, a forced gaiety. But I did not see Aluna, so I turned and, passing through one of the mahogany arched doors, crossed a silken-hung chamber, and entered another. It was dimly lighted, and I almost ran into old Shakkaru. He recoiled, and seemed much put out at meeting me, for some reason or another. I noted that his hand clutched at his robe, which Akkheba had told us, all priests wore that night in our honor.

A thought occurred to me and I voiced it.

"I wish to speak to Aluna," I said. "Where is she?"

"She is at present occupied with her duties and can not see you," he said. "Come to the temple tomorrow – "

He edged away from me, and in a vague pallor underlying his swarthy complexion, in a tremor behind his voice, I sensed that he was in deadly fear of me and wished to be rid of me. The suspicions of the barbarian flashed up in me. In an instant I had him by the throat, wrenching from his hand the long, wicked blade he drew from beneath his robe.

"Where is she, you jackal?" I snarled. "Tell me – or – "

He was dangling like a puppet in my grasp, his kicking heels clear of the floor, his head bent back almost to the snapping point. With the fear of death in his distended eyes, he jerked his head violently, and I eased my grasp a trifle.

"In the shrine of Ishtar," he gasped. "They sacrifice her to the goddess – spare my life – I will tell you all – the whole secret and plot –

But I had heard enough. Whirling him on high by girdle and knee, I dashed out his brains against a column, and leaping through an outer door, raced between rows of massive pillars, and gained the street.

A breathless silence reigned over all. No throngs were abroad that night, as one would have thought, celebrating the destruction of their enemies. The doors were shut, the windows shuttered. Hardly a light shone, and I did not even see a watchman. It was all strange and unreal; the silent, ghostly city, where the only sound was the strident, unnatural revelry rising from the great feast hall. I could see the glow of torches in the market place where our wounded lay.

I had seen old Asgrimm sitting at the head of the board, with his hands stained with dried blood, and his hacked and dusty mail showing under the silken cloak he wore; his gaunt features shadowed by the great black plumes that waved above him. All up and down the board the girls were embracing and kissing the half-drunken Æsir, lifting off their heavy helmets and easing them of their mail as they grew hot with wine.

Near the foot of the board, Kelka was tearing at a great beef-bone like a famished wolf. Some laughing girls were teasing him, coaxing him to give them his sword, until suddenly, infuriated by their sport and importunities, he dealt his foremost tormentor such a blow with the bone he was gnawing that she fell, dead or senseless, to the floor. But the high pitched laughter and wild merriment did not slacken. I likened them suddenly to vampires and skeletons, laughing over a feast of dust and ashes.

I hurried down the silent street, crossing the court and passing the houses of the priests, which seemed deserted except for slaves. Rushing into the lofty-pillared portico of the temple – I ran through the deep-lying gloom, groping in the darkness – burst into the vaguely lighted inner shrine – and halted, frozen. Lesser priests and naked women stood about the altar in positions of adoration, chanting the sacrificial song, holding golden goblets to catch the blood that ebbed down the stained grooves in the stone. And on that altar, whimpering softly as a dying doe might whimper, lay Aluna.

Shadowy was the cloud of incense smoke which gloomed the shrine; crimson as hell-fire the cloud which veiled my sight. With one inhuman yell that rang hideously to the vaulted roof, I rushed, and skulls splintered beneath my madly lashing sword. My memories of that slaughter are frenzied and chaotic. I remember frenzied screams, the whir of steel and the chop and crunch of murderous blows, the snapping of bones, spattering of blood, and the gibbering flight of figures that tore their hair and screeched to their gods as they ran – and I among them, raging in silent deadliness, like a blood-mad wolf among sheep. Some few escaped.

I remember, clear etched against a murky red background of madness, a lithe, naked woman who stood close to the altar, frozen with horror. A goblet at her lips, her eyes flaring. I caught her up with my left hand and dashed her against the marble steps with a fury that must have splintered every bone in her body. For the rest I do not well remember. There was a brief, mad whirling blast of ferocity that littered the shrine with mangled corpses. Then I stood alone among the dead, in a shrine that was a shambles, with streaks of clots and pools of blood and human fragments scattered hideously and obscenely about the dark, polished floor.

My sword trailed in a suddenly nerveless hand as I approached the altar with dragging steps. Aluna's eyelids fluttered open as I looked down at her, my hands hanging limply, my entire body sagging helplessly.

She murmured, "Hialmar!" then her eyelids sank down, the long lashes shadowing the youthful cheek, and with a little sigh, she moved her flaxen head and lay like a child just settling to sleep. All my agonized soul cried out within me, but my lips were mute with the inarticulateness of the barbarian. I sank down upon my knees beside the altar and, groping hesitantly about her slender form with my arms, I kissed her dying lips, clumsily, falteringly, as a callow stripling might have done. That one act – that one faltering kiss – was the one touch of tenderness in the whole, hard life of Hialmar of the Æsir.

Slowly I rose, and stood above the dead girl, and as slowly and mechanically I picked up my sword. At the familiar touch of the hilt, there surged through my brain again the red fury of my race.

With a terrible cry I sprang to the marble stairs. Ishtar! They had sent her spirit shuddering up to the goddess, and close on the heels of that spirit should come the avenger! No less than the bloody goddess herself should pay for Aluna. Mine was the simple cult of the barbarian. The priests had told me that Ishtar dwelt above and the steps led to her abode. Vaguely I supposed it mounted through misty realms of stars and shadows. But up I went, to a dizzy height, until below me the shrine was but a vague play of dim lights and shadows, and darkness was all around me.

Then I came suddenly, not into a broad starry expanse of the deities, but to a grill of golden bars, and beyond them I heard a woman sobbing. But it was not Aluna's naked soul which wailed before some divine throne, for dead or alive, I knew her cry.

In mad fury I gripped the bars and they bent and buckled in my hands. Like straws I tore them aside and leaped through, my killing yell trembling in my throat. In the dim light that came from a torch set high in a niche, I saw that I was in a circular, domed chamber, whose walls and ceiling seemed to be of gold. There were velvet couches there, and silken cushions, and among these lay a naked woman, weeping. I saw the weals of a whip on her white body, and I halted, bewildered. Where was the goddess, Ishtar?

I must have spoken aloud in my barbaric Khemuri, for she lifted her head and looked at me with luminous dark eyes, swimming with tears. There was a strange beauty about her, something alien and exotic beyond my reckoning.

"I am Ishtar," she answered me, and her voice was soft as distant golden chimes, though broken now with sobbing.

"You – " I gasped, "you – Ishtar – the goddess of Khemu?"

"Yes!" she rose to her knees, wringing her white hands. "Oh, man, whoever you are – grant me one touch of mercy, if there be mercy left in the world at all! Cut my head from my body and end this long agony!"

But I drew back and lowered my sword.

"I came to slay a bloody goddess," I growled. "Not to butcher a whimpering slave girl. If you be Ishtar – who – where – in Ymir's name, what madness is this?"

"Listen, and I will tell you!" she cried, hitching toward me on her knees and catching at the skirt of my corselet. "Only listen, and then grant me the little thing I ask – the stroke of your sword!

"I am Ishtar, a daughter of a king in dim Lemuria, which the sea drank so long ago. As a child I was wed to Poseidon, god of the sea, and in the awesome mysterious bridal night, when I lay floating and unharmed on the breast of the ocean, the god gave to me the gift of life everlasting, which has become a curse in the long centuries of my captivity.

"But I dwelt in purple Lemuria, young and beautiful, while my playmates grew old and grey about me. Then Poseidon wearied of Lemuria and of Atlantis. He rose and shook his foaming mane, and his white steeds raced over the walls and the spires and the crimson towers. But he lifted me gently on his bosom and bore me unharmed to a far land, where for many centuries I dwelt among a strange and kindly race.

"Then in an evil day I went upon a galley from distant Khitai, and in a hurricane it sank off this accursed coast. But as before I was borne gently ashore on the waves of my master, Poseidon, and the priests found me upon the beach. The people of Khemu claim descent from Lemuria, but they were a subject race, speaking a mongrel tongue. When I spoke to them in pure Lemurian, they cried out to the people that Poseidon had sent them a goddess and the people fell down and worshipped me. But the priests were devils then as now, necromancers and devil-worshippers, owning no gods save the demons of the Outer Gulfs. They pent me in this golden dome, and by cruelty they wrung my secret from me.

"For more than a thousand years I have been worshipped by the people, who were sometimes given faint glimpses of me, standing on the marble stair, half-hidden in the sacrificial smoke, or were allowed to hear my voice speaking in a strange tongue as oracle. But the priests – oh, gods of Mu, what I have suffered at their hands! Goddess to the people – slave to the priests!"

"Why do you not destroy them with your sorcery?" I demanded.

"I am no sorceress," she answered, "though you might deem me such, were I to tell you what mysteries the ages have unfolded to me. Yet there is one sorcery I might invoke – one terrible, overwhelming doom – if I might escape from this prison – if I might stand up naked in the dawn and call upon Poseidon. In the still nights I hear him roaring beyond the cliffs, but he sleeps and heeds not my cries. Yet if I might stand up in his sight and call upon him, he might hear and heed. The priests are crafty – they have shut me from his sight and hearing – for more than a thousand years I have not looked on the great blue monster – "

Suddenly we both started. From the city far below us welled up a strange wild clamor.

"Treachery!" she cried. "They are murdering your people in the streets! You destroyed the enemies they feared – now they turn on you!"

With a curse I raced down the stairs, cast one anguished glance at the still white form on the altar, and ran out of the temple. Down the street, beyond the houses of the priests, rose the clanging of steel, howls of death, yells of fury, and the thunderous war-cries of the Æsir. They were not dying alone. The Khemuri's cries of hate and triumph were mingled with screams of fear and pain. Ahead of me the street seethed with battling humanity, no more silent and deserted. From the doors of shops, hovels, and palaces alike swarmed screeching city folk, weapons in hand, to aid their soldiers who were locked in mad battle with the yellow-haired aliens. Flame from a score of fires lighted the frenzied scene like day.

As I neared the court adjoining the king's palace, along streets through which men ran howling, an Æsir warrior staggered toward me, drift of the storm of battle which was raging further down. He was without armor, bent almost double, and though an arrow stood out from his ribs, it was his belly he was gripping with his empty hands.

"The wine was poisoned," he groaned. "We are betrayed and doomed! We drank deep, and in our cups the women coaxed from us our swords and armor. Only Asgrimm and the Pict would not give them up. Then suddenly the women slipped away, that old vulture left the feast hall – then the pangs took hold on us! Ah, Ymir, it twists my vitals like a knotted rope! Then the doors swarmed suddenly with archers who drove their arrows upon us – the warriors of Khemu drew their swords and fell upon us – the priests who swarmed the hall tore hidden blades from their robes. Hark to the yelling in the market place where they cut the throats of the wounded! Ymir, cold steel a man may laugh at, but this – this – ah, Ymir!"

He sank to the pave, bent like a drawn bow, froth drooling from his lips, his limbs jerking in horrible convulsions. I raced into the court. On the further side, and in the street in front of the palace, was a mass of struggling figures.

Swarms of dark-skinned men in armor battled with half-naked yellow-haired giants, who smote and rent like wounded lions, though their only weapons were broken benches, arms snatched from dying foes, or their naked hands, and whose lips were flecked with the froth of the agony that knotted their entrails. I swear by Ymir, they did not die alone; mangled corpses were trodden under their feet, and they were like wild beasts whose ferocity is not quenched save with the extinguishing of the last, least spark of life.

The great feast hall was burning. In its light I saw, standing on the dais high above the conflict, old Akkheba, shaking and trembling with terror at his own treachery, with two stalwart guards on the steps below him. The fighting scattered out over the court, and I saw Kelka. He was drunk, but this did not alter his deadliness. He was the center of a struggling clump of thrusting, hacking figures, and his long knife flashed in the firelight as it ripped through throats, and bellies, spilling blood and entrails on the marble pave.

With a low, sullen roar I charged into the thick of them, and in an instant we stood alone in a ring of corpses.

He grinned wolfishly, his teeth champing spasmodically.

"There was the devil in the wine, Hialmar! It claws at my guts like a wildcat – come, let us kill some more of them before we die. Look – the Old One makes his last stand!"

I glanced quickly where, directly in front of the blazing feast hall, Asgrimm's gaunt frame loomed among the swarming pack. I saw the flash of his sword and the dropping of men about him. An instant his black plumes waved over the horde – then they vanished and over the place he had stood rolled the dark wave.

The next instant I was leaping toward the marble stairs, with Kelka close at my heels. We smote the line of warriors on the lower steps, and burst through. They surged in behind to pull us down, but Kelka wheeled and his long blade made deadly play among them. They swarmed in on him from all sides, and there he died as he had lived, slashing and slaying in silent frenzy, neither asking quarter nor giving it.

I leaped up on the steps, and old Akkheba howled at my coming. My broken sword I had left wedged in a guardsman's breastbone. With my naked hands I charged the two guardsmen at the upper steps. They sprang to meet me, stabbing hard. I caught the driving spear of one and hurled him headlong down the stairs, to dash out his brains at the bottom. The spear of the other one tore through my mail and blood gushed over the shaft. Before he could tear it free for a second thrust, I gripped his throat and tore it out with my fingers. Then wrenching forth the spear and casting it aside, I rushed at Akkheba, who screamed and sprang up, grasping the scrolled edge of the sloping stone roof behind the dais. Mad terror lent the old one strength and courage. Up the steep slope he clambered like a monkey, catching at the carved decorations with fingers and toes, and howling all the time like a beaten dog.

And I followed him. My life was ebbing out of the wound beneath my mail. It was soaked with blood, but my wild beast vitality was as yet undiminished. Up and up he climbed, shrieking, and higher and higher we rose above the city, until we swayed precariously on the level roof-ridge, five hundred feet above the howling streets. And then we were frozen, the hunted and the hunter.

A strange, haunting cry rang above the hellish tumult that raged below us, above Akkheba's frenzied howling. On the great golden dome, high above all other towers and spires, stood a naked figure, hair blown in the dawn wind, etched in the red dawn glow. It was Ishtar, waving her arms and screaming a frenzied invocation in a strange tongue. Faintly it came to us. She had escaped from the golden prison I had burst open. Now she stood on the dome, calling upon the god of her fathers, Poseidon!

But I had my own vengeance to consummate. I poised for the leap that would carry us both crashing five hundred feet to death – and under my feet the solid masonry rocked. A new frenzy rang in Akkheba's screams. With a thunderous crash the distant cliffs fell into the sea. There was a long, rumbling, cataclysmic crash, like the shattering of a world, and to my startled gaze the entire vast plain waved like a surf, gave way, and dipped southward.

Great chasms gaped in the tilting plain, and suddenly, with an indescribable rumble, a grinding thunder, and a crashing of falling walls and buckling towers, the entire city of Khemu was in motion! It was sliding in a vast, chaotic ruin down to the sea which rose, rearing, to meet it! In that sliding horror, tower crashed against tower, buckling and toppling, grinding screaming human insects to red dust, crushing them to bits with falling stones. Where I had looked out upon an ordered city, with walls and spires and roofs, all was a mad, buckled, crumpled, splintering chaos of thundering stone, where spires rocked crazily above the ruins, and came thundering down.

Still the dome rode the wrack, and the white figure upon it still screamed and gestured. Then with an awesome roar, the sea stirred and rose, and great tentacles of green foam curled mountain high and roared down over the sliding, rumbling ruins, mounting higher and higher until the entire southern side of the crushed city was hidden in swirling green waters.

For an instant the ancient roof-ridge on which we clung had risen above the ruin, holding its place. And in that instant I leaped and gripped old Akkheba. His death-shriek yowled in my ear as under my iron fingers I felt his flesh tear like rotten pulp, his thews rip from his bones, and the bones themselves splinter. The thunderings of the breaking world were in my ear, the swirling green waters at my feet, but, as the whole earth seemed to crumble and break, as the masonry dissolved beneath my feet, and the roaring green tides surged over me, drowning me in untold shimmering fathoms, my last thought was that Akkheba had died by my hand, before a wave touched him.

I sprang up with a cry, hands out thrown as if to fend off the swirling waves. I reeled, dizzy with surprise. Khemu and the eld had vanished. I stood on the oak-clad hill, and the sun hung a hand's breadth above the post-oak shinnery. Seconds only had elapsed since the woman had gestured before my eyes. Now she stood looking at me with that enigmatic smile that had less of mockery than pity.

"What is this?" I exclaimed, dazedly. "I was Hialmar – I am James Allison – the sea was the Gulf – the Great Plains ran to the shore then, and on the shore stood the accursed city of Khemu. No! I can not believe you! I can not believe my own reason. You have hypnotized me – made me dream – "

She shook her head.

"It came to pass long, long ago, Hialmar."

"Then what of Khemu?" I exclaimed.

"Its broken ruins sleep in the deep blue waters of the Gulf, whither they washed in the long ages that passed after the breaking of the land, before the waters receded and left these long rolling steppes."

"But what of the woman Ishtar, their goddess?"

"Was she not the bride of Poseidon, who heard her cry and destroyed the evil city? On his bosom he bore her unharmed. She was deathless and eternal. She wandered through many lands, and dwelt with many people, but she had learned her lesson, and she who had been a slave of priests, became their ruler. She who had been a goddess in cruel seeming, became a goddess in her right, by virtue of her ancient wisdom.

"She was Ishtar of the Assyrians, and Ashtoreth of the Phoenicians; she was Mylitta and Belit of the Babylonians, Derketo of the Philistines. Aye, and she was Isis of Egypt, and Astarte of Carthage; and she was Freya of the Saxons, and Aphrodite of the Grecians, and Venus of the Romans. The races call her by many names, and worship her in many ways, but she is one and the same, and the fires of her altars are not quenched."

As she spoke she lifted her clear, dark luminous eyes to me; the last lurid sheen of the sunset caught the rippling glory of her hair, dusky as night, framing the strange beauty of her face, alien and exotic beyond my understanding. And a cry broke from my lips.

"You! You are Ishtar! Then it is true! And you are deathless – you are the Eternal Woman – the root and the bud of Creation – the symbol of life everlasting! And I – I was Hialmar, and knew pride and battle and far lands, and the bright glory of war – "

"As truly as you shall know them all again, oh weary one," she said softly, "when, in a little while, you shall put off that misshapen mask of broken flesh and don new raiment, bright and gleaming as the armor of Hialmar!"

Then night dipped down, and whither she went I know not, but I sat alone on the thicket-clad hill, and the night wind murmured up from the sand-drifts and the shinnery, and whispered among the dreary branches of the post-oaks.

The Gods of Bal-Sagoth

Steel in the Storm

Lightning dazzled the eyes of Turlogh O'Brien and his foot slipped in a smear of blood as he staggered on the reeling deck. The clashing of steel rivaled the bellowing of the thunder, and screams of death cut through the roar of waves and wind. The incessant lightning flicker gleamed on the corpses sprawling redly, the gigantic horned figures that roared and smote like huge demons of the midnight storm, the great beaked prow looming above.

The play was quick and desperate; in the momentary illumination a ferocious bearded face shone before Turlogh, and his swift ax licked out, splitting it to the chin. In the brief, utter blackness that followed the flash, an unseen stroke swept Turlogh's helmet from his head and he struck back blindly, feeling his ax sink into flesh, and hearing a man howl. Again the fires of the raging skies sprang, showing the Gael the ring of savage faces, the hedge of gleaming steel that hemmed him in.

Back against the mainmast Turlogh parried and smote; then through the madness of the fray a great voice thundered, and in a flashing instant the Gael caught a glimpse of a giant form – a strangely familiar face. Then the world crashed into fire-shot blackness.

Consciousness returned slowly. Turlogh was first aware of a swaying, rocking motion of his whole body which he could not check. Then a dull throbbing in his head racked him and he sought to raise his hands to it. Then it was he realized he was bound hand and foot – not an altogether new experience. Clearing sight showed him that he was tied to the mast of the dragon ship whose warriors had struck him down. Why they had spared him, he could not understand, because if they knew him at all, they knew him to be an outlaw – an outcast from his clan, who would pay no ransom to save him from the very pits of Hell.

The wind had fallen greatly but a heavy sea was flowing, which tossed the long ship like a chip from gulf-like trough to foaming crest. A round silver moon, peering through broken clouds, lighted the tossing billows. The Gael, raised on the wild west coast of Ireland, knew that the serpent ship was crippled. He could tell it by the way she labored, plowing deep into the spume, heeling to the lift of the surge. Well, the tempest which had been raging on these southern waters had been enough to damage even such staunch craft as these Vikings built.

The same gale had caught the French vessel on which Turlogh had been a passenger, driving her off her course and far southward. Days and nights had been a blind, howling chaos in which the ship had been hurled, flying like a wounded bird before the storm. And in the very rack of the tempest a beaked prow had loomed in the scud above the lower, broader craft, and the grappling irons had sunk in. Surely these Norsemen were wolves and the blood-lust that burned in their hearts was not human. In the terror and roar of the storm they leaped howling to the onslaught, and while the raging heavens hurled their full wrath upon them, and each shock of the frenzied waves threatened to engulf both vessels, these sea-wolves glutted their fury to the utmost – true sons of the sea, whose wildest rages found echo in their own bosoms. It had been a slaughter rather than a fight – the Celt had been the only fighting man aboard the doomed ship – and now he remembered the strange familiarity of the face he had glimpsed just before he was struck down. Who – ?

"Good hail, my bold Dalcassian, it's long since we met!"

Turlogh stared at the man who stood before him, feet braced to the lifting of the deck. He was of huge stature, a good half head taller than Turlogh who stood well above six feet. His legs were like columns, his arms like oak and iron. His beard was of crisp gold, matching the massive armlets he wore. A shirt of scale-mail added to his war-like appearance as the horned helmet seemed to increase his height. But there was no wrath in the calm gray eyes which gazed tranquilly into the smoldering blue eyes of the Gael.

"Athelstane, the Saxon!"

"Aye – it's been a long day since you gave me this," the giant indicated a thin white scar on his temple. "We seem fated to meet on nights of fury – we first crossed steel the night you burned Thorfel's skalli. Then I fell before your ax and you saved me from Brogar's Picts – alone of all the folk who followed Thorfel. Tonight it was I who struck you down." He touched the great two-handed sword strapped to his shoulders and Turlogh cursed.

"Nay, revile me not," said Athelstane with a pained expression, "I could have slain you in the press – I struck with the flat, but knowing you Irish have cursed hard skulls, I struck with both hands. You have been senseless for hours. Lodbrog would have slain you with the rest of the merchant ship's crew but I claimed your life. But the Vikings would only agree to spare you on condition that you be bound to the mast. They know you of old."

"Where are we?"

"Ask me not. The storm blew us far out of our course. We were sailing to harry the coasts of Spain. When chance threw us in with your vessel, of course we seized the opportunity, but there was scant spoil. Now we are racing with the sea-flow, unknowing. The steer sweep is crippled and the whole ship lamed. We may be riding the very rim of the world for aught I know. Swear to join us and I will loose you."

"Swear to join the hosts of Hell!" snarled Turlogh. "Rather will I go down with the ship and sleep for ever under the green waters, bound to this mast. My only regret is that I can not send more sea-wolves to join the hundred-odd I have already sent to Purgatory!"

"Well, well," said Athelstane tolerantly, "a man must eat – here – I will loose your hands at least – now, set your teeth into this joint of meat."

Turlogh bent his head to the great joint and tore at it ravenously. The Saxon watched him a moment, then turned away. A strange man, reflected Turlogh, this renegade Saxon who hunted with the wolf-pack of the North – a savage warrior in battle, but with fibers of kindliness in his make-up which set him apart from the men with whom he consorted.

The ship reeled on blindly in the night, and Athelstane, returning with a great horn of foaming ale, remarked on the fact that the clouds were gathering again, obscuring the seething face of the sea. He left the Gael's hands unbound but Turlogh was held fast to the mast by cords about legs and body. The rovers paid no heed to their prisoner; they were too much occupied in keeping their crippled ship from going down under their feet.

At last Turlogh believed he could catch at times a deep roaring above the wash of the waves. This grew in volume, and even as the duller-eared Norsemen heard it, the ship leaped like a spurred horse, straining in every timber. As by magic the clouds, lightening for dawn, rolled away on each side, showing a wild waste of tossing gray waters, and a long line of breakers dead ahead. Beyond the frothing madness of the reefs loomed land, apparently an island. The roaring increased to deafening proportions, as the long ship, caught in the tide rip, raced headlong to her doom. Turlogh saw Lodbrog rushing about, his long beard flowing in the wind as he brandished his fists and bellowed futile commands. Athelstane came running across the deck.

"Little chance for any of us," he growled as he cut the Gael's bonds, "but you shall have as much as the rest – "

Turlogh sprang free. "Where is my ax?"

"There in that weapon-rack. But Thor's blood, man," marvelled the big Saxon, "you won't burden yourself now – "

Turlogh had snatched the ax and confidence flowed like wine through his veins at the familiar feel of the slim, graceful shaft. His ax was as much a part of him as his right hand; if he must die he wished to die with it in his grip. He hastily slung it to his girdle. All armor had been stripped from him when he had been captured.

"There are sharks in these waters," said Athelstane, preparing to doff his scale-mail. "If we have to swim – "

The ship struck with a crash that snapped her masts and shivered her prow like glass.

Her dragon beak shot high in the air and men tumbled like ten-pins from her slanted deck. A moment she poised, shuddering like a live thing, then slid from the hidden reef and went down in a blinding smother of spray.

Turlogh had left the deck in a long dive that carried him clear. Now he rose in the turmoil, fought the waves for a mad moment, then caught a piece of wreckage that the breakers flung up. As he clambered across this, a shape bumped against him and went down again. Turlogh plunged his arm deep, caught a sword-belt and heaved the man up and on his makeshift raft. For in that instant he had recognized the Saxon, Athelstane, still burdened with the armor he had not had time to remove. The man seemed dazed. He lay limp, limbs trailing.

Turlogh remembered that ride through the breakers as a chaotic nightmare. The tide tore them through, plunging their frail craft into the depths, then flinging them into the skies. There was naught to do but hold on and trust to luck. And Turlogh held on, gripping the Saxon with one hand and their raft with the other, while it seemed his fingers would crack with the strain.

Again and again they were almost swamped; then by some miracle they were through, riding in water comparatively calm and Turlogh saw a lean fin cutting the surface a yard away. It swirled in and Turlogh unslung his ax and struck. Red dyed the waters instantly and a rush of sinuous shapes made the craft rock. While the sharks tore their brother, Turlogh, paddling with his hands, urged the rude raft ashore until he could feel the bottom. He waded to the beach, half carrying the Saxon; then, iron though he was, Turlogh O'Brien sank down, exhausted and soon slept soundly.

2

Gods from the Abyss

Turlogh did not sleep long. When he awoke the sun was just risen above the sea-rim. The Gael rose, feeling as refreshed as if he had slept the whole night through, and looked about him. The broad white beach sloped gently from the water to a waving expanse of gigantic trees. There seemed no underbrush, but so close together were the huge boles, his sight could not pierce into the jungle. Athelstane was standing some distance away on a spit of sand that ran out into the sea. The huge Saxon leaned on his great sword and gazed out toward the reefs.

Here and there on the beach lay the stiff figures that had been washed ashore. A sudden snarl of satisfaction broke from Turlogh's lips. Here at his very feet was a gift from the gods; a dead Viking lay there, fully armed in the helmet and mail shirt he had not had time to doff when the ship foundered, and Turlogh saw they were his own. Even the round light buckler strapped to the Norseman's back was his. Turlogh did pause to wonder how all his accouterments had come into the possession of one man, but stripped the dead and donned the plain round helmet and the shirt of black chain mail.

Thus armed he went up the beach toward Athelstane, his eyes gleaming unpleasantly.

The Saxon turned as he approached. "Hail to you, Gael," he greeted, "We be all of Lodbrog's ship-people left alive. The hungry green sea drank them all. By Thor, I owe my life to you! What with the weight of my mail, and the crack my skull got on the rail, I had most certainly been food for the sharks but for you. It all seems like a dream now."

"You saved my life," snarled Turlogh, "I saved yours. Now the debt is paid, the accounts are squared, so up with your sword and let us make an end."

Athelstane stared. "You wish to fight me? Why – what – ?"

"I hate your breed as I hate Satan!" roared the Gael, a tinge of madness in his blazing eyes, "Your wolves have ravaged my people for five hundred years! The smoking ruins of the Southland, the seas of spilled blood call for vengeance! The screams of a thousand ravished girls are ringing in my ears, night and day! Would that the North had but a single breast for my ax to cleave!"

"But I am no Norseman," rumbled the giant in worriment.

"The more shame to you, renegade," raved the maddened Gael, "Defend yourself lest I cut you down in cold blood!"

"This is not to my liking," protested Athelstane, lifting his mighty blade, his gray eyes serious but unafraid, "Men speak truly who say there is madness in you."

Words ceased as the men prepared to go into deadly action. The Gael approached his foe, crouching panther-like, eyes ablaze. The Saxon waited the onslaught, feet braced wide apart, sword held high in both hands. It was Turlogh's ax and shield against Athelstane's two-handed sword; in a contest one stroke might end either way. Like two great jungle beasts they played their deadly, wary game, then –

Even as Turlogh's muscles tensed for the death-leap, a fearful sound split the silence! Both men started and recoiled. From the depths of the forest behind them rose a ghastly and inhuman scream. Shrill, yet of great volume, it rose higher and higher until it ceased at the highest pitch, like the triumph of a demon, like the cry of some grisly ogre gloating over its human prey.

"Thor's blood!" gasped the Saxon, letting his sword-point fall, "What was that?"

Turlogh shook his head. Even his iron nerve was slightly shaken. "Some fiend of the forest. This is a strange land in a strange sea. Mayhap Satan himself reigns here and it is the gate to Hell."

Athelstane looked uncertain. He was more pagan than Christian and his devils were heathen devils. But they were none the less grim for that.

"Well," said he, "let us drop our quarrel until we see what it may be. Two blades are better than one, whether for man or devil – "

A wild shriek cut him short. This time it was a human voice, blood-chilling in its horror and despair. Simultaneously came the swift patter of feet and the lumbering rush of some heavy body among the trees. The warriors wheeled toward the sound, and out of the deep shadows a half-naked woman came flying like a white leaf blown on the wind. Her loose hair streamed like a flame of gold behind her, her white limbs flashed in the morning sun, her eyes blazed with frenzied terror. And behind her –

Even Turlogh's hair stood up. The thing that pursued the fleeing girl was neither man nor beast. In form it was like a bird, but such a bird as the rest of the world had not seen for many an age. Some twelve feet high it towered, and its evil head with the wicked red eyes and cruel curved beak was as big as a horse's head. The long arched neck was thicker than a man's thigh and the huge taloned feet could have gripped the fleeing woman as an eagle grips a sparrow.

This much Turlogh saw in one glance as he sprang between the monster and its prey who sank down with a cry on the beach. It loomed above him like a mountain of death and the evil beak darted down, denting the shield he raised and staggering him with the impact. At the same instant he struck, but the keen ax sank harmlessly into a cushioning mass of spiky feathers. Again the beak flashed at him and his sidelong leap saved his life by a hair's breadth.

And then Athelstane ran in, and bracing his feet wide, swung his great sword with both hands and all his strength. The mighty blade sheared through one of the tree-like legs below the knee, and with an abhorrent screech, the monster sank on its side, flapping its short heavy wings wildly.

Turlogh drove the backspike of his ax between the glaring red eyes and the gigantic bird kicked convulsively and lay still.

"Thor's blood!" Athelstane's gray eyes were blazing with battle lust, "Truly we've come to the rim of the world – "

"Watch the forest lest another come forth," snapped Turlogh, turning to the woman who had scrambled to her feet and stood panting, eyes wide with wonder. She was a splendid young animal, tall, clean-limbed, slim and shapely. Her only garment was a sheer bit of silk hung carelessly about her hips. But though the scantiness of her dress suggested the savage, her skin was snowy white, her loose hair of purest gold and her eyes gray. Now she spoke hastily, stammeringly, in the tongue of the Norse, as if she had not so spoken in years.

"You – who are you men? Whence come you? What do you on the Isle of the Gods?"

"Thor's blood!" rumbled the Saxon; "she's of our own kind!"

"Not mine!" snapped Turlogh, unable even in that moment to forget his hate for the people of the North.

The girl looked curiously at the two. "The world must have changed greatly since I left it," said she, evidently in full control of herself once more, "else how is it that wolf and wild bull hunt together? By your black hair, you are a Gael, and you, big man, have a slur in your speech that can be naught but Saxon."

"We are two outcasts," answered Turlogh, "You see these dead men lining the strand? They were the crew of the dragon ship which bore us here, storm-driven. This man, Athelstane, once of Wessex, was a swordsman on that ship and I was a captive. I am Turlogh Dubh, once a chief of Clan na O'Brien. Who are you and what land is this?"

"This is the oldest land in the world," answered the girl, "Rome, Egypt, Cathay are as but infants beside it. I am Brunhild, daughter of Rane Thorfin's son, of the Orkneys, and until a few days ago, queen of this ancient kingdom."

Turlogh looked uncertainly at Athelstane. This sounded like sorcery.

"After what we have just seen," rumbled the giant, "I am ready to believe anything. But are you in truth Rane Thorfin's son's stolen child?"

"Aye!" cried the girl, "I am that one! I was stolen when Tostig the Mad raided the Orkneys and burned Rane's steading in the absence of its master – "

"And then Tostig vanished from the face of the earth – or the sea!" interrupted Athelstane, "He was in truth a madman. I sailed with him for a ship-harrying many years ago when I was but a youth."

"And his madness cast me on this island," answered Brunhild; "for after he had harried the shores of England, the fire in his brain drove him out into unknown seas – south and south and ever south until even the fierce wolves he led murmured. Then a storm drove us on yonder reef, though at another part, rending the dragon ship even as yours was rended last night. Tostig and all his strong men perished in the waves, but I clung to pieces of wreckage and a whim of the gods cast me ashore, half dead. I was fifteen years old. That was ten years ago.

"I found a strange terrible people dwelling here, a brown-skinned folk who knew many dark secrets of magic. They found me lying senseless on the beach and because I was the first white human they had ever seen, their priests divined that I was a goddess given them by the sea, whom they worship. So they put me in the temple with the rest of their curious gods and did reverence to me. And their high-priest, old Gothan – cursed be his name! – taught me many strange and fearful things. Soon I learned their language and much of their priests' inner mysteries. And as I grew into womanhood the desire for power stirred in me; for the people of the North are made to rule the folk of the world, and it is not for the daughter of a sea-king to sit meekly in a temple and accept the offerings of fruit and flowers and human sacrifices!"

She stopped for a moment, eyes blazing. Truly, she looked a worthy daughter of the fierce race she claimed.

"Well," she continued, "there was one who loved me – Kotar, a young chief. With him I plotted and at last I rose and flung off the yoke of old Gothan. That was a wild season of plot and counter-plot, intrigue, rebellion and red carnage! Men and women died like flies and the streets of Bal-Sagoth ran red – but in the end we triumphed, Kotar and I! The dynasty of Angar came to an end on a night of blood and fury and I reigned supreme on the Isle of the Gods, queen and goddess!"

She had drawn herself up to her full height, her beautiful face alight with fierce pride, her bosom heaving. Turlogh was at once fascinated and repelled. He had seen rulers rise and fall, and between the lines of her brief narrative he read the bloodshed and carnage, the cruelty and the treachery – sensing the basic ruthlessness of this girl-woman.

"But if you were queen," he asked, "how is it that we find you hunted through the forests of your domain by this monster, like a runaway serving wench?"

Brunhild bit her lip and an angry flush mounted to her cheeks. "What is it that brings down every woman, whatever her station? I trusted a man – Kotar, my lover, with whom I shared my rule. He betrayed me; after I had raised him to the highest power in the kingdom, next to my own, I found he secretly made love to another girl. I killed them both!"

Turlogh smiled coldly: "You are a true Brunhild! And then what?"

"Kotar was loved by the people. Old Gothan stirred them up. I made my greatest mistake when I let that old one live. Yet I dared not slay him. Well, Gothan rose against me, as I had risen against him, and the warriors rebelled, slaying those who stood faithful to me. Me they took captive but dared not kill; for after all, I was a goddess, they believed. So before dawn, fearing the people would change their minds again and restore me to power, Gothan had me taken to the lagoon which separates this part of the island from the other. The priests rowed me across the lagoon and left me, naked and helpless, to my fate."

"And that fate was – this?" Athelstane touched the huge carcass with his foot.

Brunhild shuddered. "Many ages ago there were many of these monsters on the isle, the legends say. They warred on the people of Bal-Sagoth and devoured them by hundreds. But at last all were exterminated on the main part of the isle and on this side of the lagoon all died but this one, who has abided here for centuries. In the old times hosts of men came against him, but he was greatest of all the devil-birds and he slew all who fought him. So the priests made a god of him and left this part of the island to him. None comes here except those brought as sacrifices – as I was. He could not cross to the main island, because the lagoon swarms with great sharks which would rend even him to pieces.

"For a while I eluded him, stealing among the trees, but at last he spied me out – and you know the rest. I owe my lives to you. Now what will you do with me?"

Athelstane looked at Turlogh and Turlogh shrugged. "What can we do, save starve in this forest?"

"I will tell you!" the girl cried in a ringing voice, her eyes blazing anew to the swift working of her keen brain. "There is an old legend among this people – that men of iron will come out of the sea and the city of Bal-Sagoth will fall! You, with your mail and helmets, will seem as iron men to these folk who know nothing of armor! You have slain Groth-golka the bird-god – you have come out of the sea as did I – the people will look on you as gods. Come with me and aid me to win back my kingdom! You shall be my right-hand men and I will heap honors on you! Fine garments, gorgeous palaces, fairest girls shall be yours!"

Her promises slid from Turlogh's mind without leaving an imprint, but the mad splendor of the proposal intrigued him. Strongly he desired to look on this strange city of which Brunhild spoke, and the thought of two warriors and one girl pitted against a whole nation for a crown stirred the utmost depths of his knight-errant Celtic soul.

"It is well," said he. "And what of you, Athelstane?"

"My belly is empty," growled the giant. "Lead me to where there is food and I'll hew my way to it, through a horde of priests and warriors."

"Lead us to this city!" said Turlogh to Brunhild.

"Hail!" she cried flinging her white arms high in wild exultation. "Now let Gothan and Ska and Gelka tremble! With ye at my side I'll win back the crown they tore from me, and this time I'll not spare my enemy! I'll hurl old Gothan from the highest battlement, though the bellowing of his demons shake the very bowels of the earth! And we shall see if the god Gol-goroth shall stand against the sword that cut Groth-golka's leg from under him. Now hew the head from this carcass that the people may know you have overcome the bird-god. Now follow me, for the sun mounts the sky and I would sleep in my own palace tonight!"

The three passed into the shadows of the mighty forest. The interlocking branches, hundreds of feet above their heads, made dim and strange such sunlight as filtered through.

No life was seen except for an occasional gayly hued bird or a huge ape. These beasts, Brunhild said, were survivors of another age, harmless except when attacked. Presently the growth changed somewhat, the trees thinned and became smaller and fruit of many kinds was seen among the branches. Brunhild told the warriors which to pluck and eat as they walked along. Turlogh was quite satisfied with the fruit, but Athelstane, though he ate enormously, did so with scant relish. Fruit was light sustenance to a man used to such solid stuff as formed his regular diet. Even among the gluttonous Danes the Saxon's capacity for beef and ale was admired.

"Look!" cried Brunhild sharply, halting and pointing. "The spires of Bal-Sagoth!"

Through the trees the warriors caught a glimmer, white and shimmery, and apparently far away. There was an illusory impression of towering battlements, high in the air, with fleecy clouds hovering about them. The sight woke strange dreams in the mystic deeps of the Gael's soul, and even Athelstane was silent as if he too were struck by the pagan beauty and mystery of the scene.

So they progressed through the forest, now losing sight of the distant city as tree tops obstructed the view, now seeing it again. And at last they came out on the low shelving banks of a broad blue lagoon and the full beauty of the landscape burst upon their eyes. From the opposite shores the country sloped upward in long gentle undulations which broke like great slow waves at the foot of a range of blue hills a few miles away. These wide swells were covered with deep grass and many groves of trees, while miles away on either hand there was seen curving away into the distance the strip of thick forest which Brunhild said belted the whole island. And among those blue dreaming hills brooded the age-old city of Bal-Sagoth, its white walls and sapphire towers clean-cut against the morning sky. The suggestion of great distance had been an illusion.

"Is that not a kingdom worth fighting for?" cried Brunhild, her voice vibrant. "Swift now – let us bind this dry wood together for a raft. We could not live an instant swimming in that shark-haunted water."

At that instant a figure leaped up from the tall grass on the other shore – a naked, brown-skinned man who stared for a moment, agape. Then as Athelstane shouted and held up the grim head of Groth-golka, the fellow gave a startled cry and raced away like an antelope.

"A slave Gothan left to see if I tried to swim the lagoon," said Brunhild with angry satisfaction. "Let him run to the city and tell them – but let us make haste and cross the lagoon before Gothan can arrive and dispute our passage."

Turlogh and Athelstane were already busy. A number of dead trees lay about and these they stripped of their branches and bound together with long vines. In a short time they had built a raft, crude and clumsy, but capable of bearing them across the lagoon. Brunhild gave a frank sigh of relief when they stepped on the other shore.

"Let us go straight to the city," said she. "The slave has reached it ere now and they will be watching us from the walls. A bold course is our only one. Thor's hammer, but I'd like to see Gothan's face when the slave tells him Brunhild is returning with two strange warriors and the head of him to whom she was given as sacrifice!"

"Why did you not kill Gothan when you had the power?" asked Athelstane.

She shook her head, her eyes clouding with something akin to fear: "Easier said than done. Half the people hate Gothan, half love him, and all fear him. The most ancient men of the city say that he was old when they were babes. The people believe him to be more god than priest, and I myself have seen him do terrible and mysterious things, beyond the power of a comman man.

"Nay, when I was but a puppet in his hands, I came only to the outer fringe of his mysteries, yet I have looked on sights that froze my blood. I have seen strange shadows flit along the midnight walls, and groping along black subterranean corridors in the dead of night I have heard un-hallowed sounds and have felt the presence of hideous beings. And once I heard the grisly slavering bellowings of the nameless Thing Gothan has chained deep in the bowels of the hills on which rests the city of Bal-Sagoth."

Brunhild shuddered.

"There are many gods in Bal-Sagoth, but the greatest of all is Gol-go-roth, the god of darkness who sits forever in the Temple of Shadows. When I overthrew the power of Gothan, I forbade men to worship Gol-goroth, and made the priests hail, as the one true deity, A-ala, the daughter of the sea-myself. I had strong men take heavy hammers and smite the image of Gol-goroth, but their blows only shattered the hammers and gave strange hurts to the men who wielded them. Gol-goroth was indestructible and showed no mar. So I desisted and shut the doors of the Temple of Shadows which were opened only when I was overthrown and Gothan, who had been skulking in the secret places of the city, came again into his own. Then Gol-goroth reigned again in his full terror and the idols of A-ala were overthrown in the Temple of the Sea, and the priests of A-ala died howling on the red-stained altar before the black god. But now we shall see!"

"Surely you are a very Valkyrie," muttered Athelstane. "But three against a nation is great odds – especially such a people as this, who must assuredly be all witches and sorcerers."

"Bah!" cried Brunhild contemptuously, "there are many sorcerers, it is true, but though the people are strange to us, they are mere fools in their own way, as are all nations. When Gothan led me captive down the streets they spat on me. Now watch them turn on Ska, the new king Gothan has given them, when it seems my star rises again! But now we approach the city gates – be bold but wary!"

They had ascended the long swelling slopes and were not far from the walls which rose immensely upward. Surely, thought Turlogh, heathen gods built this city. The walls seemed of marble and with their fretted battlements and slim watch-towers, dwarfed the memory of such cities as Rome, Damascus and Byzantium. A broad white winding road led up from the lower levels to the plateau before the gates and as they came up this road, the three adventurers felt hundreds of hidden eyes fixed on them with fierce intensity. The walls seemed deserted; it might have been a dead city. But the impact of those staring eyes was felt.

Now they stood before the massive gates, which to the amazed eyes of the warriors seemed to be of chased silver.

"Here is an emperor's ransom!" muttered Athelstane, eyes ablaze. "Thor's blood, if we had but a stout band of reavers and a ship to carry away the plunder!"

"Smite on the gate and then step back, lest something fall upon you," said Brunhild, and the thunder of Turlogh's ax on the portals woke the echoes in the sleeping hills.

The three then fell back a few paces and suddenly the mighty gates swung inward and a strange concourse of people stood revealed. The two white warriors looked on a pageant of barbaric grandeur. A throng of tall, slim, brown-skinned men stood in the gates. Their only garments were loin-cloths of silk, the fine work of which contrasted strangely with the near-nudity of the wearers. Tall waving plumes of many colors decked their heads, and armlets and leglets of gold and silver, crusted with gleaming gems, completed their ornamentation. Armor they wore none, but each carried a light shield on his left arm, made of hard wood, highly polished, and braced with silver. Their weapons were slim-bladed spears, light hatchets and slender daggers, all bladed with fine steel. Evidently these warriors depended more on speed and skill than on brute force.

At the front of this band stood three men who instantly commanded attention. One was a lean hawk-faced warrior, almost as tall as Athelstane, who wore about his neck a great golden chain from which was suspended a curious symbol in jade. One of the other men was young, evil-eyed; an impressive riot of colors in the mantle of parrot-feathers which swung from his shoulders. The third man had nothing to set him apart from the rest save his own strange personality. He wore no mantle, bore no weapons. His only garment was a plain loin-cloth. He was very old; he alone of all the throng was bearded, and his beard was as white as the long hair which fell about his shoulders. He was very tall and very lean, and his great dark eyes blazed as from a hidden fire. Turlogh knew without being told that this man was Gothan, priest of the Black God. The ancient exuded a very aura of age and mystery. His great eyes were like windows of some forgotten temple, behind which passed like ghosts his dark and terrible thoughts. Turlogh sensed that Gothan had delved too deep in forbidden secrets to remain altogether human. He had passed through doors that had cut him off from the dreams, desires and emotions of ordinary mortals. Looking into those unwinking orbs Turlogh felt his skin crawl, as if he had looked into the eyes of a great serpent.

Now a glance upward showed that the walls were thronged with silent dark-eyed folk. The stage was set; all was in readiness for the swift, red drama. Turlogh felt his pulse quicken with fierce exhilaration and Athelstane's eyes began to glow with ferocious light.

Brunhild stepped forward boldly, head high, her splendid figure vibrant. The white warriors naturally could not understand what passed between her and the others, except as they read from gestures and expressions, but later Brunhild narrated the conversation almost word for word.

"Well, people of Bal-Sagoth," said she, spacing her words slowly, "what words have you for your goddess whom you mocked and reviled?"

"What will you have, false one?" exclaimed the tall man, Ska, the king set up by Gothan; "you who mocked at the customs of our ancestors, defied the laws of Bal-Sagoth, which are older than the world, murdered your lover and defiled the shrine of Gol-goroth? You were doomed by law, king and god and placed in the grim forest beyond the lagoon – "

"And I, who am likewise a goddess and greater than any god," answered Brunhild mockingly, "am returned from the realm of horror with the head of Groth-golka!"

At a word from her, Athelstane held up the great beaked head, and a low whispering ran about the battlements, tense with fear and bewilderment.

"Who are these men?" Ska bent a worried frown on the two warriors.

"*They are iron men who have come out of the sea!*" answered Brunhild in a clear voice that carried far; "the beings who have come in response to the old prophecy, to overthrow the city of Bal-Sagoth, whose people are traitors and whose priests are false!"

At these words the fearful murmur broke out afresh all up and down the line of the walls, till Gothan lifted his vulture-head and the people fell silent and shrank before the icy stare of his terrible eyes.

Ska glared bewilderedly, his ambition struggling with his superstitious fears.

Turlogh, looking closely at Gothan, believed that he read beneath the inscrutable mask of the old priest's face. For all his inhuman wisdom, Gothan had his limitations. This sudden return of one he thought well disposed of, and the appearance of the white-skinned giants accompanying her, had caught Gothan off his guard, Turlogh believed, rightly. There had been no time to properly prepare for their reception. The people had already begun to murmur in the streets against the severity of Ska's brief rule. They had always believed in Brunhild's divinity; now that she returned with two tall men of her own hue, bearing the grim trophy that marked the conquest of another of their gods, the people were wavering. Any small thing might turn the tide either way.

"People of Bal-Sagoth!" shouted Brunhild suddenly, springing back and flinging her arms high, gazing full into the faces that looked down at her, "I bid you avert your doom before it is too late! You cast me out and spat on me; you turned to darker gods than I! Yet all this will I forgive if you return and do obeisance to me! Once you reviled me – you called me bloody and cruel! True, I was a hard mistress – but has Ska been an easy master? You said I lashed the people with whips of rawhide – has Ska stroked you with parrot feathers?

"A virgin died on my altar at the full tide of each moon – but youths and maidens die at the waxing and the waning, the rising and the setting of each moon, before Gol-goroth, on whose altar a fresh human heart forever throbs! Ska is but a shadow! Your real lord is Gothan, who sits above the city like a vulture! Once you were a mighty people; your galleys filled the seas. Now you are a remnant and that is dwindling fast! Fools! You will all die on the altar of Gol-goroth ere Gothan is done and he will stalk alone among the silent ruins of Bal-Sagoth!

"Look at him!" her voice rose to a scream as she lashed herself to an inspired frenzy, and even Turlogh, to whom the words were meaningless, shivered. "Look at him where he stands there like an evil spirit out of the past! He is not even human! I tell you, he is a foul ghost, whose beard is dabbled with the blood of a million butcheries – an incarnate fiend out of the mist of the ages come to destroy the people of Bal-Sagoth!

"Choose now! Rise up against that ancient devil and his blasphemous gods, receive your rightful queen and deity again and you shall regain some of your former greatness. Refuse, and the ancient prophesy shall be fulfilled and the sun will set on the silent and crumbled ruins of Bal-Sagoth!"

Fired by her dynamic words, a young warrior with the insignia of a chief sprang to the parapet and shouted: "Hail to A-ala! Down with the bloody gods!"

Among the multitude many took up the shout and steel clashed as a score of fights started. The crowd on the battlements and in the streets surged and eddied, while Ska glared, bewildered. Brunhild, forcing back her companions who quivered with eagerness for action of some kind, shouted: "Hold! Let no man strike a blow yet! People of Bal-Sagoth, it has been a tradition since the beginning of time that a king must fight for his crown! Let Ska cross steel with one of these warriors! If Ska wins, I will kneel before him and let him strike off my head! If Ska loses, then you shall accept me as your rightful queen and goddess!"

A great roar of approval went up from the walls as the people ceased their brawls, glad enough to shift the responsibility to their rulers.

"Will you fight, Ska?" asked Brunhild, turning to the king mockingly. "Or will you give me your head without further argument?"

"Slut!" howled Ska, driven to madness, "I will take the skulls of these fools for drinking-cups, and then I will rend you between two bent trees!"

Gothan laid a hand on his arm and whispered in his ear, but Ska had reached the point where he was deaf to all but his fury. His achieved ambition, he had found, had faded to the mere part of a puppet dancing on Gothan's string; now even the hollow bauble of his kingship was slipping from him and this wench mocked him to his face before his people. Ska went, to all practical effects, stark mad.

Brunhild turned to her two allies. "One of you must fight Ska."

"Let me be the one!" urged Turlogh, eyes dancing with eager battle-lust. "He has the look of a man quick as a wildcat, and Athelstane, while a very bull for strength, is a thought slow for such work – "

"Slow!" broke in Athelstane reproachfully. "Why, Turlogh, for a man my weight – "

"Enough," Brunhild interrupted. "He must choose for himself."

She spoke to Ska, who glared red-eyed for an instant, then indicated Athelstane, who grinned joyfully, cast aside the bird's head and unslung his sword. Turlogh swore and stepped back. The king had decided that he would have a better chance against this huge buffalo of a man who looked slow, than against the black-haired tigerish warrior, whose cat-like quickness was evident.

"This Ska is without armor," rumbled the Saxon. "Let me likewise doff my mail and helmet so that we fight on equal terms – "

"No!" cried Brunhild. "Your armor is your only chance! I tell you, this false king fights like the play of summer lightning! You will be hard put to hold your own as it is. Keep on your armor, I say!"

"Well, well," grumbled Athelstane, "I will – I will. Though I say it is scarcely fair. But let him come on and make an end of it."

The huge Saxon strode ponderously toward his foe, who warily crouched and circled away. Athelstane held his great sword in both hands before him, pointed upward, the hilt somewhat below the level of his chin, in position to strike a blow to right or left, or parry a sudden attack.

Ska had flung away his light shield, his fighting-sense telling him that it would be useless before the stroke of that heavy blade. In his right hand he held his slim spear as a man holds a throwing-dart, in his left a light, keen-edged hatchet. He meant to make a fast, shifty fight of it, and his tactics were good. But Ska, having never encountered armor before, made his fatal mistake in supposing it to be apparel or ornament through which his weapons would pierce.

Now he sprang in, thrusting Athelstane's face with his spear. The Saxon parried with ease and instantly cut tremendously at Ska's legs. The king bounded high, clearing the whistling blade, and in midair he hacked down at Athelstane's bent head. The light hatchet shivered to bits on the Viking's helmet and Ska sprang back out of reach with a blood-lusting howl.

And now it was Athelstane who rushed with unexpected quickness, like a charging bull, and before that terrible onslaught Ska, bewildered by the breaking of his hatchet, was caught off his guard – flat-footed. He caught a fleeting glimpse of the giant looming over him like an overwhelming wave and he sprang in, instead of out, stabbing ferociously. That mistake was his last. The thrusting spear glanced harmlessly from the Saxon's mail, and in that instant the great sword sang down in a stroke the king could not evade. The force of that stroke tossed him as a man is tossed by a plunging bull. A dozen feet away fell Ska, king of Bal-Sagoth, to lie shattered and dead in a ghastly welter of blood and entrails. The throng gaped, struck silent by the prowess of that deed.

"Hew off his head!" cried Brunhild, her eyes flaming as she clenched her hands so that the nails bit into the palms. "Impale that carrion's head on your sword-point so that we may carry it through the city gates with us as token of victory!"

But Athelstane shook his head, cleansing his blade: "Nay, he was a brave man and I will not mutilate his corpse. It is no great feat I have done, for he was naked and I full-armed. Else it is in my mind, the brawl had gone differently."

Turlogh glanced at the people on the walls. They had recovered from their astonishment and now a vast roar went up: "A-ala! Hail to the true goddess!" And the warriors in the gateway dropped to their knees and bowed their foreheads in the dust before Brunhild, who stood proudly erect, bosom heaving with fierce triumph. Truly, thought Turlogh, she is more than a queen – she is a shield woman, a Valkyrie, as Athelstane said.

Now she stepped aside and tearing the golden chain with its jade symbol from the dead neck of Ska, held it on high and shouted: "People of Bal-

Sagoth, you have seen how your false king died before this golden-bearded giant, who being of iron, shows no single cut! Choose now – do you receive me of your own free will?"

"Aye, we do!" the multitude answered in a great shout. "Return to your people, oh mighty and all-powerful queen!"

Brunhild smiled sardonically. "Come," said she to the warriors; "they are lashing themselves into a very frenzy of love and loyalty, having already forgotten their treachery. The memory of the mob is short!"

Aye, thought Turlogh, as at Brunhild's side he and the Saxon passed through the mighty gates between files of prostrate chieftains; aye, the memory of the mob is very short. But a few days have passed since they were yelling as wildly for Ska the liberator – scant hours had passed since Ska sat enthroned, master of life and death, and the people bowed before his feet. Now – Turlogh glanced at the mangled corpse which lay deserted and forgotten before the silver gates. The shadow of a circling vulture fell across it. The clamor of the multitude filled Turlogh's ears and he smiled a bitter smile.

The great gates closed behind the three adventurers and Turlogh saw a broad white street stretching away in front of him. Other lesser streets radiated from this one. The two warriors caught a jumbled and chaotic impression of great white stone buildings shouldering each other; of sky-lifting towers and broad stair-fronted palaces. Turlogh knew there must be an ordered system by which the city was laid out, but to him all seemed a waste of stone and metal and polished wood, without rime or reason. His baffled eyes sought the street again.

Far up the street extended a mass of humanity, from which rose a rhythmic thunder of sound. Thousands of naked, gayly plumed men and women knelt there, bending forward to touch the marble flags with their foreheads, then swaying back with an upward flinging of their arms, all moving in perfect unison like the bending and rising of tall grass before the wind. And in time to their bowing they lifted a monotoned chant that sank and swelled in a frenzy of ecstasy. So her wayward people welcomed back the goddess A-ala.

Just within the gates Brunhild stopped and there came to her the young chief who had first raised the shout of revolt upon the walls. He knelt and kissed her bare feet, saying: "Oh great king and goddess, thou knowest

Zomar was ever faithful to thee! Thou knowest how I fought for thee and barely escaped the altar of Gol-goroth for thy sake!"

"Thou hast indeed been faithful, Zomar," answered Brunhild in the stilted language required for such occasions, "nor shall thy fidelity go unrewarded. Henceforth thou art commander of my own bodyguard." Then in a lower voice she added: "Gather a band from your own retainers and from those who have espoused my cause all along, and bring them to the palace. I do not trust the people any more than I have to!"

Suddenly Athelstane, not understanding this conversation, broke in: "Where is the old one with the beard?"

Turlogh started and glanced around. He had almost forgotten the wizard. He had not seen him go – yet he was gone! Brunhild laughed ruefully.

"He's stolen away to breed more trouble in the shadows. He and Gelka vanished when Ska fell. He has secret ways of coming and going and none may stay him. Forget him for the time being; heed ye well – we shall have plenty of him anon!"

Now the chiefs brought a finely carved and highly ornamented palanquin carried by two strong slaves, and Brunhild stepped into this, saying to her companions: "They are fearful of touching you, but ask if you would be carried. I think it better that you walk, one on each side of me."

"Thor's blood!" rumbled Athelstane, shouldering the huge sword he had never sheathed, "I'm no infant! I'll split the skull of the man who seeks to carry me!"

And so up the long white street went Brunhild, daughter of Rane Thorfin's son in the Orkneys, goddess of the sea, queen of age-old Bal-Sagoth. Borne by two great slaves she went, with a white giant striding on each side with bared steel, and a concourse of chiefs following, while the multitude gave way to right and left, leaving a wide lane down which she passed. Golden trumpets sounded a fanfare of triumph, drums thundered, chants of worship echoed to the ringing skies. Surely in this riot of glory, this barbaric pageant of splendor, the proud soul of the North-born girl drank deep and grew drunken with imperial pride.

Athelstane's eyes glowed with simple delight at this flame of pagan magnificence, but to the black haired fighting-man of the West, it seemed that even in the loudest clamor of triumph, the trumpet, the drum and the shouting faded away into the forgotten dust and silence of eternity.

Kingdoms and empires pass away like mist from the sea, thought Turlogh; the people shout and triumph and even in the revelry of Belshazzar's feast, the Medes break the gates of Babylon. Even now the shadow of doom is over this city and the slow tides of oblivion lap the feet of this unheeding race. So in a strange mood Turlogh O'Brien strode beside the palanquin, and it seemed to him that he and Athelstane walked in a dead city, through throngs of dim ghosts, cheering a ghost queen.

3

The Fall of the Gods

Night had fallen on the ancient city of Bal-Sagoth. Turlogh, Athelstane and Brunhild sat alone in a room of the inner palace. The queen half reclined on a silken couch, while the men sat on mahogany chairs, engaged in the viands that slave-girls had served them on golden dishes. The walls of this room, as of all the palace, were of marble, with golden scrollwork. The ceiling was of lapis-lazuli and the floor of silver-inlaid marble tiles. Heavy velvet hangings decorated the walls and silken cushions; richly made divans and mahogany chairs and tables littered the room in careless profusion.

"I would give much for a horn of ale, but this wine is not sour to the palate," said Athelstane, emptying a golden flagon with relish. "Brunhild, you have deceived us. You let us understand it would take hard fighting to win back your crown – yet I have struck but one blow and my sword is thirsty as Turlogh's ax which has not drunk at all. We hammered on the gates and the people fell down and worshipped with no more ado. And until a little while ago, we but stood by your throne in the great palace room, while you spoke to the throngs that came and knocked their heads on the floor before you – by Thor, never have I heard such chattering and jabbering! My ears ring till now – what were they saying? And where is that old conjurer Gothan?"

"Your steel will drink deep yet, Saxon," answered the girl grimly, resting her chin on her hands and eyeing the warriors with deep moody eyes. "Had you gambled with cities and crowns as I have done, you would know that seizing a throne may be easier than keeping it. Our sudden appearance with the bird-god's head, your killing of Ska, swept the people off their

131

feet. As for the rest – I held audience in the palace as you saw, even if you did not understand, and the people who came in bowing droves were assuring me of their unswerving loyalty – ha! I graciously pardoned them all, but I am no fool. When they have time to think they will begin to grumble again. Gothan is lurking in the shadows somewhere, plotting evil to us all, you may be sure. This city is honeycombed with secret corridors and subterranean passages of which only the priests know. Even I, who have traversed some of them when I was Gothan's puppet, know not where to look for the secret doors, since Gothan always led me through them blindfolded.

"Just now, I think I hold the upper hand. The people look on you with more awe than they regard me. They think your armor and helmets are part of your bodies and that you are invulnerable. Did you not note them timidly touching your mail as we passed through the crowd, and the amazement on their faces as they felt the iron of it?"

"For a people so wise in some ways they are very foolish in others," said Turlogh. "Who are they and whence came they?"

"They are so old," answered Brunhild, "that their most ancient legends give no hint of their origin. Ages ago they were a part of a great empire which spread out over the many isles of this sea. But some of the islands sank and vanished with their cities and people. Then the red-skinned savages assailed them and isle after isle fell before them. At last only this island was left unconquered, and the people have become weaker and forgotten many ancient arts. For lack of ports to sail to, the galleys rotted by the wharves which themselves crumbled into decay. Not in the memory of man has any son of Bal-Sagoth sailed the seas. At irregular intervals the red people descend upon the Isle of the Gods, traversing the seas in their long war-canoes which bear grinning skulls on the prows. Not far away as a Viking would reckon a sea-voyage, but out of sight over the sea rim lie the islands inhabited by these red men who centuries ago slaughtered the folk who dwelt there. We have always beaten them off; they can not scale the walls, but still they come and the fear of their raid is always hovering over the isle.

"But it is not them I fear; it is Gothan, who is at this moment either slipping like a loathly serpent through his black tunnels or else brewing abominations in one of his hidden chambers. In the caves deep in the hills to which his tunnels lead, he works fearful and unholy magic. His subjects are beasts – serpents, spiders, and great apes; and men – red captives and wretches of his own race. Deep in his grisly caverns he makes beasts of men and half-men of beasts, mingling bestial with human in ghastly creation. No man dares guess at the horrors that have spawned in the darkness, or what shapes of terror and blasphemy have come into being during the ages Gothan has wrought his abominations; for he is not as other men, and has discovered the secret of life everlasting. He has at least brought into foul life one creature that even he fears, the gibbering, mowing, nameless Thing he keeps chained in the furtherest cavern that no human foot save his has trod. He would loose it against me if he dared. . . .

"But it grows late and I would sleep. I will sleep in the room next to this, which has no other opening than this door. Not even a slave-girl will I keep with me, for I trust none of these people fully. You shall keep this room, and though the outer door is bolted, one had better watch while the other sleeps. Zomar and his guardsmen patrol the corridors outside, but I shall feel safer with two men of my own blood between me and the rest of the city."

She rose, and with a strangely lingering glance at Turlogh, entered her chamber and closed the door behind her.

Athelstane stretched and yawned. "Well, Turlogh," said he lazily, "men's fortunes are unstable as the sea. Last night I was the picked swordsman of a band of reavers and you a captive. This dawn we were lost outcasts springing at each other's throats. Now we are sword brothers and right-hand men to a queen. And you, I think, are destined to become a king."

"How so?"

"Why, have you not noticed the Orkney girl's eyes on you? Faith there's more than friendship in her glances that rest on those black locks and that brown face of yours. I tell you – "

"Enough," Turlogh's voice was harsh as an old wound stung him. "Women in power are white-fanged wolves. It was the spite of a woman that – " He stopped.

"Well, well," returned Athelstane tolerantly, "there are more good women than bad ones. I know – it was the intrigues of a woman that made you an outcast. Well, we should be good comrades. I am an outlaw, too.

If I should show my face in Wessex I would soon be looking down on the countryside from a stout oak limb."

"What drove you out on the Viking path? So far have the Saxons forgotten the ocean-ways that King Alfred was obliged to hire Frisian rovers to build and man his fleet when he fought the Danes."

Athelstane shrugged his mighty shoulders and began whetting his dirk.

"I had a yearning for the sea even when I was a shock-headed child in Wessex. I was still a youth when I killed a young eorl and fled the vengeance of his people. I found refuge in the Orkneys and the ways of the Vikings were more to my liking than the ways of my own blood. But I came back to fight against Canute, and when England submitted to his rule, he gave me command of his house-carles. That made the Danes jealous because of the honor given a Saxon who had fought against them, and the Saxons remembered I had left Wessex under a cloud once, and murmured that I was overly-well favored by the conquerors. Well, there was a Saxon thane and a Danish jarl who one night at feast assailed me with fiery words and I forgot myself and slew them both.

"So England – was – again – barred – to – me. I – took – the – Viking – path – again – "

Athelstane's words trailed off. His hands slid limply from his lap and the whetstone and dirk dropped to the floor. His head fell forward on his broad chest and his eyes closed.

"Too much wine," muttered Turlogh. "But let him slumber; I'll keep watch."

Yet even as he spoke, the Gael was aware of a strange lassitude stealing over him. He lay back in the broad chair. His eyes felt heavy and sleep veiled his brain despite himself. And as he lay there, a strange nightmare vision came to him. One of the heavy hangings on the wall opposite the door swayed violently and from behind it slunk a fearful shape that crept slavering across the room. Turlogh watched it apathetically, aware that he was dreaming and at the same time wondering at the strangeness of the dream. The thing was grotesquely like a crooked gnarled man in shape, but its face was bestial. It bared yellow fangs as it lurched silently toward him, and from under penthouse brows small reddened eyed gleamed demoniacally. Yet there was something of the human in its countenance; it was neither ape nor man, but an unnatural creature horribly compounded of both.

Now the foul apparition halted before him, and as the gnarled fingers clutched his throat, Turlogh was suddenly and fearfully aware that this was no dream but a fiendish reality. With a burst of desperate effort he broke the unseen chains that held him and hurled himself from the chair. The grasping fingers missed his throat, but quick as he was, he could not elude the swift lunge of those hairy arms, and the next moment he was tumbling about the floor in a death grip with the monster, whose sinews felt like pliant steel.

That fearful battle was fought in silence save for the hissing of hard-drawn breath. Turlogh's left forearm was thrust under the apish chin, holding back the grisly fangs from his throat, about which the monster's fingers had locked. Athelstane still slept in his chair, head fallen forward. Turlogh tried to call to him, but those throttling hands had shut off his voice – were fast choking out his life. The room swam in a red haze before his distended eyes. His right hand, clenched into an iron mallet, battered desperately at the fearful face bent toward his; the beast-like teeth shattered under his blows and blood splattered, but still the red eyes gloated and the taloned fingers sank deeper and deeper until a ringing in Turlogh's ears knelled his soul's departure.

Even as he sank into semi-unconsciousness, his falling hand struck something his numbed fighting-brain recognized as the dirk Athelstane had dropped on the floor. Blindly, with a dying gesture, Turlogh struck and felt the fingers loosen suddenly. Feeling the return of life and power, he heaved up and over, with his assailant beneath him. Through red mists that slowly lightened, Turlogh Dubh saw the ape-man, now encrimsoned, writhing beneath him, and he drove the dirk home until the dumb horror lay still with wide staring eyes.

The Gael staggered to his feet, dizzy and panting, trembling in every limb. He drew in great gulps of air and his giddiness slowly cleared. Blood trickled plentifully from the wounds in his throat. He noted with amazement that the Saxon still slumbered. And suddenly he began to feel again the tides of unnatural weariness and lassitude that had rendered him helpless before. Picking up his ax, he shook off the feeling with difficulty and stepped toward the curtain from behind which the ape-man had come. Like an invisible wave a subtle power emanating from those hangings struck him, and with weighted limbs he forced his way across the room.

Now he stood before the curtain and felt the power of a terrific evil will beating upon his own, menacing his very soul, threatening to enslave him, brain and body. Twice he raised his hand and twice it dropped limply to his side. Now for the third time he made a mighty effort and tore the hangings bodily from the wall. For a flashing instant he caught a glimpse of a bizarre, half-naked figure in a mantle of parrot-feathers and a headgear of waving plumes. Then as he felt the full hypnotic blast of those blazing eyes, he closed his own eyes and struck blind. He felt his ax sink deep; then he opened his eyes and gazed at the silent figure which lay at his feet, cleft head in a widening crimson pool.

And now Athelstane suddenly heaved erect, eyes flaring bewilderedly, sword out. "What – ?" he stammered, glaring wildly, "Turlogh, what in Thor's name's happened? Thor's blood! That is a priest there, but what is this dead thing?"

"One of the devils of this foul city," answered Turlogh, wrenching his ax free, "I think Gothan has failed again. This one stood behind the hangings and bewitched us unawares. He put the spell of sleep on us – "

"Aye, I slept," the Saxon nodded dazedly. "But how came they here – ?"

"There must be a secret door behind these hangings, though I can not find it – "

"Hark!" From the room where the queen slept there came a vague scuffling sound, that in its very faintness seemed fraught with grisly potentialities.

"Brunhild!" Turlogh shouted. A strangled gurgle answered him. He thrust against the door. It was locked. As he heaved up his ax to hew it open, Athelstane brushed him aside and hurled his full weight against it. The panels crashed and through their ruins Athelstane plunged into the room. A roar burst from his lips. Over the Saxon's shoulder Turlogh saw a vision of delirium. Brunhild, queen of Bal-Sagoth, writhed helpless in midair, gripped by the black shadow of a nightmare. Then as the great black shape turned cold flaming eyes on them Turlogh saw it was a living creature. It stood, man-like, upon two tree-like legs, but its outline and face were not of a man, beast or devil. This, Turlogh felt, was the horror that even Gothan had hesitated to loose upon his foes; the arch-fiend that the demoniac priest had brought into life in his hidden caves of horror. What ghastly knowledge had been necessary, what hideous blending of human and bestial things with nameless shapes from outer voids of darkness?

Held like a babe in arms Brunhild writhed, eyes flaring with horror, and as the Thing took a misshapen hand from her white throat to defend itself, a scream of heart-shaking fright burst from her pale lips. Athelstane, first in the room, was ahead of the Gael. The black shape loomed over the giant Saxon, dwarfing and overshadowing him, but Athelstane, gripping the hilt with both hands, lunged upward. The great sword sank over half its length into the black body and came out crimson as the monster reeled back. A hellish pandemonium of sound burst forth, and the echoes of that hideous yell thundered through the palace and deafened the hearers. Turlogh was springing in, ax high, when the fiend dropped the girl and fled reeling across the room, vanishing in a dark opening that now gaped in the wall. Athelstane, clean berserk, plunged after it.

Turlogh made to follow, but Brunhild, reeling up, threw her white arms around him in a grip even he could hardly break. "No!" she screamed, eyes ablaze with terror, "do not follow them into that fearful corridor! It must lead to Hell itself! The Saxon will never return! Let you not share his fate!"

"Loose me, woman!" roared Turlogh in a frenzy, striving to disengage himself without hurting her. "My comrade may be fighting for his life!"

"Wait till I summon the guard!" she cried, but Turlogh flung her from him, and as he sprang through the secret doorway, Brunhild smote on the jade gong until the palace re-echoed. A loud pounding began in the corridor and Zomar's voice shouted: "Oh queen, are you in peril? Shall we burst the door?"

"Hasten!" she screamed, as she rushed to the outer door and flung it open.

Turlogh, leaping recklessly into the corridor, raced along in darkness for a few moments, hearing ahead of him the agonized bellowing of the wounded monster and the deep fierce shouts of the Viking. Then these noises faded away in the distance as he came into a narrow passageway faintly lighted with torches stuck into niches. Face down on the floor lay a brown man, clad in gay feathers, his skull crushed like an egg-shell.

How long Turlogh O'Brien followed the dizzy windings of the shadowy corridor he never knew. Other smaller passages led off to each side but he kept to the main corridor. At last he passed under an arched doorway and came out into a strange vasty room.

Sombre massive columns upheld a shadowy ceiling so high it seemed like a brooding cloud arched against a midnight sky. Turlogh saw that he was in a temple. Behind a black red-stained stone altar loomed a mighty form, sinister and abhorrent. The god Gol-goroth! Surely it must be he. But Turlogh spared only a single glance for the colossal figure that brooded there in the shadows. Before him was a strange tableau. Athelstane leaned on his great sword and gazed at the two shapes which sprawled in a red welter at his feet. Whatever foul magic had brought the Black Thing into life, it had taken but a thrust of English steel to hurl it back into the limbo from whence it came. The monster lay half across its last victim – a gaunt white-bearded man whose eyes were starkly evil, even in death.

"Gothan!" ejaculated the startled Gael.

"Aye, the priest – I was close behind this troll or whatever it is, all the way along the corridor, but for all its size it fled like a deer. Once one in a feather mantle tried to halt it, and it smashed his skull and paused not an instant. At last we burst into this temple, I close upon the monster's heels with my sword raised for the death-cut. But Thor's blood! When it saw the old one standing by that altar, it gave one fearful howl and tore him to pieces and died itself, all in an instant, before I could reach it and strike."

Turlogh gazed at the huge formless thing. Looking directly at it, he could form no estimate of its nature. He got only a chaotic impression of great size and inhuman evil. Now it lay like a vast shadow blotched out on the marble floor. Surely black wings beating from moonless gulfs had hovered over its birth, and the grisly souls of nameless demons had gone into its being.

And now Brunhild rushed from the dark corridor with Zomar and the guardsmen. And from outer doors and secret nooks came others silently – warriors, and priests in feathered mantles, until a great throng stood in the Temple of Darkness.

A fierce cry broke from the queen as she saw what had happened. Her eyes blazed terribly and she was gripped by a strange madness.

"At last!" she screamed, spurning the corpse of her arch-foe with her heel, "at last I am true mistress of Bal-Sagoth! The secrets of the hidden ways are mine now, and old Gothan's beard is dabbled in his own blood!"

She flung her arms high in fearful triumph, and ran toward the grim idol, screaming exultant insults like a mad-woman. And at that instant the temple rocked! The colossal image swayed outward, and then pitched suddenly forward as a tall tower falls. Turlogh shouted and leaped forward, but even as he did, with a thunder like the bursting of a world, the god Gol-goroth crashed down upon the doomed woman, who stood frozen. The mighty image splintered into a thousand great fragments, blotting from the sight of men for ever Brunhild, daughter of Rane Thorfin's son, queen of Bal-Sagoth. From under the ruins there oozed a wide crimson stream.

Warriors and priests stood frozen, deafened by the crash of that fall, stunned by the weird catastrophe. An icy hand touched Turlogh's spine. Had that vast bulk been thrust over by the hand of a dead man? As it had rushed downward it had seemed to the Gael that the inhuman features had for an instant taken on the likeness of the dead Gothan!

Now as all stood speechless, the acolyte Gelka saw and seized his opportunity.

"Gol-goroth has spoken!" he screamed. "He has crushed the false goddess! She was but a wicked mortal! And these strangers, too, are mortal! See – he bleeds!"

The priest's finger stabbed at the dried blood on Turlogh's throat and a wild roar went up from the throng. Dazed and bewildered by the swiftness and magnitude of the late events, they were like crazed wolves, ready to wipe out doubts and fear in a burst of bloodshed. Gelka bounded at Turlogh, hatchet flashing, and a knife in the hand of a satellite licked into Zomar's back. Turlogh had not understood the shout, but he realized the air was tense with danger for Athelstane and himself. He met the leaping Gelka with a stroke that sheared through the waving plumes and the skull beneath, then half a dozen lances broke on his buckler and a rush of bodies swept him back against a great pillar. Then Athelstane, slow of thought, who had stood gaping for the flashing second it had taken this to transpire, awoke in a blast of awesome fury. With a deafening roar he swung his heavy sword in a mighty arc. The whistling blade whipped off a head, sheared through a torso and sank deep into a spinal column. The three corpses fell across each other and even in the madness of the strife, men cried out at the marvel of that single stroke.

But like a brown, blind tide of fury the maddened people of Bal-Sagoth rolled on their foes. The guardsmen of the dead queen, trapped in the press, died to a man without a chance to strike a blow. But the overthrow of the two white warriors was no such easy task. Back to back they smashed and smote; Athelstane's sword was a thunderbolt of death; Turlogh's ax was lightning. Hedged close by a sea of snarling brown faces and flashing steel they hacked their way slowly toward a doorway. The very mass of the attackers hindered the warriors of Bal-Sagoth, for they had no space to guide their strokes, while the weapons of the seafarers kept a bloody ring clear in front of them.

Heaping a ghastly row of corpses as they went, the comrades slowly cut their way through the snarling press. The Temple of Shadows, witness of many a bloody deed, was flooded with gore spilled like a red sacrifice to her broken gods. The heavy weapons of the white fighters wrought fearful havoc among their naked, lighter-limbed foes, while their armor guarded their own lives. But their arms, legs and faces were cut and gashed by the frantically flying steel and it seemed the sheer number of their foes would overwhelm them ere they could reach the door.

Then they had reached it, and made desperate play until the brown warriors, no longer able to come upon them from all sides, drew back for a breathing-space, leaving a torn red heap before the threshold. And in that instant the two sprang back into the corridor and seizing the great brazen door, slammed it in the very faces of the warriors who leaped howling to prevent it. Athelstane, bracing his mighty legs, held it against their combined efforts until Turlogh had time to find and slip the bolt.

"Thor!" gasped the Saxon, shaking the blood in a red shower from his face. "This is close play! What now, Turlogh?"

"Down the corridor, quick!" snapped the Gael, "before they come on us from this way and trap us like rats against this door. By Satan, the whole city must be roused! Hark to that roaring!"

In truth, as they raced down the shadowed corridor, it seemed to them that all Bal-Sagoth had burst into rebellion and civil war. From all sides came the clashing of steel, the shouts of men, and the screams of women, overshadowed by a hideous howling. A lurid glow became apparent down the corridor and then even as Turlogh, in the lead, rounded a corner and came out into an open courtyard, a vague figure leaped at him and a heavy weapon fell with unexpected force on his shield, almost felling him. But even as he staggered he struck back and the upper-spike on his ax sank under the heart of his attacker, who fell at his feet. In the glare that illumined all, Turlogh saw his victim differed from the brown warriors he had been fighting. This man was naked, powerfully muscled and of a copperish red rather than brown. The heavy animal-like jaw, the slanting low forehead showed none of the intelligence and refinement of the brown people, but only a brute ferocity. A heavy war-club, rudely carved, lay beside him.

"By Thor!" exclaimed Athelstane, "the city burns!"

Turlogh looked up. They were standing on a sort of raised courtyard from which broad steps led down into the streets and from this vantage-point they had a plain view of the terrific end of Bal-Sagoth. Flames leaped madly higher and higher, paling the moon, and in the red glare pigmy figures ran to and fro, falling and dying like puppets dancing to the tune of the Black Gods. Through the roar of the flames and the crashing of falling walls cut screams of death and shrieks of ghastly triumph. The city was swarming with naked, copper-skinned devils who burned and ravished and butchered in one red carnival of madness.

The red men of the isles! By the thousands they had descended on the Isle of the Gods in the night, and whether stealth or treachery let them through the walls, the comrades never knew, but now they ravened through the corpse-strewn streets, glutting their blood-lust in holocaust and massacre wholesale. Not all the gashed forms that lay in the crimson-running streets were brown; the people of the doomed city fought with desperate courage, but outnumbered and caught off guard, their courage was futile. The red men were like blood-hungry tigers.

"What ho, Turlogh!" shouted Athelstane, beard a-bristle, eyes ablaze as the madness of the scene fired a like passion in his own fierce soul, "the world ends! Let us into the thick of it and glut our steel before we die! Who shall we strike for – the red or the brown?"

"Steady!" snapped the Gael. "Either people would cut our throats. We must hack our way through to the gates, and the Devil take them all. We have no friends here. This way – down these stairs. Across the roofs in yonder direction I see the arch of a gate."

The comrades sprang down the stairs, gained the narrow street below and ran swiftly in the way Turlogh indicated. About them washed a red inundation of slaughter. A thick smoke veiled all now, and in the murk

chaotic groups merged, writhed and scattered, littering the shattered flags
with gory shapes. It was like a nightmare in which demoniac figures leaped
and capered, looming suddenly in the fire-shot mist, vanishing as suddenly. The flames from each side of the streets shouldered each other,
singeing the hair of the warriors as they ran. Roofs fell in with an awesome
thunder and walls crashing into ruin filled the air with flying death. Men
struck blindly from the smoke and the seafarers cut them down and never
knew whether their skins were brown or red.

Now a new note rose in the cataclysmic horror. Blinded by the smoke,
confused by the winding streets, the red men were trapped in the snare
of their own making. Fire is impartial; it can burn the lighter as well as
the intended victim; and a falling wall is blind. The red men abandoned
their prey and ran howling to and fro like beasts, seeking escape; many,
finding this futile, turned back in a last unreasoning storm of madness as
a blinded tiger turns, and made their last moments of life a crimson burst
of slaughter.

Turlogh, with the unerring sense of direction that comes to men who
live the life of the wolf, ran toward the point where he knew an outer gate
to be; yet in the windings of the streets and the screen of smoke, doubt
assailed him. From the flame-shot murk in front of him a fearful scream
rang out. A naked girl reeled blindly into view and fell at Turlogh's feet,
blood gushing from her mutilated breast. A howling, red-stained devil,
close on her heels, jerked back her head and cut her throat a fraction of a
second before Turlogh's ax ripped the head from its shoulders and spun
it grinning into the street. And at that second a sudden wind shifted the
writhing smoke and the comrades saw the open gateway ahead of them,
aswarm with red warriors. A fierce shout, a blasting rush, a mad instant
of volcanic ferocity that littered the gateway with corpses, and they were
through and racing down the slopes toward the distant forest and the
beach beyond. Before them the sky was reddening for dawn; behind them
rose the soul-shaking tumult of the doomed city.

Like hunted things they fled, seeking brief shelter among the many
groves from time to time, to avoid groups of savages who ran toward
the city. The whole island seemed to be swarming with them; the chiefs
must have drawn on all the isles within hundreds of miles for a raid of
such magnitude. And at last the comrades reached the strip of forest, and

breathed deeply as they came to the beach and found it abandoned save for a number of long skull-decorated war canoes.

Athelstane sat down and gasped for breath. "Thor's blood! What now? What may we do but hide in these woods until those red devils hunt us out?"

"Help me launch this boat," snapped Turlogh. "We'll take our chance on the open main – "

"Ho!" Athelstane leaped erect, pointing, "Thor's blood, a ship!"

The sun was just up, gleaming like a great golden coin on the sea-rim. And limned in the sun swam a tall, high-pooped craft. The comrades leaped into the nearest canoe, shoved off and rowed like mad, shouting and waving their oars to attract the attention of the crew. Powerful muscles drove the long slim craft along at an incredible clip, and it was not long before the ship stood about and allowed them to come alongside. Dark-faced men, clad in mail, looked over the rail.

"Spaniards," muttered Athelstane. "If they recognize me, I had better stayed on the island!"

But he clambered up the chain without hesitation, and the two wanderers fronted the lean somber-faced man whose armor was that of a knight of Asturias. He spoke to them in Spanish and Turlogh answered him, for the Gael, like many of his race, was a natural linguist and had wandered far and spoken many tongues. In a few words the Dalcassian told their story and explained the great pillar of smoke which now rolled upward in the morning air from the isle.

"Tell him there is a king's ransom for the taking," put in Athelstane. "Tell him of the silver gates, Turlogh."

But when the Gael spoke of the vast loot in the doomed city, the commander shook his head.

"Good sir, we have no time to secure it, nor men to waste in the taking. Those red fiends you describe would hardly give up anything – though useless to them – without a fierce battle and neither my time nor my force is mine. I am Don Roderigo del Cortez of Castile and this ship, the *Gray Friar*, is one of a fleet that sailed to harry the Moorish Corsairs. Some days agone we were separated from the rest of the fleet in a sea skirmish and the tempest blew us far off our course. We are even now beating back to rejoin the fleet if we can find it; if not, to harry the infidel as well as we may. We serve God and the king and we can not halt for mere dross as you suggest. But you are welcome aboard this ship and we have need of such fighting men as you appear to be. You will not regret it, should you wish to join us and strike a blow for Christendom against the Moslems."

In the narrow-bridged nose and deep dark eyes, as in the lean ascetic face, Turlogh read the fanatic, the stainless cavalier, the knight errant. He spoke to Athelstane: "This man is mad, but there are good blows to be struck and strange lands to see; anyway, we have no other choice."

"One place is as good as another to masterless men and wanderers," quoth the huge Saxon. "Tell him we will follow him to Hell and singe the tail of the Devil if there be any chance of loot."

4

Empire

Turlogh and Athelstane leaned on the rail, gazing back at the swiftly receding Island of the Gods, from which rose a pillar of smoke, laden with the ghosts of a thousand centuries and the shadows and mysteries of forgotten empire, and Athelstane cursed as only a Saxon can.

"A king's ransom – and after all that blood-letting – no loot!"

Turlogh shook his head. "We have seen an ancient kingdom fall – we have seen the last remnant of the world's oldest empire sink into flames and the abyss of oblivion, and barbarism rear its brute head above the ruins. So pass the glory and the splendor and the imperial purple – in red flames and yellow smoke."

"But not one bit of plunder – " persisted the Viking.

Again Turlogh shook his head. "I brought away with me the rarest gem upon the island – something for which men and women have died and the gutters run with blood."

He drew from his girdle a small object – a curiously carved symbol of jade.

"The emblem of kingship!" exclaimed Athelstane.

"Aye – as Brunhild struggled with me to keep me from following you into the corridor, this thing caught in my mail and was torn from the golden chain that held it."

"He who bears it is king of Bal-Sagoth," ruminated the mighty Saxon. "As I predicted, Turlogh, you are a king!"

Turlogh laughed with bitter mirth and pointed to the great billowing column of smoke which floated in the sky away on the sea-rim.

"Aye – a kingdom of the dead – an empire of ghosts and smoke. I am Ard-Righ of a phantom city – I am King Turlogh of Bal-Sagoth and my kingdom is fading in the morning sky. And therein it is like all other empires in the world – dreams and ghosts and smoke."

Nekht Semerkeht

And what I am sure of is that there is not any gold nor any other metal in all that country. — Coronado

The snap of a bowstring, the shrill scream of a horse death-stricken broke the stillness. The Spanish barb reared, the feathered end of the arrow quivering behind its foreleg, and went down in a headlong plunge. The rider sprang free as it fell, and hit on his feet with a dry clang of steel. He staggered, empty hands flung wide, fighting to regain his balance. His matchlock had fallen several feet away and the match had gone out. He drew his broadsword and looked about him, trying to locate the beady black eyes he knew glittered at him from somewhere in the close-set greasewood bushes that edged the rim of the dry wash to his left. Even as he sought the slayer of his steed, the man appeared, rising upright and springing over a low shrub almost with one movement. A vengeful yell of triumph quivered in the late afternoon stillness. An instant they faced one another, with a fifty foot stretch of tawny sand between – the New World and the Old personified in them.

About them, from horizon to horizon, the naked plains swept away and away to mingle in the faint ocean-like haze that hovered along the turquoise rim of the sky. No bird cried, no beast moved. The dead horse lay motionless. In all that vast expanse those two were the only living, sentient beings – the tall, grey-bearded man in tarnished steel; the wiry, copper-skinned brave, naked in his beaded loin-clout, with his black eyes burning redly under the square-cut bang of his black mane.

Those black eyes flickered toward the matchlock, lying out of reach and useless, and the red glints grew more lurid. The Apache had learned the deadliness of the white man's guns. But now he felt that the advantage was with him. His left hand gripped a short, stout bow of bois d'arc, backed with sinew; in his right was a flint-headed dogwood arrow. He did not reach for the stone-headed hatchet at his girdle. He had no intention of coming within the sweep of that long sword which glimmered dully in the rays of the westering sun. For an instant the tableau held motionless, as he swept his fierce gaze over his enemy. He knew his flint darts would splinter on the white man's armor; but no vizor covered the bearded face. Yet he was unwilling to waste a single arrowhead, which represented hours of tedious toil. Cat-like he glided toward his prey, not in a straight line, but springing from side to side, to confuse the other, to make him shift his position and so to catch him at the end of a motion, where he could not dodge the winged death that leaped at him. The Apache did not fear a sudden sword-swinging rush. The steel-clad man could never match his own naked fleetness of foot. He had the white man at his mercy and could kill in his own way, without risk. With a short fierce cry he stopped short, whipped up the bow and jerked back the arrow – just as the white man plucked a pistol from his belt and fired point-blank.

The arrow whined erratically skyward. The bow slipped from the warrior's hands as the Apache went to his knees, choking, blood gushing between the fingers that clutched at his muscular breast. He sank down in the sand, his bloodshot, glazing eyes fixed in a last spasm of despairing hate on his slayer. The white man always had something in reserve, something unguessed. The warrior saw the armored man looming above him like a grim god, implacable and unconquerable, with bleak, pitiless eyes. In that gleaming figure he read the ultimate doom of his whole race. Weakly, as a dying snake hisses, he reared his head, spat at his slayer and slid back dead.

Hernando de Guzman sheathed his sword, reloaded the clumsy wheel-lock pistol and replaced it beside its mate, reflecting briefly that it was well for him that this particular Apache had not been familiar with the shorter arms. He sighed as he looked down at his dead horse. Like many of his race he had a fondness for fine horses and displayed toward them a kindliness seldom if ever showed to human beings. He made no move to secure the ornately decorated saddle and bridle. In the miles he must cover afoot he would find exhaustion enough without further burdening himself. The matchlock he secured, and with it resting on his shoulder he stood motionless for a moment, seeking to orient himself.

A feeling that he was already lost tugged at him – had been tugging at him for the last hour, even before his horse was killed. Veteran though he was, he had wandered further afield than was wise, in vain pursuit of an antelope, whose flaring white scud, gleaming in the sunlight, had led him like a will-o'-the-wisp over sand hills and prairie. He had tried to keep the location of the camp in his mind, but he feared that he had failed. There were no landmarks in these plains that swept without a break from sunrise to sunset. An expedition, driving its own sustenance on the hoof, was like a ship groping its way across an unknown sea, its only chance of survival lying in its self-sufficiency. A lone rider was like a man adrift in an open boat, without food or water or compass. A man afoot was a man as good as dead, unless he could reach his companions swiftly.

De Guzman briefly explored the shallow gully in hopes of finding a horse. There was none. The Apaches had not yet taken to horse-riding. Steeds strayed or stolen from the Spaniards were used as food, though he had heard tales of a terrible tribe to the north whose warriors were already horsemen.

The Spaniard chose the direction he believed to be the right one, and took up his march. He lifted his morion and ran his fingers through his damp, greying locks, but the heat of the sun made him replace it. Years of armor-wearing accustomed him to the weight and heat of the steel that cased him. Later it would add to his weariness, but it might stand him in good stead if he met other roaming warriors of the plains. The presence of the lone warrior he had killed proved that there was a whole clan somewhere in the vicinity.

The sun dipped toward the western horizon; across its red eye he moved, a tiny pygmy in the midst of the illimitable plain that mocked him in its grim vastness and silence.

The sun seemed to poise on the desert rim before it rushed from sight. A thin streamer of crimson ran north and south around the skyline. The sky seemed to expand, to deepen with the coming of sunset. Already in the east the hot volcanic blue was paling to the steel of Toledo swords.

De Guzman stopped and dropped the butt of his matchlock to the earth. It rang on the hard ground and left no print. He looked back the way he had come, unable to trace his own route over the short dry springy grass. He had passed, leaving no footprints. He might have been a phantom, drifting futilely across a sleeping, indifferent land. The plains were impervious to

148

human efforts. Man left no trace upon them; he marched, fought, struggled and died cursing the gods that betrayed him, but the plains dreamed on, with no more trace of his passing than he had left on the surface of the sea.

"Gold!" muttered de Guzman, and laughed sardonically.

He had come a long way since his horse fell. If he were going in the right direction he would have approached the camp near enough to have heard the shots that the men would be firing to guide him back. He was lost. He knew not in which direction to turn. The plains had claimed him for their own. His bones, bred of the wheat and oil and wine of Old Spain, would bleach on the dreary expanse with the bones of the Apache, the coyote and the rattlesnake. But the thought stirred in him no religious or sentimental horror. Spain was far away, a dream and a memory, a Land of Cockaigne that had been real once, in the golden glow of youth and desire, but now had no more reality than a ghost-continent lost in a sea of mist.

Spanish blood was no more sacred than the blood of other races; blood was only blood, and he had seen oceans of it spilled: Spanish blood, English blood, Huguenot blood, Inca blood, Aztec blood – the royal blood of Montezuma dripping from the parapets of Tenochtitlan – blood running ankle-deep in the plaza of Cajamarca, about the frantic feet of doomed Atahualpa.

But the will to live burned fiercely in his breast, the blind, black instinct toward life, which has no relation to intellect or reason or anything else. As such he recognized and obeyed it. He had no more illusions concerning existence. He knew, as all men know who have bared its core, that the game was not worth the candle. Men rationalize the blind instinct of self preservation, and build glib air-castles explaining why it is better to live than to die, when their boasted – but ignored – intellect is, in every phase, a negation of life. But civilized men hate and fear their instincts, as they hate and fear every heritage from the blind, squalling pit of primordial beginnings that bred them. Dogs, apes, elephants, these creatures obey instincts and live only because instinct bids them live. Man's urge toward life is no less blind and reasonless, but, abhorring his kinship with those creatures who had the misfortune not to be made in the Deity's image – having no prophets to declare it – fondles his favorite delusion that *he* is guided wholly by reason, even when reason tells him it is better to die than to live. It is not the intellect he boasts that bids him live, but the blind, black, unreasoning beast-instinct.

This de Guzman knew and admitted. He did not try to deceive himself into believing that there was any intellectual reason why he should not give up the agonizing struggle, place the muzzle of a pistol to his head and quit an existence whose savor had long ago become less than its pain. If by some miracle he found his way back to Coronado's camp, and at last to Mexico or fabled Quivira, there was no reason to believe life would be any less sordid or more desirable than it had been before he marched northward in search of the Seven Cities of Gold. But that blind instinct bade him fight for life to its last gagging gasp, to live in spite of hell or the actions of his fellow men. It burned as strongly now as it had that long-past day in his youth when he fought shoulder to shoulder with Cortez and saw the plumed hordes of Montezuma roll in like a wave to engulf the desperate handful which defied them.

To live! Not for love, nor profit, nor ambition, nor for a cause – all these things were wisps of mist, phantoms conjured up by men to explain the unexplainable. To live, because in his being there was implanted too deeply a blind black urge to live, that was in itself question and answer, desire and goal, beginning and end, and the answer to all the riddles in the universe.

And so the Conquistador laughed sardonically, shouldered his clumsy matchlock and prepared to take up anew his futile march, into ultimate oblivion and silence.

Then he heard the drum.

Even, deliberate, unhurried, its voice rolled across the plains, as mellow as the booming of waves of wine on a golden coast. He posed a moment, an image in steel, straining his ears. It came from the east, he decided, and it was no Apache drum. It was alien, exotic, like a drum he had heard that night when he stood on a flat roof in Cajamarca and watched the myriad fires of the great Inca's army twinkling through the night, while near by the passionless voice of the Bastard Pizarro spun black webs of treachery and infamy.

He closed his eyes, rubbed a hand across them; opened them, listened, with his head tilted sidewise, wondering if the heat and silence were already melting his brain and giving birth to phantasies. No! It was no mirage framed in sound. Steady as the pulse in his own temple it throbbed and throbbed, touching obscure chords in his brain until his whole being thrummed with the call of mystery. For a moment dead ashes flickered into flame, as if his dead youth were for the moment revived. In that mellow sound were magic and allure. He felt again, for a moment, as he had felt so long ago when he gripped a ship's rail with hot eager hands and saw the golden fabled coast of Mexico loom out of the morning mist, and felt the lure of adventure and plunder that was like the blast of a golden trumpet ringing down the wind.

It passed, but a pulse in his temple beat swift staccato so that he laughed at himself. And without pausing to argue the matter with himself he turned and strode eastward.

The sun had set; the brief twilight of the plains glowed and faded. The stars blinked out, great, white cold stars, indifferent to the tiny figure plodding across the shadowless vastness. The sparse shrubs crouched like nameless beasts waiting for the wanderer to stumble and fall. The drum pulsed steadily on and on, booming its golden wavelets of sound across the wasteland. It roused memories long faded, alien and exotic, of flaming gardens of great blossoms, steaming jungles, tinkling fountains, and always an undertone of golden drops tinkling on a golden paving.

Gold! Again he was following a quest of gold – the same, old, threadbare quest that had led him around the world over seas, through jungles, and through the smoke and flame of butchered cities. Like Coronado, sleeping somewhere on these plains and wrapped in fantastic dreams, he was following a call of gold, and one as tangible as that which maddened Francisco's dreams. Coronado, seeking vainly for the cities of Cibolo, with their lofty houses and glittering treasures, where even the slaves ate from golden dishes! De Guzman smiled bitterly, with his parched, thirst-twisted lips, reflecting that in future years Coronado would become a symbol for the chasing of will-o'-the-wisps. Historians to come, wise with the blatant wisdom of hindsight, would mock at him as a visionary and a fool. His name would become a taunt for treasure-seekers. Yet with what reason? Why should not a Spaniard search for gold in the countries north of the Rio Grande? Why refuse to credit the tales of Cibolo? They were no more incredible than the tales of Peru and Mexico had been, less than a generation ago. There was as much reason to believe Cibolo existed as there had been to believe that Peru existed, before the swineherd Pizarro sailed southward.

But the world judges by failure or success. Coronado was of the same hard-headed, heavy-handed breed as Pizarro and Cortez. But they found gold and would go down in history as robbers and plunderers; Coronado found no gold and would go down in history as a visionary, a credulous believer in myths, a chaser of non-existent rainbows. De Guzman laughed, and his laughter was not pleasant, embodying his personal opinion of the human race, which was not flattering.

So through the night he followed the mellow booming of the drum which grew subtly louder as he advanced. In the small hours of morning, when his feet seemed weighted not with steel but with lead, and sleep filled his eyes like dust, so that he kept blinking continually, he was aware of a vague bulk looming among the stars on the eastern horizon, and lights twinkled which might have been stars, but which he believed to be fires. And the drum was not far away now; he caught minor notes and under-tones he had not heard before, strange rustlings and murmurings, like the swish of the skirts of dark-eyed Aztec women, or the soft low gurglings of their laughter that tinkled among the silvery fountains in the gardens of Tenochtitlan before the Spanish swords reddened those gardens with blood. Why should a drum speak with such voices in this naked, northern land, bringing the lures and mysteries of the faraway south?

On either hand he made out the faint outlines of a long ridge. He was aware that he had made a slow, gradual descent. He knew that he had entered a broad, shallow valley, probably one marking the course of a sunken river. The ridges drew nearer as he advanced, and increased in height.

Just before dawn he stumbled upon a small stream which ran south-eastward as all the streams in this land seemed to run. Willows and cottonwoods and straggling bushes grew thick along it. He drank deeply and lay there near the water's edge, waiting for dawn. The drum pulsed once more, and ceased. Only a single fire twinkled in the dark bulk before him. Silence lay over the ancient land.

With the first streak of milky light in the east, he saw before him the towers and flat roofs of a walled city.

He had roamed too far and seen too many incredible sights to be greatly surprised at anything he saw, yet he lay there wondering at the sight. The city was built of adobe, like the pueblos they had encountered far to the west, but there the resemblance ceased. The walls were sheathed in an enamel-like glaze, decorated with intricate designs in blue, purple, and crimson. It was not large in extent, but the houses, three or four stories in height, did not resemble the beehive huts of the pueblos. The whole city was dominated by a towering structure that gleamed in the dawn-light, and was somewhat like a teocalla, save that it was topped by a dome. He blinked at that. He had never seen anything like it, in Peru, Yucatan or Mexico. The architecture of the city was baffling, obviously allied to that of the Aztecs, yet curiously unlike, as if Aztec hands had reared what an alien brain had conceived.

The city sat in a broad fan-shaped valley, which narrowed and deepened to the east; or rather the cliffs grew higher, for the valley floor remained level. Here once, thousands, perhaps millions of years ago, a great river had cut its channel in the plain and plunged out of sight, leaving a V-shaped valley, walled on three sides by cliffs which grew tall and steep at the apex. The city faced westward, toward the broad opening of the valley, where the ridges dwindled until they vanished. Any enemy must approach from the west, but there was no barrier to guard the city in that direction, where the dwindling ridges were more than a mile apart. The stream entered the broad mouth and wound past the walls at a few hundred yards distance, until it plunged into a cavern in the cliffs. Beyond the city, to the southeast, it flowed through a checkerboard of irrigated fields in which he recognized corn, grapes, berries, nuts and melons. The soil of these barren plains was fertile; all it lacked was water to produce food in abundance. Here the water was supplied. As he watched a small gate in the southeast wall opened and people came into the fields to work, small brown people, well-formed, the men clad in loin-cloths, the women in short sleeveless tunics which left the left breast bare, and came scarcely below mid-thigh.

As he lay there watching, he heard a rumbling to the west, a sound he knew. He jerked his head about and, peering through the intertwining willows, he saw a cloud of dust rising in the valley mouth. Through the dust appeared a long low black line, which grew swiftly as it advanced. The line became a swiftly rolling mass which was seen to be formed of shaggy dark animals with huge, horned heads. It was a stampede of buffalo, the cattle of the plains. The people in the fields ran for the gate which swung open to receive them. The beasts came on blindly, perhaps a thousand of them. Heads appeared along the walls of the city, and a trumpet blared barbarically. De Guzman had seen buffalo stampede before, but he did not understand why they should charge so blindly toward the city. On they came, in a black, bellowing wave, until it seemed they would dash themselves against the foot of the walls. But three hundred yards from the walls they split as on an unseen barrier, and broke away to the north and south, some crashing through the willows and splashing madly across the stream. Then de Guzman saw the reason for their stampede.

Their dividing unmasked three hundred Apaches, painted for war, with bows in their hands. They had driven the buffalo before them and running behind and among them, fleet-footed and untiring as wolves, had used the rushing herd as a cover to come within bow-shot of the city.

Now with wild yells they rushed for the gate, showing a recklessness de Guzman did not associate with the Apaches. He believed they had been drugged with tizwin. No arrows came from the wall, but a strange misty cloud rolled over the wall and floated toward the Apaches. It enveloped them, and their yells ceased. No brave rushed out of the cloud. A stark silence reigned. Then the cloud dispersed and he saw them again – lying where they had fallen, their naked brown bodies gleaming in the rising sun, their feathers stirring in the faint wind.

De Guzman's flesh crawled. This was necromancy! Men were coming from the gate, now; tall, sinewy men, clad in plumed helmets and beaded loin-clouts. And de Guzman felt the old blood-stir of the Conquistador, for those helmets gleamed in the sun as only pure gold can gleam.

The warriors fastened ropes to the ankles of the fallen braves and dragged them inside the gates. The gates were closed and again the workers came into the fields. De Guzman lay undecided among the willows.

He had satisfied his thirst, but he was ravenously hungry. Yet he hesitated to show himself to these people, who had showed themselves possessed of what was undoubtedly a gift of the Devil. De Guzman doubted the existence of a Lord of Evil, but he recognized diabolatry nevertheless.

He lay there, and despite himself, he slept. He awoke with a start. A girl had parted the willows and was staring down at him. She was clad in the scanty cotton tunic of the workers in the field, but she did not seem the sort of woman who would have been wearing such a garment. Silks and jewels would have seemed more appropriate. There was an Aztec look about her, but a subtle difference. She was tall, slender but voluptuously formed, and the careless abandon with which she wore her scanty garment left few of her generous contours wholly concealed. De Guzman felt a quickening of the pulse as he had when he saw the gold of the strange city. His greying beard was no indication of the fire that still burned in the Conquistador's veins. She was like the strange, exotic women who had intoxicated him in his youth when he first followed the iron captains in hot, unknown lands.

She spoke, stammering in her surprise: "Who are you?"

She had spoken in Aztec, scarcely familiar with its alien enunciations.

He was on his feet in a flash, armor and all, and grasped her wrist as she recoiled. She did not struggle, feeling the iron in his grip. She stared up at him, amazement mirrored more than fear in her wide dark eyes. A subtle perfume filled his nostrils and his head reeled momentarily.

"What does a woman like you at work in the fields?" he muttered.

She ignored his question. "I know what manner of man you are! You are a Spaniard! One of those who slew Montezuma and destroyed his kingdom! You ride beasts called horses, and make thunder and the red flame of death flash out of a metal war-club!"

Eagerly she ran her fingers over his dented breastplate. The touch of her soft warm fingers against his beard sent tingles of pleasure through his iron frame. He smiled to himself, sardonically. What new thing could there be for him to learn about women, who could not even remember how many he had held in his arms during his wild career? But his instincts drew him to her, and he did not resist or question them.

"Word came to the North," she said. "Word of the slaughter made in Mexico – I was but a baby then. Men doubted – but no more tribute came from Montezuma – "

"Tribute?" The word was startled out of him. "Tribute? From Montezuma, the emperor of all Mexico?"

"Aye. He and his fathers paid tribute to Nekht Semerkeht for a thousand years – slaves, gold, pelts."

"Nekht Semerkeht!" It had a strange, alien ring. It was not Aztec, that was certain. Where had he heard it? Dimly, its echo reverberated in the shadowy recesses back of his mind. It seemed somehow associated with a deafening noise, the reek of gunpowder and the reek of spilt blood.

"I have seen men like you!" she said. "Once, when I was ten, I wandered outside the city, and the Apaches caught me and sold me to the Lipans, who sold me to the Karankawas who dwell on the coast far to the south, and are cannibals. Once a great war-canoe with wings came sailing by the coast, and the Karankawa braves went out in their dug-outs and shot their arrows at it. There were men in steel on the deck, like you. They turned great war-clubs of metal toward the canoes and blew them out of the water. I ran away in the confusion and came to a camp of the Tonkewas, who brought me home again for the Tonkewas are our servants. What is your name?"

He told her; she turned it about her tongue, lisping it in her attempts to pronounce it.

"And who are you?" he demanded. He had never released her wrist and now his steel-clad arm slipped about her supple waist. She started at the contact and tried to draw away.

"I am a princess," she answered haughtily.

"Then what are you doing in a slave's garment?" he demanded, taking hold of the garment and raising it – possibly to call her attention to it.

Her fine dark eyes filled suddenly with tears and she drooped her head in a sort of wrathful humility.

"I forgot. I am a slave. A toiler in the fields, bearing the weals of the overseer's whip!"

In angry scorn at herself, she turned lithely and exhibited them to him.

"I, the daughter of kings, whipped like a common slave!"

She spoke rapidly: "Listen, I am Nezahualca, daughter of a line of kings. Nekht Semerkeht reigns in Tlasceltec, but beneath him is a governor, the *tlacatecatl*, Lord of the Fighting Men. Atzcaputzalco was governor; my lover, Acamapichtli, was an officer under him. I desired that my lover become governor. We intrigued – I have – *had* – power in the city. But Nekht did not desire it. My lover was fed to the *feeders from the sky*. I was degraded to the status of a public slave – one of the Totonacs whom my ancestors brought with them centuries ago when they came northward."

"When was that?" he asked.

"Long ago, when Nekht Semerkeht first came to Tenochtitlan. He reigned there for a space, then he gathered many people and came northward, to found this city. He took only young men and women, newly married."

De Guzman suddenly remembered where he had heard that name Nekht

Semerkeht – a cry from the bloody lips of an Aztec priest falling in the darkness of the terrible battle on the *noche triste*, as men, in their last extremity invoke a devil instead of a god.

He remembered, too, vague tales of a city far to the North – from which, he believed grew the tales of Cibolo. He had thought it a legend; but here was the reality.

"Who is Nekht Semerkeht?" he asked. The name was not Aztec.

She gestured vaguely eastward. "He came across the blue ocean, long ago. He is a mighty magician, mightier than the priests of the Toltecs. He came alone and made himself ruler of Mexico. But he grew weary and came north – listen to me, iron man!

"Nekht Semerkeht does not know of your race. Even his magic can not prevail against the thunder of your war-club. Help me to kill him! There are warriors who will follow me, in spite of all. I will gather them in a chamber of his temple. Tonight I will open a gate to you, will lead you into the temple. The overseer who guards the slaves at night, he is a young man who has fallen in love with me. He will do anything I ask. Will you aid me?"

He nodded. "But bring me food."

"I will bring food and leave it among the bushes. But I must return to the gardens now, before I am missed."

So all day he lay hidden among the willows, and at night he rose and moved like a steel-clad phantom, dim in the starlight, across the silent gardens until he came to the door she had mentioned. It was opened and she appeared, limned in the faint glow of a tiny hand-cresset, in her scanty garment. With her was a young man in the garments of an overseer.

She caught his steel-gloved hand in her slim fingers.

"Come! The warriors await!"

She led him through narrow streets and shadowy courtyards to a small door in the great temple. Along a dark corridor they moved until they came into a chamber, where ten men waited. Nezahualca cried out sharply. The ten men sat each in his ebon chair, in rigid, unseeing attitudes.

The light went out. Nezahualca screamed in the dark. The young overseer gasped. De Guzman's matchlock was wrenched from his hands. He drew his sword and stood tense and listening in the silence which followed. Then a soft hand touched his. He almost struck with his sword before he recognized the feel of a woman's slim hand. The fingers closed supply about his, and tugged gently. He followed, gliding as silently as he could in his armor. He was led through a door, along a darkened corridor, on and on. Suddenly, somewhere, a woman screamed, in the voice of Nezahualca.

Smitten by a grisly thought, he ran his fingers along the wrist of the hand that held his. They encountered a few inches of soft smooth wrist, then a hairy, wiry arm! A peal of demoniac laughter burst out in the darkness. Gagging with horror he heaved up his sword and smote blindly, and the horrible guffaw broke in an agonized gurgle.

Something thrashed and flopped in the darkness at his feet, and he turned back, his flesh crawling. That nameless monstrosity with the soft hands of a woman was not leading him anywhere he should go. He turned aside, found a door, and presently, moving at random along another corridor, saw a faint gleam of light far ahead of him.

He was looking down into a chamber, from a sort of balcony. He could see a throne of black ebony, with a back and canopy which hid the occupant, but he knew someone or *something* sat there. He saw the young overseer and Nezahualca. Stark naked, he hung suspended from a golden chain by his ankles from the ceiling, over a gold brazier which sent up clouds of purple smoke which from time to time hid him completely as high as his waist. He made no sound, but writhed weakly.

Nezahualca, as naked as the youth, lay on a gold, gem-crusted altar directly beneath a circular opening in the dome which showed a disk of blue-black star-clustered night-sky. Her lovely eyes were dilated with fear, her wrists and ankles confined by slender golden chains. She stared wildly up through the roof.

A voice was speaking from the throne, calm, passionless, and merciless: "You were a fool to place trust in a barbarian with a thunder-club. Its necromancy is less than mine. He lost his thunder-club and a child of darkness led him to his doom among the rattlesnakes. And your flesh shall glut the *feeders from the sky*."

A despairing cry broke from the girl's throat.

De Guzman turned and groped his way down the stairs, a pistol in each hand. Just as he reached a lower landing, he heard the girl cry out again, with greater poignancy, and with the cry the dry rustle of great wings. He came through a door and saw a nightmare shape settling down on the altar – a dragon-like thing from the upper spaces of the air, whose raids on the lower levels, ages ago, gave rise to tales of harpies and vampires.

De Guzman stepped through the door and fired point-blank with his right-hand pistol, and the monster rolled to the floor, its head blasted. He wheeled. A man had risen from the throne, and though he had expected to see a monstrosity, the Spaniard's flesh crawled – not because the man was hideous, for he was handsome with a terrible dark beauty; but because of the ageless evil in his luminous dark eyes.

"Fool!" said he, calmly, "I am Nekht Semerkeht of Egypt!"

Even as he glimpsed the motion de Guzman fired point-blank with his left-hand pistol, and Nekht Semerkeht reeled with a choking cry. He staggered back and vanished through the wall. De Guzman unbound the girl. She cried out for him to follow. He followed, through strange corridors until he came to a vast chamber where about the walls were ranged bodies of men upright, and turned to stone – Toltecs, Aztecs, Totonacs, Tonkewas, Lipans, Apaches, warriors of tribes unfamiliar to the Spaniard.

Nekht Semerkeht sat at a smooth stone table, a slight smile of seeming self-mockery on his dark lips, his red-stained hand against his breast.

"You have conquered," he said. "I am dying." De Guzman sat the cresset on the table. "I am Nekht Semerkeht of Egypt. The Ptolemies drove me from Egypt long ago. My galley was wrecked off the coast of Mexico. My arts were strong then. They are stronger now. I made myself lord of Mexico, but I wearied of its rule and came northward. I have heard how your race slew Montezuma. But here in this city are greater treasures of gold than ever Cortez took from Tenochtitlan."

As they talked de Guzman was aware of a magic web surrounding him. He broke it, leaped up, and Nekht Semerkeht was on him with a curved sword.

"Fool!" roared the Egyptian. "Did you think a pellet of lead could slay Nekht Semerkeht?"

His blade was a white flame about the Spaniard's bare head, and as de Guzman parried and smote, he saw the cresset was dimming, going out. He rushed, smiting desperately to strike down this dark fiend before the blackness engulfed them. Sparks rang and Nekht Semerkeht cried out as he pitched backward into the blackness yawning at his feet. Blood spurting he toppled and vanished. The trap door closed, and de Guzman stood alone in the hall of the warriors.

He turned and ran out of the accursed place. The great doors were rushing shut. He sprang through and they clanged behind him.

He sought Nezahualca and claimed his part of the kingship. She resisted but he overpowered her. Then as he slept Nekht Semerkeht came to him and assumed the likeness of a strange Indian warrior and told the Spaniard he would bring the Comanches upon the city by means of a dream, and that his race would never be able to conquer them. The Comanches came upon them and Nekht Semerkeht, dying, dragged himself upon the palace tower and smote on a gong until a section of the wall fell. The Comanches swarmed in and butchered everyone in the city. De Guzman fell fighting fiercely.

Black Vulmea's Vengeance

Out of the *Cockatoo*'s cabin staggered Black Terence Vulmea, pipe in one hand and flagon in the other. He stood with booted legs wide, teetering slightly to the gentle lift of the lofty poop. He was bareheaded and his shirt was open, revealing his broad hairy chest. He emptied the flagon and tossed it over the side with a gusty sigh of satisfaction, then directed his somewhat blurred gaze on the deck below. From poop ladder to forecastle it was littered by sprawling figures. The ship smelt like a brewery. Empty barrels, with their heads stove in, stood or rolled between the prostrate forms. Vulmea was the only man on his feet. From galley-boy to first mate the rest of the ship's company lay senseless after a debauch that had lasted a whole night long. There was not even a man at the helm.

But it was lashed securely and in that placid sea no hand was needed on the wheel. The breeze was light but steady. Land was a thin blue line to the east. A stainless blue sky held a sun whose heat had not yet become fierce.

Vulmea blinked indulgently down upon the sprawled figures of his crew, and glanced idly over the larboard side. He grunted incredulously and batted his eyes. A ship loomed where he had expected to see only naked ocean stretching to the skyline. She was little more than a hundred yards away, and was bearing down swiftly on the *Cockatoo*, obviously with the intention of laying her alongside. She was tall and square-rigged, her white canvas flashing dazzlingly in the sun. From the maintruck the flag of England whipped red against the blue. Her bulwarks were lined with tense figures, bristling with boarding-pikes and grappling irons, and through her open ports the astounded pirate glimpsed the glow of the burning matches the gunners held ready.

"All hands to battle-quarters!" yelled Vulmea confusedly. Reverberant snores answered the summons. All hands remained as they were.

"Wake up, you lousy dogs!" roared their captain. "Up, curse you! A king's ship is at our throats!"

His only response came in the form of staccato commands from the frigate's deck, barking across the narrowing strip of blue water.

"Damnation!"

Cursing luridly he lurched in a reeling run across the poop to the swivel-gun which stood at the head of the larboard ladder. Seizing this he swung it about until its muzzle bore full on the bulwark of the approaching frigate. Objects wavered dizzily before his bloodshot eyes, but he squinted along its barrel as if he were aiming a musket.

"Strike your colors, you damned pirate!" came a hail from the trim figure that trod the warship's poop, sword in hand.

"Go to hell!" roared Vulmea, and knocked the glowing coals of his pipe into the vent of the gun-breech. The falcon crashed, smoke puffed out in a white cloud, and the double handful of musket balls with which the gun had been charged mowed a ghastly lane through the boarding party clustered along the frigate's bulwark. Like a clap of thunder came the answering broadside and a storm of metal raked the *Cockatoo*'s decks, turning them into a red shambles.

Sails ripped, ropes parted, timbers splintered, and blood and brains mingled with the pools of liquor spilt on the decks. A round shot as big as a man's head smashed into the falcon, ripping it loose from the swivel and dashing it against the man who had fired it. The impact knocked him backward headlong across the poop where his head hit the rail with a crack that was too much even for an Irish skull. Black Vulmea sagged senseless to the boards. He was as deaf to the triumphant shouts and the stamp of victorious feet on his red-streaming decks as were his men who had gone from the sleep of drunkenness to the black sleep of death without knowing what had hit them.

Captain John Wentyard, of his Majesty's frigate the *Redoubtable*, sipped his wine delicately and set down the glass with a gesture that in another man would have smacked of affectation. Wentyard was a tall man, with a narrow, pale face, colorless eyes, and a prominent nose. His costume was almost sober in comparison with the glitter of his officers who sat in respectful silence about the mahogany table in the main cabin.

"Bring in the prisoner," he ordered, and there was a glint of satisfaction in his cold eyes.

They brought in Black Vulmea, between four brawny sailors, his hands manacled before him and a chain on his ankles that was just long enough to allow him to walk without tripping. Blood was clotted in the pirate's thick black hair. His shirt was in tatters, revealing a torso bronzed by the sun and rippling with great muscles. Through the stern-windows, he could see the topmasts of the *Cockatoo*, just sinking out of sight. That close-range broadside had robbed the frigate of a prize. His conquerors were before him and there was no mercy in their stares, but Vulmea did not seem at all abashed or intimidated. He met the stern eyes of the officers with a level gaze that reflected only a sardonic amusement. Wentyard frowned. He preferred that his captives cringe before him. It made him feel more like Justice personified, looking unemotionally down from a great height on the sufferings of the evil.

"You are Black Vulmea, the notorious pirate?"

"I'm Vulmea," was the laconic answer.

"I suppose you will say, as do all these rogues," sneered Wentyard, "that you hold a commission from the Governor of Tortuga? These privateer commissions from the French mean nothing to his Majesty. You – "

"Save your breath, fish-eyes!" Vulmea grinned hardly. "I hold no commission from anybody. I'm not one of your accursed swashbucklers who hide behind the name of buccaneer. I'm a pirate, and I've plundered English ships as well as Spanish – and be damned to you, heron-beak!"

The officers gasped at this effrontery, and Wentyard smiled a ghastly, mirthless smile, white with the anger he held in rein.

"You know that I have the authority to hang you out of hand?" he reminded the other.

"I know," answered the pirate softly. "It won't be the first time you've hanged me, John Wentyard."

"What?" The Englishman stared.

A flame grew in Vulmea's blue eyes and his voice changed subtly in tone and inflection; the brogue thickened almost imperceptibly.

"On the Galway coast it was, years ago, captain. You were a young officer then, scarce more than a boy – but with all your present characteristics already fully developed. There were some wholesale evictions, with the military to see the job was done, and the Irish were mad enough to make a fight of it – poor, ragged, half-starved peasants, fighting with sticks against full-armed English soldiers and sailors. After the massacre and the usual hangings, a boy crept into a thicket to watch – a lad of ten, who didn't even know what it was all about. You spied him, John Wentyard, and had your dogs drag him forth and string him up alongside the kicking bodies of the others. 'He's Irish,' you said as they heaved him aloft. 'Little snakes grow into big ones.' I was that boy. I've looked forward to this meeting, you English dog!"

Vulmea still smiled, but the veins knotted in his temples and the great muscles stood out distinctly on his manacled arms. Ironed and guarded though the pirate was, Wentyard involuntarily drew back, daunted by the stark and naked hate that blazed from those savage eyes.

"How did you escape your just desserts?" he asked coldly, recovering his poise.

Vulmea laughed shortly.

"Some of the peasants escaped the massacre and were hiding in the thickets. As soon as you left they came out, and not being civilized, cultured Englishmen, but only poor, savage Irishry, they cut me down along with the others, and found there as still a bit of life in me. We Gaels are hard to kill, as you Britons have learned to your cost."

"You fell into our hands easily enough this time," observed Wentyard.

Vulmea grinned. His eyes were grimly amused now, but the glint of murderous hate still lurked in their deeps.

"Who'd have thought to meet a king's ship in these western seas? It's been weeks since we sighted a sail of any kind, save for the carrack we took yesterday, with a cargo of wine bound for Panama from Valparaiso. It's not the time of year for rich prizes. When the lads wanted a drinking bout, who was I to deny them? We drew out of the lanes the Spaniards mostly follow, and thought we had the ocean to ourselves. I'd been sleeping in my cabin for some hours before I came on deck to smoke a pipe or so, and saw you about to board us without firing a shot."

"You killed seven of my men," harshly accused Wentyard.

"And you killed all of mine," retorted Vulmea. "Poor devils, they'll wake up in hell without knowing how they got there."

He grinned again, fiercely. His toes dug hard against the floor, unnoticed by the men who gripped him on either side. The blood was rioting through his veins, and the berserk feel of his great strength was upon him. He knew he could, in a sudden, volcanic explosion of power, tear free from the men who held him, clear the space between him and his enemy with one bound, despite his chains, and crush Wentyard's skull with a smashing swing of his manacled fists. That he himself would die an instant later mattered not at all. In that moment he felt neither fears nor regrets – only a reckless, ferocious exultation and a cruel contempt for these stupid Englishmen about him. He laughed in their faces, joying in the knowledge that they did not know why he laughed. So they thought to chain the tiger, did they? Little they guessed of the devastating fury that lurked in his catlike thews.

He began filling his great chest, drawing in his breath slowly, imperceptibly, as his calves knotted and the muscles of his arms grew hard. Then Wentyard spoke again.

"I will not be overstepping my authority if I hang you within the hour. In any event you hang, either from my yard-arm or from a gibbet on the Port Royal wharves. But life is sweet, even to rogues like you, who notoriously cling to every moment granted them by outraged society. It would gain you a few more months of life if I were to take you back to Jamaica to be sentenced by the governor. This I might be persuaded to do, on one condition."

"What's that?" Vulmea's tensed muscles did not relax; imperceptibly he began to settle into a semi-crouch.

"That you tell me the whereabouts of the pirate, Van Raven."

In that instant, while his knotted muscles went pliant again, Vulmea unerringly gauged and appraised the man who faced him, and changed his plan. He straightened and smiled.

"And why the Dutchman, Wentyard?" he asked softly. "Why not Tranicos, or Villiers, or McVeigh, or a dozen others more destructive to English trade than Van Raven? Is it because of the treasure he took from the Spanish plate-fleet? Aye, the king would like well to set his hands on that hoard, and there's a rich prize would go the captain lucky or bold enough to find Van Raven and plunder him. Is that why you came all the way around the Horn, John Wentyard?"

"We are at peace with Spain," answered Wentyard acidly. "As for the purposes of an officer in his Majesty's navy, they are not for you to question."

Vulmea laughed at him, the blue flame in his eyes.

"Once I sank a king's cruiser off Hispaniola," he said. "Damn you and your prating of 'His Majesty'! Your English king is no more to me than so much rotten driftwood. Van Raven? He's a bird of passage. Who knows where he sails? But if it's treasure you want, I can show you a hoard that would make the Dutchman's loot look like a peat-pool beside the Caribbean Sea!"

A pale spark seemed to snap from Wentyard's colorless eyes, and his officers leaned forward tensely. Vulmea grinned hardly. He knew the credulity of navy men, which they shared with landsmen and honest mariners, in regard to pirates and plunder. Every seaman not himself a rover, believed that every buccaneer had knowledge of vast hidden wealth. The loot the men of the Red Brother took from the Spaniards, rich enough as it was, was magnified a thousand times in the telling, and rumor made every swaggering sea-rat the guardian of a treasure-trove.

Coolly plumbing the avarice of Wentyard's hard soul, Vulmea said: "Ten days' sail from here there's a nameless bay on the coast of Ecuador. Four years ago Dick Harston, the English pirate and I anchored there, in a quest of a hoard of ancient jewels called the Fangs of Satan. An Indian swore he had found them, hidden in a ruined temple in an uninhabited jungle a day's march inland, but superstitious fear of the old gods kept him from helping himself. But he was willing to guide us there.

"We marched inland with both crews, for neither of us trusted the other. To make a long tale short, we found the ruins of an old city, and beneath an ancient, broken altar, we found the jewels – rubies, diamonds, emeralds, sapphires, bloodstones, big as hen eggs, making a quivering flame of fire about the crumbling old shrine!"

The flame grew in Wentyard's eyes. His white fingers knotted about the slender stem of his wine glass.

"The sight of them was enough to madden a man," Vulmea continued, watching the captain narrowly. "We camped there for the night, and, one way or another, we fell out over the division of the spoil, though there was enough to make every man of us rich for life. We came to blows, though, and whilst we fought among ourselves, there came a scout running with word that a Spanish fleet had come into the bay, driven our ships away, and sent five hundred men ashore to pursue us. By Satan, they were on us before the scout ceased the telling! One of my men snatched the plunder away and hid it in the old temple, and we scattered, each band for itself. There was no time to take the plunder. We barely got away with our naked lives. Eventually I, with most of my crew, made my way back to the coast and was picked up by my ship which came slinking back after escaping from the Spaniards.

"Harston gained his ship with a handful of men, after skirmishing all the way with the Spaniards who chased him instead of us, and later was slain by savages on the coast of California.

"The Dons harried me all the way around the Horn, and I never had an opportunity to go back after the loot – until this voyage. It was there I was going when you overhauled me. The treasure's still there. Promise me my life and I'll take you to it."

"That is impossible," snapped Wentyard. "The best I can promise you is trial before the governor of Jamaica."

"Well," said Vulmea, "Maybe the governor might be more lenient than you. And much may happen between here and Jamaica."

Wentyard did not reply, but spread a map on the broad table.

"Where is this bay?"

Vulmea indicated a certain spot on the coast. The sailors released their grip on his arms while he marked it, and Wentyard's head was within reach, but the Irishman's plans were changed, and they included a chance for life – desperate, but nevertheless a chance.

"Very well. Take him below."

Vulmea went out with his guards, and Wentyard sneered coldly.

"A gentleman of His Majesty's navy is not bound by a promise to such a rogue as he. Once the treasure is aboard the *Redoubtable*, gentlemen, I promise you he shall swing from a yard-arm."

Ten days later the anchors rattled down in the nameless bay Vulmea had described.

It seemed desolate enough to have been the coast of an uninhabited continent. The bay was merely a shallow indentation of the shore-line. Dense jungle crowded the narrow strip of white sand that was the beach. Gay-plumed birds flitted among the broad fronds, and the silence of primordial savagery brooded over all. But a dim trail led back into the twilight vistas of green-walled mystery.

Dawn was a white mist on the water when seventeen men marched down the dim path. One was John Wentyard. On an expedition designed to find treasure, he would trust the command to none but himself. Fifteen were soldiers, armed with hangers and muskets. The seventeenth was Black Vulmea. The Irishman's legs, perforce, were free, and the irons had been removed from his arms. But his wrists were bound before him with cords, and one end of the cord was in the grip of a brawny marine whose other hand held a cutlass ready to chop down the pirate if he made any move to escape.

"Fifteen men are enough," Vulmea had told Wentyard. "Too many! Men go mad easily in the tropics, and the sight of the Fangs of Satan is enough to madden any man, king's man or not. The more that see the jewels, the greater chance of mutiny before you raise the Horn again. You don't need more than three or four. Who are you afraid of? You said England was at peace with Spain, and there are no Spaniards anywhere near this spot, in any event."

"I wasn't thinking of Spaniards," answered Wentyard coldly. "I am providing against any attempt you might make to escape."

"Well," laughed Vulmea, "do you think you need fifteen men for that?"

"I'm taking no chances," was the grim retort. "You are stronger than two or three ordinary men, Vulmea, and full of wiles. My men will march with pieces ready, and if you try to bolt, they will shoot you down like the dog you are – should you, by any chance, avoid being cut down by your guard. Besides, there is always the chance of savages."

The pirate jeered.

"Go beyond the Cordilleras if you seek real savages. There are Indians there who cut off your head and shrink it no bigger than your fist. But they never come on this side of the mountains. As for the race that built the temple, they've all been dead for centuries. Bring your armed escort if you want to. It will be of no use. One strong man can carry away the whole hoard."

"One strong man!" murmured Wentyard, licking his lips as his mind reeled at the thought of the wealth represented by a load of jewels that required the full strength of a strong man to carry. Confused visions of knighthood and admiralty whirled through his head. "What about the path?" he asked suspiciously. "If this coast is uninhabited, how comes it there?"

"It was an old road, centuries ago, probably used by the race that built the city. In some places you can see where it was paved. But Harston and I were the first to use it for centuries. And you can tell it hasn't been used since. You can see where the young growth has sprung up above the scars of the axes we used to clear a way."

Wentyard was forced to agree. So now, before sunrise, the landing party was swinging inland at a steady gait that ate up the miles. The bay and the ship were quickly lost to sight. All morning they tramped along through steaming heat, between green, tangled jungle walls where gay-hued birds flitted silently and monkeys chattered. Thick vines hung low across the trail, impeding their progress, and they were sorely annoyed by gnats and other insects. At noon they paused only long enough to drink some water and eat the ready-cooked food they had brought along. The men were stolid veterans, inured to long marches, and Wentyard would allow them no more rest than was necessary for their brief meal. He was afire with savage eagerness to view the hoard Vulmea had described.

The trail did not twist as much as most jungle paths. It was overgrown with vegetation, but it gave evidence that it had once been a road, well-built and broad. Pieces of paving were still visible here and there. By mid-afternoon the land began to rise slightly to be broken by low, jungle-choked hills. They were aware of this only by the rising and dipping of the trail. The dense walls on either hand shut off their view.

Neither Wentyard nor any of his men glimpsed the furtive, shadowy shapes which now glided along through the jungle on either hand. Vulmea was aware of their presence, but he only smiled grimly and said nothing. Carefully and so subtly that his guard did not suspect it, the pirate worked at the cords on his wrists, weakening and straining the strands by continual tugging and twisting. He had been doing this all day, and he could feel them slowly giving way.

The sun hung low in the jungle branches when the pirate halted and pointed to where the old road bent almost at right angles and disappeared into the mouth of a ravine.

"Down that ravine lies the old temple where the jewels are hidden."

"On, then!" snapped Wentyard, fanning himself with his plumed hat. Sweat trickled down his face, wilting the collar of his crimson, gilt-embroidered coat. A frenzy of impatience was on him, his eyes dazzled by the imagined glitter of the gems Vulmea had so vividly described. Avarice makes for credulity, and it never occurred to Wentyard to doubt Vulmea's tale. He saw in the Irishman only a hulking brute eager to buy a few months more of life. Gentlemen of his Majesty's navy were not accustomed to analyzing the character of pirates. Wentyard's code was painfully simple: a heavy hand and a roughshod directness. He had never bothered to study or try to understand outlaw types.

They entered the mouth of the ravine and marched on between cliffs fringed with overhanging fronds. Wentyard fanned himself with his hat and gnawed his lip with impatience as he stared eagerly about for some sign of the ruins described by his captive. His face was paler than ever, despite the heat which reddened the bluff faces of his men, tramping ponderously after him. Vulmea's brown face showed no undue moisture. He did not tramp; he moved with the sure, supple tread of a panther, and without a suggestion of a seaman's lurching roll. His eyes ranged the walls above them and when a frond swayed without a breath of wind to move it, he did not miss it.

The ravine was some fifty feet wide, the floor carpeted by a low, thick growth of vegetation. The jungle ran densely along the rims of the walls, which were some forty feet high. They were sheer for the most part, but here and there natural ramps ran down into the gulch, half-covered with tangled vines. A few hundred yards ahead of them they saw that the ravine bent out of sight around a rocky shoulder. From the opposite wall there jutted a corresponding crag. The outlines of these boulders were blurred by moss and creepers, but they seemed too symmetrical to be the work of nature alone.

Vulmea stopped, near one of the natural ramps that sloped down from the rim. His captors looked at him questioningly.

"Why are you stopping?" demanded Wentyard fretfully. His foot struck something in the rank grass and he kicked it aside. It rolled free and grinned up at him – a rotting human skull. He saw glints of white in the green all about him – skulls and bones almost covered by the dense vegetation.

"Is this where you piratical dogs slew each other?" he demanded crossly. "What are you waiting on? What are you listening for?"

Vulmea relaxed his tense attitude and smiled indulgently.

"That used to be a gateway there ahead of us," he said. "Those rocks on each side are really gate-pillars. This ravine was a roadway, leading to the city when people lived there. It's the only approach to it, for it's surrounded by sheer cliffs on all sides." He laughed harshly. "This is like the road to Hell, John Wentyard: easy to go down – not so easy to go up again."

"What are you maundering about?" snarled Wentyard, clapping his hat viciously on his head. "You Irish are all babblers and mooncalves! Get on with – "

From the jungle beyond the mouth of the ravine came a sharp twang. Something whined venomously down the gulch, ending its flight with a vicious thud. One of the soldiers gulped and started convulsively. His musket clattered to the earth and he reeled, clawing at his throat from which protruded a long shaft, vibrating like a serpent's head. Suddenly he pitched to the ground and lay twitching.

"Indians!" yelped Wentyard, and turned furiously on his prisoner. "Dog! Look at that! You said there were no savages hereabouts!"

Vulmea laughed scornfully.

"Do you call them savages? Bah! Poor-spirited dogs that skulk in the jungle, too fearful to show themselves on the coast. Don't you see them slinking among the trees? Best give them a volley before they grow too bold."

Wentyard snarled at him, but the Englishman knew the value of a display of firearms when dealing with natives, and he had a glimpse of brown figures moving among the green foliage. He barked an order and fourteen muskets crashed, and the bullets rattled among the leaves. A few severed fronds drifted down; that was all. But even as the smoke puffed out in a cloud, Vulmea snapped the frayed cords on his wrists, knocked his guard staggering with a buffet under the ear, snatched his cutlass and was gone, running like a cat up the steep wall of the ravine. The soldiers with their empty muskets gaped helplessly after him, and Wentyard's pistol banged futilely, an instant too late. From the green fringe above them came a mocking laugh.

"Fools! You stand in the door of Hell!"

"Dog!" yelled Wentyard, beside himself, but with his greed still uppermost in his befuddled mind. "We'll find the treasure without your help!"

"You can't find something that doesn't exist," retorted the unseen pirate. "There never were any jewels. It was a lie to draw you into a trap. Dick Harston never came here. I came here, and the Indians butchered all my crew in that ravine, as those skulls in the grass there testify."

"Liar!" was all Wentyard could find tongue for. "Lying dog! You told me there were no Indians hereabouts!"

"I told you the head-hunters never came over the mountains," retorted Vulmea. "They don't either. I told you the people who built the city were all dead. That's so, too. I didn't tell you that a tribe of brown devils live in the jungle near here. They never go down to the coast, and they don't like to have white men come into the jungle. I think they were the people who wiped out the race that built the city, long ago. Anyway, they wiped out my men, and the only reason I got away was because I'd lived with the red men of North America and learned their woodscraft. You're in a trap you won't get out of, Wentyard!"

"Climb that wall and take him!" ordered Wentyard, and half a dozen men slung their muskets on their backs and began clumsily to essay the rugged ramp up which the pirate had run with such catlike ease.

"Better trim sail and stand by to repel boarders," Vulmea advised him from above. "There are hundreds of red devils out there – and no tame dogs to run at the crack of a caliver, either."

"And you'd betray white men to savages!" raged Wentyard.

"It goes against my principles," the Irishman admitted, "but it was my only chance for life. I'm sorry for your men. That's why I advised you to bring only a handful. I wanted to spare as many as possible. There are enough Indians out there in the jungle to eat your whole ship's company. As for you, you filthy dog, what you did in Ireland forfeited any consideration you might expect as a white man. I gambled on my neck and took my chances with all of you. It might have been me that arrow hit."

The voice ceased abruptly, and just as Wentyard was wondering if there were no Indians on the wall above them, the foliage was violently agitated, there sounded a wild yell, and down came a naked brown body, all asprawl, limbs revolving in the air. It crashed on the floor of the ravine and lay motionless – the figure of a brawny warrior, naked but for a loin-cloth of bark. The dead man was deep-chested, broad-shouldered, and muscular, with features not unintelligent, but hard and brutal. He had been slashed across the neck.

The bushes waved briefly, and then again, further along the rim, which agitation Wentyard believed marked the flight of the Irishman along the ravine wall, pursued by the companions of the dead warrior, who must have stolen up on Vulmea while the pirate was shouting his taunts.

The chase was made in deadly silence, but down in the ravine conditions were anything but silent. At the sight of the falling body a blood-curdling ululation burst forth from the jungle outside the mouth of the ravine, and a storm of arrows came whistling down it. Another man fell, and three more were wounded, and Wentyard called down the men who were laboriously struggling up the vine-matted ramp. He fell back down the ravine, almost to the bend where the ancient gate-posts jutted, and beyond that point he feared to go. He felt sure that the ravine beyond the Gateway was filled with lurking savages. They would not have hemmed him in on all sides and then left open an avenue of escape.

At the spot where he halted there was a cluster of broken rocks that looked as though as they might once have formed the walls of a building of some sort. Among them Wentyard made his stand. He ordered his men to lie prone, their musket barrels resting on the rocks. One man he detailed to watch for savages creeping up the ravine from behind them, the others watched the green wall visible beyond the path that ran into the mouth of the ravine. Fear chilled Wentyard's heart. The sun was already lost behind the trees and the shadows were lengthening. In the brief dusk of the tropic twilight, how could a white man's eye pick out a swift, flitting brown body, or a musket ball find its mark? And when darkness fell – Wentyard shivered despite the heat.

Arrows kept singing down the ravine, but they fell short or splintered on the rocks. But now bowmen hidden on the walls drove down their shafts, and from their vantage point the stones afforded little protection. The screams of men skewered to the ground rose harrowingly.

Wentyard saw his command melting away under his eyes. The only thing that kept them from being instantly exterminated was the steady fire he had them keep up at the foliage on the cliffs. They seldom saw their foes; they only saw the fronds shake, had an occasional glimpse of a brown arm. But the heavy balls, ripping through the broad leaves, made the hidden archers wary, and the shafts came at intervals instead of in volleys. Once a piercing death yell announced that a blind ball had gone home, and the English raised a croaking cheer.

Perhaps it was this which brought the infuriated warriors out of the jungle. Perhaps, like the white men, they disliked fighting in the dark, and wanted to conclude the slaughter before night fell. Perhaps they were ashamed longer to lurk hidden from a handful of men.

At any rate, they came out of the jungle beyond the trail suddenly, and by the scores, not scrawny primitives, but brawny, hard-muscled warriors, confident of their strength and physically a match for even the sinewy Englishmen. They came in a wave of brown bodies that suddenly flooded the ravine, and others leaped down the walls, swinging from the lianas. They were hundreds against the handful of Englishmen left. These rose from the rocks without orders, meeting death with the bulldog stubbornness of their breed. They fired a volley full into the tide of snarling faces that surged upon them, and then drew hangers and clubbed empty muskets. There was no time to reload. Their blast tore lanes in the onsweeping human torrent, but it did not falter; it came on and engulfed the white men in a snarling, slashing, smiting whirlpool.

Hangers whirred and bit through flesh and bone, clubbed muskets rose and fell, spattering brains. But copper-headed axes flashed dully in the twilight, war-clubs made a red ruin of the skulls they kissed, and there were a score of red arms to drag down each struggling white man. The ravine was choked with a milling, eddying mass, revolving about a fast-dwindling cluster of desperate, white-skinned figures.

Not until his last man fell did Wentyard break away, blood smeared on his arms, dripping from his sword. He was hemmed in by a surging ring of ferocious figures, but he had one loaded pistol left. He fired it full in a painted face surmounted by a feathered chest and saw it vanish in red ruin. He clubbed a shaven head with the empty barrel, and rushed through the gap made by the falling bodies. A wild figure leaped at him, swinging a war-club, but the sword was quicker. Wentyard tore the blade free as the savage fell. Dusk was ebbing swiftly into darkness, and the figures swirling about him were becoming indistinct, vague of outline. Twilight waned quickly in the ravine and darkness had settled there before it veiled the jungle outside. It was the darkness that saved Wentyard, confusing his attackers. As the sworded Indian fell he found himself free, though men were rushing on him from behind, with clubs lifted.

Blindly he fled down the ravine. It lay empty before him. Fear lent wings to his feet. He raced through the stone abutted Gateway. Beyond it he saw the ravine widen out; stone walls rose ahead of him, almost hidden by vines and creepers, pierced with blank windows and doorways. His flesh crawled with the momentary expectation of a thrust in the back. His heart was pounding so loudly, the blood hammering so agonizingly in his temples that he could not tell whether or not bare feet were thudding close behind him.

His hat and coat were gone, his shirt torn and blood-stained, though somehow he had come through that desperate melee unwounded. Before him he saw a vine-tangled wall, and an empty doorway. He ran reelingly into the door and turned, falling to his knee from sheer exhaustion. He shook the sweat from his eyes, panting gaspingly as he fumbled to reload his pistols. The ravine was a dim alleyway before him, running to the rock-buttressed bend. Moment by moment he expected to see it thronged with fierce faces, with swarming figures. But it lay empty and fierce cries of the victorious warriors drew no nearer. For some reason they had not followed him through the Gateway.

Terror that they were creeping on him from behind brought him to his feet, pistols cocked, staring this way and that.

He was in a room whose stone walls seemed ready to crumble. It was roofless, and grass grew between the broken stones of the floor. Through the gaping roof he could see the stars just blinking out, and the frond-fringed rim of the cliff. Through a door opposite the one by which he crouched he had a vague glimpse of other vegetation-choked, roofless chambers beyond.

Silence brooded over the ruins, and now silence had fallen beyond the bend of the ravine. He fixed his eyes on the blur that was the Gateway and waited. It stood empty. Yet he knew that the Indians were aware of his flight. Why did they not rush in and cut his throat? Were they afraid of his pistols? They had shown no fear of his soldiers' muskets. Had they gone away, for some inexplicable reason? Were those shadowy chambers behind him filled with lurking warriors? If so, why in God's name were they waiting?

He rose and went to the opposite door, craned his neck warily through it, and after some hesitation, entered the adjoining chamber. It had no outlet into the open. All its doors led into other chambers, equally ruinous, with broken roofs, cracked floors and crumbling walls. Three or four he traversed, his tread, as he crushed down the vegetation growing among the broken stones, seeming intolerably loud in the stillness. Abandoning his explorations – for the labyrinth seemed endless – he returned to the room that opened toward the ravine. No sound came up the gulch, but it was so dark under the cliff that men could have entered the Gateway and been crouching near him, without his being able to see them.

At last he could endure the suspense no longer. Walking as quietly as he was able, he left the ruins and approached the Gateway, now a well of blackness. A few moments later he was hugging the left-hand abutment and straining his eyes to see into the ravine beyond. It was too dark to see anything more than the stars blinking over the rims of the walls. He took a cautious step beyond the Gateway – it was the swift swish of feet through the vegetation on the floor that saved his life. He sensed rather than saw a black shape loom out of the darkness, and he fired blindly and point-blank. The flash lighted a ferocious face, falling backward, and beyond it the Englishman dimly glimpsed other figures, solid ranks of them, surging inexorably toward him.

With a choked cry he hurled himself back around the gate-pillar, stumbled and fell and lay dumb and quaking, clenching his teeth against the sharp agony he expected in the shape of a spear-thrust. None came. No figure came lunging after him. Incredulously he gathered himself to his feet, his pistols shaking in his hands. They were waiting, beyond that bend, but they would not come through the Gateway, not even to glut their blood-lust. This fact forced itself upon him, with its implication of inexplicable mystery.

Stumblingly he made his way back to the ruins and groped into the black doorway, overcoming an instinctive aversion against entering the roofless chamber. Starlight shone through the broken roof, lightening the gloom a little, but black shadows clustered along the walls and the inner door was an ebon wall of mystery. Like most Englishmen of his generation, John Wentyard more than half believed in ghosts, and he felt that if ever there was a place fit to be haunted by the phantoms of a lost and forgotten race, it was these sullen ruins.

He glanced fearfully through the broken roof at the dark fringe of overhanging fronds on the cliffs above, hanging motionless in the breathless air, and wondered if moonrise, illuminating his refuge, would bring arrows questing down through the roof. Except for the far lone cry of a nightbird, the jungle was silent. There was not so much as the rustle of a leaf. If there were men on the cliffs there was no sign to show it. He was aware of hunger and an increasing thirst; rage gnawed at him, and a fear that was already tinged with panic.

He crouched at the doorway, pistols in his hands, naked sword at his knee, and after awhile the moon rose, touching the overhanging fronds with silver long before it untangled itself from the trees and rose high enough to pour its light over the cliffs. Its light invaded the ruins, but no arrows came from the cliff, nor was there any sound from beyond the Gateway. Wentyard thrust his head through the door and surveyed his retreat.

The ravine, after it passed between the ancient gate-pillars, opened into a broad bowl, walled by cliffs, and unbroken except for the mouth of the gulch. Wentyard saw the rim as a continuous, roughly circular line, now edged with the fire of moonlight. The ruins in which he had taken refuge almost filled this bowl, being built against the cliffs on one side. Decayed and smothering vines had almost obliterated the original architectural plan. He saw the structure as a maze of roofless chambers, the outer doors opening upon the broad space left between it and the opposite wall of the cliff. This space was covered with low, dense vegetation, which also choked some of the chambers.

Wentyard saw no way of escape. The cliffs were not like the walls of the ravine. They were of solid rock and sheer, even jutting outward a little at the rim. No vines trailed down them. They did not rise many yards above the broken roofs of the ruins, but they were as far out of his reach as if they had towered a thousand feet. He was caught like a rat in a trap. The only way out was up the ravine, where the blood-lusting warriors waited with grim patience. He remembered Vulmea's mocking warning: " – Like the road to Hell: easy to go down; not so easy to go up again!" Passionately he hoped that the Indians had caught the Irishman and slain him slowly and painfully. He could have watched Vulmea flayed alive with intense satisfaction.

Presently, despite hunger and thirst and fear, he fell asleep, to dream of ancient temples where drums muttered and strange figures in parrot-feather mantles moved through the smoke of sacrificial fires; and he dreamed at last of a silent, hideous shape which came to the inner door of his roofless chamber and regarded him with cold, inhuman eyes.

It was from this dream that he awakened, bathed in cold sweat, to start up with an incoherent cry, clutching his pistols. Then, fully awake, he stood in the middle of the chamber, trying to gather his scattered wits. Memory of the dream was vague but terrifying. Had he actually seen a shadow sway in the doorway and vanish as he awoke, or had it been only part of his nightmare? The red, lopsided moon was poised on the western rim of the cliffs, and that side of the bowl was in thick shadow, but still an illusive light found its way into the ruins. Wentyard peered through the inner doorway, pistols cocked. Light floated rather than streamed down from above, and showed him an empty chamber beyond. The vegetation on the floor was crushed down, but he remembered having walked back and forth across it several times.

Cursing his nervous imagination he returned to the outer doorway. He told himself that he chose that place the better to guard against an attack from the ravine, but the real reason was that he could not bring himself to select a spot deeper in the gloomy interior of the ancient ruins.

He sat down cross-legged just inside the doorway, his back against the wall, his pistols beside him and his sword across his knees. His eyes burned and his lips felt baked with the thirst that tortured him. The sight of the heavy globules of dew that hung on the grass almost maddened him, but he did not seek to quench his thirst by that means, believing as he did that it was rank poison. He drew his belt closer, against his hunger, and told himself that he would not sleep. But he did sleep, in spite of everything.

CHAPTER 3

It was a frightful scream close at hand that awakened Wentyard. He was on his feet before he was fully awake, glaring wildly about him. The moon had set and the interior of the chamber was dark as Egypt, in which the outer doorway was but a somewhat lighter blur. But, outside it there sounded a blood-chilling gurgling, the heaving and flopping of a heavy body. Then silence.

It was a human being that had screamed. Wentyard groped for his pistols, found his sword instead, and hurried forth, his taut nerves thrumming. The starlight in the bowl, dim as it was, was less Stygian than the absolute blackness of the ruins. But he did not see the figure stretched in the grass until he stumbled over it. That was all he saw, then – just that dim form stretched on the ground before the doorway. The foliage hanging over the cliff rustled a little in the faint breeze. Shadows hung thick under the wall and about the ruins. A score of men might have been lurking near him, unseen. But there was no sound.

After a while, Wentyard knelt beside the figure, straining his eyes in the starlight. He grunted softly. The dead man was not an Indian, but a black man, a brawny ebon giant, clad, like the red men, in a bark loin clout, with a crest of parrot feathers on his kinky head. A murderous copper-headed axe lay near his hand, and a great gash showed in his muscular breast, a lesser wound under his shoulder blade. He had been stabbed so savagely that the blade had transfixed him and come out through his back.

Wentyard swore at the accumulated mystery of it. The presence of the black man was not inexplicable. Negro slaves, fleeing from Spanish masters, frequently took to the jungle and lived with the natives. This black evidently did not share in whatever superstition or caution kept the Indians outside the bowl; he had come in alone to butcher the victim they had at bay. But the mystery of his death remained. The blow that had impaled him had been driven with more than ordinary strength. There was a sinister suggestion about the episode, though the mysterious killer had saved Wentyard from being brained in his sleep – it was as if some inscrutable being, having claimed the Englishman for its own, refused to be robbed of its prey. Wentyard shivered, shaking off the thought.

Then he realized that he was armed only with his sword. He had rushed out of the ruins half asleep, leaving his pistols behind him, after a brief fumbling that failed to find them in the darkness. He turned and hurried back into the chamber and began to grope on the floor, first irritably, then with growing horror. The pistols were gone.

At this realization panic overwhelmed Wentyard. He found himself out in the starlight again without knowing just how he had got there. He was sweating, trembling in every limb, biting his tongue to keep from screaming in hysterical terror.

Frantically he fought for control. It was not imagination, then, which peopled those ghastly ruins with furtive, sinister shapes that glided from room to shadowy room on noiseless feet, and spied upon him while he slept. Something besides himself had been in that room – something that had stolen his pistols either while he was fumbling over the dead negro outside, or – grisly thought! – while he slept. He believed the latter had been the case. He had heard no sound in the ruins while he was outside. But why had it not taken his sword as well? Was it the Indians, after all, playing a horrible game with him? Was it their eyes he seemed to feel burning upon him from the shadows? But he did not believe it was the Indians. They would have no reason to kill their black ally.

Wentyard felt that he was near the end of his rope. He was nearly frantic with thirst and hunger, and he shrank from the contemplation of another day of heat in that waterless bowl. He went toward the ravine mouth, grasping his sword in desperation, telling himself that it was better to be speared quickly than haunted to an unknown doom by unseen phantoms, or perish of thirst. But the blind instinct to live drove him back from the rock-buttressed Gateway. He could not bring himself to exchange an uncertain fate for certain death. Faint noises beyond the bend told him that men, many men, were waiting there, and he retreated, cursing weakly.

In a futile gust of passion he dragged the black man's body to the Gateway and thrust it through. At least he would not have it for a companion to poison the air when it rotted in the heat.

He sat down about half-way between the ruins and the ravine-mouth, hugging his sword and straining his eyes into the shadowy starlight, and felt that he was being watched from the ruins; he sensed a Presence there, inscrutable, inhuman, waiting – waiting –

He was still sitting there when dawn flooded jungle and cliffs with grey light, and a brown warrior, appearing in the Gateway, bent his bow and sent an arrow at the figure hunkered in the open space. The shaft cut into the grass near Wentyard's foot, and the white man sprang up stiffly and ran into the doorway of the ruins. The warrior did not shoot again. As if frightened by his own temerity, he turned and hurried back through the Gateway and vanished from sight.

Wentyard spat dryly and swore. Daylight dispelled some of the phantom terrors of the night, and he was suffering so much from thirst that his fear was temporarily submerged. He was determined to explore the ruins by each crevice and cranny and bring to bay whatever was lurking among them. At least he would have daylight by which to face it.

To this end he turned toward the inner door, and then he stopped in his tracks, his heart in his throat. In the inner doorway stood a great gourd, newly cut and hollowed, and filled with water; beside it was a stack of fruit, and in another calabash there was meat, still smoking faintly. With a stride he reached the door and glared through. Only an empty chamber met his eyes.

Sight of water and scent of food drove from his mind all thoughts of anything except his physical needs. He seized the water-gourd and drank gulpingly, the precious liquid splashing on his breast. The water was fresh and sweet, and no wine had ever given him such delirious satisfaction. The meat he found was still warm. What it was he neither knew nor cared. He ate ravenously, grasping the joints in his fingers and tearing away the flesh with his teeth. It had evidently been roasted over an open fire, and without salt or seasoning, but it tasted like food of the gods to the ravenous man. He did not seek to explain the miracle, nor to wonder if the food were poisoned. The inscrutable haunter of the ruins which had saved his life that night, and which had stolen his pistols, apparently meant to preserve him for the time being, at least, and Wentyard accepted the gifts without question.

And having eaten he lay down and slept. He did not believe the Indians would invade the ruins; he did not care much if they did, and speared him in his sleep. He believed that the unknown being which haunted the rooms could slay him any time it wished. It had been close to him again and again and had not struck. It had showed no signs of hostility so far, except to steal his pistols. To go searching for it might drive it into hostility.

Wentyard, despite his slaked thirst and full belly, was at the point where he had a desperate indifference to consequences. His world seemed to have crumbled about him. He had led his men into a trap to see them butchered; he had seen his prisoner escape; he was caught like a caged rat himself; the wealth he had lusted after and dreamed about had proved a lie. Worn out with vain ragings against his fate, he slept.

The sun was high when he awoke and sat up with a startled oath. Black Vulmea stood looking down at him.

"Damn!" Wentyard sprang up, snatching at his sword. His mind was a riot of maddening emotions, but physically he was a new man, and nerved to a rage that was tinged with near-insanity.

"You dog!" he raved. "So the Indians didn't catch you, on the cliffs!"

"Those red dogs?" Vulmea laughed. "They didn't follow me past the Gateway. They don't come on the cliffs overlooking these ruins. They've got a cordon of men strung through the jungle, surrounding this place, but I can get through any time I want to. I cooked your breakfast – and mine – right under their noses, and they never saw me."

"My breakfast!" Wentyard glared wildly. "You mean it was you brought water and food for me?"

"Who else?"

"But – but why?" Wentyard was floundering in a maze of bewilderment.

Vulmea laughed, but he laughed only with his lips. His eyes were burning. "Well, at first I thought it would satisfy me if I saw you get an arrow through your guts. Then when you broke away and got in here, I said, 'Better still! They'll keep the swine there until he starves, and I'll lurk about and watch him die slowly.' I knew they wouldn't come in after you. When they ambushed me and my crew in the ravine, I cut my way through them and got in here, just as you did, and they didn't follow me in. But I got out of here the first night. I made sure you wouldn't get out the way I did that time, and then settled myself to watch you die. I could come or go as I pleased after nightfall, and you'd never see or hear me."

"But in that case, I don't see why – "

"You probably wouldn't understand!" snarled Vulmea. "But just watching you starve wasn't enough. I wanted to kill you myself – I wanted to see your blood gush, and watch your eyes glaze!" The Irishman's voice thickened with his passion, and his great hands clenched until the knuckles showed white. "And I didn't want to kill a man half-dead with want. So I went back up into the jungle on the cliffs and got water and fruit and knocked a monkey off a limb with a stone, and roasted him. I brought you a good meal and set it there in the door while you were sitting outside the ruins. You couldn't see me from where you were sitting, and of course you didn't hear anything. You English are all dull-eared."

"And it was you who stole my pistols last night!" muttered Wentyard, staring at the butts jutting from Vulmea's Spanish girdle.

"Aye! I took them from the floor beside you while you slept. I learned stealth from the Indians of North America. I didn't want you to shoot me when I came to pay my debt. While I was getting them I heard somebody sneaking up outside, and saw a black man coming toward the doorway. I didn't want him to be robbing me of my revenge, so I stuck my cutlass through him. You awakened when he howled, and ran out, as you'll remember, but I stepped back around the corner and in at another door. I didn't want to meet you except in broad open daylight and you in fighting trim."

"Then it was you who spied on me from the inner door," muttered Wentyard. "You whose shadow I saw just before the moon sank behind the cliffs."

"Not I!" Vulmea's denial was genuine. "I didn't come down into the ruins until after moonset, when I came to steal your pistols. Then I went back up on the cliffs, and came again just before dawn to leave your food."

"But enough of this talk!" he roared gustily, whipping out his cutlass. "I'm mad with thinking of the Galway coast and dead men kicking in a row, and a rope that strangled me! I've tricked you, trapped you, and now I'm going to kill you!"

Wentyard's face was a ghastly mask of hate, livid, with bared teeth and glaring eyes.

"Dog!" with a screech he lunged, trying to catch Vulmea off guard.

But the cutlass met and deflected the straight blade, and Wentyard bounded back just in time to avoid the decapitating sweep of the pirate's steel. Vulmea laughed fiercely and came on like a storm, and Wentyard met him with a drowning man's desperation.

Like most officers of the British navy, Wentyard was proficient in the use of the long straight sword he carried. He was almost as tall as Vulmea, and though he looked slender beside the powerful figure of the pirate, he believed that his skill would offset the sheer strength of the Irishman.

He was disillusioned within the first few moments of the fight. Vulmea was neither slow nor clumsy. He was as quick as a wounded panther, and his sword-play was no less crafty than Wentyard's. It only seemed so, because of the pirate's furious style of attack, showering blow on blow with what looked like sheer recklessness. But the very ferocity of his attack was his best defense, for it gave his opponent no time to launch a counterattack.

The power of his blows, beating down on Wentyard's blade, rocked and shook the Englishman to his heels, numbing his wrist and arm with their impact. Blind fury, humiliation, naked fright combined to rob the captain of his poise and cunning. A stamp of feet, a louder clash of steel, and Wentyard's blade whirred into a corner. The Englishman reeled back, his face livid, his eyes like those of a madman.

"Pick up your sword!" Vulmea was panting, not so much from exertion as from rage. Wentyard did not seem to hear him.

"Bah!" Vulmea threw aside his cutlass in a spasm of disgust. "Can't you even fight? I'll kill you with my bare hands!"

He slapped Wentyard viciously first on one side of the face and then on the other. The Englishman screamed wordlessly and launched himself at the pirate's throat, and Vulmea checked him with a buffet in the face and knocked him sprawling with a savage smash under the heart. Wentyard got to his knees and shook the blood from his face, while Vulmea stood over him, his brows black and his great fists knotted.

"Get up!" muttered the Irishman thickly. "Get up, you hangman of peasants and children!"

Wentyard did not heed him. He was groping inside his shirt, from which he drew out something he stared at with painful intensity.

"Get up, damn you, before I set my boot-heels on your face – "

Vulmea broke off, glaring incredulously. Wentyard, crouching over the object he had drawn from his shirt, was weeping in great, racking sobs.

"What the hell!" Vulmea jerked it away from him, consumed by wonder to learn what could bring tears from John Wentyard. It was a skillfully painted miniature. The blow he had struck Wentyard had cracked it, but not enough to obliterate the soft gentle faces of a pretty young woman and child which smiled up at the scowling Irishman.

"Well, I'm damned!" Vulmea stared from the broken portrait in his hand to the man crouching miserably on the floor. "Your wife and daughter?"

Wentyard, his bloody face sunk in his hands, nodded mutely. He had endured much within the last night and day. The breaking of the portrait he always carried over his heart was the last straw; it seemed like an attack on the one soft spot in his hard soul, and it left him dazed and demoralized.

Vulmea scowled ferociously, but it somehow seemed forced.

"I didn't know you had a wife and child." he said almost defensively.

"The lass is but five years old," gulped Wentyard. "I haven't seen them in nearly a year. My God, what's to become of them now? A navy captain's pay is none so great. I've never been able to save anything. It was for them I sailed in search of Van Raven and his treasure. I hoped to get a prize that would take care of them if aught happened to me. Kill me!" he cried shrilly, his voice cracking at the highest pitch. "Kill me and be done with it, before I lose my manhood with thinking of them, and beg for my life like a craven dog!"

But Vulmea stood looking down at him with a frown. Varying expressions crossed his dark face, and suddenly he thrust the portrait back in the Englishman's hand.

"You're too poor a creature for me to soil my hands with!" he sneered, and turning on his heel, strode through the inner door.

Wentyard stared dully after him, then, still on his knees, began to caress the broken picture, whimpering softly like an animal in pain as if the breaks in the ivory were wounds in his own flesh. Men break suddenly and unexpectedly in the tropics, and Wentyard's collapse was appalling.

He did not look up when the swift stamp of boots announced Vulmea's sudden return, without the pirate's usual stealth. A savage clutch on his shoulder raised him to stare stupidly into the Irishman's convulsed face.

"You're an infernal dog!" snarled Vulmea, in a fury that differed strangely from his former murderous hate. He broke into lurid imprecations, cursing Wentyard with all the proficiency he had acquired during his years at sea. "I ought to split your skull," he wound up. "For years I've dreamed of it, especially when I was drunk. I'm a cursed fool not to stretch you dead on the floor. I don't owe you any consideration, blast you! Your wife and daughter don't mean anything to me. But I'm a fool, like all the Irish, a blasted, chicken-hearted, sentimental fool, and I can't be the cause of a helpless woman and her colleen starving. Get up and quit sniveling!"

Wentyard looked up at him stupidly.

"You – you came back to help me?"

"I might as well stab you as leave you here to starve!" roared the pirate, sheathing his sword. "Get up and stick your skewer back in its scabbard. Who'd have ever thought that a scraun like you would have womenfolk like those innocents? Hell's fire! You ought to be shot! Pick up your sword. You may need it before we get away. But remember, I don't trust you any further than I can throw a whale by the tail, and I'm keeping your pistols. If you try to stab me when I'm not looking I'll break your head with my cutlass hilt."

Wentyard, like a man in a daze, replaced the painting carefully in his bosom and mechanically picked up his sword and sheathed it. His numbed wits began to thaw out, and he tried to pull himself together.

"What are we to do now?" he asked.

"Shut up!" growled the pirate. "I'm going to save you for the sake of the lady and the lass, but I don't have to talk to you!" With rare consistency he then continued: "We'll leave this trap the same way I came and went.

"Listen: four years ago I came here with a hundred men. I'd heard rumors of a ruined city up here, and I thought there might be loot hidden in it. I followed the old road from the beach, and those brown dogs let me and my men get in the ravine before they started butchering us. There must have been five or six hundred of them. They raked us from the walls, and then charged us – some came down the ravine and others jumped down the walls behind us and cut us off. I was the only one who got away, and I managed to cut my way through them, and ran into this bowl. They didn't follow me in, but stayed outside the Gateway to see that I didn't get out.

"But I found another way – a slab had fallen away from the wall of a room that was built against the cliff, and a stairway was cut in the rock. I followed it and came out of a sort of trap door up on the cliffs. A slab of rock was over it, but I don't think the Indians knew anything about it anyway, because they never go up on the cliffs that overhang the basin. They never come in here from the ravine, either. There's something here they're afraid of – ghosts, most likely.

"The cliffs slope down into the jungle on the outer sides, and the slopes and the crest are covered with trees and thickets. They had a cordon of men strung around the foot of the slopes, but I got through at night easily enough, made my way to the coast and sailed away with the handful of men I'd left aboard my ship.

"When you captured me the other day, I was going to kill you with my manacles, but you started talking about treasure, and a thought sprang in my mind to steer you into a trap that I might possibly get out of. I remembered this place, and I mixed a lot of truth in with some lies. The Fangs of Satan are no myth; they are a hoard of jewels hidden somewhere on this coast, but this isn't the place. There's no plunder about here.

"The Indians have a ring of men strung around this place, as they did before. I can get through, but it isn't going to be so easy getting you through. You English are like buffaloes when you start through the brush. We'll start just after dark and try to get through before the moon rises.

"Come on; I'll show you the stair."

Wentyard followed him through a series of crumbling, vine-tangled chambers, until he halted before a doorway that gaped in the wall that was built against the cliff. A thick slab leaned against the wall which obviously served as a door. The Englishman saw a flight of narrow steps, carved in the solid rock, leading upward through a shaft tunneled in the cliff.

"I meant to block the upper mouth by heaping big rocks on the slab that covers it," said Vulmea. "That was when I was going to let you starve. I knew you might find the stair. I doubt if the Indians know anything about it, as they never come in here or go up on the cliffs. But they know a man might be able to get out over the cliffs some way, so they've thrown that cordon around the slopes.

"That nigger I killed was a different proposition. A slave ship was wrecked off this coast a year ago, and the blacks escaped and took to the jungle. There's a regular mob of them living somewhere near here. This particular black man wasn't afraid to come into the ruins. If there are more of his kind out there with the Indians, they may try again tonight. But I believe he was the only one, or he wouldn't have come alone."

"Why don't we go up the cliff now and hide among the trees?" asked Wentyard.

"Because we might be seen by the men watching below the slopes, and they'd guess that we were going to make a break tonight, and redouble their vigilance. After awhile I'll go and get some more food. They won't see me."

The men returned to the chamber where Wentyard had slept. Vulmea grew taciturn, and Wentyard made no attempt at conversation. They sat in silence while the afternoon dragged by. An hour or so before sundown Vulmea rose with a curt word, went up the stair, and emerged on the cliffs. Among the trees he brought down a monkey with a dextrously-thrown stone, skinned it, and brought it back into the ruins along with a calabash of water from a spring on the hillside. For all his woodscraft he was not aware that he was being watched; he did not see the fierce black face that glared at him from a thicket that stood where the cliffs began to slope down into the jungle below.

Later, when he and Wentyard were roasting the meat over a fire built in the ruins, he raised his head and listened intently.

"What do you hear?" asked Wentyard.

"A drum," grunted the Irishman.

"I hear it," said Wentyard after a moment. "Nothing unusual about that."

"It doesn't sound like an Indian drum," answered Vulmea. "Sounds more like an African drum."

Wentyard nodded agreement; his ship had lain off the mangrove swamps of the Slave Coast, and he had heard such drums rumbling to one another through the steaming night. There was a subtle difference in the rhythm and timbre that distinguished it from an Indian drum.

Evening came on and ripened slowly to dusk. The drum ceased to throb. Back in the low hills, beyond the ring of cliffs, a fire glinted under the dusky trees, casting brown and black faces into sharp relief.

An Indian whose ornaments and bearing marked him as a chief squatted on his hams, his immobile face turned toward the ebony giant who stood facing him. This man was nearly a head taller than any other man there, his proportions overshadowing both the Indians squatting about

188

the fire and the black warriors who stood in a close group behind him. A jaguar-skin mantle was cast carelessly over his brawny shoulders, and copper bracelets ornamented his thickly-muscled arms. There was an ivory ring on his head, and parrot-feathers stood up from his kinky hair. A shield of hard wood and toughened bull-hide was on his left arm, and in his right hand he gripped a great spear whose hammered iron head was as broad as a man's hand.

"I came swiftly when I heard the drum," he said gutturally, in the bastard-Spanish that served as a common speech for the savages of both colors. "I knew it was N'Onga who called me. N'Onga had gone from my camp to fetch Ajumba, who was lingering with your tribe. N'Onga told me by the drum-talk that a white man was at bay, and Ajumba was dead. I came in haste. Now you tell me that you dare not enter the Old City."

"I have told you a devil dwells there," answered the Indian doggedly. "He has chosen the white man for his own. He will be angry it you try to take him away from him. It is death to enter his kingdom."

The black chief lifted his great spear and shook it defiantly.

"I was a slave to the Spaniards long enough to know that the only devil is a white man! I do not fear your devil. In my land his brothers are big as he, and I have slain one with a spear like this. A day and a night have passed since the white man fled into the Old City. Why has not the devil devoured him, or this other who lingers on the cliffs?"

"The devil is not hungry," muttered the Indian. "He waits until he is hungry. He has eaten recently. When he is hungry again he will take them. I will not go into his lair with my men. You are a stranger in this country. You do not understand these things."

"I understand that Bigomba who was a king in his own country fears nothing, neither man nor demon," retorted the black giant. "You tell me that Ajumba went into the Old City by night, and died. I have seen his body. The devil did not slay him. One of the white men stabbed him. If Ajumba could go into the Old City and not be seized by the devil, then I and my thirty men can go. I know how the big white man comes and goes between the cliffs and the ruins. There is a hole in the rock with a slab for a door over it. N'Onga watched from the bushes high up on the slopes and saw him come forth and later return through it. I have placed men there to watch it. If the white men come again through that hole, my warriors will spear them. If they do not come, we will go in as soon as the moon rises. Your men hold the ravine, and they can not flee that way. We will hunt them like rats through the crumbling houses."

CHAPTER 4

"Easy now," muttered Vulmea. "It's as dark as Hell in this shaft." Dusk had deepened into early darkness. The white men were groping their way up the steps cut in the rock. Looking back and down Wentyard made out the lower mouth of the shaft only as a slightly lighter blur in the blackness. They climbed on, feeling their way, and presently Vulmea halted with a muttered warning. Wentyard, groping, touched his thigh and felt the muscles tensing upon it. He knew that Vulmea had placed his shoulders under the slab that closed the upper entrance, and was heaving it up. He saw a crack appear suddenly in the blackness above him, limning the Irishman's bent head and foreshortened figure.

The stone came clear and starlight gleamed through the aperture, laced by the overhanging branches of the trees. Vulmea let the slab fall on the stone rim, and started to climb out of the shaft. He had emerged head, shoulders and hips when without warning a black form loomed against the stars and a gleam of steel hissed downward at his breast.

Vulmea threw up his cutlass and the spear rang against it, staggering him on the steps with the impact. Snatching a pistol from his belt with his left hand he fired point-blank and the black man groaned and fell, head and arms dangling in the opening. He struck the pirate as he fell, destroying Vulmea's already precarious balance. He toppled backward down the steps, carrying Wentyard with him. A dozen steps down they brought up in a sprawling heap, and staring upward, saw the square well above them fringed with indistinct black blobs they knew were heads outlined against the stars.

"I thought you said the Indians never – " panted Wentyard.

"They're not Indians," growled Vulmea, rising. "They're negroes. Cimarroons! The same dogs who escaped from the slave ship. That drum we heard was one of them calling the others. Look out!"

Spears came whirring down the shaft, splintering on the steps, glancing from the walls. The white men hurled themselves recklessly down the steps at the risk of broken limbs. They tumbled through the lower doorway and Vulmea slammed the heavy slab in place.

"They'll be coming down it next," he snarled. "We've got to heap enough rocks against it to hold it – no, wait a minute! If they've got the guts to come at all, they'll come by the ravine if they can't get in this way, or on ropes hung from the cliffs. This place is easy enough to get into – not so damned easy to get out of. We'll leave the shaft open. If they come this way we can get them in a bunch as they try to come out."

He pulled the slab aside, standing carefully away from the door.

"Suppose they come from the ravine and this way, too?"

"They probably will," growled Vulmea, "but maybe they'll come this way first, and maybe if they come down in a bunch we can kill them all. There may not be more than a dozen of them. They'll never persuade the Indians to follow them in."

He set about reloading the pistol he had fired, with quick sure hands in the dark. It consumed the last grain of powder in the flask. The white men lurked like phantoms of murder about the doorway of the stair, waiting to strike suddenly and deadly. Time dragged. No sound came from above. Wentyard's imagination was at work again, picturing an invasion from the ravine, and dusky figures gliding about them, surrounding the chamber. He spoke of this and Vulmea shook his head.

"When they come I'll hear them; nothing on two legs can get in here without my knowing it."

Suddenly Wentyard was aware of a dim glow pervading the ruins. The moon was rising above the cliffs. Vulmea swore.

"No chance of our getting away tonight. Maybe those black dogs were waiting for the moon to come up. Go into the chamber where you slept and watch the ravine. If you see them sneaking in that way, let me know. I can take care of any that come down the stair."

Wentyard felt his flesh crawl as he made his way through those dim chambers. The moonlight glinted down through vines tangled across the broken roofs, and shadows lay thick across his path. He reached the chamber where he had slept, and where the coals of the fire still glowed dully. He started across toward the outer door when a soft sound brought him whirling around. A cry was wrenched from his throat.

Out of the darkness of a corner rose a swaying shape; a great wedge-shaped head and an arched neck were outlined against the moonlight. In one brain-staggering instant the mystery of the ruins became clear to him; he knew what had watched him with lidless eyes as he lay sleeping, and what had glided away from his door as he awoke – he knew why the Indians would not come into the ruins or mount the cliffs above them. He was face to face with the devil of the deserted city, hungry at last – and that devil was a giant anaconda!

In that moment John Wentyard experienced such fear and loathing horror as ordinarily come to men only in foul nightmares. He could not run, and after that first scream his tongue seemed frozen to his palate. Only when the hideous head darted toward him did he break free from the paralysis that engulfed him and then it was too late.

He struck at it wildly and futilely, and in an instant it had him – lapped and wrapped about with coils which were like huge cables of cold, pliant steel. He shrieked again, fighting madly against the crushing constriction – he heard the rush of Vulmea's boots – then the pirate's pistols crashed together and he heard plainly the thud of the bullets into the great snake's body. It jerked convulsively and whipped from about him, hurling him sprawling to the floor, and then it came at Vulmea like the rush of a hurricane through the grass, its forked tongue licking in and out in the moonlight, and the noise of its hissing filling the chamber.

Vulmea avoided the battering-ram stroke of the blunt nose with a sidewise spring that would have shamed a starving jaguar, and his cutlass was a sheen in the moonlight as it hewed deep into the mighty neck. Blood spurted and the great reptile rolled and knotted, sweeping the floor and dislodging stones from the wall with its thrashing tail. Vulmea leaped high, clearing it as it lashed but Wentyard, just climbing to his feet, was struck and knocked sprawling into a corner. Vulmea was springing in again, cutlass lifted, when the monster rolled aside and fled through the inner door, with a loud rushing sound through the thick vegetation.

Vulmea was after it, his berserk fury fully roused. He did not wish the wounded reptile to crawl away and hide, perhaps to return later and take them by surprise. Through chamber after chamber the chase led, in a direction neither of the men had followed in his former explorations, and at last into a room almost choked by tangled vines. Tearing these aside Vulmea stared into a black aperture in the wall, just in time to see the monster vanishing into its depths. Wentyard, trembling in every limb, had followed, and now looked over the pirate's shoulder. A reptilian reek came from the aperture, which they now saw as an arched doorway, partly masked by thick vines. Enough moonlight found its way through the roof to reveal a glimpse of stone steps leading up into darkness.

"I missed this," muttered Vulmea. "When I found the stair I didn't look any further for an exit. Look how the door-sill glistens with scales that have been rubbed off that brute's belly. He uses it often. I believe those steps lead to a tunnel that goes clear through the cliffs. There's nothing in this bowl that even a snake could eat or drink. He has to go out into the jungle to get water and food. If he was in the habit of going out by the way of the ravine, there'd be a path worn away through the vegetation, like there is in the room. Besides, the Indians wouldn't stay in the ravine. Unless there's some other exit we haven't found, I believe that he comes and goes this way, and that means it lets into the outer world. It's worth trying, anyway."

"You mean to follow that fiend into that black tunnel?" ejaculated Wentyard aghast.

"Why not? We've got to follow and kill him anyway. If we run into a nest of them – well, we've got to die some time, and if we wait here much longer the Cimarroons will be cutting our throats. This is a chance to get away, I believe. But we won't go in the dark."

Hurrying back to the room where they had cooked the monkey, Vulmea caught up a fagot, wrapped a torn strip of his shirt about one end and set it smouldering in the coals which he blew into a tiny flame. The improvised torch flickered and smoked, but it cast light of a sort. Vulmea strode back to the chamber where the snake had vanished, followed by Wentyard who stayed close within the dancing ring of light, and saw writhing serpents in every vine that swayed overhead.

The torch revealed blood thickly spattered on the stone steps. Squeezing their way between the tangled vines which did not admit a man's body as easily as a serpent's, they mounted the steps warily. Vulmea went first, holding the torch high and ahead of him, his cutlass in his right hand. He had thrown away the useless, empty pistols. They climbed half a dozen steps and came into a tunnel some fifteen feet wide and perhaps ten feet high from the stone floor to the vaulted roof. The serpent-reek and the glisten of the floor told of long occupancy by the brute, and the blood-drops ran on before them.

The walls, floor, and roof of the tunnel were in a much better state of preservation than were the ruins outside, and Wentyard found time to marvel at the ingenuity of the ancient race which had built it.

Meanwhile, in the moonlit chamber they had just quitted, a giant black man appeared as silently as a shadow. His great spear glinted in the moonlight, and the plumes on his head rustled as he turned to look about him. Four warriors followed him.

"They went into that door," said one of these, pointing to the vine-tangled entrance. "I saw their torch vanish into it. But I feared to follow them, alone as I was, and I ran to tell you, Bigomba."

"But what of the screams and the shot we heard just before we descended the shaft?" asked another uneasily.

"I think they met the demon and slew it," answered Bigomba. "Then they went into this door. Perhaps it is a tunnel which leads through the cliffs. One of you go gather the rest of the warriors who are scattered through the rooms searching for the white dogs. Bring them after me. Bring torches with you. As for me, I will follow with the other three, at once. Bigomba sees like a lion in the dark."

As Vulmea and Wentyard advanced through the tunnel Wentyard watched the torch fearfully. It was not very satisfactory, but it gave some light, and he shuddered to think of its going out or burning to a stump and leaving them in darkness. He strained his eyes into the gloom ahead, momentarily expecting to see a vague, hideous figure rear up amidst it. But when Vulmea halted suddenly it was not because of an appearance of the reptile. They had reached a point where a smaller corridor branched off the main tunnel, leading away to the left.

"Which shall we take?"

Vulmea bent over the floor, lowering his torch.

"The blood-drops go to the left," he grunted. "That's the way he went."

"Wait!" Wentyard gripped his arm and pointed along the main tunnel. "Look! There ahead of us! Light!"

Vulmea thrust his torch behind him, for its flickering glare made the shadows seem blacker beyond its feeble radius. Ahead of them, then, he saw something like a floating gray mist, and knew it was moonlight finding its way somehow into the tunnel. Abandoning the hunt for the wounded reptile, the men rushed forward and emerged into abroad square chamber, hewn out of solid rock. But Wentyard swore in bitter disappointment. The moonlight was coming, not from a door opening into the jungle, but from a square shaft in the roof, high above their heads.

An archway opened in each wall, and the one opposite the arch by which they had entered was fitted with a heavy door, corroded and eaten by decay. Against the wall to their right stood a stone image, taller than a man, a carven grotesque, at once manlike and bestial. A stone altar stood before it, its surface channeled and darkly stained. Something on the idol's breast caught the moonlight in a frosty sparkle.

"The devil!" Vulmea sprang forward and wrenched it away. He held it up – a thing like a giant's necklace, made of jointed plates of hammered gold, each as broad as a man's palm and set with curiously-cut jewels.

"I thought I lied when I told you there were gems here," grunted the pirate. "It seems I spoke the truth unwittingly! These are not the Fangs of Satan, but they'll fetch a tidy fortune anywhere in Europe."

"What are you doing?" demanded Wentyard, as the Irishman laid the huge necklace on the altar and lifted his cutlass. Vulmea's reply was a stroke that severed the ornament into equal halves. One half he thrust into Wentyard's astounded hands.

"If we get out of here alive that will provide for the wife and child," he grunted.

"But you – " stammered Wentyard. "You hate me – yet you save my life and then give me this – "

"Shut up!" snarled the pirate. "I'm not giving it to you; I'm giving it to the girl and her baby. Don't you venture to thank me, curse you! I hate you as much as I – "

He stiffened suddenly, wheeling to glare down the tunnel up which they had come. He stamped out the torch and crouched down behind the altar, drawing Wentyard with him.

"Men!" he snarled. "Coming down the tunnel, I heard steel clink on stone. I hope they didn't see the torch. Maybe they didn't. It wasn't much more than a coal in the moonlight."

They strained their eyes down the tunnel. The moon hovered at an angle above the open shaft which allowed some of its light to stream a short way down the tunnel. Vision ceased at the spot where the smaller corridor branched off. Presently four shadows bulked out of the blackness beyond, taking shape gradually like figures emerging from a thick fog. They halted, and the white men saw the largest one – a giant who towered above the others – point silently with his spear, up the tunnel, then down the corridor. Two of the shadowy shapes detached themselves from the group and moved off down the corridor out of sight. The giant and the other man came on up the tunnel.

"The Cimarroons, hunting us," muttered Vulmea. "They're splitting their party to make sure they find us. Lie low; there may be a whole crew right behind them."

They crouched lower behind the altar while the two blacks came up the tunnel, growing more distinct as they advanced. Wentyard's skin crawled at the sight of the broad-bladed spears held ready in their hands. The biggest one moved with the supple tread of a great panther, head thrust forward, spear poised, shield lifted. He was a formidable image of rampant barbarism, and Wentyard wondered if even such a man as Vulmea could stand before him with naked steel and live.

They halted in the doorway, and the white men caught the white flash of their eyes as they glared suspiciously about the chamber. The smaller black seized the giant's arm convulsively and pointed, and Wentyard's heart jumped into his throat. He thought they had been discovered, but the negro was pointing at the idol. The big man grunted contemptuously. However slavishly in awe he might be of the fetishes of his native coast, the gods and demons of other races held no terrors for him.

But he moved forward majestically to investigate, and Wentyard realized that discovery was inevitable.

Vulmea whispered fiercely in his ear: "We've got to get them, quick! Take the brave. I'll take the chief. Now!"

They sprang up together, and the blacks cried out involuntarily, recoiling from the unexpected apparitions. In that instant the white men were upon them.

The shock of their sudden appearance had stunned the smaller black. He was small only in comparison with his gigantic companion. He was as tall as Wentyard and the great muscles knotted under his sleek skin. But he was staggering back, gaping stupidly, spear and shield lowered on limply hanging arms. Only the bite of steel brought him to his senses, and then it was too late. He screamed and lunged madly, but Wentyard's sword had girded deep into his vitals and his lunge was wild. The Englishman side-stepped and thrust again and yet again, under and over the shield, fleshing his blade in groin and throat. The black man swayed in his rush, his arms fell, shield and spear clattered to the floor and he toppled down upon them.

Wentyard turned to stare at the battle waging behind him, where the two giants fought under the square beam of moonlight, black and white, spear and shield against cutlass.

Bigomba, quicker-witted than his follower, had not gone down under the unexpected rush of the white man. He had reacted instantly to his fighting instinct. Instead of retreating he had thrown up his shield to catch the down-swinging cutlass, and had countered with a ferocious lunge that scraped blood from the Irishman's neck as he ducked aside.

Now they fought in grim silence, while Wentyard circled about them, unable to get in a thrust that might not imperil Vulmea. Both moved with the sure-footed quickness of tigers. The black man towered above the white, but even his magnificent proportions could not overshadow the sinewy physique of the pirate. In the moonlight the great muscles of both men knotted, rippled and coiled in response to their herculean exertions. The play was bewildering, almost blinding the eye that tried to follow it.

Again and again the pirate barely avoided the dart of the great spear, and again and again Bigomba caught on his shield a stroke that otherwise would have shorn him asunder. Speed of foot and strength of wrist alone saved Vulmea, for he had no defensive armor. But repeatedly he either dodged or side-stepped the savage thrusts, or beat aside the spear with his blade. And he rained blow on blow with his cutlass, slashing the bull-hide to ribbons, until the shield was little more than a wooden framework through which, slipping in a lightning-like thrust, the cutlass drew first blood as it raked through the flesh across the black chief's ribs.

At that Bigomba roared like a wounded lion, and like a wounded lion he leaped. Hurling the shield at Vulmea's head he threw all his giant body behind the arm that drove the spear at the Irishman's breast. The muscles leaped up in quivering bunches on his arm as he smote, and Wentyard cried out, unable to believe that Vulmea could avoid the lunge. But chain-lightning was slow compared to the pirate's shift. He ducked, side-stepped, and as the spear whipped past under his arm-pit, he dealt a cut that found no shield in the way. The cutlass was a blinding flicker of steel in the moonlight, ending its arc in a butcher-shop crunch. Bigomba fell as a tree falls and lay still. His head had been all but severed from his body.

Vulmea stepped back, panting. His great chest heaved under the tattered shirt, and sweat dripped from his face. At last he had met a man almost his match, and the strain of that terrible encounter left the tendons of his thighs quivering.

"We've got to get out of here before the rest of them come," he gasped, catching up his half of the idol's necklace. "That smaller corridor must lead to the outside, but those niggers are in it, and we haven't any torch. Let's try this door. Maybe we can get out that way."

The ancient door was a rotten mass of crumbling panels and corroded copper bands. It cracked and splintered under the impact of Vulmea's heavy shoulder, and through the apertures the pirate felt the stir of fresh air, and caught the scent of a damp river-reek. He drew back to smash again at the door, when a chorus of fierce yells brought him about snarling like a trapped wolf. Swift feet pattered up the tunnel, torches waved, and barbaric shouts re-echoed under the vaulted roof. The white men saw a mass of fierce faces and flashing spears, thrown into relief by the flaring torches, surging up the tunnel. The light of their coming streamed before them. They had heard and interpreted the sounds of combat as they hurried up the tunnel, and now they had sighted their enemies, and they burst into a run, howling like wolves.

"Break the door, quick!" cried Wentyard.

"No time now," grunted Vulmea. "They'd be on us before we could get through. We'll make our stand here."

He ran across the chamber to meet them before they could emerge from the comparatively narrow archway, and Wentyard followed him. Despair gripped the Englishman and in a spasm of futile rage he hurled the half-necklace from him. The glint of its jewels was mockery. He fought down the sick memory of those who waited for him in England as he took his place at the door beside the giant pirate.

As they saw their prey at bay the howls of the oncoming blacks grew wilder. Spears were brandished among the torches – then a shriek of different timbre cut the din. The foremost blacks had almost reached the point where the corridor branched off the tunnel – and out of the corridor raced a frantic figure. It was one of the black men who had gone down it exploring. And behind him came a blood-smeared nightmare. The great serpent had turned at bay at last.

It was among the blacks before they knew what was happening. Yells of hate changed to screams of terror, and in an instant all was madness, a clustering tangle of struggling black bodies and limbs, and that great sinuous cable-like trunk writhing and whipping among them, the wedge-shaped head darting and battering. Torches were knocked against the walls, scattering sparks. One man, caught in the squirming coils, was crushed and killed almost instantly, and others were dashed to the floor or hurled with bone-splintering force against the walls by the battering-ram head, or the lashing, beam-like tail. Shot and slashed as it was, wounded mortally, the great snake clung to life with the horrible vitality of its kind, and in the blind fury of its death-throes it became an appalling engine of destruction.

Within a matter of moments the blacks who survived had broken away and were fleeing down the tunnel, screaming their fear. Half a dozen limp and broken bodies lay sprawled behind them, and the serpent, unlooping himself from these victims, swept down the tunnel after the living who fled from him. Fugitives and pursuer vanished into the darkness, from which frantic yells came back faintly.

"God!" Wentyard wiped his brow with a trembling hand. "That might have happened to us!"

"Those niggers who went groping down the corridor must have stumbled onto him lying in the dark," muttered Vulmea. "I guess he got tired of running. Or maybe he knew he had his death-wound and turned back to kill somebody before he died. He'll chase those niggers until either he's killed them all, or died himself. They may turn on him and spear him to death when they get into the open. Pick up your part of the necklace. I'm going to try that door again."

Three powerful drives of his shoulder were required before the ancient door finally gave way. Fresh, damp air poured through, though the interior was dark. But Vulmea entered without hesitation, and Wentyard followed him. After a few yards of groping in the dark, the narrow corridor turned sharply to the left, and they emerged into a somewhat wider passage, where a familiar, nauseating reek made Wentyard shudder.

"The snake used this tunnel," said Vulmea. "This must be the corridor that branches off the tunnel on the other side of the idol-room. There must be a regular network of subterranean rooms and tunnels under these cliffs. I wonder what we'd find if we explored all of them."

Wentyard fervently disavowed any curiosity in that direction, and an instant later jumped convulsively when Vulmea snapped suddenly: "Look there!"

"Where? How can a man look anywhere in this darkness?"

"Ahead of us, damn it! It's light at the other end of this tunnel!"

"Your eyes are better than mine," muttered Wentyard, but he followed the pirate with new eagerness, and soon he too could see the tiny disk of grey that seemed set in a solid black wall. After that it seemed to the Englishman that they walked for miles. It was not that far in reality, but the disk grew slowly in size and clarity, and Wentyard knew that they had come along way from the idol-room when at last they thrust their heads through a round, vine-crossed opening and saw the stars reflected in the black water of a sullen river flowing beneath them.

"This is the way he came and went, all right," grunted Vulmea.

The tunnel opened in the steep bank and there was a narrow strip of beach below it, probably existent only in dry seasons. They dropped down to it and looked about at the dense jungle walls which hung over the river.

"Where are we?" asked Wentyard helplessly, his sense of direction entirely muddled.

"Beyond the foot of the slopes," answered Vulmea, "and that means we're outside the cordon the Indians have strung around the cliffs. The coast lies in that direction; come on!"

The sun hung high above the western horizon when two men emerged from the jungle that fringed the beach, and saw the tiny bay stretching before them.

Vulmea stopped in the shadow of the trees.

"There's your ship, lying at anchor where we left her. All you've got to do now is hail her for a boat to be sent ashore, and your part of the adventure is over."

Wentyard looked at his companion. The Englishman was bruised, scratched by briars, his clothing hanging in tatters. He could hardly have been recognized as the trim captain of the *Redoubtable*. But the change was not limited to his appearance. It went deeper. He was a different man than the one who marched his prisoner ashore in quest of a mythical hoard of gems.

"What of you? I owe you a debt that I can never – "

"You owe me nothing," Vulmea broke in. "I don't trust you, Wentyard."

The other winced. Vulmea did not know that it was the cruelest thing he could have said. He did not mean it as cruelty. He was simply speaking his mind, and it did not occur to him that it would hurt the Englishman.

"Do you think I could ever harm you now, after this?" exclaimed Wentyard. "Pirate or not, I could never – "

"You're grateful and full of the milk of human kindness now," answered Vulmea, and laughed hardly. "But you might change your mind after you got back on your decks. John Wentyard lost in the jungle is one man; Captain Wentyard aboard his king's warship is another."

"I swear – " began Wentyard desperately, and then stopped, realizing the futility of his protestations. He realized, with an almost physical pain, that a man can never escape the consequences of a wrong, even though the victim may forgive him. His punishment now was an inability to convince Vulmea of his sincerity, and it hurt him far more bitterly than the Irishman could ever realize. But he could not expect Vulmea to trust him, he realized miserably. In that moment he loathed himself for what he had been, and for the smug, self-sufficient arrogance which had caused him to ruthlessly trample on all who fell outside the charmed circle of his approval. At that moment there was nothing in the world he desired more than the firm hand-clasp of the man who had fought and wrought so tremendously for him; but he knew he did not deserve it. "You can't stay here!" he protested weakly

"The Indians never come to this coast," answered Vulmea. "I'm not afraid of the Cimarroons. Don't worry about me." He laughed again, at what he considered the jest of anyone worrying about his safety. "I've lived in the wilds before now. I'm not the only pirate in these seas. There's a rendezvous you know nothing about. I can reach it easily. I'll be back on the Main with a ship and a crew the next time you hear about me."

And turning supply, he strode into the foliage and vanished, while Wentyard, dangling in his hand a jeweled strip of gold, stared helplessly after him.

The Strange Case of Josiah Wilbarger

Even amid the stark realities of frontier life, the fantastic and unexplainable had its place. There was no event stranger than the case of the man whose scalped and bloody head came thrice to a woman in a dream.

One early morning in autumn, 1833, five men were cooking their breakfast of venison over a campfire on the banks of a stream some miles south of what is now the city of Austin, Texas. They were Josiah Wilbarger, Thomas Christian, Maynie, William Strother, and Standifer. They had been out on a land prospecting trip and were returning to the settlements. Wilbarger's cabin was on the Colorado River, near the present site of Bastrop, and only one family – the Hornsbys – lived above him.

As the party busied themselves over their meal, there came a sudden interruption – common enough in those perilous days.

From the surrounding thickets and trees crashed a volley of shots, a whistling flight of arrows. Unseen, the red-skinned painted warriors had stolen up and trapped their prey. Three of the men dropped, riddled. The other two, miraculously untouched by the missiles whistling about them, sprang to their horses, broke through the ambush and out-ran their attackers. Looking back as they rode, they saw the bodies of their three companions lying motionless in pools of blood. One of these was Wilbarger, and they plainly saw the feathered end of an arrow standing up from his body.

They drove in the spurs and raced madly through the thickets, striving to shut out from their horrified ears the triumphant and fiendish yells of their barbaric attackers.

These had not long pursued the fleeing survivors; they returned to the bodies which lay by the small fire which still burned cheerfully, lighting that scene of horror. They gathered about, those lean, naked men, hideously painted, with shaven heads, and bearing tomahawks in their beaded girdles. They stripped the bodies and then, as a hunter might strip the pelt from a trapped animal, they took the symbols of their victory – the scalps of their victims.

This horrible practice, which the English settlers first introduced to the red man, and which did not originate with him, varied with different tribes. Some only took a small part of the scalp. Some ripped off the entire scalp. The braves who had surprised the land prospectors took the whole scalp. Josiah Wilbarger, struck once by an arrow and twice by bullets, was not dead, though he lay like a lifeless corpse. He was only semi-conscious, dimly aware of what was going on about him. He felt rude hands ripping the clothing from his body, and he saw, as in a dream, the gory scalps ripped from the heads of his dead companions. Then he felt a lean muscled hand locked in his own hair, pulling back his head at an agonizing angle. It is fantastic that he could have so feigned death as to fool the keen hunters in whose hands he lay.

He realized the horror of his position, but he lay like a man struck dumb and paralyzed. He felt the keen edge of the scalping knife slice through his skin, and perhaps he would have cried out, but he could not. He felt the knife circle his head above the ears, though he experienced only a vague stinging. Then his head was almost wrenched from his body as his tormentor ripped the scalp away with ferocious force. Still he felt no unusual agony, numbed as he was by his desperate wounds, but the noise of the scalp leaving his head sounded in his ears like a clap of thunder. And his remaining shred of consciousness was blanked out.

Had he been capable of any distinct thought, as he sank into senselessness, it must have been that this, at last, was death. Yet again he opened his eyes upon the bloody scene and the naked, scalped corpses about the dead ashes of the fire – how much later he had no interest in even speculating about. Now all was silent and deserted; the red slayers had gone as silently and swiftly as they had come.

And in this wounded and mutilated man awoke dimly the instinct to live, so powerful in the men of the raw frontier. He began to crawl, slowly, painfully, toward the direction of the settlements. To seek to depict her agonies of that ghastly journey would be but to display the frailty of the mere written word. Flies hung in clouds over his bloody head and he left red smears on the ground and the rocks. A quarter of a mile he dragged himself, then even his steely frame rebelled, and he reposed unconscious beneath a giant post-oak tree.

Now the occult element enters into the tale. The survivors of the massacre had ridden through the wide-flung settlements, bearing the tale of the crime. They had passed the cabin of the Hornsbys, which was the only cabin on the river above that of Josiah Wilbarger.

The following night, Mrs. Hornsby lay sleeping and she dreamed. The tale of the massacre was in her mind, and it is not strange that she dreamed of her neighbor, Josiah Wilbarger. Not strange, even, that in her dream she saw him naked and scalped, since the survivors had told her he had been killed, and she was familiar with Indian customs. But what was strange is that, in her dream, she saw him, not at the camping place, but beneath a great post-oak tree, some distance from where he was struck down – and alive.

Awakened by the terror of the nightmare, she told her husband, who soothed her and told her to go back to sleep.

Again she slept, again she dreamed and again she saw Wilbarger, naked, wounded and scalped – but living – under the oak tree. Once again she awoke, and again her husband soothed her distress, and again she slept. But when she dreamed the same dream for the third time she refused any longer to doubt. She began assembling things that might be needed to bandage the wounds of a wounded man, and her vehemence convinced her husband, who gathered a party and set out. First they went to the place where the attack had occurred: they saw the two dead men there and the track Wilbarger had made in dragging his wounded body away. And beneath the great post-oak tree, they found Wilbarger, alive – but just barely!

Josiah Wilbarger lived twelve years thereafter, but his wounds never fully healed, and at last he met his death – by a dream. In a nightmare he again experienced the horror of his scalping, and leaping up, struck his head with terrific force against the bedpost. This blow, coupled with his other wounds, finally caused his death.

Marking the spot where Josiah Pugh Wilbarger of Austin's Colony was stabbed and scalped by the Indians, is a marker placed there by the State of Texas, in 1936, which explains that while Wilbarger was attacked and scalped in 1833, he died on April 11, 1845.

A footnote to the story has it that Wilbarger told his rescuers that he had seen, in a vision, his sister Margaret, at the time when he was sure he would bleed to death without help. She urged him not to give up, that help was on the way, and that he would be found – friends would find him. Three months later, it was learned that about the time Wilbarger had this *visitation*, and as nearly as they could figure out at the same hour – Margaret died in her home in Missouri.

The chronicles of the Middle Ages can offer no stranger tale, yet its truth is well substantiated, and it is, perhaps the most unexplainable event in Texas history.

The Valley of the Lost

As a wolf spies upon its hunters, John Reynolds watched his pursuers. He lay close in a thicket on the slope, an inferno of hate seething in his heart. He had ridden hard; up the slope behind him, where the dim path wound up out of Lost Valley, his crank-eyed mustang stood, head drooping, trembling, after the long run. Below him, not more than eighty yards away, stood his enemies, fresh come from the slaughter of his kinsmen.

In the clearing fronting Ghost Cave they had dismounted and were arguing among themselves. John Reynolds knew them all with an old, bitter hate. The black shadow of feud lay between them and himself.

The feuds of early Texas have been neglected by chroniclers who have sung the feuds of the Kentucky mountains, though the men who first settled the Southwest were of the same breed as those mountaineers. But there was a difference; in the mountain country feuds dragged on for generations; on the Texas frontier they were short, fierce, and appallingly bloody.

The Reynolds-McCrill feud was long, as Texas feuds went: fifteen years had passed since old Esau Reynolds stabbed young Braxton McCrill to death with his bowie knife in the saloon at Antelope Wells, in a quarrel over range rights. For fifteen years the Reynoldses and their kin – the Brills, Allisons, and Donnellys – had been at open war with the McCrills and their kin – the Killihers, the Fletchers, and the Ords. There had been ambushes in the hills, murders on the open range, and gun-fights on the streets of the little cowtowns. Each clan had rustled the other's cattle wholesale. Gunmen and outlaws called in by both sides to participate for pay, had spread a reign of terror and lawlessness throughout the vicinity. Settlers shunned the war-torn range; the feud became a red obstacle in the way of progress and development, a savage retrogression which was demoralizing the whole countryside.

Little John Reynolds cared. He had grown up in the atmosphere of the feud, and it had become a burning obsession with him. The war had taken fearful toll on both clans, but the Reynolds clan had suffered most. John was the last of the fighting Reynoldses, for Esau, the grim old patriarch who ruled the clan, would never again walk or sit in a saddle, with his legs paralyzed by McCrill bullets. John had seen his brothers shot down from ambush or killed in pitched battles.

Now the last stroke had nearly wiped out the waning clan. John Reynolds cursed as he thought of the trap into which they had walked in the saloon at Antelope Wells; the hidden foes had opened their murderous fire without warning. There had fallen his cousin, Bill Donnelly; his sister's son, young Jonathon Brill; his brother-in-law, Job Allison; and Steve Kerney, the hired gunman. How he himself had shot his way through and gained the hitching rack, untouched by the blasting hail of lead, John Reynolds hardly knew. They had pressed him so closely he had not time to mount his long-limbed rangy bay, but had been forced to take the first horse he came to – the crank-eyed, speedy, but short-winded mustang of the dead Jonathon Brill.

He had distanced his pursuers for a while, had gained the uninhabited hills, and swung back into mysterious Lost Valley, with its silent thickets and crumbling stone columns, where he intended to double back over the hills and gain the country of the Reynolds. But the mustang had failed him. He had tied it up the slope, out of sight of the valley floor, and crept back – to see his enemies ride into the valley. There were five of them: old Jonas McCrill, with the perpetual snarl twisting his wolfish lips; Saul Fletcher, with his black beard and the limping, dragging gait that a fall in his youth from a wild mustang had left him; Bill Ord and Peter Ord, brothers; and the outlaw Jack Solomon.

Jonas McCrill's voice came up to the silent watcher. "And I tell yuh he's a-hidin' somewhere in this valley. He was a-ridin' that mustang and it didn't never have no guts. I'm bettin' it give plumb out on him time he got this far."

"Well," came the voice of Saul Fletcher, "what're we a-standin' 'round pow-wowin' for? Why don't we start huntin' him?"

"Not so fast," growled old Jonas. "Remember it's John Reynolds we're a-chasin'. We got plenty time."

John Reynolds' fingers hardened on the stock of his single-action .45.

There were two cartridges unfired in the cylinder. He pushed the muzzle through the stems of the thicket in front of him, his thumb drawing back the wicked fanged hammer. His grey eyes narrowed and became opaque as ice as he sighted down the long blue barrel. An instant he weighed his hatred, and chose Saul Fletcher. All the hate in his soul centered for an instant on that brutal, black-bearded face, and the limping tread he had heard that night he lay wounded in a besieged corral, with his brother's riddled corpse beside him, and fought off Saul and his brothers.

John Reynolds' finger crooked and the crash of the shot broke the echoes of the sleeping hills. Saul Fletcher swayed, flinging his black beard drunkenly upward, and crashed face-down and headlong. The others, with the quickness of men accustomed to frontier warfare, dropped behind rocks, and their answering shots roared back as they combed the slope blindly. The bullets tore through the thickets, whistling over the unseen killer's head. High up on the slope the mustang, out of sight of the men in the valley but frightened by the noise, screamed shrilly, and, rearing, snapped the reins that held him and fled away up the hill path. The drum of his hoofs on the stones dwindled in the distance.

Silence reigned for an instant, then came Jonas McCrill's wrathful voice: "I told yuh he was a-ridin' here! Come outa there; he's got clean away."

The old fighter's rangy frame rose up from behind the rock where he had taken refuge. Reynolds, grinning fiercely, took steady aim; then some instinct of self-preservation held his hand. The others came out into the open.

"What are we a-waitin' on?" yelled young Bill Ord, tears of rage in his eyes. "Here that coyote's done shot Saul and's ridin' hell-for-leather away from here, and we're a-standin' 'round jawin'. I'm a goin' to . . ." he started ed for his horse.

"Yuh're a-goin' to listen to me!" roared old Jonas. "I warned yuh to go slow, but yuh would come lickety-split along like a bunch of blind buzzards, and now Saul's layin' there dead. If we ain't careful, John Reynolds'll kill all of us. Didn't I tell yuh – all he was here? Likely stopped to rest his horse. He can't go far. This here's a long hunt, like I told yuh at first. Let him get a good start. Long as he's ahead of us, we got to watch for ambushes. He'll try to get back onto the Reynolds range. Well, we're a-goin' after him slow and easy and keep him hazed back all the time. We'll be a-ridin' the inside of a big half-circle and he can't get by us-not on that shortwinded mustang. We'll just foller him and gather him in when his horse can't do no more. And I purty well know where he'll come to bay at – Blind Horse Canyon."

"We'll have to starve him out, then," growled Jack Solomon.

"No, we won't," grinned old Jonas. "Bill, you hightail it back to Antelope and git five or six sticks of dynamite. Then you git a fresh horse and follow our trail. If we catch him before he gits to the canyon, all right. If he beats us there and holds up, we'll wait for yuh, and then blast him out."

"What about Saul?" growled Peter Ord.

"He's dead," grunted Jonas. "Nothin' we can do for him now. No time to take him back." He glanced up at the sky, where already black dots wheeled against the blue. His gaze drifted to the walled-up mouth of the cavern in the steep cliff which rose at right angles to the slope up which the path wandered.

"We'll break open the cave and put him in it," he said. "We'll pile up the rocks again and the wolves and buzzards can't git to him. Maybe several days before we git back."

"That cave's ha'nted," muttered Bill Ord, uneasily. "The Injuns said if yuh put a dead man in there, he'd come walkin' out at midnight."

"Shet up and help pick up pore Saul," snapped Jonas. "Here's your own kin a-layin' dead, and his murderer a-ridin' further away every second, and you talk about ha'nts."

As they lifted the corpse, Jonas drew the long-barreled six-shooter from the holster and shoved the weapon into his own waistband.

"Pore Saul," he grunted. "He's shore dead. Shot plumb through the heart. Dead before he hit the ground, I reckon. Well, we'll make that damned Reynolds pay for it."

They carried the dead man to the cave, and, laying him down, attacked the rocks which blocked the entrance. These were soon torn aside, and Reynolds saw the men carry the body inside. They emerged almost immediately, minus their burden, and mounted their horses. Young Bill Ord swung away down the valley and vanished among the trees; the rest cantered along the winding trail that led up into the hills. They passed within a hundred feet of his refuge and John Reynolds hugged the earth, fearing discovery. But they did not glance in his direction. He heard the dwindling of their hoofs over the rocky path; then silence settled again over the ancient valley.

John Reynolds rose cautiously, looked about him as a hunted wolf looks, then made his way quickly down the slope. He had a very definite purpose in mind. A single unfired cartridge was all his ammunition; but about the dead body of Saul Fletcher was a belt well filled with .45 caliber cartridges.

As he attacked the rocks heaped in the cave's mouth, there hovered in his mind the curious dim speculations which the cave and the valley itself roused in him. Why had the Indians named it the Valley of the Lost – which white men shortened to Lost Valley? Why had the red men shunned it? Once in the memory of white men, a band of Kiowas, fleeing the vengeance of Bigfoot Wallace and his rangers, had taken up their abode there and fallen on evil times. The survivors of the tribe had fled, telling wild tales in which murder, fratricide, insanity, vampirism, slaughter, and cannibalism had played grim parts. Then six white men, brothers – Stark by name – had settled in Lost Valley. They had re-opened the cave which the Kiowas had blocked up. Horror had fallen on them and in one night five died by one another's hands. The survivor had walled up the cave mouth again and departed, where none knew. Word had drifted through the settlements of a man named Stark who had come among the remnants of those Kiowas who had once lived in Lost Valley, and, after a long talk with them, had cut his own throat with his bowie knife.

What was the mystery of Lost Valley, if not a web of lies and legends? What the meaning of those crumbling stones, which, scattered all over the valley, half hidden in the climbing growth, bore a curious symmetry, especially in the moonlight, so that some people believed when the Indians swore they were the half destroyed columns of a prehistoric city which once stood in Lost Valley? Before it crumbled into a heap of grey dust, Reynolds himself had seen a skull unearthed at the base of a cliff by a wandering prospector. It seemed neither Caucasian nor Indian – a curious, peaked skull, which but for the formation of the jaw bones might have been that of some unknown antediluvian animal.

Such thoughts flitted vaguely and momentarily through John Reynolds' mind as he dislodged the boulders, which the McCrills had put back loosely – just firmly enough to keep a wolf or buzzard from squeezing through. In the main his thoughts were engrossed with the cartridges in dead Saul Fletcher's belt. A fighting chance! A lease on life! He would fight his way out of the hills yet; would bring in more gunmen and cut-throats for striking back. He would flood the whole range with blood, and bring the countryside to ruin, if by those means he might be avenged. For years he had been the moving factor in the feud. When even old Esau had weakened and wished for peace, John Reynolds had kept the flame of hate blazing. The feud had become his own driving motive, his one interest in life and reason for existence. The last boulders fell aside.

John Reynolds stepped into the semi-gloom of the cavern. It was not large, but the shadows seemed to cluster there in almost tangible sub-stance. Slowly his eyes accustomed themselves, and an involuntary excla-mation broke from his lips – the cave was empty! He swore in bewilder-ment. He had seen men carry Saul Fletcher's corpse into the cave and come out again, empty handed. Yet no corpse lay on the dusty cavern floor. He went to the back of the cave, glanced at the straight, even wall, bent and examined the smooth rock floor. His keen eyes, straining in the gloom, made out a dull smear of blood on the stone. It ended abruptly at the back wall, and there was no stain on the wall.

Reynolds leaned closer, supporting himself by a hand propped against the stone wall. And suddenly, shockingly, the sensation of solidity and stability vanished. The wall gave way beneath his propping hand; a section swung inward, precipitating him headlong through a black gaping open-ing. His cat-like quickness could not save him. It was as if the yawning shadows reached tenuous and invisible hands to jerk him headlong into the darkness.

He did not fall far. His out-flung hands struck what seemed to be steps carved in the stone, and on them he scrambled and floundered for an instant. Then he righted himself and turned back to the opening through which he had fallen. But the secret door had closed, and only a smooth stone wall met his groping fingers. He fought down a rising panic. How the McCrills had come to know of this secret chamber he could not say, but quite evidently they had placed Saul Fletcher's body in it. And there, trapped like a rat, they would find John Reynolds when they returned. Then a grim smile curled Reynolds' thin lips. When they opened the secret door, he would be hidden in the darkness, while they would be etched against the dim light of the outer cave. Where could he find a more perfect ambush? But first he must find the body and secure the cartridges.

He turned to grope his way down the steps and his first stride brought him to a level floor. It was a sort of narrow tunnel, he decided, for though he could not touch the roof, a stride to the right or the left and his outstretched hand encountered a wall, seemingly too even and symmetrical to have been the work of nature. He went slowly, groping in the darkness, keeping in touch with the walls and momentarily expecting to stumble on Saul Fletcher's body. And as he did not, a dim horror began to grow in his soul. The McCrills had not been in the cavern long enough to carry the body so far back into the darkness. A feeling was rising in John Reynolds that the McCrills had not entered the tunnel at all – that they were not aware of its existence. Then where in the name of sanity was Saul Fletcher's corpse?

He stopped short, jerking out his six-shooter. Something was coming up the dark tunnel – something that walked upright and lumberingly.

John Reynolds knew it was a man, wearing high-heeled riding boots; no other footwear makes the same stilted sound. He caught the jingle of the spurs. And a dark tide of nameless horror moved sluggishly in John Reynolds' mind as he heard that halting tread approach, and remembered the night when he had lain at bay in the old corral, with the younger brother dying beside him, and heard a limping, dragging footstep, out in the night where Saul Fletcher led his wolves and sought for a way to come upon his back.

Had the man only been wounded? These steps sounded stiff and blundering, such as a wounded man might make. No – John Reynolds had seen too many men die; he knew that his bullet had gone straight through Saul Fletcher's heart, possibly tearing the heart out, certainly killing him instantly. Besides, he had heard old Jonas McCrill declare the man was dead. No – Saul Fletcher lay lifeless somewhere in this black cavern. It was some other lame man who was coming up that silent tunnel.

Now the tread ceased. The man was fronting him, separated only by a few feet of utter blackness. What was there in that to quicken the iron pulse of John Reynolds, who had unflinchingly faced death times without number? – what to make his flesh crawl and his tongue freeze to his palate? – to awake sleeping instincts of fear as a man senses the presence of an unseen serpent, and make him feel that somehow the other was aware of his presence with eyes that pierced the darkness?

In the silence John Reynolds heard the staccato pounding of his own heart. And with shocking suddenness the man lunged. Reynolds' straining ears caught the first movement of that lunge and he fired pointblank. And he screamed – a terrible animal-like scream. Heavy arms locked upon him and unseen teeth worried at his flesh; but in the frothing frenzy of his fear, his own strength was superhuman. For in the flash of the shot he had seen a bearded face with a slack hanging mouth and staring dead eyes. *Saul Fletcher!* The dead, come back from hell.

As in a nightmare, Reynolds entered a fiendish battle in the dark where the dead sought to drag down the living. He was flung with bone-shattering force against the stone walls. Dashed to the floor, the silent horror squatted ghoul-like upon him, its horrid fingers sinking deep into his throat.

In that nightmare, John Reynolds had no time to doubt his own sanity. He knew that he was battling a dead man. The flesh of his foe was cold with a charnel house clamminess. Under the torn shirt he had felt the round bullet-hole, caked with clotted blood. No single sound came from the loose lips.

Choking and gasping, John Reynolds tore the strangling hands aside and flung the thing off. For an instant the darkness again separated them; then the horror came hurtling toward him again. As the thing lunged, Reynolds caught blindly and gained the wrestling hold he wished; and hurling all his power behind the attack, he dashed the horror headlong, falling upon it with his full weight. Saul Fletcher's spine snapped like a rotten branch and the tearing hands went limp, the straining limbs relaxed. Something flowed from the lax body and whispered away through the darkness like a ghostly wind, and John Reynolds instinctively knew that at last Saul Fletcher was truly dead.

Panting and shaken, Reynolds rose. The tunnel remained in utter darkness. But down it, in the direction from which the walking corpse had come stalking, there whispered a faint throbbing that was hardly sound at all, yet had in its pulsing a dark weird music. Reynolds shuddered and the sweat froze on his body. The dead man lay at his feet in the thick darkness, and faintly to his ears came that unbearably sweet, unbearably evil echo, like devil-drums beating faint and far in the dim caverns of hell.

Reason urged him to turn back – to fight against that blind door until he burst its stone, if human power could burst it; but he realized that reason and sanity had been left behind him. A single step had plunged him from a normal world of material realities into a realm of nightmare and lunacy. He decided that he was mad, or else dead and in hell. Those dim tom-toms drew him; they tugged at his heart-strings eerily. They repelled him and filled his soul with shadowy and monstrous conjectures, yet their call was irresistible. He fought the mad impulse to shriek and fling his arms wildly aloft, and run down the black tunnel as a rabbit runs down the prairie dog's burrow into the jaws of the waiting rattler.

Fumbling in the dark, he found his revolver, and still fumbling he loaded it with cartridges from Saul Fletcher's belt. He felt no more aversion now, at touching the body, than he would have felt at handling any dead flesh. Whatever unholy power had animated the corpse, it had left it when the snapping of the spine had unraveled the nerve centers and disrupted the roots of the muscular system.

Then, revolver in hand, John Reynolds went down the tunnel, drawn by a power he could not fathom, toward a doom he could not guess.

The throb of the tom-toms grew only slightly in volume as he advanced. How far below the hills he was, he could not know, but the tunnel slanted downward and he had gone a long way. Often his groping hands encountered doorways – corridors leading off the main tunnel, he believed. At last he was aware that he had left the tunnel and had come out into a vast open space. He could see nothing, but he somehow felt the vastness of the place. And in the darkness a faint light began. It throbbed as the drums throbbed, waning and waxing in time to their pulsing, but it grew slowly, casting a weird glow that was more like green than any color Reynolds had ever seen – but was not really green, nor any other sane or earthly color.

Reynolds approached it. It widened. It cast a shimmering radiance over the smooth stone floor, illuminating fantastic mosaics. It cast its sheen high in the hovering shadows, but he could see no roof. Now he stood bathed in its weird glow, so that his flesh looked like a dead man's. Now he saw the roof, high and vaulted, brooding far above him like a dusky midnight sky, and towering walls, gleaming and dark, sweeping up to tremendous heights, their bases fringed with squat shadows from which glittered other lights, small and scintillant.

He saw the source of the illumination, a strange carven stone altar on which burned what appeared to be a giant jewel of an unearthly hue, like the light it emitted. Greenish flame jetted from it; it burned as a bit of coal might burn, but it was not consumed. Just behind it a feathered serpent reared from its coils, a fantasy carven of some clear crystalline substance, the tints of which in the weird light were never the same, but which pulsed and shimmered and changed as the drums – now on all sides of him – pulsed and throbbed.

Abruptly something alive moved beside the altar and John Reynolds, though he was expecting anything, recoiled. At first he thought it was a huge reptile which slithered about the altar, then he saw that it stood upright as a man stands. As he met the menacing glitter of its eyes, he fired pointblank and the thing went down like a slaughtered ox, its skull shattered. Reynolds wheeled as a sinister rustling rose on his ears – at least these beings could be killed – then checked the lifted muzzle. The fringing shadows had moved out from the darkness at the base of the walls, and drawn about him a wide ring. And though at first glance they possessed the semblance of men, he knew they were not human.

The weird light flickered and danced over them, and back in the deeper darkness the soft, evil drums whispered their accompanying undertone everlastingly. John Reynolds stood aghast at what he saw.

It was not their dwarfish figures which caused his shudder, nor even the unnaturally made hands and feet – it was their heads. He knew now, of what race was the skull found by the prospector. Like it, these heads were peaked and malformed, curiously flattened at the sides. There was no sign of ears, as if their organs of hearing, like a serpent's, were beneath the skin. The noses were like a python's snout, the mouth and jaws much less human in appearance than his recollection of the skull would have led him to suppose. The eyes were small, glittering, and reptilian. The squamous lips writhed back, showing pointed fangs, and John Reynolds felt that their bite would be as deadly as a rattlesnake's. Garments they wore none, nor did they bear any weapons.

He tensed himself for the death struggle, but no rush came. The snake-people sat down cross-legged about him in a great circle, and beyond the circle he saw them massed thick. And now he felt a stirring in his consciousness, an almost tangible beating of wills upon his senses. He was distinctly aware of a concentrated invasion of his innermost mind, and realized that these fantastic beings were seeking to convey their commands or wishes to him by medium of thought. On what common plane could he meet these inhuman creatures? Yet in some dim, strange, telepathic way they made him understand some of their meaning; and he realized with a grisly shock that, whatever these things were now, they had once been at least partly human, else they had never been able to so bridge the gulf between the completely human and the completely bestial.

He understood that he was the first living man to come into their innermost realm, the first to look on the shining serpent, the Terrible Nameless One who was older than the world; that before he died, he was to know all which had been denied to the sons of men concerning the mysterious valley, that he might take this knowledge into Eternity with him, and discuss these matters with those who had gone before him.

The drums rustled, the strange light leaped and shimmered, and before the altar came one who seemed in authority – an ancient monstrosity whose skin was like the whitish hide of an old serpent, and who wore on his peaked skull a golden circlet, set with weird gems. He bent and made suppliance to the feathered snake. Then with a sharp implement of some sort which left a phosphorescent mark, he drew a cryptic triangular figure on the floor before the altar, and in the figure he strewed some sort of glimmering dust. From it reared up a thin spiral which grew to a gigantic shadowy serpent, feathered and horrific, and then changed and faded and became a cloud of greenish smoke. This smoke billowed out before John Reynolds' eyes and hid the serpent-eyed ring, and the altar, and the cavern itself. All the universe dissolved into the green smoke, in which titanic scenes and alien landscapes rose and shifted and faded, and monstrous shapes lumbered and leered.

Abruptly the chaos crystallized. He was looking into a valley which he did not recognize. Somehow he knew it was Lost Valley, but in it towered a gigantic city of dully gleaming stone. John Reynolds was a man of the outlands and the waste places. He had never seen the great cities of the world; but he knew that nowhere in the world today such a city reared up to the sky.

Its towers and battlements were those of an alien age. Its outline baffled his gaze with its unnatural aspects; it was a city of lunacy to the normal human eye, with its hints of alien dimensions and abnormal principles of architecture. Through it moved strange figures – human, yet of a humanity definitely different from his own. They were clad in robes; their hands and feet were less abnormal, their ears and mouths more like those of normal humans; yet there was an undoubted kinship between them and the monsters of the cave. It showed in the curious peaked skull, though this was less pronounced and bestial in the people of the city.

He saw them in the twisting streets, and in their colossal buildings, and he shuddered at the inhumanness of their lives. Much they did was beyond his ken; he could understand their actions and motives no more than a Zulu savage might understand the events of modern London. But he did understand that these people were very ancient and very evil. He saw them enact rituals that froze his blood with horror, obscenities and blasphemies beyond his understanding. He grew sick with a sensation of contamination. Somehow he knew that this city was the remnant of an outworn age – that this people represented the survival of an epoch lost and forgotten.

Then a new people came upon the scene. Over the hills came wild men clad in hides and feathers, armed with bows and flint-tipped weapons. They were, Reynolds knew, Indians – and yet not Indians as he knew them. They were slant-eyed, and their skins were yellowish rather than copper-colored. Somehow he knew that these were the nomadic ancestors of the Toltecs, wandering and conquering on their long trek before they settled in upland valleys far to the south and evolved their own special type and civilization. These were still close to the primal Mongolian rootstock, and he gasped at the gigantic vistas of time this realization evoked.

Reynolds saw the warriors move like a giant wave on the towering walls. He saw the defenders man the towers and deal death in strange and grisly forms to them. He saw the invaders reel back again and again, then come on once more with the blind ferocity of the primitive. This strange evil city, filled with mysterious people of a different order, was in their path, and they could not pass until they had stamped it out.

Reynolds marveled at the fury of the invaders, who wasted their lives like water, matching the cruel and terrible science of an unknown civilization with sheer courage and the might of manpower. Their bodies littered the plateau, but not all the forces of hell could keep them back. They rolled like a wave to the foot of the towers. They scaled the walls in the teeth of sword and arrow and death in ghastly forms; they gained the parapets; they met their enemies hand-to-hand. Bludgeons and axes beat down the lunging spears, the thrusting swords. The tall figures of the barbarians towered over the smaller forms of the defenders.

Red hell raged in the city. The siege became a street battle, the battle a rout, the rout a slaughter. Smoke rose and hung in clouds over the doomed city.

The scene changed. Reynolds looked on charred and ruined walls from which smoke still rose. The conquerors had passed on; the survivors gathered in the red-stained temple before their curious god, a crystalline serpent on a fantastic stone altar. Their age had ended; their world crumbled suddenly. They were the remnants of an otherwise extinct race. They could not rebuild their marvelous city and they feared to remain within its broken walls, a prey to every passing tribe. Reynolds saw them take up their altar and its god and follow an ancient man clad in a mantle of feathers and wearing on his head a gem-set circlet of gold. He led them across the valley to a hidden cave. They entered and squeezing through a narrow rift in the back wall, came into a vast network of caverns honeycombing the hills. Reynolds saw them at work, exploring these labyrinths, excavating and enlarging, hewing the walls and floors smooth, enlarging the rift that let into the outer cavern and setting therein a cunningly hung door, so that it seemed part of the solid wall.

Then an ever-shifting panorama denoted the passing of many centuries. The people lived in the caverns, and as time passed they adapted themselves more and more to their surroundings, each generation going less frequently into the outer sunlight. They learned to obtain their food in shuddersome ways from the earth. Their ears grew smaller, their bodies more dwarfish, their eyes more catlike. John Reynolds stood aghast as he watched the race changing through the ages.

Outside in the valley the deserted city crumbled and fell into ruins, becoming prey to lichen and weed and tree. Men came and briefly meditated among these ruins – tall Mongolian warriors, and dark inscrutable little people men call the Mound Builders. And as the centuries passed, the visitors conformed more and more to the type of Indian as he knew it, until at last the only men who came were painted red men with stealthy feet and feathered scalp-locks. None ever tarried long in that haunted place with its cryptic ruins.

Meanwhile, in the caverns, the Old People abode and grew strange and terrible. They fell lower and lower in the scale of humanity, forgetting first their written language, and gradually their human speech. But in other ways they extended the boundaries of life. In their nighted kingdom they discovered other, older caverns, which led them into the very bowels of the earth. They learned lost secrets, long-forgotten or never known by men, sleeping in the blackness far below the hills. Darkness is conducive to silence, so they gradually lost the power of speech, a sort of telepathy taking its place. And with each grisly gain they lost more of their human attributes: Their ears vanished; their noses grew snoutlike; their eyes became unable to bear the light of the sun, and even the stars. They had long abandoned the use of fire, and the only light they used was the weird gleams evoked from their gigantic jewel on the altar, and even this they did not need. They changed in other ways. John Reynolds, watching, felt the cold sweat bead his body. For the slow transmutation of the Old People was horrible to behold, and many and hideous were the shapes which moved among them before their ultimate mold and nature were evolved.

Yet they remembered the sorcery of their ancestors and added to this their own black wizardry developed far below the hills. And at last they attained the peak of that necromancy. John Reynolds had had horrific inklings of it in fragmentary glimpses of the olden times, when the wizards of the Old People had sent forth their spirits from their sleeping bodies to whisper evil things in the ears of their enemies.

A tribe of tall painted warriors came into the valley, bearing the body of a great chief, slain in tribal warfare.

Long eons had passed. Of the ancient city only scattered columns stood among the trees. A landslide had laid bare the entrance of the outer cavern. This the Indians found and therein they placed the body of their chief with his weapons broken beside him. Then they blocked up the cave mouth with stones, and took up their journey, but night caught them in the valley.

Through all the ages, the Old People had found no other entrance or exit to or from the pits, save the small outer cave; it was the one doorway between their grim realm and the world they had so long abandoned. Now they came through the secret door into the outer cavern, whose dim light they could endure, and John Reynolds' hair stood up at what he saw. For they took the corpse and laid it before the altar of the feathered serpent, and an ancient wizard lay upon it, his mouth against the mouth of the dead. Above them tom-toms pulsed and strange fires flickered, and the voiceless votaries with soundless chants invoked gods forgotten before the birth of Egypt, until unhuman voices bellowed in the outer darkness and the sweep of monstrous wings filled the shadows. And slowly life ebbed from the sorcerer and stirred the limbs of the dead chief. The body of the wizard rolled limply aside and the corpse of the chief stood up stiffly; and with puppetlike steps and glassy staring eyes it went up the dark tunnel and through the secret door into the outer cave. Its dead hands tore aside the stones, and into the starlight stalked the Horror.

Reynolds saw it walk stiffly under the shuddering trees while the night things fled gibbering. He saw it come into the camp of the warriors. The rest was horror and madness, as the dead thing pursued its former companions and tore them limb from limb. The valley became a shambles before one of the braves, conquering his terror, turned on his pursuer and hewed through its spine with a stone ax.

And even as the twice-slain corpse crumpled, Reynolds saw, on the floor of the cavern before the carven serpent, the form of the wizard quicken and live as his spirit returned to him from the corpse he had caused it to animate.

The soundless glee of incarnate demons shook the crawling blackness of the pits, and Reynolds shrank before the verminous fiends gloating over their newfound power to deal horror and death to the sons of men, their ancient enemies.

But the word spread from clan to clan, and men came not to the Valley of the Lost. For many a century it lay dreaming and deserted beneath the sky. Then came mounted braves with trailing war-bonnets, painted with the colors of the Kiowas, warriors of the north who knew nothing of the mysterious valley. They pitched their camps in the very shadows of those sinister monoliths which were now no more than shapeless stones.

They placed their dead in the cavern. And Reynolds saw the horrors that took place when the dead came ravening by night among the living to slay and devour – and to drag screaming victims into the nighted caverns and the demoniac doom that awaited them. The legions of hell were loosed in the Valley of the Lost, where chaos reigned and nightmare and madness stalked. Those who were left alive and sane walled up the cavern and rode out of the hills like men riding from hell.

Once more Lost Valley lay gaunt and naked to the stars. Then again the coming of men broke the primal solitude, and smoke rose among the trees. And John Reynolds caught his breath with a start of horror as he saw these were white men, clad in the buckskins of an earlier day – six of them, so much alike that he knew they were brothers.

He saw them fell trees and build a cabin in the clearing. He saw them hunt game in the mountains and begin clearing a field for corn. And all the time he saw the vermin of the hills waiting with ghoulish lust in the darkness. They could not look from their caverns with their nighted eyes, but by their godless sorcery they were aware of all that took place in the valley. They could not come forth in their own bodies in the light, but they waited with the patience of night and the still places.

Reynolds saw one of the brothers find the cavern and open it. He entered and the secret door hung open. The man went into the tunnel. He could not see, in the darkness, the shapes of horror that stole slavering about him, but in sudden panic he lifted his muzzleloading rifle and fired blindly, screaming as the flash showed him the hellish forms that ringed him in. In the utter blackness following the vain shot they rushed, overthrowing him by the power of their numbers, sinking their snaky fangs into his flesh. As he died, he slashed half a dozen of them to pieces with his bowie knife, but the poison did its work quickly.

Reynolds saw them drag the corpse before the altar; he saw again the horrible transmutation of the dead, which rose grinning vacantly and stalked forth. The sun had set in a welter of dull crimson. Night had fallen. To the cabin where his brothers slept, wrapped in their blankets, stalked the dead. Silently the groping hands swung open the door. The Horror crouched in the gloom, its bared teeth shining, its dead eyes gleaming glassily in the starlight. One of the brothers stirred and mumbled, then sat up and stared at the motionless shape in the doorway. He called the dead man's name – then he shrieked hideously – the Horror sprang . . .

From John Reynolds' throat burst a cry of intolerable horror. Abruptly the pictures vanished, with the smoke. He stood in the weird glow before the altar, the tom-toms throbbing softly and evilly, the fiendish faces hemming him in. And now from among them crept, on his belly like the serpent he was, the one which wore the gemmed circlet, venom dripping from his bared fangs. Loathsomely he slithered toward John Reynolds, who fought the temptation to leap upon the foul thing and stamp out its life. There was no escape; he could send his bullets crashing through the swarm and mow down all in front of the muzzle, but those would be as nothing beside the hundreds which hemmed him in. He would die there in the waning light, and they would send his corpse blundering forth, lent a travesty of life by the spirit of the wizard, just as they had sent Saul Fletcher. John Reynolds grew tense as steel as his wolf-like instinct to live rose above the maze of horror into which he had fallen.

And suddenly his human mind rose above the vermin who threatened him, as he was electrified by a swift thought that was like an inspiration. With a fierce inarticulate cry of triumph, he bounded sideways just as the crawling monstrosity lunged. It missed him, sprawling headlong, and Reynolds snatched from the altar the carven serpent, and holding it on high, thrust against it the muzzle of his cocked pistol. He did not need to speak. In the dying light his eyes blazed madly. The Old People wavered back. Before them lay he whose peaked skull Reynolds' pistol had shattered. They knew a crook of his trigger finger would splinter their fantastic god into shining bits.

For a tense space the tableau held. Then Reynolds felt their silent surrender. Freedom in exchange for their god. It was again borne on him that these beings were not truly bestial, since true beasts know no gods. And this knowledge was the more terrible, for it meant that these creatures had evolved into a type neither bestial nor human, a type outside of nature and sanity.

The snakish figures gave back on each side, and the waning light sprang up again. As he went up the tunnel they were close at his heels, and in the dancing uncertain glow he could not be sure whether they walked as a man walks or crawled as a snake crawls. He had a vague impression that their gait was hideously compounded of both. He swerved far aside to avoid the sprawling bulk that had been Saul Fletcher, and so, with his gun muzzle pressed hard against the shining brittle image borne in his left hand, he came to the short flight of steps which led up to the secret door. There they came to a standstill. He turned to face them. They ringed him in a close half-circle, and he understood that they feared to open the secret door lest he dash, with their image, through the cavern into the sunlight, where they could not follow. Nor would he set down the god until the door was opened.

At last they withdrew several yards, and he cautiously set the image on the floor at his feet where he could snatch it up in an instant. How they opened the door he never knew, but it swung wide, and he backed slowly up the steps, his gun trained on the glittering god. He had almost reached the door – one backthrown hand gripped the edge – when the light went out suddenly and the rush came. A volcanic burst of effort shot him backward through the door, which was already rushing shut. As he leaped he emptied his gun full into the fiendish faces that suddenly filled the dark opening. They dissolved in red ruin, and as he raced madly from the outer cavern he heard the soft closing of the secret door, shutting that realm of horror from the human world.

In the glow of the westering sun, John Reynolds staggered drunkenly, clutching at stones and trees as a madman clutches at realities. The keen tenseness that had held him when he fought for his life fell from him and left him a quivering shell of disrupted nerves. An insane titter broke through his lips, and he rocked to and fro in ghastly laughter he could not check.

Then the clink of hoofs on stone sent him leaping behind a cluster of boulders. It was some hidden instinct which led him to take refuge; his conscious mind was too dazed and chaotic for thought or action.

Into the clearing rode Jonas McCrill and his followers – and a sob tore through Reynolds' throat. At first he did not recognize them – did not realize that he had ever seen them before. The feud, with all other sane and normal things, lay lost and forgotten far back in dim vistas beyond the black tunnels of madness.

Two figures rode from the other side of the clearing – Bill Ord and one of the outlaw followers of the McCrills. Strapped to Ord's saddle were several sticks of dynamite, done into a compact package.

"Well, gee whiz," hailed young Ord, "I shore didn't expect to meet yuh-all here. Did yuh git him?"

"Naw," snapped old Jonas," he's done fooled us again. We came up with his horse, but he wasn't on it. The rein was snapped like he'd had it tied and it'd broke away. I dunno where he is, but we'll git him. I'm a-goin' on to Antelope to git some more of the boys. Yuh-all git Saul's body outa that cave and foller me as fast as yuh can."

He reined away and vanished through the trees, and Reynolds, his heart in his mouth, saw the other four approach the cavern.

"Well, by God!" exclaimed Jack Solomon fiercely, "somebody's done been here! Look! Them rocks are torn down!"

John Reynolds watched as one paralyzed. If he sprang up and called to them they would shoot him down before he could voice his warning. Yet it was not that which held him as in a vise; it was sheer horror which robbed him of thought and action, and froze his tongue to the roof of his mouth. His lips parted but no sound came forth. As in a nightmare he saw his enemies disappear into the cavern. Their voices, muffled, came back to him.

"By golly, Saul's gone!"

"Look here, boys, here's a door in the back wall!"

"By thunder, it's open!"

"Let's take a look!"

Suddenly from within the bowels of the hills crashed a fusillade of shots – a burst of hideous screams. Then silence closed like a clammy fog over the Valley of the Lost.

John Reynolds, finding voice at last, cried out as a wounded beast cries, and beat his temples with his clenched fists. He brandished them to the heavens, shrieking wordless blasphemies.

Then he ran staggeringly to Bill Ord's horse which grazed tranquilly with the others beneath the trees. With clammy hands he tore away the package of dynamite, and without separating the sticks he punched a hole in the end of the middle stick with a twig. Then he cut a short – a very short – piece of fuse, and slipped a cap over one end which he inserted into the hole in the dynamite. In a pocket of the rolled up slicker bound behind the saddle he found a match, and lighting the fuse he hurled the bundle into the cavern. Hardly had it struck the back wall when with an earthquake roar it exploded.

The concussion nearly hurled him off his feet. The whole mountain rocked, and with a thunderous crash the cave roof fell. Tons and tons of shattered rock crashed down to obliterate all marks of Ghost Cave, and to shut the door to the pits forever.

John Reynolds walked slowly away; and suddenly the whole horror swept upon him. The earth seemed hideously alive under his feet, the sun foul and blasphemous over his head. The light was sickly, yellowish and evil, and all things were polluted by the unholy knowledge locked in his skull, like hidden drums beating ceaselessly in the blackness beneath the hills.

He had closed one Door forever, but what other nightmare shapes might lurk in hidden places and the dark pits of the earth, gloating over the souls of men? His knowledge was a reeking blasphemy which would never let him rest; forever in his soul would whisper the drums that throbbed in those dark pits where lurked demons that had once been men. He had looked on ultimate foulness, and his knowledge was a taint which would never let him stand clean before men again, or touch the flesh of any living thing without a shudder. If man, molded of divinity, could sink to such verminous obscenities, who could contemplate his eventual destiny unshaken?

And if such beings as the Old People existed, what other horrors might not lurk beneath the visible surface of the universe? He was suddenly aware that he had glimpsed the grinning skull beneath the mask of life, and that that glimpse made life intolerable. All certainty and stability had been swept away, leaving a mad welter of lunacy, nightmare, and stalking horror.

John Reynolds drew his gun and his horny thumb drew back the heavy hammer. Thrusting the muzzle against his temple, he pulled the trigger. The shot crashed echoing through the hills, and the last of the fighting Reynoldses pitched headlong.

Old Jonas McCrill, galloping back at the sound of the blast, found him where he lay, and wondered that his face should be that of an old, old man, his hair white as hoar-frost.

Kelly the Conjure-Man

There are strange tales told when the full moon shines
Of voodoo nights when the ghost-things ran –
But the strangest figure among the pines
Was Kelly the conjure-man.

About seventy-five miles north-east of the great Smackover oil field of Arkansas lies a densely wooded country of pinelands and rivers, rich in folklore and tradition. Here, in the early 1850s came a sturdy race of Scotch-Irish pioneers pushing back the frontier and hewing homes in the tangled wilderness.

Among the many picturesque characters of those early days, one figure stands out, sharply, yet dimly limned against a background of dark legendry and horrific fable – the sinister figure of Kelly, the black conjurer.

Son of a Congo ju-ju man, legend whispered, Kelly, born a slave, exercised in his day unfathomed power among the darkest of the Ouachita pinelands. Where he came from is not exactly known; he drifted into the country shortly after the Civil War and mystery was attendant on his coming as upon all his actions.

Kelly did little work with his hands, and he did not mingle overmuch with his kind. They came to him; he never came to them. His cabin stood on the banks of Tulip Creek, a dark, serpent-like stream winding through the deep overhanging shadows of the pines, and there Kelly lived apart in dark and silent majesty.

A fine figure of barbaric manhood he was, perhaps six foot in height, mighty shouldered, supple like a great black panther. He always wore a vivid red flannel shirt, and great gold rings in his ears and nose heightened the bizarre and fantastic imagery of his appearance. He had little to say to white men or black. Silently, like an uncrowned king of dark Africa he stalked along the roads, looming like a dark inscrutable wizard among the pinelands. His eyes were deep, murky, far-seeing, and his skin was black as tropical night. The very aura of the jungle hung about him and people feared him, perhaps sensing something sinister, something abysmal that lurked in the black waters of his soul and peered through his murky eyes.

He was, indeed, incongruous in his environments. He belonged in another age – another lands – another setting. He belonged in the haunted shadows of a fetish hut, lapped by the monstrous, brutish slumber of ancient Africa.

Kelly the "conjer man" they called him, and to his cabin on lonely Tulip Creek came the black people on mysterious errands. Furtively they stole like shadows through the sombre blackness of the pinelands but what went on in that dim cabin no white man ever knew.

Kelly was a professed dealer in charms, and a dispeller of "conjers". The black folk came to him to have spells lifted from their souls where enemies had placed them by curses and incantations. More, he was a healer-at least he claimed to heal the black people of their diseases. Tuberculosis was rare among white people in that locality, but negroes were subject to its ravages, and these victims Kelly professed to heal. His methods were unique; he burnt snake bones to powder and sifted the powder in an incision made in the victim's arm by means of a lancet made from an old razor. It is a matter of doubt whether anyone was ever healed by these methods – in fact, there is reason to believe the results were appallingly opposite.

Perhaps Kelly did not himself believe he could combat tuberculosis in this manner; perhaps it was but a ruse to get the victim in his power; this is but a supposition, but primitive peoples have strange ways of bringing their fellows under their sway. Among some tribes it is but necessary to procure a lock of hair, a finger nail, a drop of blood, over which to utter certain incantations and perform certain rituals. Then, in the mind of the spell-weaver, and in the mind of the victim as well, the latter is completely under control. And there is the magic of molding a figure of the intended victim from clay. Pins stuck in this figure cause the human model to die agonizingly; place the clay figure in a stream, and as the water dissolves it, the human victim withers and fades away into slow dissolution. All these things are solemn truths in the minds of the voodooists.

Be that as it may, Kelly soon began to exercise unusual powers over the darkies of the locality. From a dispeller of "conjers" he became, it would seem, a weaver of spells himself. Negroes began to go violently insane, a rumor laid their obsessions at Kelly's door. Whether the cause of their insanity was physical or mental was not known, but that their minds were affected by some uncanny thing was well evident. They were obsessed by the horrible belief that their stomachs were full of living snakes, created by the spell of some master conjurer, and at the mention of this nameless wizard, suspicion turned to Kelly. Was it hypnosis, some obscure malady or maddening drug, or the action of sheer fear? No white man knew, yet the victims were indisputably mad.

In every community of whites and blacks, at least in the South, a deep, dark current flows forever, out of sight of the whites who but dimly suspect its existence. A dark current of colored folks' thoughts, deeds, ambitions and aspirations, like a river flowing unseen through the jungle. No white man ever knew why Kelly – if Kelly it were – drove black men and black women mad. What was the secret of grim power, what the secret of his dark ambitions, no white man ever knew.

And Kelly never spoke of them, certainly; he went his way, silent, brooding, darkly majestic, that satanic something growing in his shadowy eyes until he seemed to look on white people as if they too were blind mewling puppets in the hollow of his black hand.

Then, in the late '70s, Kelly vanished. The word is to be taken literally. His cabin on Tulip Creek stood empty, the slab door sagging open on the wooden hinges, and he was seen no more, stalking like a dark ghost through the pinelands. Perhaps the colored people knew, but they never spoke. He had come in mystery, in mystery he lived, and in mystery he went and no man knew the road of his going. At least no man ever admitted that he knew. Perhaps the gloomy waters knew. Perhaps Kelly's victims turned on him at last. That lonely cabin in the black shadows of the moaning pines might have known a grisly midnight crime; the dusky waters of Tulip Creek might have received a form that splashed soggily and silently sank.

Or perhaps the conjure-man merely went his mysterious way in the night for reasons of his own, and on some other river pursued his fantastic career. None knows. Mystery hangs over his coming and his going, like a cloud impenetrable as night among the piney-woods, than which there is no blacker darkness this side of Oblivion.

But even today his shadow haunts the long dim river-reaches and when the wind drones through the black pines under the stars, the old black people will tell you it is the spirit of the conjure-man whispering to the dead in the black shadows of the pinelands.

Black Canaan

Call from Canaan

"Trouble on Tularoosa Creek!" A warning to send cold fear along the spine of any man who was raised in that isolated back-country, called Canaan, that lies between Tularoosa and Black River – to send him racing back to that swamp-bordered region, wherever the word might reach him.

It was only a whisper from the withered lips of a shuffling black crone, who vanished among the throng before I could seize her; but it was enough. No need to seek confirmation; no need to inquire by what mysterious, black-folk way the word had come to her. No need to inquire what obscure forces worked to unseal those wrinkled lips to a Black River man. It was enough that the warning had been given – and understood.

Understood? How could any Black River man fail to understand that warning? It could have but one meaning-old hates seething again in the jungle-deeps of the swamplands, dark shadows slipping through the cypress, and massacre stalking out of the black, mysterious village that broods on the moss-festooned shore of sullen Tularoosa.

Within an hour New Orleans was falling further behind me with every turn of the churning wheel. To every man born in Canaan, there is always an invisible tie that draws him back whenever his homeland is imperiled by the murky shadow that has lurked in its jungled recesses for more than half a century.

The fastest boats I could get seemed maddeningly slow for that race up the big river, and up the smaller, more turbulent stream. I was burning with impatience when I stepped off on the Sharpsville landing, with the last fifteen miles of my journey yet to make. It was past midnight, but I hurried to the livery stable where, by tradition half a century old, there is always a Buckner horse, day or night.

As a sleepy black boy fastened the cinches, I turned to the owner of the stable, Joe Lafely, yawning and gaping in the light of the lantern he upheld. "There are rumors of trouble on Tularoosa?"

He paled in the lantern-light.

"I don't know. I've heard talk. But you people in Canaan are a shut-mouthed clan. No one *outside* knows what goes on in there – "

The night swallowed his lantern and his stammering voice as I headed west along the pike.

The moon set red through the black pines. Owls hooted away off in the woods, and somewhere a hound howled his ancient wistfulness to the night. In the darkness that foreruns dawn I crossed Nigger Head Creek, a streak of shining black fringed by walls of solid shadows. My horse's hoof splashed through the shallow water and clinked on the wet stones, startlingly loud in the stillness. Beyond Nigger Head Creek began the country men called Canaan.

Heading in the same swamp, miles to the north, that gives birth to Tularoosa, Nigger Head flows due south to join Black River a few miles west of Sharpsville, while the Tularoosa runs westward to meet the same river at a higher point. The trend of Black River is from northwest to southeast; so these three streams from the great irregular triangle known as Canaan.

In Canaan lived the sons and daughters of the white frontiersmen who first settled the country, and the sons and daughters of their slaves. Joe Lafely was right; we were an isolated, shut-mouthed breed, self-sufficient, jealous of our seclusion and independence.

Beyond Nigger Head the woods thickened, the road narrowed, winding through unfenced pinelands, broken by live-oaks and cypresses. There was no sound except the soft clop-clop of hoofs in the thin dust, the creak of the saddle. Then someone laughed throatily in the shadows.

I drew up and peered into the trees. The moon had set and dawn was not yet come, but a faint glow quivered among the trees, and by it I made out a dim figure under the moss-hung branches. My hand instinctively sought the butt of one of the dueling-pistols I wore, and the action brought another low, musical laugh, mocking yet seductive. I glimpsed a brown face, a pair of scintillant eyes, white teeth displayed in an insolent smile.

"Who the devil are you?" I demanded.

"Why do you ride so late, Kirby Buckner?" Taunting laughter bubbled in the voice. The accent was foreign and unfamiliar; a faintly negroid twang was there, but it was rich and sensuous as the rounded body of its owner. In the lustrous pile of dusky hair a great white blossom glimmered palely in the darkness.

"What are you doing here?" I demanded. "You're a long way from any darky cabin. And you're a stranger to me."

"I came to Canaan since you went away," she answered. "My cabin is on the Tularoosa. But now I've lost my way. And my poor brother has hurt his leg and cannot walk."

"Where is your brother?" I asked, uneasily. Her perfect English was disquieting to me, accustomed as I was to the dialect of the black folk.

"Back in the woods, there – far back!" She indicated the black depths with a swaying motion of her supple body rather than a gesture of her hand, smiling audaciously as she did so.

I knew there was no injured brother, and she knew I knew it, and laughed at me. But a strange turmoil of conflicting emotions stirred in me. I had never before paid any attention to a black or brown woman. But this quadroon girl was different from any I had ever seen. Her features were regular as a white woman's, and her speech was not that of a common wench. Yet she was barbaric, in the open lure of her smile, in the gleam of her eyes, in the shameless posturing of her voluptuous body. Every gesture, every motion she made set her apart from the ordinary run of women; her beauty was untamed and lawless, meant to madden rather than to soothe, to make a man blind and dizzy, to rouse in him all the unreined passions that are his heritage from his ape ancestors.

I hardly remember dismounting and tying my horse. My blood pounded suffocatingly through the veins in my temples as I scowled down at her, suspicious yet fascinated.

"How do you know my name? Who *are* you?"

With a provocative laugh, she seized my hand and drew me deeper into the shadows. Fascinated by the lights gleaming in her dark eyes, I was hardly aware of her action.

"Who does not know Kirby Buckner?" she laughed. "All the people of

Canaan speak of you, white or black. Come! My poor brother longs to look upon you!" And she laughed with malicious triumph.

It was this brazen effrontery that brought me to my senses. Its cynical mockery broke the almost hypnotic spell in which I had fallen.

I stopped short, throwing her hand aside, snarling: "What devil's game are you up to wench?"

Instantly the smiling siren was changed to a blood-mad jungle cat. Her eyes flamed murderously, her red lips writhed in a snarl as she leaped back, crying out shrilly. A rush of bare feet answered her call. The first faint light of dawn struck through the branches, revealing my assailants, three gaunt black giants. I saw the gleaming whites of their eyes, their bare glistening teeth, the sheen of naked steel in their hands.

My first bullet crashed through the head of the tallest man, knocking him dead in full stride. My second pistol snapped – the cap had somehow slipped from the nipple. I dashed it into a black face, and as the man fell, half stunned, I whipped out my bowie knife and closed with the other. I parried his stab and my counter-stroke ripped across his belly-muscles. He screamed like a swamp-panther and made a wild grab for my knife wrist, but I struck him in the mouth with my clenched left fist, and felt his lips split and teeth crumble under the impact as he reeled backward, his knife waving wildly. Before he could regain his balance I was after him, thrusting, and got home under his ribs. He groaned and slipped to the ground in a puddle of his own blood.

I wheeled about, looking for the other. He was just rising, blood streaming down his face and neck. As I started for him he sounded a panicky yell and plunged into the underbrush. The crashing of his blind flight came back to me, muffled with distance. The girl was gone.

2

The Stranger on Tularoosa

The curious glow that had first showed me the quadroon girl had vanished. In my confusion I had forgotten it. But I did not waste time on vain conjecture as to its source, as I groped my way back to the road. Mystery had come to the pinelands and a ghostly light that hovered among the trees was only part of it.

My horse snorted and pulled against his tether, frightened by the smell of blood that hung in the heavy damp air. Hoofs clattered down the road, forms bulked in the growing light. Voices challenged.

"Who's that? Step out and name yourself, before we shoot!"

"Hold on, Esau!" I called. "It's me – Kirby Buckner!"

"Kirby Buckner, by thunder!" ejaculated Esau McBride, lowering his pistol. The tall rangy forms of the other riders loomed behind him.

"We heard a shot," said McBride. "We was ridin' patrol on the roads around Grimesville like we've been ridin' every night for a week now – ever since they killed Ridge Jackson."

"Who killed Ridge Jackson?"

"The swamp niggers. That's all we know. Ridge come out of the woods early one mornin' and knocked at Cap'n Sorley's door. Cap'n says he was the color of ashes. He hollered for the Cap'n for God's sake to let him in, he had somethin' awful to tell him. Well, the Cap'n started down to open the door, but before he'd got down the stairs he heard an awful row among the dogs outside, and a man screamed he reckoned was Ridge. And when he got to the door, there wasn't nothin' but a dead dog layin' in the yard with his head knocked in, and the others all goin' crazy. They found Ridge later, out in the pines a few hundred yards from the house. From the way the ground and the bushes was tore up, he'd been dragged that far by four or five men. Maybe they got tired of haulin' him along. Anyway, they beat his head into a pulp and left him layin' there."

"I'll be damned!" I muttered. "Well, there's a couple of niggers lying back there in the brush. I want to see if you know them. I don't."

A moment later we were standing in the tiny glade, now white in the growing dawn. A black shape sprawled on the matted pine needles, his head in a pool of blood and brains. There were wide smears of blood on the ground and bushes on the other side of the little clearing, but the wounded black was gone.

McBride turned the carcass with his foot.

"One of them niggers that came in with Saul Stark," he muttered.

"Who the devil's that?" I demanded.

"Strange nigger that moved in since you went down the river last time. Come from South Carolina, he says. Lives in that old cabin in the Neck – you know, the shack where Colonel Reynolds' niggers used to live."

"Suppose you ride on to Grimesville with me, Esau," I said, "and tell me about this business as we ride. The rest of you might scout around and see if you can find a wounded nigger in the brush."

They agreed without question; the Buckners have always been tacitly considered leaders in Canaan, and it came natural for me to offer suggestions. Nobody gives *orders* to white men in Canaan.

"I reckoned you'd be showin' up soon," opined McBride, as we rode along the whitening road. "You usually manage to keep up with what's happenin' in Canaan."

"What is happening?" I inquired. "I don't know anything. An old black woman dropped me the word in New Orleans that there was trouble. Naturally I came home as fast as I could. Three strange niggers waylaid me – " I was curiously disinclined to mention the woman. "And now you tell me somebody killed Ridge Jackson. What's it all about?"

"The swamp niggers killed Ridge to shut his mouth," announced McBride. "That's the only way to figure it. They must have been close behind him when he knocked on Cap'n Sorley's door. Ridge worked for Cap'n Sorley most of his life; he thought a lot of the old man. Some kind of deviltry's bein' brewed up in the swamps, and Ridge wanted to warn the Cap'n. That's the way I figure it."

"Warn him about what?"

"We don't know," confessed McBride. "That's why we're all on edge. It must be an uprisin'."

That word was enough to strike chill fear into the heart of any Canaan-dweller. The blacks had risen in 1845, and the red terror of that revolt was not forgotten, nor the three lesser rebellions before it, when the slaves rose and spread fire and slaughter from Tularoosa to the shores of Black River. The fear of a black uprising lurked for ever in the depths of that forgotten back-country; the very children absorbed it in their cradles.

"What makes you think it might be an uprising?" I asked.

"The niggers have all quit the fields, for one thing. They've all got business in Goshen. I ain't seen a nigger nigh Grimesville for a week. The town niggers have pulled out."

In Canaan we still draw a distinction born in antebellum days. "Town-niggers" are descendents of the house-servants of the old days, and most of them live in or near Grimesville. There are not many, compared to the mass of "swamp-niggers" who dwell on tiny farms along the creeks and the edge of the swamps, or in the black village of Goshen, on the Tularoosa. They are descendants of the field-hands of other days, and, untouched by the mellow civilization which refined the natures of the house-servants, they remain as primitive as their African ancestors.

"Where have the town-niggers gone?" I asked.

"Nobody knows. They lit out a week ago. Probably hidin' down on Black River. If we win, they'll come back. If we don't, they'll take refuge in Sharpsville."

I found his matter-of-factness a bit ghastly, as if the actuality of the uprising were an assured fact.

"Well, what have you done?" I demanded.

"Ain't much we could do," he confessed. "The niggers ain't made no open move, outside of killin' Ridge Jackson; and we couldn't prove who done that, or why they done it.

"They ain't done nothin' but clear out. But that's mighty suspicious. We can't keep from thinkin' Saul Stark's behind it."

"Who is this fellow?" I asked.

"I told you all I know, already. He got permission to settle in that old deserted cabin on the Neck; a great big black devil that talks better English than I like to hear a nigger talk. But he was respectful enough. He had three or four big south Carolina bucks with him, and a brown wench which we don't know whether she's his daughter, sister, wife or what. He ain't been in to Grimesville but that one time, and a few weeks after he came to Canaan, the niggers begun actin' curious. Some of the boys wanted to ride over to Goshen and have a show-down, but that's takin' a desperate chance."

I knew he was thinking of a ghastly tale told us by our grandfathers of how a punitive expedition from Grimesville was once ambushed and butchered among the dense thickets that masked Goshen, then a rendezvous for runaway slaves, while another red-handed band devastated Grimesville, left defenseless by that reckless invasion.

"Might take all the men to get Saul Stark," said McBride. "And we don't dare leave the town unprotected. But we'll soon have to – hello, what's this?"

We had emerged from the trees and were just entering the village of

Grimesville, the community center of the white population of Canaan. It was not pretentious. Log cabins, neat and whitewashed, were plentiful enough. Small cottages clustered about big, old-fashioned houses which sheltered the rude aristocracy of that backwoods democracy. All the "planter" families lived "in town." "The country" was occupied by their tenants, and by the small independent farmers, white and black.

A small log cabin stood near the point where the road wound out of the deep forest. Voices emanated from it, in accents of menace, and a tall lanky figure, rifle in hand, stood at the door.

"Howdy, Esau!" this man hailed us. "By golly, if it ain't Kirby Buckner! Glad to see you, Kirby."

"What's up, Dick?" asked McBride.

"Got a nigger in the shack, tryin' to make him talk. Bill Reynolds seen him sneakin' past the edge of town about daylight, and nabbed him."

"Who is it?" I asked.

"Tope Sorley. John Willoughby's gone after a blacksnake."

With a smothered oath I swung off my horse and strode in, followed by McBride. Half a dozen men in boots and gun-belts clustered about a pathetic figure cowering on an old broken bunk. Tope Sorley (his forebears had adopted the name of the family that owned them, in slave days) was a pitiable sight just then. His skin was ashy, his teeth chattered spasmodically, and his eyes seemed to be trying to roll back into his head.

"Here's Kirby!" ejaculated one of the men as I pushed my way through the group. "I'll bet he'll make the coon talk!"

"Here comes John with the blacksnake!" shouted someone, and a tremor ran through Tope Sorley's shivering body.

I pushed aside the butt of the ugly whip thrust eagerly into my hand.

"Tope," I said, "you've worked one of my father's farms for years. Has any Buckner ever treated you any way but square?"

"Nossuh," came faintly.

"Then what are you afraid of? Why don't you speak up? Something's going on in the swamps. You know, and I want you to tell us why the town niggers have all run away, why Ridge Jackson was killed, why the swamp niggers are acting so mysteriously."

"And what kind of devilment that cussed Saul Stark's cookin' up over on Tularoosa!" shouted one of the men.

238

Tope seemed to shrink into himself as the mention of Stark.

"I don't dast," he shuddered. "He'd put me in the swamp!"

"Who?" I demanded. "Stark? Is Stark a conjer man?"

Tope sank his head in his hands and did not answer. I laid my hand on his shoulder.

"Tope," I said, "you know if you'll talk, we'll protect you. If you don't talk, I don't think Stark can treat you much rougher than these men are likely to. Now spill it – what's it all about?"

He lifted desperate eyes.

"You-all got to lemme stay here," he shuddered. "And guard me, and gimme money to git away on when de trouble's over."

"We'll do all that," I agreed instantly. "You can stay right here in this cabin, until you're ready to leave for New Orleans or wherever you want to go."

He capitulated, collapsed, and words tumbled from his livid lips.

"Saul Stark's a conjer man. He come here because it's way off in back-country. He aim to kill all de white folks in Canaan – "

A growl rose from the group, such a growl as rises unbidden from the throat of the wolf pack that scents peril.

"He aim to make hisself king of Canaan. He sent me to spy dis mornin' to see if Mistah Kirby got through. He sent men to waylay him on de road, cause he knowed Mistah Kirby was comin' back to Canaan. Niggers makin' voodoo on Tularoosa, for weeks now. Ridge Jackson was goin' to tell Cap'n Sorley; so Stark's niggers foller him and kill him. That make Stark mad. He ain't want to kill Ridge; he want to put him in de swamp with Tunk Bixby and de others."

"What are you talking about?" I demanded.

Far out in the woods rose a strange, shrill cry, like the cry of a bird. But no such bird ever called before in Canaan. Tope cried out as if in answer, and shivered into himself. He sank down on the bunk in a veritable palsy of fear.

"That was a signal!" I snapped. "Some of you go out there."

Half a dozen men hastened to follow my suggestion, and I returned to the task of making Tope renew his revelations. It was useless. Some hideous fear had sealed his lips. He lay shuddering like a stricken animal, and did not even seem to hear our questions. No one suggested the use of the blacksnake. Anyone could see the negro was paralyzed with terror.

Presently the searchers returned empty-handed. They had seen no one, and the thick carpet of pine needles showed no foot-prints. The men looked at me expectantly. As Colonel Buckner's son, leadership was expected of me.

"What about it, Kirby?" asked McBride. "Breckinridge and the others have just rode in. They couldn't find that nigger you cut up."

"There was another nigger I hit with a pistol," I said. "Maybe he came back and helped him." Still I could not bring myself to mention the brown girl. "Leave Tope alone. Maybe he'll get over his scare after a while. Better keep a guard in the cabin all the time. The swamp niggers may try to get him as they got Ridge Jackson. Better scour the roads around town, Esau; there may be some of them hiding in the woods."

"I will. I reckon you'll want to be gettin' up to the house, now, and seein' your folks."

"Yes. And I want to swap these toys for a couple of .44s. Then I'm going to ride out and tell the country people to come into Grimesville. If it's to be an uprising, we don't know when it will commence."

"You're not goin' alone!" protested McBride.

"I'll be all right," I answered impatiently. "All this may not amount to anything, but it's best to be on the safe side. That's why I'm going after the country folks. No, I don't want anybody to go with me. Just in case the niggers do get crazy enough to attack the town, you'll need every man you've got. But if I can get hold of some of the swamp niggers and talk to them, I don't think there'll be any attack."

"You won't get a glimpse of them," McBride predicted.

3

Shadows Over Canaan

It was not yet noon when I rode out of the village westward along the old road. Thick woods swallowed me quickly. Dense walls of pines marched with me on either hand, giving way occasionally to fields enclosed with straggling rail fences, with the log cabins of the tenants or owners close by, with the usual litters of tow-headed children and lank hound dogs.

Some of the cabins were empty. The occupants, if white, had already gone into Grimesville; if black they had gone into the swamps, or fled to the hidden refuge of the town niggers, according to their affiliations. In any event, the vacancy of their hovels was sinister in its suggestion.

A tense silence brooded over the pinelands, broken only by the occasional wailing call of a plowman. My progress was not swift, for from time to time I turned off the main road to give warning to some lonely cabin huddled on the bank of one of the many thicket-fringed creeks. Most of these farms were south of the road; the white settlements did not extend far to the north; for in that direction lay Tularoosa Creek with its jungle-grown marshes that stretched inlets southward like groping fingers.

The actual warning was brief; there was no need to argue or explain. I called from the saddle: "Get into town; trouble's brewing on Tularoosa." Faces paled, and people dropped whatever they were doing: the men to grab guns and jerk mules from the plow to hitch to the wagons, the women to bundle necessary belongings together and shrill the children in from their play. As I rode I heard the cow-horns blowing up and down the creeks, summoning men from distant fields – blowing as they had not blown for a generation, a warning and a defiance which I knew carried to such ears as might be listening in the edges of the swamplands. The country emptied itself behind me, flowing in thin but steady streams toward Grimesville.

The sun was swinging low among the topmost branches of the pines when I reached the Richardson cabin, the westernmost "white" cabin in Canaan. Beyond it lay the Neck, the angle formed by the junction of Tularoosa with Black River, a jungle-like expanse occupied only by scattered negro huts.

Mrs. Richardson called to me anxiously from the cabin stoop.

"Well, Mr. Kirby, I'm glad to see you back in Canaan! We been hearin' the horns all evenin', Mr. Kirby. What's it mean? It – it ain't – "

"You and Joe better get the children and light out for Grimesville," I answered. "Nothing's happened yet, and may not, but it's best to be on the safe side. All the people are going."

"We'll go right now!" she gasped, paling, as she snatched off her apron. "Lord, Mr. Kirby, you reckon they'll cut us off before we can git to town?"

I shook my head. "They'll strike at night, if at all. We're just playing safe. Probably nothing will come of it."

"I bet you're wrong there," she predicted, scurrying about in desperate activity. "I been hearin' a drum beatin' off toward Saul Stark's cabin, off and on, for a week now. They beat drums back in the Big Uprisin'. My pappy's told me about it many's the time. The niggers skinned his brother alive. The horns was blowin' all up and down the creeks, and the drums was beatin' louder'n the horns could blow. You'll be ridin' back with us, won't you, Mr. Kirby?"

"No; I'm going to scout down along the trail a piece."

"Don't go too far. You're liable to run into old Saul Stark and his devils. Lord! *Where* is that man? Joe! *Joe!*"

As I rode down the trail her shrill voice followed me, thin-edged with fear.

Beyond the Richardson farm, pines gave way to live-oaks. The underbrush grew ranker. A scent of rotting vegetation impregnated the fitful breeze. Occasionally I sighted a nigger hut, half hidden under the trees, but always it stood silent and deserted. Empty nigger cabins meant but one thing: the blacks were collecting at Goshen, some miles to the east on the Tularoosa; and that gathering, too, could have but one meaning.

My goal was Saul Stark's hut. My intention had been formed when I heard Tope Sorley's incoherent tale. There could be no doubt that Saul Stark was the dominant figure in this web of mystery. With Saul Stark I meant to deal. That I might be risking my life was a chance any man must take who assumes the responsibility of leadership.

The sun slanted through the lower branches of the cypresses when I reached it – a log cabin set against a background of gloomy tropical jungle. A few steps beyond it began the uninhabitable swamp in which Tularoosa emptied its murky current into Black River. A reek of decay hung in the air; gray moss bearded the trees, and poisonous vines twisted in rank tangles.

I called: "Stark! Saul Stark! Come out here!"

There was no answer. A primitive silence hovered over the tiny clearing. I dismounted, tied my horse and approached the crude, heavy door. Perhaps this cabin held a clue to the mystery of Saul Stark; at least it doubtless contained the implements and paraphernalia of his noisome craft. The faint breeze dropped suddenly. The stillness became so intense it was like a physical impact. I paused, startled; it was as if some inner instinct had shouted urgent warning.

As I stood there every fiber of me quivered in response to that sub-conscious warning; some obscure, deep-hidden instinct sensed peril, as a man senses the presence of the rattlesnake in the darkness, or the swamp panther crouching in the bushes. I drew a pistol, sweeping the trees and bushes, but saw no shadow or movement to betray the ambush I feared. But my instinct was unerring; what I sensed was not lurking in the woods about me; it was inside the cabin – *waiting*. Trying to shake off the feeling, and irked by a vague half-memory that kept twitching at the back of my brain, I again advanced. And again I stopped short, with one foot on the tiny stoop, and a hand half advanced to pull open the door. A chill shivering swept over me, a sensation like that which shakes a man to whom a flicker of lightning has revealed the black abyss into which another blind step would have hurled him. For the first time in my life I knew the meaning of fear; I knew that black horror lurked in that sullen cabin under the moss-bearded cypresses – a horror against which every primitive instinct that was my heritage cried out in panic.

And that insistent half-memory woke suddenly. It was the memory of a story of how voodoo men leave their huts guarded in their absence by a powerful ju-ju spirit to deal madness and death to the intruder. White men ascribed such deaths to superstitious fright and hypnotic suggestion. But in that instant I understood my sense of lurking peril; I comprehended the horror that breathed like an invisible mist from that accursed hut. I sensed the reality of the ju-ju, of which the grotesque wooden images which voodoo men place in their huts are only a symbol.

Saul Stark was gone; but he had left a Presence to guard his hut.

I backed away, sweat beading the backs of my hands. Not for a bag of gold would I have peered into the shuttered windows or touched that unbolted door. My pistol hung in my hand, useless I knew against the Thing in that cabin. What it was I could not know, but I knew it was some brutish, soulless entity drawn from the black swamps by the spells of voodoo. Man and the natural animals are not the only sentient beings that haunt this planet. There are invisible Things – black spirits of the deep swamps and the slimes of the river beds – the negroes know of them . . .

My horse was trembling like a leaf and he shouldered close to me as if seeking security in bodily contact. I mounted and reined away, fighting a panicky urge to strike in the spurs and bolt madly down the trail.

I breathed an involuntary sigh of relief as the somber clearing fell away behind me and was lost from sight. I did not, as soon as I was out of sight of the cabin, revile myself for a silly fool. My experience was too vivid in my mind. It was not cowardice that prompted my retreat from the empty hut; it was the natural instinct of self-preservation, such as keeps a squirrel from entering the lair of a rattlesnake.

My horse snorted and shied violently. A gun was in my hand before I saw what had startled me. Again a rich musical laugh taunted me.

She was leaning against a bent tree-trunk, her hands clasped behind her sleek head, insolently posing her sensuous figure. The barbaric fascination of her was not dispelled by daylight; if anything, the glow of the low-hanging sun enhanced it.

"Why did you not go into the ju-ju cabin, Kirby Buckner?" she mocked, lowering her arms and moving insolently out from the tree.

She was clad as I had never seen a swamp woman, or any other woman, dressed. Snakeskin sandals were on her feet, sewn with tiny sea-shells that were never gathered on this continent. A short silken skirt of flaming crimson molded her full hips, and was upheld by a broad bead-worked girdle. Barbaric anklets and armlets clashed as she moved, heavy ornaments of crudely hammered gold that were as African as her loftily piled coiffure. Nothing else she wore, and on her bosom, between her arching breasts, I glimpsed the faint lines of tattooing on her brown skin.

She posed derisively before me, not in allure, but in mockery. Triumphant malice blazed in her dark eyes; her red lips curled with cruel mirth. Looking at her then I found it easy to believe all the tales I had heard of torture and mutilations inflicted by the women of savage races on wounded enemies. She was alien, even in this primitive setting; she needed a grimmer, more bestial background, a background of steaming jungle, reeking black swamps, flaring fires and cannibal feasts, and the bloody altars of abysmal tribal gods.

"Kirby Buckner!" She seemed to caress the syllables with her red tongue, yet the very intonation was an obscene insult. "Why did you not enter Saul Stark's cabin? It was not locked! Did you fear what you might see there?

Did you fear you might come out with your hair white like an old man's, and the drooling lips of an imbecile?"

"What's in that hut?" I demanded.

She laughed in my face, and snapped her fingers with a peculiar gesture.

"One of the ones which come oozing like black mist out of the night when Saul Stark beats the ju-ju drum and shrieks the black incantation to the gods that crawl on their bellies in the swamp."

"What is he doing here? The black folk were quiet until he came."

Her red lips curled disdainfully. "Those black dogs? They are his slaves. If they disobey he kills them, *or puts them in the swamp.* For long we have looked for a place to begin our rule. We have chosen Canaan. You whites must go. And since we know that white people can never be driven away from their land, we must kill you all."

It was my turn to laugh, grimly.

"They tried that, back in '45."

"They did not have Saul Stark to lead them, then," she answered calmly.

"Well, suppose they won? Do you think that would be the end of it? Other white men would come into Canaan and kill them all."

"They would have to cross water," she answered. "We can defend the rivers and creeks. Saul Stark will have many *servants in the swamps* to do his bidding. He will be king of dark Canaan. No one can cross the waters to come against him. He will rule his tribe, as his fathers ruled their tribes in the Ancient Land."

"Mad as a loon!" I muttered. Then curiosity impelled me to ask: "Who is this fool? What are you to him?"

"He is the son of a Kongo witch-finder, and he is the greatest voodoo priest out of the Ancient Land," she answered, laughing at me again. "I? You shall learn who I am, tonight in the swamp, in the House of Damballah."

"Yes?" I grunted. "What's to prevent me from taking you into Grimesville with me? You know the answers to questions I'd like to ask."

Her laughter was like the slash of a velvet whip.

"*You* drag me to the village of the whites? Not all death and hell could keep me from the Dance of the Skull, tonight in the House of Damballah. You are my captive, already." She laughed derisively as I started and glared into the shadows about me. "No one is hiding there. I am alone, and you are the strongest man in Canaan. Even Saul Stark fears you, for he sent me with three men to kill you before you could reach the village. Yet you are my captive. I have but to beckon, so" – she crooked a contemptuous finger – "and you will follow to the fires of Damballah and the knives of the torturers."

I laughed at her, but my mirth rang hollow. I could not deny the incredible magnetism of this brown enchantress; it fascinated and impelled, drawing me toward her, beating at my will-power. I could not fail to recognize it any more than I could fail to recognize the peril of the ju-ju hut.

My agitation was apparent to her, for her eyes flashed with unholy triumph.

"Black men are fools, all but Saul Stark," she laughed. "White men are fools, too. I am the daughter of a white man, who lived in the hut of a black king and mated with his daughters. I know the strength of white men, and their weakness. I failed last night when I met you in the woods, but now I cannot fail!" Savage exultation thrummed in her voice. "By the blood in your veins I have snared you. The knife of the man you killed scratched your hand – seven drops of blood that fell on the pine needles have given me your soul! I took that blood, and Saul Stark gave me the man who ran away. Saul Stark hates cowards. With his hot, quivering heart, and seven drops of your blood, Kirby Buckner, deep in the swamps I have made such magic as none but a Bride of Damballah can make. Already you feel its urge! Oh, you are strong! The man you fought with the knife died less than an hour later. But you cannot fight me. Your blood makes you my slave. I have put a conjurement upon you."

By heaven, it was not mere madness she was mouthing! Hypnotism, magic, call it what you will, I felt its onslaught on my brain and will – a blind, senseless impulse that seemed to be rushing me against my will to the brink of some nameless abyss.

"I have made a charm you cannot resist!" she cried. "When I call you, you will come! Into the deep swamps you will follow me. You will see the Dance of the Skull, and you will see the doom of a poor fool who sought to betray Saul Stark – who dreamed he could resist the Call of Damballah when it came. Into the swamp he goes tonight, with Tunk Bixby and the other four fools who opposed Saul Stark. You shall see that. You shall know and understand your own doom. And then you too shall go into the swamp, into darkness and silence deep as the darkness of nighted Africa! But before the darkness engulfs you there will be sharp knives, and little fires – oh, you will scream for death, even for the death that is beyond death!"

With a choking cry I whipped out a pistol and leveled it full at her breast. It was cocked and my finger was on the trigger. At that range I could not miss. But she looked full into the black muzzle and laughed – laughed – laughed, in wild peals that froze the blood in my veins.

And I sat there like an image pointing a pistol I could not fire! A frightful paralysis gripped me. I knew, with numbing certainty, that my life depended on the pull of that trigger, but I could not crook my finger – not though every muscle in my body quivered with the effort and sweat broke out on my face in clammy beads.

She ceased laughing, then, and stood looking at me in a manner indescribably sinister.

"You cannot shoot me, Kirby Buckner," she said quietly. "I have enslaved your soul. You cannot understand my power, but it has ensnared you. It is the Lure of the Bride of Damballah – the blood I have mixed with the mystic waters of Africa drawing the blood in your veins. Tonight you will come to me, in the House of Damballah."

"You lie!" My voice was an unnatural croak bursting from dry lips. "You've hypnotized me, you she-devil, so I can't pull this trigger. But you can't drag me across the swamps to you."

"It is you who lie," she returned calmly. "You know you lie. Ride back towards Grimesville or wherever you will, Kirby Buckner. But when the sun sets and the black shadows crawl out of the swamps, you will see me beckoning you, and you will follow me. Long I have planned your doom, Kirby Buckner, since first I heard the white men of Canaan talking of you. It was I who sent the word down the river that brought you back to Canaan. Not even Saul Stark knows of my plans for you.

"At dawn Grimesville shall go up in flames, and the heads of the white men will be tossed in the blood-running streets. But tonight is the Night of Damballah, and a white sacrifice shall be given to the black gods. Hidden among the trees you shall watch the Dance of the Skull – and then I shall call you forth – to die! And now, go fool! Run as far and as fast as you will.

At sunset, wherever you are, you will turn your footsteps toward the House of Damballah!"

And with the spring of a panther she was gone into the thick brush, and as she vanished the strange paralysis dropped from me. With a gasped oath I fired blindly after her, but only a mocking laugh floated back to me.

Then in a panic I wrenched my horse about and spurred him down the trail. Reason and logic had momentarily vanished from my brain, leaving me in the grasp of blind primitive fear. I had confronted sorcery beyond my power to resist. I had felt my will mastered by the mesmerism in a brown woman's eyes. And now one driving urge overwhelmed me – a wild desire to cover as much distance as I could before that low-hanging sun dipped below the horizon and the black shadows came crawling from the swamps.

And yet I knew I could not outrun the grisly specter that menaced me. I was like a man fleeing in a nightmare, trying to escape from a monstrous phantom which kept pace with me despite my desperate speed.

I had not reached the Richardson cabin when above the drumming of my flight I heard the clop of hoofs ahead of me, and an instant later, sweeping around a kink in the trail, I almost rode down a tall, lanky man on an equally gaunt horse.

He yelped and dodged back as I jerked my horse to its haunches, my pistol presented at his breast.

"Look out, Kirby! It's me – Jim Braxton! My God, you look like you'd seen a ghost! What's chasin' you?"

"Where are you going?" I demanded, lowering my gun.

"Lookin' for you. Folks got worried as it got late and you didn't come in with the refugees. I 'lowed I'd light out and look for you. Miz Richardson said you rode into the Neck. Where in tarnation you been?"

"To Saul Stark's cabin."

"You takin' a big chance. What'd you find there?"

The sight of another white man had somewhat steadied my nerves. I opened my mouth to narrate my adventure, and was shocked to hear myself saying, instead: "Nothing. He wasn't there."

"Thought I heard a gun crack, a while ago," he retorted, glancing sharply at me sidewise.

"I shot at a copperhead," I answered, and shuddered. This reticence regarding the brown woman was compulsory; I could no more speak of her than I could pull the trigger of the pistol aimed at her. And I cannot describe the horror that beset me when I realized this. The conjer spells the black men feared were not lies, I realized sickly; demons in human form *did* exist who were able to enslave men's will and thoughts.

Braxton was eyeing me strangely.

"We're lucky the woods ain't full of black copperheads," he said. "Tope Sorley's pulled out."

"What do you mean?" By an effort I pulled myself together.

"Just that. Tom Breckinridge was in the cabin with him. Tope hadn't said a word since you talked to him. Just laid on that bunk and shivered. Then a kind of holler begun way out in the woods, and Tom went to the door with his rifle-gun, but couldn't see nothin'. Well, while he was standin' there he got a lick on the head from *behind*, and as he fell he seen that crazy nigger Tope jump over him and light out for the woods. Tom he taken a shot at him, but missed. Now what you make of that?"

"The Call of Damballah!" I muttered, a chill perspiration beading my body. "God! The poor devil!"

"Huh? What's that?"

"For God's sake let's not stand here mouthing! The sun will soon be down!" In a frenzy of impatience I kicked my mount down the trail. Braxton followed me, obviously puzzled. With a terrific effort I got a grip on myself. How madly fantastic it was that Kirby Buckner should be shaking in the grip of unreasoning terror! It was so alien to my whole nature that it was no wonder Jim Braxton was unable to comprehend what ailed me.

"Tope didn't go of his own free will," I said. "That call was a summons he couldn't resist. Hypnotism, black magic, voodoo, whatever you want to call it. Saul Stark has some damnable power that enslaves men's will-power. The blacks are gathered somewhere in the swamp, for some kind of a devilish voodoo ceremony, which I have reason to believe will culminate in the murder of Tope Sorley. We've got to get to Grimesville if we can. I expect an attack at dawn."

Braxton was pale in the dimming light. He did not ask me where I got my knowledge.

"We'll lick 'em when they come; but it'll be a slaughter."

I did not reply. My eyes were fixed with savage intensity on the sinking sun, and as it slid out of sight behind the trees I was shaken with an icy tremor. In vain I told myself that no occult power could draw me against my will. If she had been able to compel me, why had she not forced me to accompany her from the glade of the ju-ju hut? A grisly whisper seemed to tell me that she was but playing with me, as a cat allows a mouse almost to escape, only to be pounced upon again.

"Kirby, what's the matter with you?" I scarcely heard Braxton's anxious voice. "You're sweatin' and shakin' like you had the aggers. What – hey, what you stoppin' for?"

I had not consciously pulled on the rein, but my horse halted, and stood trembling and snorting, before the mouth of a narrow trail which meandered away at right angles from the road we were following – a trail that led north.

"Listen!" I hissed tensely.

"What is it?" Braxton drew a pistol. The brief twilight of the pinelands was deepening into dusk.

"Don't you hear it?" I muttered. "Drums! Drums beating in Goshen!"

"I don't hear nothin'," he mumbled uneasily. "If they was beatin' drums in Goshen you couldn't hear 'em this far away."

"Look there!" My sharp sudden cry made him start. I was pointing down the dim trail, at the figure which stood there in the dusk less than a hundred yards away. There in the dusk I saw her, even made out the gleam of her strange eyes, the mocking smile on her red lips. "Saul Stark's brown wench!" I raved, tearing at my scabbard. "My God, man, are you stone-blind? Don't you see her?"

"I don't see nobody!" he whispered, livid. "What are you talkin' about, Kirby?"

With eyes glaring I fired down the trail, and fired again, and yet again. This time no paralysis gripped my arm. But the smiling face still mocked me from the shadows. A slender, rounded arm lifted, a finger beckoned imperiously; and then she was gone and I was spurring my horse down the narrow trail, blind, deaf and dumb, with a sensation as of being caught in a black tide that was carrying me with it as it rushed on to a destination beyond my comprehension.

Dimly I heard Braxton's urgent yells, and then he drew up beside me with a clatter of hoofs, and grabbed my reins, setting my horse back on its haunches. I remember striking at him with my gun-barrel, without realizing what I was doing. All the black rivers of Africa were surging and foaming within my consciousness, roaring into a torrent that was sweeping me down to engulf me in an ocean of doom.

"Kirby, are you crazy? This trail leads to Goshen!"

I shook my head dazedly. The foam of the rushing waters swirled in my brain, and my voice sounded far away. "Go back! Ride for Grimesville! I'm going to Goshen."

"Kirby, you're mad!"

"Mad or sane, I'm going to Goshen this night," I answered dully. I was fully conscious. I knew what I was saying, and what I was doing. I realized the incredible folly of my action, and I realized my inability to help myself. Some shred of sanity impelled me to try to conceal the grisly truth from my companion, to offer a rational reason for my madness. "Saul Stark is in Goshen. He's the one who's responsible for all this trouble. I'm going to kill him. That will stop the uprising before it starts."

He was trembling like a man with the ague.

"Then I'm goin' with you."

"You must go on to Grimesville and warn the people," I insisted, holding to sanity, but feeling a strong urge begin to seize me, and irresistible urge to be in motion – to be riding in the direction toward which I was so horribly drawn.

"They'll be on their guard," he said stubbornly. "They won't need my warnin'. I'm goin' with you. I don't know what's got in you, but I ain't goin' to let you die alone among these black woods."

I did not argue. I could not. The blind rivers were sweeping me on – on – on! And down the trail, dim in the dusk, I glimpsed a supple figure, caught the gleam of uncanny eyes, the crook of a lifted finger. . . . Then I was in motion, galloping down the trail, and I heard the drum of Braxton's horse's hoofs behind me.

4

The Dwellers in the Swamp

Night fell and the moon shone through the trees, blood-red behind the black branches. The horses were growing hard to manage.

"They got more sense'n us, Kirby," muttered Braxton.

"Panther, maybe," I replied absently, my eyes searching the gloom of the trail ahead.

"Naw, t'ain't. Closer we get to Goshen, the worse they git. And every time we swing nigh to a creek they shy and snort."

The trail had not yet crossed any of the narrow, muddy creeks that criss-crossed that end of Canaan, but several times it had swung so close to one of them that we glimpsed the black streak that was water glinting dully in the shadows of the thick growth. And each time, I remembered, the horses showed signs of fear.

But I had hardly noticed, wrestling as I was with the grisly compulsion that was driving me. Remember, I was not like a man in a hypnotic trance. I was fully awake, fully conscious. Even the daze in which I had seemed to hear the roar of black rivers had passed, leaving my mind clear, my thoughts lucid. And that was the sweating hell of it: to realize my folly clearly and poignantly, but to be unable to conquer it. Vividly I realized that I was riding to torture and death, and leading a faithful friend to the same end. But on I went. My efforts to break the spell that gripped me almost unseated my reason, but on I went. I cannot explain my compulsion, any more than I can explain why a sliver of steel is drawn to a magnet. It was a black power beyond the ring of white man's knowledge; a basic, elemental thing of which formal hypnotism is but scanty crumbs, spilled at random. A power beyond my control was drawing me to Goshen, and beyond; more I cannot explain, any more than the rabbit could explain why the eyes of the swaying serpent draw him into its gaping jaws.

We were not far from Goshen when Braxton's horse unseated its rider, and my own began snorting and plunging.

"They won't go no closer!" gasped Braxton, fighting at the reins.

I swung off, threw the reins over the saddle-horn.

"Go back, for God's sake, Jim! I'm going on afoot."

I heard him whimper an oath, then his horse was galloping after mine, and he was following me on foot. The thought that he must share my doom sickened me, but I could not dissuade him; and ahead of me a supple form was dancing in the shadows, luring me on – on – on. . . .

I wasted no more bullets on that mocking shape. Braxton could not see it, and I knew it was part of my enchantment, no real woman of flesh and blood, but a hell-born will-o'-the-wisp, mocking me and leading me through the night to a hideous death. A "sending," the people of the Orient, who are wiser than we, call such a thing.

Braxton peered nervously at the black forest walls about us, and I knew his flesh was crawling with the fear of sawed-off shotguns blasting us suddenly from the shadows. But it was no ambush of lead or steel I feared as we emerged into the moonlit clearing that housed the cabins of Goshen.

The double line of log cabins faced each other across the dusty street. One line backed against the bank of Tularoosa Creek. The back stoops almost overhung the black waters. Nothing moved in the moonlight. No lights showed, no smoke oozed up from the stick-and-mud chimneys. It might have been a dead town, deserted and forgotten.

"It's a trap!" hissed Braxton, his eyes blazing slits. He bent forward like a skulking panther, a gun in each hand. "They're layin' for us in them huts!"

Then he cursed, but followed me as I strode down the street. I did not hail the silent huts. I knew Goshen was deserted. I felt its emptiness. Yet there was a contradictory sensation as of spying eyes fixed upon us. I did not try to reconcile these opposite convictions.

"They're gone," muttered Braxton, nervously. "I can't smell 'em. I can always smell niggers, if they're a lot of 'em, or if they're right close. You reckon they've already gone to raid Grimesville?"

"No," I muttered. "They're in the House of Damballah."

He shot a quick glance at me.

"That's a neck of land in the Tularoosa about three miles west of here. My grandpap used to talk about it. The niggers held their heathen palavers there back in slave times. You ain't – Kirby – you – "

"Listen!" I wiped the icy sweat from my face. "Listen!"

Through the black woodlands the faint throb of a drum whispered on the wind that glided up the shadowy reaches of the Tularoosa.

Braxton shivered. "It's them, all right. But for God's sake, Kirby – look out!"

With an oath he sprang toward the houses on the bank of the creek. I was after him just in time to glimpse a dark clumsy object scrambling or tumbling down the sloping bank into the water. Braxton threw up his long pistol, then lowered it, with a baffled curse. A faint splash marked the disappearance of the creature. The shiny black surface crinkled with spreading ripples.

"What was it?" I demanded.

"A nigger on his all-fours!" swore Braxton. His face was strangely pallid in the moonlight. "He was crouched between them cabins there, watchin' us!"

"It must have been an alligator." What a mystery is the human mind! I was arguing for sanity and logic, I, the blind victim of a compulsion beyond sanity and logic. "A nigger would have to come up for air."

"He swum under the water and come up in the shadder of the bresh where we couldn't see him," maintained Braxton. "Now he'll go warn Saul Stark."

"Never mind!" The pulse was thrumming in my temples again, the roar of foaming waters rising irresistibly in my brain. "I'm going – straight through the swamp. For the last time, go back!"

"No! Sane or mad, I'm goin' with you!"

The pulse of the drum was fitful, growing more distant as we advanced. We struggled through jungle-thick growth; tangled vines tripped us; our boots sank in scummy mire. We were entering the fringe of the swamp which grew deeper and denser until it culminated in the uninhabitable morass where the Tularoosa flowed into Black River, miles farther to the west.

The moon had not yet set, but the shadows were black under the interlacing branches with their mossy beards. We plunged into the first creek we must cross, one of the many muddy streams flowing into the Tularoosa. The water was only thigh-deep, the moss-clogged bottom fairly firm. My foot felt the edge of a sheer drop, and I warned Braxton: "Look out for a deep hole; keep right behind me."

His answer was unintelligible. He was breathing heavily, crowding close behind me. Just as I reached the sloping bank and pulled myself up by the slimy, projecting roots, the water was violently agitated behind me. Braxton cried out incoherently, and hurled himself up the bank, almost upsetting me. I wheeled, gun in hand, but saw only the black water seething and whirling, after his thrashing rush through it.

"What the devil, Jim?"

"Somethin' grabbed me!" he panted. "Somethin' out of the deep hole. I tore loose and busted up the bank. I tell you, Kirby, something's follerin' us! Somethin' that swims under the water."

"Maybe it was that nigger you saw. These swamp people swim like fish. Maybe he swam up under the water to try to drown you."

He shook his head, staring at the black water, gun in hand.

"It *smelt* like a nigger, and the little I saw of it *looked* like a nigger. But it didn't *feel* like any kind of a human."

"Well, it was an alligator then," I muttered absently as I turned away. As always when I halted, even for a moment, the roar of peremptory and imperious rivers shook the foundations of my reason.

He splashed after me without comment. Scummy puddles rose about our ankles, and we stumbled over moss-grown cypress knees. Ahead of us there loomed another, wider creek, and Braxton caught my arm.

"Don't do it, Kirby!" he gasped. "If we go into that water, it'll git us sure!"

"What?"

"I don't know. Whatever it was that flopped down that bank back there in Goshen. The same thing that grabbed me in that creek back yonder. Kirby, let's go back."

"Go back?" I laughed in bitter agony. "I wish to God I could! I've got to go on. Either Saul Stark or I must die before dawn."

He licked dry lips and whispered. "Go on, then; I'm with you, come heaven or hell." He thrust his pistol back into its scabbard, and drew a long keen knife from his boot. "Go ahead!"

I climbed down the sloping bank and splashed into the water that rose to my hips. The cypress branches bent a gloomy, moss-trailing arch over the creek. The water was black as midnight. Braxton was a blur, toiling behind me. I gained the first shelf of the opposite bank and paused, in water knee-deep, to turn and look back at him.

Everything happened at once, then. I saw Braxton halt short, staring at something on the bank behind me. He cried out, whipped out a gun and fired, just as I turned. In the flash of the gun I glimpsed a supple form reeling backward, a brown face fiendishly contorted. Then in the momentarily blindness that followed the flash, I heard Jim Braxton scream.

Sight and brain cleared in time to show me a sudden swirl of the murky water, a round, black object breaking the surface behind Jim – and then Braxton gave a strangled cry and went under with a frantic thrashing and splashing. With an incoherent yell I sprang into the creek, stumbled and went to my knees, almost submerging myself. As I struggled up I saw Braxton's head, now streaming blood, break the surface for an instant, and I lunged toward it. It went under and another head appeared in its place, a shadowy black head. I stabbed at it ferociously, and my knife cut only the blank water as the thing dipped out of sight.

I staggered from the wasted force of the blow, and when I righted myself, the water lay unbroken about me. I called Jim's name, but there was no answer. Then panic laid a cold hand on me, and I splashed to the bank, sweating and trembling. With the water no higher than my knees I halted and waited, for I knew not what. But presently, down the creek a short distance, I made out a vague object lying in the shallow water near the shore.

I waded to it, through the clinging mud and crawling vines. It was Jim Braxton, and he was dead. It was not the wound in his head which had killed him. Probably he had struck a submerged rock when he was dragged under. But the marks of strangling fingers showed black on his throat. At the sight a nameless horror oozed out of that black swamp water and coiled itself clammily about my soul; for no human fingers ever left such marks as those.

I had seen a head rise in the water, a head that looked like that of a negro, though the features had been indistinct in the darkness. But no man, white or black, ever possessed the fingers that had crushed the life out of Jim Braxton. The distant drum grunted as if in mockery.

I dragged the body up on the bank and left it. I could not linger longer, for the madness was foaming in my brain again, driving me with white-hot spurs. But as I climbed the bank, I found blood on the bushes, and was shaken by the implication.

I remembered the figure I had seen staggering in the flash of Braxton's gun. *She* had been there, waiting for me on the bank, then – not a spectral illusion, but the woman herself, in flesh and blood! Braxton had fired at her, and wounded her. But the wound could not have been mortal; for no corpse lay among the bushes, and the grim hypnosis that dragged me onward was unweakened. Dizzily I wondered if she could be killed by mortal weapons.

The moon had set. The starlight scarcely penetrated the interwoven branches. No more creeks barred my way, only shallow streams, through which I splashed with sweating haste. Yet I did not expect to be attacked. Twice the dweller in the depths had passed me by to attack my companion. In icy despair I knew I was being saved for a grimmer fate. Each stream I crossed might be hiding the monster that killed Jim Braxton. Those creeks were all connected in a network of winding waterways. It could follow me easily. But my horror of it was less than the horror of the jungle-born magnetism that lurked in a witch-woman's eyes.

As I stumbled through the tangled vegetation, I heard the drum rumbling ahead of me, louder and louder, in demoniacal mockery. Then a human voice mingled with its mutter, in a long-drawn cry of horror and agony that set every fiber of me quivering with sympathy. Sweat coursed down my clammy flesh; soon my own voice might be lifted like that, under unnamable torture. But on I went, my feet moving like automatons, apart from my body, motivated by a will not my own.

The drum grew loud, and a fire glowed among the black trees. Presently, crouching among the bushes, I stared across the stretch of black water that separated me from a nightmare scene. My halting there was as compulsory as the rest of my actions had been. Vaguely I knew the stage for horror had been set, but the time for my entry upon it was not yet. When the time had come, I would receive my summons.

A low, wooded island split the black creek, connected with the shore opposite me by a narrow neck of land. At its lower end the creek split into a network of channels threading their way among hummocks and rotting logs and moss-grown, vine-tangled clumps of trees. Directly across from my refuge the shore of the island was deeply indented by an arm of open, deep black water. Bearded trees walled a small clearing, and partly hid a hut. Between the hut and the shore burned a fire that sent up weird twisting snake-tongues of green flames. Scores of black people squatted under the shadows of the overhanging branches. When the green fire lit their faces it lent them the appearance of drowned corpses.

In the midst of the glade stood a giant negro, an awesome statue in black marble. He was clad in ragged trousers, but on his head was a band of beaten gold set with a huge red jewel, and on his feet were barbaric sandals. His features reflected titanic vitality no less than his huge body. But he was all negro – flaring nostrils, thick lips, ebony skin. I knew I looked upon Saul Stark, the conjure man.

He was regarding something that lay in the sand before him, something dark and bulky that moaned feebly. Presently, lifting his head, he rolled out a sonorous invocation across the black waters. From the blacks huddled under the trees there came a shuddering response, like a wind wailing through midnight branches. Both invocation and response were framed in an unknown tongue – a guttural, primitive language.

Again he called out, this time a curious high-pitched wail. A shuddering sigh swept the black people. All eyes were fixed on the dusky water. And presently an object rose slowly from the depths. A sudden trembling shook me. It looked like the head of a negro. One after another it was followed by similar objects until five heads reared above the black, cypress-shadowed water. They might have been five negroes submerged except for their heads – but I knew this was not so. There was something diabolical here. Their silence, motionless, their whole aspect was unnatural. From the trees came the hysterical sobbing of women, and someone whimpered a man's name.

The Saul Stark lifted his hands, and the five heads silently sank out of sight. Like a ghostly whisper I seemed to hear the voice of the African witch: "He puts them in the swamp!"

Stark's deep voice rolled out across the narrow water: "And now the Dance of the Skull, to make the conjer sure!"

What had the witch said? "Hidden among the trees you shall watch the dance of the Skull!"

The drum struck up again, growling and rumbling. The blacks swayed on their haunches, lifting a wordless chant. Saul Stark paced measuredly about the figure on the sand, his arms weaving cryptic patterns. Then he wheeled and faced toward the other end of the glade. By some sleight of hand he now grasped a grinning human skull, and this he cast upon the wet sand beyond the body. "Bride of Damballah!" he thundered. "The sacrifice awaits!"

There was an expectant pause; the chanting sank. All eyes were glued on the farther end of the glade. Stark stood waiting, and I saw him scowl as if puzzled. The as he opened his mouth to repeat the call, a barbaric figure moved out of the shadows.

At the sight of her a chill shuddering shook me. For a moment she stood motionless, the firelight glinting on her gold ornaments, her head hanging on her breast. A tense silence reigned and I saw Saul Stark, staring at her sharply. She seemed to be detached, somehow, standing aloof and withdrawn, head bent strangely.

Then, as if rousing herself, she began to sway with a jerky rhythm, and presently whirled into the mazes of a dance that was ancient when the ocean drowned the black kings of Atlantis. I cannot describe it. It was bestiality and diabolism set to motion, framed in a writhing, spinning whirl of posturing and gesturing that would have appalled a dancer of the Pharaohs. And that cursed skull danced with her; rattling and clashing on the sand, it bounded and spun like a live thing in time with her leaps and prancings.

But there was something amiss. I sensed it. Her arms hung limp, her drooping head swayed. Her legs bent and faltered, making her lurch drunkenly and out of time. A murmur rose from the people, and bewilderment etched Saul Stark's black countenance. For the domination of a conjure man is a thing hinged on a hair-trigger. Any trifling dislocation of formula or ritual may disrupt the whole web of his enchantment.

As for me, I felt the perspiration freeze on my flesh as I watched the grisly dance. The unseen shackles that bound me to that gyrating she-devil were strangling, crushing me. I knew she was approaching a climax, when she would summon me from my hiding-place, to wade through the black waters to the House of Damballah, to my doom.

Now she whirled to a floating stop, and when she halted, poised on her toes, she faced toward the spot where I lay hidden, and I knew that she could see me as plainly as if I stood in the open; knew, too, somehow, that only she knew of my presence. I felt myself toppling on the edge of the abyss. She raised her head and I saw the flame of her eyes, even at that distance. Her face was lit with awful triumph. Slowly she raised her hand,

and I felt my limbs began to jerk in response to that terrible magnetism. She opened her mouth –

But from that open mouth sounded only a choking gurgle, and suddenly her lips were dyed crimson. And suddenly, without warning, her knees gave way and she pitched headlong in the sands.

And as she fell, so I too fell, sinking into the mire. Something burst in my brain with a shower of flame. And then I was crouching among the trees, weak and trembling, but with such a sense of freedom and lightness of limb as I never dreamed a man could experience. The black spell that gripped me was broken; the foul incubus lifted from my soul. It was as if light had burst upon a night blacker than African midnight.

At the fall of the girl a wild cry rose from the blacks, and they sprang up, trembling on the verge of panic. I saw their rolling white eyeballs, their bared teeth glistening in the firelight. Saul Stark had worked their primitive natures up to a pitch of madness, meaning to turn this frenzy, at the proper time, into a fury of battle. It could as easily turn into an hysteria of terror. Stark shouted sharply at them.

But just then the girl in a last convulsion, rolled over on the wet sand, and the firelight shone on a round hole between her breasts, which still oozed crimson. Jim Braxton's bullet had found its mark.

From the first I had felt that she was not wholly human; some black jungle spirit sired her, lending her the abysmal subhuman vitality that made her what she was. She had said that neither death nor hell could keep her from the Dance of the Skull. And, shot through the heart and dying, she had come through the swamp from the creek where she had received her death-wound to the House of Damballah. And the Dance of the Skull had been her death dance.

Dazed as a condemned man just granted a reprieve, at first I hardly grasped the meaning of the scene that now unfolded before me.

The blacks were in a frenzy. In the sudden, and to them inexplicable, death of the sorceress they saw a fearsome portent. They had no way of knowing that she was dying when she entered the glade. To them, their prophetess and priestess had been struck down under their very eyes, by an invisible death. This was magic blacker than Saul Stark's wizardry – and obviously hostile to them.

Like fear-maddened cattle they stampeded. Howling, screaming, tearing at one another they blundered through the trees, heading for the neck of land and the shore beyond. Saul Stark stood transfixed, heedless of them as he stared down at the brown girl, dead at last. And suddenly I came to myself, and with my awakened manhood came cold fury and the lust to kill. I drew a gun, and aiming in the uncertain firelight, pulled the trigger. Only a click answered me. The powder in the cap-and-ball pistols was wet.

Saul Stark lifted his head and licked his lips. The sounds of flight faded in the distance, and he stood alone in the glade. His eyes rolled whitely toward the black woods around him. He bent, grasped the man-like object that lay on the sand, and dragged it into the hut. The instant he vanished I started toward the island, wading through the narrow channels at the lower end. I had almost reached the shore when a mass of driftwood gave way with me and I slid into a deep hole.

Instantly the water swirled about me, and a head rose beside me; a dim face was close to mine – the face of a negro – *the face of Tunk Bixby*. But now it was inhuman; as expressionless and soulless as that of a catfish; the face of a being no longer human, and no longer mindful of its human origin.

Slimy, misshapen fingers gripped my throat, and I drove my knife into the sagging mouth. The features vanished in a wave of blood; mutely the thing sank out of sight, and I hauled myself up on the bank, under the thick bushes.

Stark had run from his hut, a pistol in his hand. He was staring wildly about, alarmed by the noise he had heard, but I knew he could not see me. His ashy skin glistened with perspiration. He who had ruled by fear was now ruled by fear. He feared the unknown hand that had slain his mistress; feared the negroes who had fled from him; feared the abysmal swamp which had sheltered him, and the monstrosities he had created. He lifted a weird call that quavered with panic. He called again as only four heads broke the water, but he called in vain.

But the four heads began to move toward the shore and the man who stood there. He shot them one after another. They made no effort to avoid the bullets. They came straight on, sinking one by one. He had fired six shots before the last head vanished. The shots drowned the sound of my approach. I was close behind him when he turned at last.

I know he knew me; recognition flooded his face and fear went with it, at the knowledge that he had a human being to deal with. With a scream he hurled his empty pistol at me and rushed after it with a lifted knife.

I ducked, parried his lunge, and countered with a thrust that bit deep into his ribs. He caught my wrist and I gripped his, and there we strained, breast to breast. His eyes were like a mad dog's in the starlight, his muscles like steel cords.

I ground my heel down on his bare foot, crushing the instep. He howled and lost balance, and I tore my knife hand free and stabbed him in the belly. Blood spurted and he dragged me down with him. I jerked loose and rose, just as he pulled himself up on his elbow and hurled his knife. It sang past my ear, and I stamped on his breast. His ribs caved in under my heel. In a red killing-haze I knelt, jerked back his head and cut his throat ear to ear.

There was a pouch of dry powder in his belt. Before I moved further I reloaded my pistols. Then I went into the hut with a torch. And there I understood the doom the brown witch had meant for me. Tope Sorley lay moaning on a bunk. The transmutation that was to make him a mindless, soulless semi-human dweller in the water was not complete, but his mind was gone. Some of the physical changes had been made – by what godless sorcery out of Africa's black abyss I have no wish to know. His body was rounded and elongated, his legs dwarfed; his feet were flattened and broadened, his fingers horribly long, and *webbed*. His neck was inches longer than it should be. His features were not altered, but the expression was no more human that that of a great fish. And there, but for the loyalty of Jim Braxton, lay Kirby Buckner. I placed my pistol muzzle against Tope's head in grim mercy and pulled the trigger.

And so the nightmare closed, and I would not drag out the grisly narration. The white people of Canaan never found anything on the island except the bodies of Saul Stark and the brown woman. They think to this day that a swamp negro killed Jim Braxton, after he had killed the brown woman, and that I broke up the threatened uprising by killing Saul Stark. I let them think it. They will never know the shapes the black water of Tularoosa hides. That is a secret I share with the cowed and terror-haunted black people of Goshen, and of it neither they nor I have ever spoken.

Kirby Buckner, gambling and ruffling it in New Orleans, received a warning from an old negro hag who had gotten the news in some mysterious African way. "Trouble on Black River!" He knew that meant that the negroes were restless in the pine covered back country, and returned at once, by steamboat and by horse, to that isolated country lying between Black River and Nigger Head Creek, a country of pines and cypresses, of forests and swamps, where the people lived their own lives and followed their own laws, a hardy breed, sons of the frontiersmen. According to tradition half a century old, a Buckner horse was always kept in the stable at Sharpsville. Buckner rode the fifteen miles that lay between the steamboat landing and the village of Grimesville, crossing Nigger Head Creek, which ran into Cypress Creek, which in turn ran into Black River, forming an irregular triangle which practically isolated the inhabitants. Nigger Head Creek had once had another name, but, since a negro rebellion years before, when the head of the ring-leader had been nailed to a tree at the crossing, it had been known as Nigger Head. It was a black, narrow creek, lined with trees hung with Spanish moss. On the other side, among the pines, he meet a strange quadroon woman, who spoke with a Spanish accent, and tried to lure him deep into the woods. When she failed he was attacked by three negroes. He had only a pair of dueling pistols and his bowie knife. One he shot, but the cap had slipped from the other pistol. He wounded another with his knife, and the other fled. Riding on, it being then just about dawn, he encountered Esau McBride, one of the villagers, who had heard the shot and was investigating. They said that the negroes in the village on Cypress Creek had been acting strangely recently, and spoke of drums beating in the swamps, and chants of wild worship. They attributed the unrest to a strange negro from South Carolina, Saul Claver. With him had come a brazen young wench, sister, wife or daughter none knew.

Pigeons from Hell

The Whistler in the Dark

Griswell awoke suddenly, every nerve tingling with a premonition of imminent peril. He stared about wildly, unable at first to remember where he was, or what he was doing there. Moonlight filtered in through the dusty windows, and the great empty room with its lofty ceiling and gaping black fireplace was spectral and unfamiliar. Then as he emerged from the clinging cobwebs of his recent sleep, he remembered where he was and how he came to be there. He twisted his head and stared at his companion. Sleeping on the floor near him, John Branner was but a vaguely bulking shape in the darkness that the moon scarcely grayed.

Griswell tried to remember what had awakened him. There was no sound in the house, no sound outside except the mournful hoot of an owl, far away in the piny woods. Now he had captured the illusive memory. It was a dream, a nightmare so filled with dim terror that it had frightened him awake. Recollection flooded back, vividly etching the abnormal vision.

Or was it a dream? Certainly it must have been, but it had blended so curiously with recent actual events that it was difficult to know where reality left off and fantasy began.

Dreaming, he had seemed to relive his past few waking hours, in accurate detail. The dream had begun, abruptly, as he and John Branner came in sight of the house where they now lay. They had come rattling and bouncing over the stumpy, uneven old road that led through the pinelands, he and John Branner, wandering far afield from their New England home, in search of vacation pleasure. They had sighted the old house with its balustraded galleries rising amidst a wilderness of weeds and bushes, just as the sun was setting behind it. It dominated their fancy, rearing black and stark and gaunt against the low lurid rampart of sunset, barred by the black pines.

They were tired, sick of bumping and pounding all day over woodland roads. The old deserted house stimulated their imagination with its suggestion of antebellum splendor and ultimate decay. They left the automobile beside the rutty road, and as they went up the winding walk of crumbling bricks, almost lost in the tangle of rank growth, pigeons rose from the balustrades in a fluttering, feathery crowd and swept away with a low thunder of beating wings.

The oaken door sagged on broken hinges. Dust lay thick on the floor of the wide, dim hallway, on the broad steps of the stair that mounted up from the hall. They turned into a door opposite the landing, and entered a large room, empty, dusty, with cobwebs shining thickly in the corners. Dust lay thick over the ashes in the great fireplace.

They discussed gathering wood and building a fire, but decided against it. As the sun sank, darkness came quickly, the thick, black, absolute darkness of the pinelands. They knew that rattlesnakes and copperheads haunted Southern forests, and they did not care to go groping for firewood in the dark. They ate frugally from tins, then rolled in their blankets fully clad before the empty fireplace, and went instantly to sleep.

This, in part, was what Griswell had dreamed. He saw again the gaunt house looming stark against the crimson sunset; saw the flight of the pigeons as he and Branner came up the shattered walk. He saw the dim room in which they presently lay, and he saw the two forms that were himself and his companion, lying wrapped in their blankets on the dusty floor. Then from that point his dream altered subtly, passed out of the realm of the commonplace and became tinged with fear. He was looking into a vague, shadowy chamber, lit by the gray light of the moon which streamed from some obscure source. For there was no window in that room. But in the gray light he saw three silent shapes that hung suspended in a row, and their stillness and their outlines woke chill horror in his soul. There was no sound, no word, but he sensed a Presence of fear and lunacy crouching in a dark corner. . . . Abruptly he was back in the dusty, high-ceilinged room, before the great fireplace.

He was lying in his blankets, staring tensely through the dim door and across the shadowy hall, to where a beam of moonlight fell across the balustraded stair, some seven steps up from the landing. And there was something on the stair, a bent, misshapen, shadowy thing that never moved fully into the beam of light. But a dim yellow blur that might have been a face was turned toward him, as if *something* crouched on the stair, regarding him and his companion. Fright crept chilly through his veins, and it was then that he awoke – if indeed he had been asleep.

He blinked his eyes. The beam of moonlight fell across the stair just as he had dreamed it did; but no figure lurked there. Yet his flesh still crawled from the fear the dream or vision had roused in him; his legs felt as if they had been plunged in ice-water. He made an involuntary movement to awaken his companion, when a sudden sound paralyzed him.

It was the sound of whistling on the floor above. Eerie and sweet it rose, not carrying any tune, but piping shrill and melodious. Such a sound in a supposedly deserted house was alarming enough; but it was more than the fear of a physical invader that held Griswell frozen. He could not himself have defined the horror that gripped him. But Branner's blankets rustled, and Griswell saw he was sitting upright. His figure bulked dimly in the soft darkness, the head turned toward the stair as if the man were listening intently. More sweetly and more subtly evil rose that weird whistling.

"John!" whispered Griswell from dry lips. He had meant to shout – to tell Branner that there was somebody upstairs, somebody who could mean them no good; that they must leave the house at once. But his voice died dryly in his throat.

Branner had risen. His boots clumped on the floor as he moved toward the door. He stalked leisurely into the hall and made for the lower landing, merging with the shadows that clustered black about the stair.

Griswell lay incapable of movement, his mind a whirl of bewilderment. Who was that whistling upstairs? Griswell saw him pass the spot where the moonlight rested, he saw his head tilted back as if he were looking at something Griswell could not see, above and beyond the stair. But his face was like that of a sleep-walker. He moved across the bar of moonlight and vanished from Griswell's view, even as the latter tried to shout to him to come back. A ghastly whisper was the only result of his effort.

The whistling sank to a lower note, died out. Griswell heard the stairs creaking under Branner's measured tread. Now he had reached the hall-way above, for Griswell heard the clump of his feet moving along it. Sud-denly the footfalls halted, and the whole night seemed to hold its breath. Then an awful scream split the stillness, and Griswell started up, echoing the cry.

The strange paralysis that had held him was broken. He took a step toward the door, then checked himself. The footfalls were resumed. Bran-ner was coming back. He was not running. The tread was even more de-liberate and measured than before. Now the stairs began to creak again. A groping hand, moving along the balustrade, came into the bar of moon-light; then another , and a ghastly thrill went through Griswell as he saw that the other hand gripped a hatchet – a hatchet which dripped blackly. *Was* that Branner who was coming down that stair?

Yes! The figure had moved into the bar of moonlight now, and Griswell recognized it. Then he saw Branner's face, and a shriek burst from Gris-well's lips. Branner's face was bloodless, corpse-like; gouts of blood drip-ped darkly down it; his eyes were glassy and set, and blood oozed from the great gash *which cleft the crown of his head!*

Griswell never remembered exactly how he got out of that accursed house. Afterward he retained a mad, confused impression of smashing his way through a dusty cobwebbed window, of stumbling blindly across the weed-choked lawn, gibbering his frantic horror. He saw the black wall of the pines, and the moon floating in a blood-red mist in which there was neither sanity nor reason.

Some shred of sanity returned to him as he saw the automobile beside the road. In a world gone suddenly mad, that was an object reflecting prosaic reality; but even as he reached for the door, a dry chilling whir sounded in his ears, and he recoiled from the swaying undulating shape that arched up from its scaly coils on the driver's seat and hissed sibilantly at him, darting a forked tongue in the moonlight.

With a sob of horror he turned and fled down the road, as a man runs in a nightmare. He ran without purpose or reason. His numbed brain was incapable of conscious thought. He merely obeyed the blind primitive urge to run – run – run until he fell exhausted.

The black walls of the pines flowed endlessly past him; so he was seized with the illusion that he was getting nowhere. But presently a sound penetrated the fog of his terror – the steady, inexorable patter of feet behind him. Turning his head, he saw *something* loping after him – wolf or dog, he could not tell which, but its eyes glowed like balls of green fire. With a gasp he increased his speed, reeled around a bend in the road, and heard a horse snort; saw it rear and heard its rider curse; saw the gleam of blue steel in the man's lifted hand.

He staggered and fell, catching at the rider's stirrup.

"For God's sake, help me!" he panted. "The thing! It killed Branner – it's coming after me! *Look!*"

Twin balls of fire gleamed in the fringe of bushes at the turn of the road. The rider swore again, and on the heels of his profanity came the smashing report of his six-shooter – again and yet again. The fire-sparks vanished, and the rider, jerking his stirrup free from Griswell's grasp, spurred his horse at the bend. Griswell staggered up, shaking in every limb. The rider was out of sight only a moment; then he came galloping back.

"Took to the brush. Timber wolf, I reckon, though I never heard of one chasin' a man before. Do you know what it was?"

Griswell could only shake his head weakly.

The rider, etched in the moonlight, looked down at him, smoking pistol still lifted in his right hand. He was a compactly-built man of medium height, and his broad-brimmed planter's hat and his boots marked him as a native of the country as definitely as Griswell's garb stamped him as a stranger.

"What's this all about anyway?"

"I don't know," Griswell answered helplessly. "My name's Griswell. John Branner – my friend who was traveling with me – we stopped at a deserted house back down the road to spend the night. Something – " at the memory he was choked by a rush of horror. "My God!" he screamed. "I must be mad! *Something* came and looked over the balustrade of the stair – something with a yellow face! I thought I dreamed it, but it must have been real. Then somebody began whistling upstairs, and Branner rose and went up the stairs walking like a man in his sleep, or hypnotized. I heard him scream – or somebody screamed; then he came down the stair again with a bloody hatchet in his hand – and my God, sir, he was *dead!* His head had been split open. I saw his brains and clotted blood oozing down his face, and his face was that of a dead man. *But he came down the stair!* As God is my witness, John Branner was murdered in that dark upper hallway, and then his dead body came stalking down the stairs with a hatchet in his hand – to kill me!"

The rider made no reply; he sat his horse like a statue, outlined against the stars, and Griswell could not read his expression, his face shadowed by his hatbrim.

"You think I'm mad," he said hopelessly. "Perhaps I am."

"I don't know what to think," answered the rider. "If it was any house but the old Blassenville Manor – well, we'll see. My name's Buckner. I'm sheriff of this county. Took a nigger over to the county-seat in the next county and was ridin' back late."

He swung off his horse and stood beside Griswell, shorter than the lanky New Englander, but much harder knit. There was a natural manner of decision and certainty about him, and it was easy to believe that he would be a dangerous man in any sort of a fight.

"Are you afraid to go back to the house?" he asked, and Griswell shuddered, but shook his head, the dogged tenacity of Puritan ancestors asserting itself.

"The thought of facing that horror again turns me sick. But poor Branner – " he choked again. "We must find his body. My God!" he cried, unmanned by the abysmal horror of the thing; "*what* will we find? If a dead man walks, what – "

"We'll see." The sheriff caught the reins in the crook of his left elbow and began filling the empty chambers of his big blue pistol as they walked along.

As they made the turn Griswell's blood was ice at the thought of what they might see lumbering up the road with bloody, grinning death-mask, but they saw only the house looming spectrally among the pines, down the road. A strong shudder shook Griswell.

"God, how *evil* that house looks, against those black pines! It looked sinister from the very first – when we went up the broken walk and saw those pigeons fly up from the porch – "

"Pigeons?" Buckner cast him a quick glance. "You saw the pigeons?"

"Why, yes! Scores of them perching on the porch railing."

They strode on for a moment in silence, before Buckner said abruptly: "I've lived in this country all my life. I've passed the old Blassenville place

269

a thousand times, I reckon, at all hours of the day and night. But I never saw a pigeon anywhere around it, or anywhere else in these woods."

"There were scores of them," repeated Griswell, bewildered.

"I've seen men who swore they'd seen a flock of pigeons perched along the balusters just at sundown," said Buckner slowly. "Niggers, all of them except one man. A tramp. He was buildin' a fire in the yard, aimin' to camp there that night. I passed along there about dark, and he told me about the pigeons. I came back by there the next mornin'. The ashes of his fire were there, and his tin cup, and skillet where he'd fried pork, and his blankets looked like they'd been slept in. Nobody ever saw him again. That was twelve years ago. The niggers say they can see the pigeons, but no nigger would pass along this road between sundown and sun-up. They say the pigeons are the souls of the Blassenvilles, let out of hell at sunset. The niggers say the red glare in the west is the light from hell, because then the gates of hell are open, and the Blassenvilles fly out."

"Who were the Blassenvilles?" asked Griswell, shivering.

"They owned all this land here. French-English family. Came here from the West Indies before the Louisiana Purchase. The Civil War ruined them, like it did so many. Some were killed in the War; most of the others died out. Nobody's lived in the Manor since 1890 when Miss Elizabeth Blassenville, last of the line, fled from the old house one night like it was a plague spot, and never came back to it – this your auto?"

They halted beside the car, and Griswell stared morbidly at the grim house. Its dusty panes were empty and blank; but they did not seem blind to him. It seemed to him that ghastly eyes were fixed hungrily on him through those darkened panes. Buckner repeated his question.

"Yes. Be careful. There's a snake on the seat – or there was."

"Not there now," grunted Buckner, tying his horse and pulling an electric torch out of the saddle-bag. "Well, let's have a look."

He strode up the broken brick-walk as matter-of-factly as if he were paying a social call on friends. Griswell followed close at his heels, his heart pounding suffocatingly. A scent of decay and moldering vegetation blew on the faint wind, and Griswell grew faint with nausea, that rose from a frantic abhorrence of these black woods, these ancient plantation houses that hid forgotten secrets of slavery and bloody pride and mysterious intrigues. He had thought of the South as a sunny, lazy land washed by soft breezes laden with spice and warm blossoms, where life ran tranquilly to the rhythm of black folk singing in sun-bathed cotton-fields. But now he had discovered another, unsuspected side – a dark, brooding, fearhaunted side, and the discovery repelled him.

The oaken door sagged as it had before. The blackness of the interior was intensified by the beam of Buckner's light playing on the sill. That beam sliced through the darkness of the hall-way and roved up the stair, and Griswell held his breath, clenching his fists. But no shape of lunacy leered down at them. Buckner went in, walking light as a cat, torch in one hand, gun in the other.

As he swung his light into the room across from the stairway, Griswell cried out – and cried out again, almost fainting with the intolerable sickness at what he saw. A trail of blood drops led across the floor, crossing the blankets Branner had occupied, which lay between the door and those in which Griswell had lain. And Griswell's blankets had a terrible occupant. John Branner lay there, face down, his cleft head revealed in merciless clarity in the steady light. His out-stretched hand still gripping the haft of a hatchet, and the blade was imbedded deep in the blanket and the floor beneath, just where Griswell's head had lain when he slept there.

A momentary rush of blackness engulfed Griswell. He was not aware that he staggered, or that Buckner caught him. When he could see and hear again, he was violently sick and hung his head against the mantel, retching miserably.

Buckner turned the light full on him, making him blink. Buckner's voice came from behind the blinding radiance, the man himself unseen.

"Griswell, you've told me a yarn that's hard to believe. I saw something chasin' you, but it might have been a timber wolf, or a mad dog.

"If you're holdin' back anything, you better spill it. What you told me won't hold up in any court. You're bound to be accused of killin' your partner. I'll have to arrest you. If you'll give me the straight goods now, it'll make it easier. Now, didn't you kill this fellow, Branner?

"Wasn't it something like this: you quarreled, he grabbed a hatchet and swung at you, but you dodged and then let him have it?"

Griswell sank down and hid his face in his hands, his head swimming.

"Great God, man, I didn't murder John! Why, we've been friends ever since we were children in school together. I've told you the truth. I don't blame you for not believing me. But God help me, it is the truth!"

The light swung back to the gory head again, and Griswell closed his eyes.

He heard Buckner grunt.

"I believe this hatchet in his hand is the one he was killed with. Blood and brains plastered on the blade, and hairs stickin' to it – hairs exactly the same color as his. This makes it tough for you, Griswell."

"How so?" the New Englander asked dully.

"Knocks any plea of self-defense in the head. Branner couldn't have swing at you with this hatchet after you split his skull with it. You must have pulled the ax out of his head, stuck it into the floor and clamped his fingers on it to make it look like he'd attacked you. And it would have been damned clever – if you'd used another hatchet."

"But I didn't kill him," groaned Griswell. "I have no intention of pleading self-defense."

"That's what puzzles me," Buckner admitted frankly, straightening. "What murderer would rig up such a crazy story as you've told me, to prove his innocence? Average killer would have told a logical yarn, at least. Hmmm! Blood drops leadin' from the door. The body was dragged – no, couldn't have been dragged. The floor isn't smeared. You must have carried it here, after killin' him in some other place. But in that case, why isn't there any blood on your clothes? Of course you could have changed clothes and washed your hands. But the fellow hasn't been dead long."

"He walked downstairs and across the room," said Griswell hopelessly. "He came to kill me, I knew he was coming to kill me when I saw him lurching down the stair. He struck where I would have been, if I hadn't awakened. That window – I burst out at it. You see it's broken."

"I see. But if he walked then, why isn't he walkin' now?"

"I don't know! I'm too sick to think straight. I've been fearing that he'd rise up from the floor where he lies and come at me again. When I heard that wolf running up the road after me, I thought it was John chasing me – John, running through the night with his bloody ax and his bloody head, and his death-grin!"

His teeth chattered as he lived that horror over again.

Buckner let his light play across the floor.

"The blood drops lead into the hall. Come on. We'll follow them."

Griswell cringed. "They lead upstairs."

Buckner's eyes were fixed hard on him.

"Are you afraid to go upstairs, with me?"

Griswell's face was gray.

"Yes. But I'm going, with you or without you. The thing that killed poor John may still be hiding up there."

"Stay behind me," ordered Buckner. "If anything jumps us, I'll take care of it. But for your own sake, I warn you that I shoot quicker than a cat jumps, and I don't often miss. If you've got any ideas of layin' me out from behind, forget them."

"Don't be a fool!" Resentment got the better of his apprehension, and this outburst seemed to reassure Buckner more than any of his protestations of innocence.

"I want to be fair," he said quietly. "I haven't indicted and condemned you in my mind already. If only half of what you're tellin' me is the truth, you've been through a hell of an experience and I don't want to be too hard on you. But you can see how hard it is for me to believe all you've told me."

Griswell wearily motioned for him to lead the way, unspeaking. They went out into the hall, paused at the landing. A thin string of crimson drops, distinct in the thick dust, led up the steps.

"Man's tracks in the dust," grunted Buckner. "Go slow. I've got to be sure of what I see, because we're obliteratin' them as we go up. Hmmm! One set goin' up, one set comin' down. Same man. Not your tracks. Branner was a bigger man than you are. Blood drops all the way – blood on the banisters like a man had laid his bloody hand there – a smear of stuff that looks – brains. Now what – "

"He walked down the stair, a dead man," shuddered Griswell. "Groping with one hand – the other gripping the hatchet that killed him."

"Or was carried," muttered the sheriff. "But if somebody carried him – *where are the tracks?*"

They came out into the upper hallway, a vast, empty space of dust and shadows where time-crusted windows repelled the moonlight and the ring of Buckner's torch seemed inadequate. Griswell trembled like a leaf. Here, in darkness and horror, John Branner had died.

Somebody whistled up here," he muttered. "John came, as if he were being called."

Buckner's eyes were blazing strangely in the light.

"The footprints lead down the hall," he muttered. "Same as on the stair—one set going, one coming. Same prints—*Judas!*"

Behind him Griswell stifled a cry, for he had seen what prompted Buckner's exclamation. A few feet from the head of the stair Branner's footprints stopped abruptly, then returned, treading almost in the other tracks. And where the trail halted there was a great splash of blood on the dusty floor—and other tracks met it—tracks of bare feet, narrow but with splayed toes. They too receded in a second line from the spot.

Bucker bent over them, swearing.

"The tracks meet! And where they meet there's blood and brains on the floor! Branner must have been killed on that spot—with a blow from a hatchet. Bare feet coming out of the darkness to meet shod feet—then both turned away again; the shod feet went downstairs, the bare feet went back down the hall." He directed his light down the hall. The footprints faded into darkness, beyond the reach of the beam. On either hand the closed doors of chambers were cryptic portals of mystery.

"Suppose your crazy tale *was* true," Buckner muttered, half to himself. "These aren't your tracks. They look like a woman's. Suppose somebody did whistle, and Branner went upstairs to investigate. Suppose somebody met him here in the dark and split his head. The signs and tracks would have been, in that case, just as they really are. But if that's so, why isn't Branner lyin' here where he was killed? Could he have lived long enough to take the hatchet away from whoever killed him, and stagger downstairs with it?"

"No, no!" Recollection gagged Griswell. "I *saw* him on the stair. He was dead. No man could live a minute after receiving such a wound."

"I believe it," muttered Buckner. "But—it's madness! Or else it's *too* clever—yet, what sane man would think up and work out such an elaborate and utterly insane plan to escape punishment for murder, when a simple plea of self-defense would have been so much more effective? No court would recognize that story. Well, let's follow these other tracks. They lead down the hall—here, what's this?"

With an icy clutch at his soul, Griswell saw the light was beginning to grow dim.

"This battery is new," muttered Buckner, and for the first time Griswell caught an edge of fear in his voice. "Come on – out of here quick!"

The light had faded to a faint red glow. The darkness seemed straining into them, creeping with black cat-feet. Buckner retreated, pushing Griswell stumbling behind him as he walked backward, pistol cocked and lifted, down the dark hall. In the growing darkness Criswell heard what sounded like the stealthy opening of a door. And suddenly the blackness about them was vibrant with menace. Griswell knew Buckner sensed it as well as he, for the sheriff's hard body was tense and taut as a stalking panther's.

But without haste he worked his way to the stair and backed down it, Griswell preceding him, and fighting the panic that urged him to scream and burst into mad flight. A ghastly thought brought icy sweat out of his flesh. *Suppose the dead man were creeping up the stair behind them in the dark, face frozen in the death-grin, blood-caked hatchet lifted to strike?*

This possibility so overpowered him that he was scarcely aware when his feet struck the level of the lower hallway, and he was only then aware that the light had grown brighter as they descended, until it now gleamed with its full power – but when Buckner turned it back up the stairway, it failed to illuminate the darkness that hung like a tangible fog at the head of the stair.

The damn thing was conjured," muttered Buckner. "Nothin' else. It couldn't act like that naturally."

"Turn the light into the room." Begged Griswell. "See if John – if John is – "

He could not put the ghastly thought into words, but Buckner understood.

He swung the beam around, and Griswell had never dreamed that the sight of the gory body of a murdered man could bring such relief.

"He's still there," grunted Buckner. "If he walked after he was killed, he hasn't walked since. But that thing –

Again he turned the light up the stair, and stood chewing his lip and scowling. Three times he half lifted his gun. Griswell read his mind. The sheriff was tempted to plunge back up the stair, take his chance with the unknown. But common sense held him back.

"I wouldn't have a chance in the dark," he muttered. "And I've got a hunch the light would go out again."

He turned and faced Griswell squarely.

"There's no use dodgin' the question. There's somethin' hellish in this house, and I believe I have an inklin' of what it is. I don't believe you killed Branner. Whatever killed him is up there – now. There's a lot about your yarn that don't sound sane; but there's nothin' sane about a flashlight goin' out like this one did. I don't believe that thing upstairs is human. I never met anything I was afraid to tackle in the dark before, but I'm not goin' up there until daylight. It's not long until dawn. We'll wait for it out there on that gallery."

The stars were already paling when they came out on the broad porch. Buckner seated himself on the balustrade, facing the door, his pistol dangling in his fingers. Griswell sat down near him and leaned back against a crumbling pillar. He shut his eyes, grateful for the faint breeze that seemed to cool his throbbing brain. He experienced a dull sense of unreality. He was a stranger in a strange land, a land that had become suddenly imbued with black horror. The shadow of the noose hovered above him, and in that dark house lay John Branner, with his butchered head – like the figments of a dream these facts spun and eddied in his brain until all merged in a gray twilight as sleep came uninvited to his weary soul.

He awoke to a cold white dawn and full memory of the horrors of the night. Mists curled about the stems of the pines, crawled in smoky wisps up the broken walk. Buckner was shaking him.

"Wake up! It's daylight."

Griswell rose, wincing at the stiffness of his limbs. His face was gray and old.

"I'm ready. Let's go upstairs."

"I've already been!" Buckner's eyes burned in the early dawn. "I didn't wake you up. I went as soon as it was light. I found nothin'."

"The tracks of the bare feet – "

"Gone!"

"Gone?"

"Yes, gone! The dust had been disturbed all over the hall, from the point where Branner's tracks ended; swept into corners. No chance of trackin' anything there now. Something obliterated those tracks while we sat here, and I didn't hear a sound. I've gone through the whole house. Not a sign of anything."

Griswell shuddered at the thought of himself sleeping alone on the porch while Buckner conducted his exploration.

"What shall we do?" he asked listlessly. "With those tracks gone, there goes my only chance of proving my story."

"We'll take Branner's body into the county-seat," answered Buckner. "Let me do the talkin'. If the authorities knew the facts as they appear, they'd insist on you being confined and indicted. I don't believe you killed Branner – but neither a district attorney, judge nor jury would believe what you told me, or what happened to us last night. I'm handlin' this thing my own way. I'm not goin' to arrest you until I've exhausted every other possibility.

"Say nothin' about what's happened here, when we get to town. I'll simply tell the district attorney that John Branner was killed by a party or parties unknown, and that I'm workin' on the case.

"Are you game to come back with me to this house and spend the night here, sleepin' in that room as you and Branner slept last night?"

Griswell went white, but answered as stoutly as his ancestors might have expressed their determination to hold their cabins in the teeth of the Pequots: "I'll do it."

"Let's go then; help me pack the body out to your auto."

Griswell's soul revolted at the sight of John Branner's bloodless face in the chill white dawn, and the feel of his clammy flesh. The gray fog wrapped wispy tentacles about their feet as they carried their grisly burden across the lawn.

2

The Snake's Brother

Again the shadows were lengthening over the pinelands, and again two men came bumping along the old road in a car with a New England license plate.

Buckner was driving. Griswell's nerves were too shattered for him to trust himself at the wheel. He looked gaunt and haggard, and his face was still palid. The strain of the day spent at the county-seat was added to the horror that still rode his soul like the shadow of a black-winged vulture. He had not slept, had not tasted what he had eaten.

"I told you I'd tell you about the Blassenvilles," said Buckner. "They were proud folks, haughty, and pretty damn ruthless when they wanted their way. They didn't treat their niggers as well as the other planters did – got their ideas in the West Indies, I reckon. There was a streak of cruelty in them – especially Miss Celia, the last one of the family to come to these parts. That was long after the slaves had been freed, but she used to whip her mulatto maid just like she was a slave, the old folks say. . . . The niggers said when a Blassenville died, the devil was always waitin' for him out in the black pines.

"Well, after the Civil War they died off pretty fast, livin' in poverty on the plantation which was allowed to go to ruin. Finally only four girls were left, sisters, livin' in the old house and ekin' out a bare livin', with a few niggers livin' in the old slave huts and workin' the fields of the share. They kept to themselves, bein' proud, and ashamed of their poverty. Folks wouldn't see them for months at a time. When they needed supplies they sent a nigger to town after them.

"But folks knew about it when Miss Celia came to live with them. She came from somewhere in the West Indies, where the whole family originally had its roots – a fine, handsome woman, they say, in the early thirties. But she didn't mix with folks any more than the girls did. She brought a mulatto maid with her, and the Blassenville cruelty cropped out in her treatment of this maid. I knew an old nigger, years ago, who swore he saw Miss Celia tie this girl up to a tree, stark naked, and whip her with a horsewhip. Nobody was surprised when she disappeared. Everybody figured she'd run away, of course.

"Well, one day in the spring of 1890 Miss Elizabeth, the youngest girl, came into town for the first time in maybe a year. She came after supplies. Said the niggers had all left the place. Talked a little more, too, a bit wild. Said Miss Celia had gone, without leaving any word. Said her sisters thought she'd gone back to the West Indies, but she believed her aunt *was* still in the house. She didn't say what she meant. Just got her supplies and pulled out for the Manor.

"A month went past, and a nigger came into town and said that Miss

Elizabeth was livin' at the Manor alone. Said her three sisters weren't there any more, that they'd left one by one without givin' any word or explanation. She didn't know where they'd gone, and was scared to stay there alone, but didn't know where else to go. She'd never known anything but the Manor, and had neither relatives nor friends. But she was in mortal terror of *something*. The nigger said she locked herself in her room at night and kept candles burnin' all night. . . .

"It was a stormy spring night when Miss Elizabeth came tearin' into town on the one horse she owned, nearly dead from fright. She fell from her horse in the square; when she could talk she said she'd found a secret room in the Manor that had been forgotten for a hundred years. And she said that there she found her three sisters, dead, and hangin' by their necks from the ceilin'. She said *something* chased her and nearly brained her with an ax as she ran out the front door, but somehow she got to the horse and got away. She was crazy with fear, and didn't know what it was that chased her – said it looked like a woman with a yellow face.

"About a hundred men rode out there, right away. They searched the house from top to bottom, but they didn't find any secret room, or the remains of the sisters. But they did find a hatchet stickin' in the doorjamb downstairs, with some of Miss Elizabeth's hairs stuck on it, just as she'd said. She wouldn't go back there and show them how to find the secret door; almost went crazy when they suggested it.

"When she was able to travel, the people made up some money and loaned it to her – she was still too proud to accept charity – and she went to California. She never came back, but later it was learned, when she sent back to repay the money they'd loaned her, that she'd married out there.

"Nobody ever bought the house. It stood there just as she'd left it, and as the years passed folks stole all the furnishings out of it, poor white trash, I reckon. A nigger wouldn't go about it. But they came after sun-up and left long before sundown."

"What did the people think about Miss Elizabeth's story?" asked Griswell.

"Well, most folks thought she'd gone a little crazy, livin' in that old house alone. But some people believed that mulatto girl, Joan, didn't run away, after all. They believe she'd hidden in the woods, and glutted her hatred of the Blassenvilles by murderin' Miss Celia and the three girls.

They beat up the woods with bloodhounds, but never found a trace of her. If there was a secret room in the house, she might have been hidin' there – if there was anything to that theory."

She couldn't have been hiding there all these years," muttered Griswell. "Anyway, the thing in the house now isn't human."

Buckner wrenched the wheel around and turned into a dim trace that left the main road and meandered off through the pines.

"Where are you going?"

"There's an old nigger that lives off this way a few miles. I want to talk to him. We're up against something that takes more than white man's sense. The black people know more than we do about some things. The old man is nearly a hundred years old. His master educated him when he was a boy, and after he was freed he traveled more extensively than most white men do. They say he's a voodoo man."

Griswell shivered at the phrase, staring uneasily at the green forest walls that shut them in. The scent of the pines was mingled with the odors of unfamiliar plants and blossoms. But underlying all was a reek of rot and decay. Again a sick abhorrence of these dark mysterious woodlands almost overpowered him.

"Voodoo!" he muttered. "I'd forgotten about that – I never could think of black magic in connection with the South. To me witchcraft was always associated with old crooked streets in waterfront towns, overhung by gabled roofs that were old when they were hanging witches in Salem; dark musty alleys where black cats and other things might steal at night. Witchcraft always meant the old towns of New England to me – but all this is more terrible than any New England legend – these somber pines, old deserted houses, lost plantations, mysterious black people, old tales of madness and horror – God, what frightful, ancient terrors there are on this continent fools call 'young'!"

"Here's old Jacob's hut," announced Buckner, bringing the automobile to a halt.

Griswell saw a clearing and a small cabin squatting under the shadows of the huge trees. There pines gave way to oaks and cypresses, bearded with gray trailing moss, and behind the cabin lay the edge of a swamp that ran away under the dimness of the trees, choked with rank vegetation. A thin wisp of blue smoke curled up from the stick-and-mud chimney.

He followed Buckner to the tiny stoop, where the sheriff pushed open the leather-hinged door and strode in. Griswell blinked in the comparative dimness of the interior. A single small window let in a little daylight. An old negro crouched beside the hearth, watching a pot stew over the open fire. He looked up as they entered, but did not rise. He seemed incredibly old. His face was a mass of wrinkles, and his eyes, dark and vital, were filmed momentarily at times as if his mind wandered.

Buckner motioned Griswell to sit down in a string-bottomed chair, and himself took a rudely-made bench near the hearth, facing the old man.

"Jacob," he said bluntly, "The time's come for you to talk. I know you know the secret of Blassenville Manor. I've never questioned you about it, because it wasn't in my line. But a man was murdered there last night, and this man here may hang for it, unless you tell me what haunts that old house of the Blassenvilles."

The old man's eyes gleamed, then grew misty as if clouds of extreme age drifted across his brittle mind.

"The Blassenvilles," he murmured, and his voice was mellow and rich, his speech not the patois of the piny woods darky. "They were proud people, sirs – proud and cruel. Some died in the war, some were killed in duels – the menfolks, sirs. Some died in the Manor – the old Manor – " His voice trailed off into unintelligible mumblings.

"What of the Manor?' asked Buckner patiently.

"Miss Celia was the proudest of them all," the old man muttered. "The proudest and the cruelest. The black people hated her; Joan most of all. Joan had white blood in her, and she was proud too. Miss Celia whipped her like a slave."

"What is the secret of Blassenville Manor?" persisted Buckner.

The film faded from the old man's eyes; they were dark as moonlit wells.

"What secret, sir? I do not understand."

"Yes, you do. For years that old house has stood there with its mystery. You know the key to its riddle."

The old man stirred the stew. He seemed perfectly rational now.

"Sir, life is sweet, even to an old black man."

"You mean somebody would kill you if you told me?"

But the old man was mumbling again, his eyes clouded.

"Not somebody. No human. No human being. The black gods of the swamps. My secret is inviolate, guarded by the Big Serpent, the god above all gods. He would send a little brother to kiss me with his cold lips – a little brother with a white crescent moon on his head. I sold my soul to the Big Serpent when he made me a maker of *zuvembies* – "

Buckner stiffened.

"I heard that word once before," he said softly, "from the lips of a dying black man, when I was a child. What does it mean?"

Fear filled the eyes of old Jacob.

"What have I said? No-no! I said nothing."

"Zuvembies," prompted Buckner.

"Zuvembies," mechanically repeated the old man, his eyes vacant. "A *zuvembie* was once a woman – on the Slave Coast they know of them. The drums that whisper by night in the hills of Haiti tell of them. The makers of *zuvembies* are honored of the people of Damballah. It is death to speak of it to a white man – it is one of the Snake God's forbidden secrets."

"You speak of the *zuvembies*," said Buckler softly.

"I must not speak of it," mumbled the old man, and Griswell realized he was thinking aloud, too far gone in his dotage to be aware that he was speaking at all. "No white man must know that I danced in the Black Ceremony of the voodoo, and was made a maker of *zombies* and *zuvembies*. The Big Snake punishes loose tongues with death."

"A *zuvembie* is a woman?" prompted Buckner.

"*Was* a woman," the old negro muttered. "*Sh*e knew I was a maker of *zuvembies* – she came and stood in my hut and asked for the awful brew – the brew of ground snake-bones, and the blood of vampire bats, and the dew from a nighthawk's wings, and other elements unnamable. She had danced in the Black Ceremony – she was ripe to become a *zuvembie* – the Black Brew was all that was needed – the other was beautiful – I could not refuse her."

"Who?" demanded Buckner tensely, but the old man's head was sunk on his withered breast, and he did not reply. He seemed to slumber as he sat. Buckner shook him. "You gave a brew to make a woman a *zuvembie* – what is a *zuvembie*?"

The old man stirred resentfully and muttered drowsily.

"A *zuvembie* is no longer human. It knows neither relatives nor friends. It is one with the people of the Black World. It commands the natural demons – owls, bats, snakes, and werewolves, and can fetch darkness to blot out a little light. It can be slain by lead or steel, but unless it is slain thus, it lives for ever, and it eats no such food as humans eat. It dwells like a bat in a cave or an old house. Times means naught to the *zuvembie*; an hour, a day, a year, all is one. It cannot speak human words, nor think as a human thinks, but it can hypnotize the living by the sound of its voice, and when it slays a man, it can command his lifeless body until the flesh is cold. As long as the blood flows, the corpse is its slave. Its pleasure lies in the slaughter of human beings."

"And why should one become a *zuvembie*?" asked Buckner softly.

"Hate," whispered the old man. "Hate! Revenge!"

"Was her name Joan?" murmured Buckner.

It was as if the name penetrated the fogs of senility that clouded the voodoo-man's mind. He shook himself and the film faded from his eyes, leaving them hard and gleaming as wet black marble.

"Joan?" he said slowly. "I have not heard that name for the span of a generation. I seem to have been sleeping, gentleman; I do not remember – I ask your pardon. Old men fall asleep before the fire, like old dogs. You asked me of Blassenville Manor? Sir, if I were to tell you why I cannot answer you, you would deem it mere superstition. Yet the white man's God be my witness – "

As he spoke he was reaching across the hearth for a piece of firewood, groping among the heaps of sticks there. And his voice broke in a scream, as he jerked back his arm convulsively. And a horrible, thrashing, trailing *thing* came with it. Around the voodoo-man's arm a mottled length of that shape was wrapped and a wicked wedge-shaped head stuck again in silent fury.

The old man fell on the hearth, screaming, upsetting the simmering pot and scattering the embers, and then Buckner caught up a billet of firewood and crushed the flat head. Cursing, he kicked aside the knotting, twisting trunk, glaring briefly at the mangled head. Old Jacob had ceased screaming and writhing; he lay still, staring ghastly upward.

"Dead?" whispered Griswell.

"Dead as Judas Iscariot," snapped Buckner, frowning at the twitching reptile. "That infernal snake crammed enough poison into his veins to kill a dozen men his age. But I think it was the shock and fright that killed him."

"What shall we do?" asked Griswell, shivering.

"Leave the body on that bunk. Nothin' can hurt it, if we bolt the door so the wild hogs can't get in, or any cat. We'll carry it into town tomorrow. We've got work to do tonight. Let's get goin'."

Griswell shrank from touching the corpse, but he helped Buckner lift it on the rude bunk, and then stumbled hastily out of the hut. The sun was hovering above the horizon, visible in dazzling red flame through the black stems of the trees.

They climbed into the car in silence, and went bumping back along the stumpy train.

"He said the Big Snake would send one of his brothers," muttered Griswell.

"Nonsense!" snorted Buckner. "Snakes like warmth, and that swamp is full of them. It crawled in and coiled up among that firewood. Old Jacob disturbed it, and it bit him. Nothin' supernatural about that." After a short silence he said, in a different voice, "That was the first time I ever saw a rattler strike without singin'; and the first time I ever saw a snake *with a white crescent moon on its head.*"

They were turning in to the main road before either spoke again.

"You think that the mulatto Joan has skulked in the house all these years?" Griswell asked.

"You heard what old Jacob said," answered Buckner grimly. "Time means nothin' to a *zuvembie.*"

As they made the last turn in the road, Griswell braced himself against the sight of Blassenville Manor looming black against the red sunset. When it came into view he bit his lip to keep from shrieking. The suggestion of cryptic horror came back in all its power.

"Look!" he whispered from the dry lips as they came to a halt beside the road. Buckner grunted.

From the balustrades of the gallery rose a whirling cloud of pigeons that swept away into the sunset, black against the lurid glare.

The Call of Zuvembie

Both men sat rigid for a few moments after the pigeons had flown.

"Well, I've seen them at last," muttered Buckner.

"Only the doomed see them, perhaps," whispered Griswell. "That tramp saw them – "

"Well, we'll see," returned the Southerner tranquilly, as he climbed out of the car, but Griswell noticed him unconsciously hitch forward his scabbarded gun.

The oaken door sagged on broken hinges. Their feet echoed on the broken brick walk. The blind windows reflected the sunset in sheets of flame. As they came into the broad hall Griswell saw the string of black marks that ran across the floor and into the chamber, marking the path of a dead man.

Buckner had brought blankets out of the automobile. He spread them before the fireplace.

"I'll lie next to the door," he said. "You lie where you did last night."

"Shall we light a fire in the grate?" asked Griswell, dreading the thought of the blackness that would cloak the woods when the brief twilight had died.

"No. You've got a flashlight and so have I. We'll lie here in the dark and see what happens. Can you use that gun I gave you?"

"I suppose so. I never fired a revolver, but I know how it's done."

"Well, leave the shootin' to me, if possible." The sheriff seated himself cross-legged on his blankets and emptied the cylinder of his big blue Colt, inspecting each cartridge with a critical eye before he replaced it.

Griswell prowled nervously back and forth, begrudging the slow fading of the light as a miser begrudges the waning of his gold. He leaned with one hand against the mantelpiece, staring down into the dust-covered ashes. The fire that produced those ashes must have been builded by Elizabeth Blassenville, more than forty years before. The thought was depressing. Idly he stirred the dusty ashes with his toe. Something came to view among the charred debris-a bit of paper, stained and yellowed. Still idly he bent and drew it out of the ashes. It was a note-book with moldering cardboard backs.

"What have you found?" asked Buckner, squinting down the gleaming barrel of his gun.

"Nothing but an old note-book. Looks like a diary. The pages are covered with writing – but the ink is so faded, and the paper is in such a state of decay that I can't tell much about it. How do you suppose it came in the fireplace, without being burned up?"

"Thrown in long after the fire was out," surmised Buckner. "Probably found and tossed in the fireplace by somebody who was in here stealin' furniture. Likely somebody who couldn't read."

Griswell fluttered the crumbling leaves listlessly, straining his eyes in the fading light over the yellowed scrawls. Then he stiffened.

"Here's an entry that's legible! Listen!" He read:

" 'I know someone is in the house besides myself. I can hear someone prowling about at night when the sun has set and the pines are black outside. Often in the night I hear it fumbling at my door. *Who* is it? Is it one of my sisters? Is it Aunt Celia? If it is either of these, why does she steal so subtly about the house? Why does she tug at my door, and glide away when I call to her? No, no! I dare not! I am afraid. Oh God, what shall I do? I dare not stay here – but where am I to go?' "

"By God!" ejaculated Buckner. "That must be Elizabeth Blassingville's diary! Go on!"

"I can't make out the rest of the pages," answered Griswell. "But a few pages further on I can make out some lines." He read:

" 'Why did the negroes all run away when Aunt Celia disappeared? My sisters are dead. I know they are dead. I seem to sense that they died horribly, in fear and agony. But why? *Why?* If someone murdered Aunt Celia, why should that person murder my poor sisters? They were always kind to the black people. Joan – ' " He paused, scowling futilely.

"A piece of the page is torn out. Here's another entry under another date – at least if I judge it's a date; I can't make it out for sure.

" ' – the awful thing that the old negress hinted at? She named Jacob Blount, and Joan, but she would not speak plainly; perhaps she feared to – ' Part of it gone here, then: 'No, no! How can it be? *She* is dead – or gone away. Yet – she was born and raised in the West Indies, and from hints she let fall in the past, I know she delved into the mysteries of the voodoo. I believe she even danced in one of their horrible ceremonies – how could she have been such a beast? And this – this horror. God, can such things be? I know not what to think. If it is *she* who roams the house at night, who fumbles at my door, who *whistles* so weirdly and sweetly – no, no, I must be going mad. If I stay here alone I shall die as hideously as my sisters must have died. Of that I am convinced.' "

The incoherent chronicle ended as abruptly as it had begun. Griswell was so engrossed in deciphering the scraps that he was not aware that darkness had stolen upon them, hardly aware that Buckner was holding his electric torch for him to read by. Waking from his abstraction he started and darted a quick glance at the black hallway.

"What do you make of it?"

"What I've suspected all the time," answered Buckner. "That mulatto maid Joan turned *zuvembie* to avenge herself of Miss Celia. Probably hated the whole family as much as she did her mistress. She'd taken part in voodoo ceremonies on her native island until she was 'ripe,' as old Jacob said. All she needed was the Black Brew – he supplied that. She killed Miss Celia and the three older girls, and would have gotten Elizabeth but for chance. She's been lurkin' in this old house all these years, like a snake in a ruin."

"But why should she murder a stranger?"

"You heard what old Jacob said," reminded Buckner. "A *zuvembie* finds satisfaction in the slaughter of humans. She called Branner up the stair and split his head and stuck the hatchet in his hand, and sent him downstairs to murder you. No court will ever believe that, but if we can produce her body, that will be evidence enough to prove your innocence. My word will be taken, that she murdered Branner. Jacob said a *zuvembie* could be killed . . . in reporting this affair I don't have to be too accurate in detail."

"She came and peered over the balustrade of the stair at us," muttered Griswell. "But why didn't we find her tracks on the stair?"

"Maybe you dreamed it. Maybe a *zuvembie* can project her spirit – hell! why try to rationalize something that's outside the bounds of rationality? Let's begin our watch."

"Don't turn out the light!" exclaimed Griswell involuntarily. Then he added: "Of course. Turn it out. We must be in the dark as" – he gagged a bit – "as Branner and I were."

But fear like a physical sickness assailed him when the room was plunged into darkness. He lay trembling and his heart beat so heavily he felt as if he would suffocate.

"The West Indies must be the plague spot of the world," muttered Buckner, a blur on his blankets. "I've heard of zombies. Never knew before what a zuvembie was. Evidently some drug concocted by the voodoo-men to induce madness in women. That doesn't explain the other things, though; the hypnotic powers, the abnormal longevity, the ability to control corpses – no, a zuvembie can't be merely a madwoman. It's a monster, something more and less than a human being, created by the magic that spawns in black swamps and jungles – well, we'll see."

His voice ceased, and in the silence Griswell heard the pounding of his own heart. Outside in the black woods a wolf howled eerily, and owls hooted. Then silence fell again like a black fog.

Griswell forced himself to lie still on his blankets. Time seemed at a standstill. He felt as if he were choking. The suspense was growing unendurable; the effort he made to control his crumbling nerves bathed his limbs in sweat. He clenched his teeth until his jaws ached and almost locked, and the nails of his fingers bit deeply into his palms.

He did not know what he was expecting. The fiend would strike again – but how? Would it be horrible, sweet whistling, bare feet steeling down the creaking steps, or a sudden hatchet-stroke in the dark? Would it choose him or Buckner? *Was Buckner already dead?* He could see nothing in the blackness, but he heard the man's steady breathing. The Southerner must have nerves of steel. Or was that Buckner breathing beside him, separated by a narrow strip of darkness? Had the fiend already struck in silence, and taken the sheriff's place, there to lie in ghoulish glee until it was ready to strike? – a thousand hideous fancies assailed Griswell tooth and claw.

He began to feel that he would go mad if he did not leap to his feet, screaming, and burst frenziedly out of that accursed house – not even the fear of the gallows could keep him lying there in the darkness any longer – the rhythm of Buckner's breathing was suddenly broken, and Griswell felt as if a bucket of ice-water had been poured over him. From somewhere above them rose a sound of weird, sweet whistling. . . .

Griswell's control snapped, plunging his brain into darkness deeper than the physical blackness which engulfed him. There was a period of absolute blankness, in which a realization of *motion* was his first sensation of awakening consciousness. He was running, madly, stumbling over an incredibly rough road. All was darkness about him, and he ran blindly. Vaguely he realized that he must have bolted from the house, and fled for perhaps miles before his overwrought brain begun to function. He did not care; dying on the gallows for a murder he never committed did not terrify him half as much as the thought of returning to that house of horror. He was overpowered by the urge to run – run – run as he was running now, blindly, until he reached the end of his endurance. The mist had not yet fully lifted from his brain, but he was aware of a dull wonder that he could not see the stars through the black branches. He wished vaguely that he could see where he was going. He believed he must be climbing a hill, and that was strange, for he knew there were no hills within miles of the Manor. Then above and ahead of him a dim glow began.

He scrambled toward it, over ledge-like projections that were more and more and more taking on a disquieting symmetry. Then he was horror-stricken to realize that a sound was impacting on his ears – *a weird mocking whistle.* The sound swept the mists away. Why, what was this? *Where was he?* Awakening and realization came like the stunning stroke of a butcher's maul. He was not fleeing along a road, or climbing a hill; he was mounting a stair. He was still in Blassenville Manor! *And he was climbing the stair!*

An inhuman scream burst from his lips. Above it the mad whistling rose in a ghoulish piping of demoniac triumph. He tried to stop – to turn back – even to fling himself over the balustrade. His shrieking rang unbearably in his own ears. But his will-power was shattered to bits. It did not exist. He had no will. He had dropped his flashlight, and he had forgotten the gun in his pocket. He could not command his own body. His legs, moving stiffly, worked like pieces of mechanism detached from his brain, obeying an outside will. Clumping methodically they carried him shrieking up the stair toward the witch-fire glow shimmering above him.

"Buckner!" he screamed. "Buckner! Help, for God's sake!"

His voice strangled in his throat. He had reached the upper landing. He was tottering down the hallway. The whistling sank and ceased, but its impulsion still drove him on. He could not see from what source the dim glow came. It seemed to emanate from no central focus. But he saw a vague figure shambling toward him. It looked like a woman, but no human woman ever walked with that skulking gait, and no human woman ever had that face of horror, that leering yellow blur of lunacy – he tried to scream at the sight of that face, at the glint of keen steel in the uplifted claw-like hand – but his tongue was frozen.

Then something crashed deafeningly behind him; the shadows were split by a tongue of flame which lit a hideous figure falling backward. Hard on the heels of the report rang an inhuman squawk.

In the darkness that followed the flash Griswell fell to his knees and covered his face with his hands. He did not hear Buckner's voice. The Southerner's hand on his shoulder shook him out of his swoon.

A light in his eyes blinded him. He blinked, shaded his eyes, looked up into Buckner's face, bending at the rim of the circle of light. The sheriff was pale.

"Are you hurt? God, man, are you hurt? There's a butcher knife there on the floor – "

"I'm not hurt," mumbed Griswell. "You fired just in time – the fiend! Where is it? Where did it go?"

"Listen!"

Somewhere in the house there sounded a sickening flopping and flapping as of something that thrashed and struggled in its death convulsions.

"Jacob was right," said Buckner grimly. "Lead can kill them. I hit her, all right. Didn't dare use my flashlight, but there was enough light. When that whistlin' started you almost walked over me gettin' out. I knew you were hypnotized, or whatever it is. I followed you up the stairs. I was right behind you, but crouchin' low so she wouldn't see me, and maybe get away again. I almost waited too long before I fired – but the sight of her almost paralyzed me. Look!"

He flashed his light down the hall, and now it shone bright and clear. And it shone on an aperture gaping in the wall where no door had showed before.

"The secret panel Miss Elizabeth found!" Buckner snapped. "Come on!"

He ran across the hallway and Griswell followed him dazedly. The flopping and thrashing came from beyond that mysterious door, and now the sounds had ceased.

The light revealed a narrow, tunnel-like corridor that evidently led through one of the thick walls. Buckner plunged into it without hesitation.

"Maybe it couldn't think like a human," he muttered, shining his light ahead of him. "But it had sense enough to erase its tracks last night so we couldn't trail it to that point in the wall and maybe find the secret panel. There's a room ahead – the secret room of the Blassenvilles!"

And Griswell cried out: "My God! It's the windowless chamber I saw in my dream, with the three bodies hanging – ahhhhh!"

Buckner's light playing about the circular chamber became suddenly motionless. In that wide ring of light three figures appeared, three dried, shriveled, mummy-like shapes, still clad in the moldering garments of the last century. Their slippers were clear of the floor as they hung by their withered necks from chains suspended from the ceiling.

"The three Blassenville sisters!" muttered Buckner. "Miss Elizabeth wasn't crazy, after all."

"Look!" Griswell could barely make his voice intelligible. "There – over there in the corner!"

The light moved, halted.

"Was that thing a woman once?" whispered Griswell. "God, look at that face, even in death. Look at those claw-like hands, with black talons like those of a beast. Yes, it was human, though – even the rags of an old ballroom gown. Why should a mulatto maid wear such a dress, I wonder?"

"This has been her lair for over forty years," muttered Buckner, brooding over the grinning grisly thing sprawling in the corner. "This clears you, Griswell – a crazy woman with a hatchet – that's all the authorities need to know. God, what a revenge! – what a foul revenge! Yet what a bestial nature she must have had, in the beginnin', to delve into voodoo as she must have done – "

"The mulatto woman?" whispered Griswell, dimly sensing a horror that overshadowed all the rest of the terror.

Buckner shook his head. "We misunderstood old Jacob's maunderin's, and the things Miss Elizabeth wrote – *she* must have known, but family pride sealed her lips. Griswell, I understand now; the mulatto woman had her revenge, but not as we supposed. She didn't drink the Black Brew old Jacob fixed for her. It was for somebody else, to be given secretly in her food, or coffee no doubt. Then Joan ran away, leavin' the seeds of the hell she'd sowed to grow."

"That – that's not the mulatto woman?" whispered Griswell.

"When I saw her out there in the hallway I knew she was no mulatto. And those distorted features still reflect a family likeness. I've seen her portrait, and I can't be mistaken. There lies the creature that was once Celia Blassenville."

Old Garfield's Heart

I was sitting on the porch when my grandfather hobbled out and sank down on his favorite chair with the cushioned seat, and began to stuff tobacco in his old corncob-pipe.

"I thought you'd be goin' to the dance," he said.

"I'm waiting for Doc Blaine," I answered. "I'm going over to old man Garfield's with him."

My grandfather sucked at his pipe awhile before he spoke again.

"Old Jim purty bad off?"

"Doc says he hasn't a chance."

"Who's takin' care of him?"

"Joe Braxton – against Garfield's wishes. But somebody had to stay with him."

My grandfather sucked his pipe noisily, and watched the heat lightning playing away off up in the hills; then he said: "You think old Jim's the biggest liar in this county, don't you?"

"He tells some pretty tall tales," I admitted. "Some of the things he claimed he took part in, must have happened before he was born."

"I came from Tennessee to Texas in 1870," my grandfather said abruptly. "I saw this town of Lost Knob grow up from nothin'. There wasn't even a log-hut store here when I came. But old Jim Garfield was here, livin' in the same place he lives now, only then it was a log cabin. He didn't look a day older now than he did the first time I saw him."

"You never mentioned that before," I said in some surprise.

"I knew you'd put it down to an old man's maunderin's," he answered. "Old Jim was the first white man to settle in this country. He built his cabin a good fifty miles west of the frontier. God knows how he done it, for these hills swarmed with Comanches then.

"I remember the first time I ever saw him. Even then everybody called him 'old Jim.'

"I remember him tellin' me the same tales he's told you – how he was at the battle of San Jacinto when he was a youngster, and how he'd rode with Ewen Cameron and Jack Hayes. Only I believe him, and you don't.

"That was so long ago – " I protested.

"The last Indian raid through this country was in 1874," said my grandfather, engrossed in his own reminiscences. "I was in on that fight, and so was old Jim. I saw him knock old Yellow Tail off his mustang at seven hundred yards with a buffalo rifle.

"But before that I was with him in a fight up near the head of Locust Creek. A band of Comanches came down Mesquital, lootin' and burnin', rode through the hills and started back up Locust Creek, and a scout of us were hot on their heels. We ran on to them just at sundown in a mesquite flat. We killed seven of them, and the rest skinned out through the brush on foot. But three of our boys were killed, and Jim Garfield got a thrust in the breast with a lance.

"It was an awful wound. He lay like a dead man, and it seemed sure nobody could live after a wound like that. But an old Indian came out of the brush, and when we aimed our guns at him, he made the peace sign and spoke to us in Spanish. I don't know why the boys didn't shoot him in his tracks, because our blood was heated with the fightin' and killin', but somethin' about him made us hold our fire. He said he wasn't a Comanche, but was an old friend's of Garfield's, and wanted to help him. He asked us to carry Jim into a clump of mesquite, and leave him alone with him, and to this day I don't know why we did, but we did. It was an awful time – the wounded moanin' and callin' for water, the starin' corpses strewn about the camp, night comin' on, and no way of knowin' that the Indians wouldn't return when dark fell.

"We made camp right there, because the horses were fagged out, and we watched all night, but the Comanches didn't come back. I don't know what went on out in the mesquite where Jim Garfield's body lay, because I never saw that strange Indian again, but durin' the night I kept hearin' a weird moanin' that wasn't made by the dyin' men, and an owl hooted from midnight till dawn.

"And at sunrise Jim Garfield came walkin' out of the mesquite, pale and haggard, but alive, and already the wound in his breast had closed and begun to heal. And since then he's never mentioned that wound, nor that fight, nor the strange Indian who came and went so mysteriously. And he hasn't aged a bit; he looks now just like he did then – a man of about fifty."

In the silence that followed, a car began to purr down the road, and twin shafts of light cut through the dusk.

"That's Doc Blaine," I said. "When I come back I'll tell you how Garfield is."

Doc Blaine was prompt with his predictions as we drove the three miles of post-oak covered hills that lay between Lost Knob and the Garfield farm.

"I'll be surprised to find him alive," he said, "smashed up like he is. A man his age ought to have more sense than to try to break a young horse."

"He doesn't look so old," I remarked.

"I'll be fifty, my next birthday," answered Doc Blaine. "I've know him all my life, and he must have been at least fifty the first time I ever saw him. His looks are deceiving."

Old Garfield's dwelling-place was reminiscent of the past. The boards of the low squat house had never known paint. Orchard fence and corrals were built of rails.

Old Jim lay on his rude bed, tended crudely but efficiently by the man Doc Blaine had hired over the old man's protests. As I looked at him, I was impressed anew by his evident vitality. His frame was stooped but unwithered, his limbs rounded out with springy muscles. In his corded neck and in his face, drawn though it was with suffering, was apparent an innate virility. His eyes, though partly glazed with pain, burned with the same unquenchable element.

"He's been ravin'," said Joe Braxton stolidly.

"First white man in this country," muttered old Jim, becoming intelligible. "Hills no white man ever set foot in before. Gettin' too old. Have to settle down. Can't move on like I used to. Settle down here. Good country before it filled up with cow-men and squatters. Wish Ewen Cameron could see this country. The Mexicans shot him. Damn 'em!"

Doc Blaine shook his head. "He's all smashed up inside. He won't live till daylight."

Garfield unexpectedly lifted his head and looked at us with clear eyes.

"Wrong, Doc," he wheezed, his breath whistling with pain. "I'll live. What's broken bones and twisted guts? Nothin'! It's the heart that counts.

295

Long as the heart keeps pumpin', a man can't die. My heart's sound. Listen to it! Feel of it!"

He groped painfully for Doc Blaine's wrist, dragged his hand to his bosom and held it there, staring up into the doctor's face with avid intensity.

"Regular dynamo, ain't it?" he gasped. "Stronger'n a gasoline engine!"

Blaine beckoned me. "Lay your hand here," he said, placing my hand on the old man's bare breast. "He does have a remarkable heart action."

I noted, in the light of the coal-oil lamp, a great livid scar as might be made by a flint-headed spear. I laid my hand directly on this scar, and an exclamation escaped my lips.

Under my hand old Jim Garfield's heart pulsed, but its throb was like no other heart action I have ever observed. Its power was astounding; his ribs vibrated to its steady throb. It felt more like the vibrating of a dynamo than the action of a human organ. I could feel its amazing vitality radiating from his breast, stealing up into my hand and up my arm, until my own heart seemed to speed up in response.

"I can't die," old Jim gasped. "Not so long as my heart's in my breast. Only a bullet through the brain can kill me. And even then I wouldn't be rightly dead, as long as my heart beats in my breast. Yet it ain't rightly mine, either. It belongs to Ghost Man, the Lipan chief. It was the heart of a god the Lipans worshiped before the Comanches drove 'em out of their native hills.

"I knew Ghost Man down on the Rio Grande, when I was with Ewen Cameron. I saved his life from the Mexicans once. He tied the string of ghost wampum between him and me – the wampum no man but me and him can see or feel. He came when he knowed I needed him, in that fight up on the headwaters of Locust Creek, when I got this scar.

"I was dead as a man can be. My heart was sliced in two, like the heart of a butchered beef steer.

"All night Ghost Man did magic, callin' my ghost back from spirit-land. I remember that flight, a little. It was dark, and gray-like, and I drifted through gray mists and heard the dead wailin' past me in the mist. But Ghost Man brought me back.

"He took out what was left of my mortal heart, and put the heart of the god in my bosom. But it's his, and when I'm through with it, he'll come for it. It's kept me alive and strong for the lifetime of a man. Age can't touch me. What do I care if these fools around here call me an old liar? What I know, I know. But hark'ee!"

His fingers became claws, clamping fiercely on Doc Blaine's wrist. His old eyes, old yet strangely young, burned fierce as those of an eagle under his bushy brows.

"If by some mischance I *should* die, now or later, promise me this! Cut into my bosom and take out the heart Ghost Man lent me so long ago! It's his. And as long as it beats in my body, my spirit'll be tied to that body, though my head be crushed like an egg underfoot! A livin' thing in a rottin' body! Promise!"

"All right, I promise," replied Doc Blaine, to humor him, and old Jim Garfield sank back with a whistling sigh of relief.

He did not die that night, nor the next, nor the next. I well remember the next day, because it was that day that I had the fight with Jack Kirby.

People will take a good deal from a bully, rather than to spill blood. Because nobody had gone to the trouble of killing him, Kirby thought the whole countryside was afraid of him.

He had bought a steer from my father, and when my father went to collect for it, Kirby told him that he had paid the money to me – which was a lie. I went looking for Kirby, and came upon him in a bootleg joint, boasting of his toughness, and telling the crowd that he was going to beat me up and make me say that he had paid me the money, and that I had stuck it into my own pocket. When I heard him say that, I saw red, and ran in on him with a stockman's knife, and cut him across the face, and in the neck, side, breast, and belly, and the only thing that saved his life was the fact that the crowd pulled me off.

There was a preliminary hearing, and I was indicted on a charge of assault, and my trial was set for the following term of court. Kirby was as tough-fibered as a post-oak country bully ought to be, and he recovered, swearing vengeance, for he was vain of his looks, though God knows why, and I had permanently impaired them.

And while Jack Kirby was recovering, old man Garfield recovered too, to the amazement of everybody, especially Doc Blaine.

I well remember the night Doc Blaine took me again out to old Jim Garfield's farm. I was in Shifty Corlan's joint, trying to drink enough of the slop he called beer to get a kick out of it, when Doc Blaine came in and persuaded me to go with him.

As we drove along the winding old road in Doc's car, I asked: "Why are you insistent that I go with you this particular night? This isn't a professional call, is it?"

"No," he said. "You couldn't kill old Jim with a post-oak maul. He's completely recovered from injuries that ought to have killed an ox. To tell you the truth, Jack Kirby is in Lost Knob, swearing he'll shoot you on sight."

"Well, for God's sake!" I exclaimed angrily. "Now everybody'll think I left town because I was afraid of him. Turn around and take me back, damn it!"

"Be reasonable," said Doc. "Everybody knows you're not afraid of Kirby. Nobody's afraid of him now. His bluff's broken, and that's why he's so wild against you. But you can't afford to have any more trouble with him now, and your trial only a short time off."

I laughed and said: "Well, if he's looking for me hard enough, he can find me as easily at old Garfield's as in town, because Shifty Corlan heard you say where we were going. And Shifty's hated me ever since I skinned him in that horse-swap last fall. He'll tell Kirby where I went."

"I never thought of that," said Doc Blaine, worried.

"Hell, forget it," I advised. "Kirby hasn't got guts enough to do anything but blow."

But I was mistaken. Puncture a bully's vanity and you touch his one vital spot.

Old Jim had not gone to bed when we got there. He was sitting in the room opening on to his sagging porch, the room which was at once living-room and bedroom, smoking his old cob pipe and trying to read a newspaper by the light of his coal-oil lamp. All the windows and doors were wide open for the coolness, and the insects which swarmed in and fluttered around the lamp didn't seem to bother him.

We sat down and discussed the weather – which isn't so inane as one might suppose, in a country where men's livelihood depends on sun and rain, and is at the mercy of wind and drouth. The talk drifted into the other kindred channels, and after some time, Doc Blaine bluntly spoke of something that hung in his mind.

"Jim," he said, "that night I thought you were dying, you babbled a lot of stuff about your heart, and an Indian who lent you his. How much of that was delirium?"

"None, Doc," said Garfield, pulling at his pipe. "It was gospel truth. Ghost Man, the Lipan priest of the Gods of Night, replaced my dead, torn heart with one from somethin' he worshipped. I ain't sure myself just what that somethin' is – somethin' from away back and a long way off, he said. But bein' a god, it can do without a heart for awhile. But when I die – if I ever got my head smashed so my consciousness is destroyed – the heart must be given back to Ghost Man."

"You mean you were in earnest about the cutting out your heart?" demanded Doc Blaine.

"It has to be," answered old Garfield. "A livin' thing in a dead thing is opposed to nat'er. That's what Ghost Man said."

"Who the devil *was* Ghost Man?"

"I told you. A witch-doctor of the Lipans, who dwelt in this country before the Comanches came down from the Staked Plains and drove 'em south across the Rio Grande. I was a friend to 'em. I reckon Ghost Man is the only one left alive."

"Alive? Now?"

"I dunno," confessed old Jim. "I dunno whether he's alive or dead. I dunno whether he was alive when he came to me after the fight on Locust Creek, or even if he was alive when I knowed him in the southern country. Alive as we understand life, I mean."

"What balderdash is this?" demanded Doc Blaine uneasily, and I felt a slight stirring in my hair. Outside was stillness, and the stars, and the black shadows of the post-oak woods. The lamp cast old Garfield's shadow grotesquely on the wall, so that it did not at all resemble that of a human, and his words were strange as words heard in a nightmare.

"I knowed you wouldn't understand," said old Jim. "I don't understand myself, and I ain't got the words to explain them things I feel and know without understandin'. The Lipans were kin to the Apaches, and the Apaches learnt curious things from the Pueblos. Ghost Man *was* – that's all I can say – alive or dead, I don't know, but he *was*. What's more, he *is*."

"Is it you or me that's crazy?" asked Doc Blaine.

"Well," said old Jim, "I'll tell you this much – Ghost Man knew Coronado."

"Crazy as a loon!" murmured Doc Blaine. Then he lifted his head. "What's that?"

"Horse turning in from the road," I said. "Sounds like it stopped."

I stepped to the door, like a fool, and stood etched in the light behind me. I got a glimpse of a shadowy bulk I knew to be a man on a horse; then Doc Blaine yelled: "Look out!" and threw himself against me, knocking us both sprawling. At the same instant I heard the smashing report of a rifle, and old Garfield grunted and fell heavily.

"Jack Kirby!" screamed Doc Blaine. "He's killed Jim!"

I scrambled up, hearing the clatter of retreating hoofs, snatched old Jim's shotgun from the wall, rushed recklessly out on to the sagging porch and let go both barrels at the fleeing shape, dim in the starlight. The charge was too light to kill at that range, but the bird-shot stung the horse and maddened him. He swerved, crashed headlong through a rail fence and charged across the orchard, and a peach tree limb knocked his rider out of the saddle. He never moved after he hit the ground. I ran out there and looked down at him. It was Jack Kirby, right enough, and his neck was broken like a rotten branch.

I let him lie, and ran back to the house. Doc Blaine had stretched old Garfield out on a bench he'd dragged in from the porch, and Doc's face was whiter than I'd ever seen it. Old Jim was a ghastly sight; he had been shot with an old-fashioned .45-70, and at that range the heavy ball had literally torn off the top of his head. His features were masked with blood and brains. He had been directly behind me, poor old devil, and he had stopped the slug meant for me.

Doc Blaine was trembling, though he was anything but a stranger to such sights.

"Would you pronounce him dead?" he asked.

"That's for you to say," I answered. "But even a fool could tell that he's dead."

"He *is* dead," said Doc Blaine in a strained unnatural voice. "Rigor mortis is already setting in. But feel his heart!"

I did, and cried out. The flesh was already cold and clammy; but beneath it that mysterious heart still hammered steadily away, like a dynamo in a deserted house. No blood coursed through those veins; yet the heart pounded, pounded, pounded, like the pulse of Eternity.

"A living thing in a dead thing," whispered Doc Blaine, cold sweat on his face. "This is opposed to nature. I am going to keep the promise I made him. I'll assume full responsibility. This is too monstrous to ignore."

Our implements were a butcher-knife and a hack-saw. Outside only the still stars looked down on the black post-oak shadows and the dead man that lay in the orchard. Inside, the oil lamp flickered, making strange shadows move and shiver and cringe in the corners, and glistened on the blood on the floor, and the red-dabbled figure on the bench. The only sound inside was the crunch of the saw-edge in bone; outside an owl began to hoot weirdly.

Doc Blaine thrust a red-stained hand into the aperture he had made, and drew out a red, pulsing object that caught the lamplight. With a choked cry he recoiled, and the thing slipped from his fingers and fell on the table. And I too cried out involuntarily. For it did not fall with a soft meaty thud, as a piece of flesh should fall. It *thumped* hard on the table.

Impelled by an irresistible urge, I bent and gingerly picked up old Garfield's heart. The feel of it was brittle, unyielding, like steel or stone, but smoother than either. In size and shape it was the duplicate of a human heart, but it was slick and smooth, and its crimson surface reflected the lamplight like a jewel more lambent than any ruby; and in my hand it still throbbed mightily, sending vibratory radiations of energy up my arm until my own heart seemed swelling and bursting in response. It was cosmic *power*, beyond my comprehension, concentrated into the likeness of a human heart.

The thought came to me that here was a dynamo of life, the nearest approach to immortality that is possible for the destructible human body, the materialization of a cosmic secret more wonderful than the fabulous fountain sought for by Ponce de Leon. My soul was drawn into that unterrestrial gleam, and I suddenly wished passionately that it hammered and thundered in my own bosom in place of my paltry heart of tissue and muscle.

Doc Blaine ejaculated incoherently. I wheeled.

The noise of his coming had been no greater than the whispering of a night wind through the corn. There in the doorway he stood, tall, dark, inscrutable – an Indian warrior, in the paint, war bonnet, breech-clout, and moccasins of an elder age. His dark eyes burned like fires gleaming deep under fathomless black lakes. Silently he extended his hand, and I dropped Jim Garfield's heart into it. Then without a word he turned and stalked into the night. But when Doc Blaine and I rushed out into the yard an instant later, there was no sign of any human being. He had vanished like a phantom of the night, and only something that looked like an owl was flying, dwindling from sight, into the rising moon.

The Horror from the Mound

Steve Brill did not believe in ghosts or demons. Juan Lopez did. But neither the caution of the one nor the sturdy skepticism of the other was shield against the horror that fell upon them – the horror forgotten by men for more than three hundred years – a screaming fear monstrously resurrected from the black lost ages.

Yet as Steve Brill sat on his sagging stoop that last evening, his thoughts were as far from uncanny menaces as the thoughts of man can be. His ruminations were bitter but materialistic. He surveyed his farmland and he swore. Brill was tall, rangy and tough as boot-leather – true son of the iron-bodied pioneers who wrenched West Texas from the wilderness. He was browned by the sun and strong as a long-horned steer. His lean legs and the boots on them showed his cowboy instincts, and now he cursed himself that he had ever climbed off the hurricane deck of his crank-eyed mustang and turned to farming. He was no farmer, the young puncher admitted profanely.

Yet his failure had not been his fault. Plentiful rain in the winter – so rare in West Texas – had given promise of good crops. But as usual, things had happened. A late blizzard had destroyed all the budding fruit. The grain which had looked so promising was ripped to shreds and battered into the ground by terrific hailstorms just as it was turning yellow. A period of intense dryness, followed by another hailstorm, finished the corn.

Then the cotton, which had somehow struggled through, fell before a swarm of grasshoppers which stripped Brill's field almost over night. So Brill sat and swore that he would not renew his lease – he gave fervent thanks that he did not own the land on which he had wasted his sweat, and that there were still broad rolling ranges to the west where a strong young man could make his living riding and roping.

Now as Brill sat glumly, he was aware of the approaching form of his nearest neighbor, Juan Lopez, a taciturn old Mexican who lived in a hut just out of sight over the hill across the creek, and grubbed for a living. At present he was clearing a strip of land on an adjoining farm, and in returning to his hut he crossed a corner of Brill's pasture.

Brill idly watched him climb through the barbed-wire fence and trudge along the path he had worn in the short dry grass. He had been working at his present job for over a month now, chopping down tough gnarly mesquite trees and digging up their incredibly long roots, and Brill knew that he always followed the same path home. And watching, Brill noted him swerving far aside, seemingly to avoid a low rounded hillock which jutted above the level of the pasture. Lopez went far around this knoll and Brill remembered that the old Mexican always circled it at a distance. And another thing came into Brill's idle mind – Lopez always increased his gait when he was passing the knoll, and he always managed to get by it before sundown – yet Mexican laborers generally worked from the first light of dawn to the last glint of twilight, especially at these grubbing jobs, when they were paid by the acre and not by the day. Brill's curiosity was aroused.

He rose, and sauntering down the slight slope on the crown of which his shack sat, hailed the plodding Mexican.

"Hey, Lopez, wait a minute."

Lopez halted, looked about, and remained motionless but unenthusiastic as the white man approached.

"Lopez," said Brill lazily, "it ain't none of my business, but I just wanted to ask you – how come you always go so far around that old Indian mound?"

"No *sabe*," grunted Lopez shortly.

"You're a liar," responded Brill genially. "You savvy all right; you speak English as good as me. What's the matter – you think that mound 's ha'nted or somethin'?"

Brill could speak Spanish himself and read it, too, but like most Anglo-Saxons he much preferred to speak his own language.

Lopez shrugged his shoulders.

"It is not a good place, *no bueno*," he muttered, avoiding Brill's eye. "Let hidden things rest."

"I reckon you're scared of ghosts," Brill bantered. "Shucks, if that is an Indian mound, them Indians been dead so long their ghosts 'ud be plumb wore out by now."

Brill knew that the illiterate Mexicans looked with superstitious aversion on the mounds that are found here and there through the Southwest – relics of a past and forgotten age, containing the moldering bones of chiefs and warriors of a lost race.

"Best no to disturb what is hidden in the earth," grunted Lopez.

"Bosh," said Brill. "Me and some boys busted into one of them mounds over in the Palo Pinto country and dug up pieces of a skeleton with some beads and flint arrowheads and the like. I kept some of the teeth a long time till I lost 'em, and I ain't never been ha'nted."

"Indians?" snorted Lopez unexpectedly. "Who spoke of Indians? There have been more than Indians in this country. In the old times strange things happened here. I have heard the tales of my people, handed down from generation to generation. And my people were here long before yours, Señor Brill."

"Yeah, you're right," admitted Steve. "First white men in this country was Spaniards, of course. Coronado passed along not very far from here, I hear tell, and Hernando de Estrada's expedition came through here – away back yonder – I dunno how long ago."

"In 1545," said Lopez. "They pitched camp yonder where your corral stands now."

Brill turned to glance at his rail-fenced corral, inhabited now by his saddle-horse, a pair of work-horses, and a scrawny cow.

"How come you know so much about it?" he asked curiously.

"One of my ancestors marched with de Estrada," answered Lopez. "A soldier, Porfirio Lopez; he told his son of that expedition, and he told his son, and so down the family line to me, who have no son to whom I can tell the tale."

"I didn't know you were so well connected," said Brill. "Maybe you know somethin' about the gold de Estrada was supposed to hid around here somewhere."

"There was no gold," growled Lopez. "De Estrada's soldiers bore only their arms, and they fought their way through hostile country – many left their bones along the trail. Later – many years later – a mule train from Santa Fe was attacked not many miles from here by Comanches and they hid their gold and escaped; so the legends got mixed up. But even their gold is not there now, because Gringo buffalo-hunters found it and dug it up."

Brill nodded abstractedly, hardly heeding. Of all the continent of North America there is no section so haunted by tales of lost or hidden treasure as is the Southwest. Uncounted wealth passed back and forth over the hills and plains of Texas and New Mexico in the old days when Spain owned the gold and silver mines of the New World and controlled the rich fur trade of the West, and echoes of that wealth linger on in tales of golden caches. Some such vagrant dream, born of failure and pressing poverty, rose in Brill's mind.

Aloud he spoke: "Well, anyway, I got nothin' else to do and I believe I'll dig into that old mound and see what I can find."

The effect of that simple statement on Lopez was nothing short of shocking. He recoiled and his swarthy brown face went ashy; his black eyes flared and he threw up his arms in a gesture of intense expostulation.

"*Dios, no!*" he cried. "Don't do that, Señor Brill! There is a curse – my grandfather told me – "

"Told you what?" asked Brill.

Lopez lapsed into sullen silence.

"I can not speak," he muttered. "I am sworn to silence. Only to an eldest son could I open my heart. But believe me when I say better had you cut your throat than to break into that accursed mound."

"Well," said Brill, impatient of Mexican superstitions, "if it's so bad why don't you tell me about it? Gimme a logical reason for not bustin' into it."

"I can not speak!" cried the Mexican desperately. "I *know!* – but I swore to silence on the Holy Crucifix, just as every man of my family has sworn. It is a thing so dark, it is to risk damnation even to speak of it! Were I to tell you, I would blast the soul from your body. But I have sworn – and I have no son, so my lips are sealed for ever."

"Aw, well," said Brill sarcastically, "why don't you write it out?"

Lopez started, stared, and to Steve's surprise, caught at the suggestion.

"I will! *Dios* be thanked the good priest taught me to write when I was a child. My oath said nothing of writing. I only swore not to speak. I will write out the whole thing for you, if you will swear not to speak of it afterward, and to destroy the paper as soon as you have read it."

"Sure," said Brill to humor him, and the old Mexican seemed much relieved.

"*Bueno!* I will go at once and write. Tomorrow as I go to work I will bring you the paper and you will understand why no one must open that accursed mound!"

And Lopez hurried along his homeward path, his stooped shoulders swaying with the effort of his unwonted haste. Steve grinned after him, shrugged his shoulders and turned back toward his own shack. Then he halted, gazing back at the low rounded mound with its grass-grown sides. It must be an Indian tomb, he decided, what with its symmetry and its similarity to other Indian mounds he had seen. He scowled as he tried to figure out the seeming connection between the mysterious knoll and the martial ancestor of Juan Lopez.

Brill gazed after the receding figure of the old Mexican. A shallow valley, cut by a half-dry creek, bordered with trees and underbrush, lay between Brill's pasture and the low sloping hill beyond which lay Lopez's shack. Among the trees along the creek bank the old Mexican was disappearing. And Brill came to a sudden decision.

Hurrying up the slight slope, he took a pick and a shovel from the tool shed built on to the back of his shack. The sun had not yet set and Brill believed he could open the mound deep enough to determine its nature before dark. If not, he could work by lantern-light. Steve, like most of his breed, lived mostly by impulse, and his present urge was to tear into that mysterious hillock and find what, if anything, was concealed therein. The thought of treasure came again to his mind.

What if, after all, that grassy heap of brown earth hid riches – virgin ore from forgotten mines, or the minted coinage of old Spain? Was it not possible that the musketeers of de Estrada had themselves reared that pile above a treasure they could not bear away, molding it in the likeness of an Indian mound to fool seekers? Did old Lopez know that? It would not be strange if, knowing of treasure there, the old Mexican refrained from disturbing it. Ridden with grisly superstitious fears, he might well live out a life of barren toil rather than risk the wrath of lurking ghosts or devils – for the Mexicans say that hidden gold is always accursed, and surely there was supposed to be some especial doom resting on this mound. Well, Brill meditated, Latin-Indian devils had no terrors for the Anglo-Saxon, tormented by the demons of drouth and storm and crop failure.

Steve set to work with the savage energy characteristic of his breed. The task was no light one; the soil, baked by the fierce sun, was iron-hard, and mixed with rocks and pebbles. Brill sweated profusely and grunted with his efforts, but the fire of the treasure-hunter was on him. He shook the sweat out of his eyes and drove in the pick with mighty strokes that ripped and crumbled the close-packed dirt.

The sun went down, and in the long dreamy summer twilight he worked on, almost oblivious of time or space. He began to be convinced that the mound was a genuine Indian tomb, as he found traces of charcoal in the soil. The ancient people which reared these sepulchers had kept fires burning upon them for days, at some point in the building. All the mounds Steve had ever opened had contained a solid stratum of charcoal a short distance below the surface. But the charcoal traces he found now were scattered about through the soil.

His idea of a Spanish-built treasure-trove faded, but he persisted. Who knows? Perhaps that strange folk men now called Mound-Builders had treasure of their own which they laid away with the dead.

Then Steve yelped in exultation as his pick rang on a bit of metal. He snatched it up and held it close to his eyes, straining in the waning light. It was caked and corroded with rust, worn almost paper-thin, but he knew it for what it was – a spur-rowel, unmistakably Spanish with its long cruel points. And he halted completely bewildered. No Spaniard ever reared this mound, with its undeniable marks of aboriginal workmanship. Yet how came that relic of Spanish caballeros hidden deep in the packed soil?

Brill shook his head and set to work again. He knew that in the center of the mound, if it were indeed an aboriginal tomb, he would find a narrow chamber built of heavy stones, containing the bones of the chief for whom the mound had been reared and the victims sacrificed above it. And in the gathering darkness he felt his pick strike heavily against something granite-like and unyielding. Examination, by sense of feel as well as by sight, proved it to be a solid block of stone, roughly hewn. Doubtless it formed one of the ends of the death-chamber. Useless to try to shatter it. Brill chipped and pecked about it, scraping the dirt and pebbles away from the corners until he felt that wrenching it out would be but a matter of sinking the pick-point underneath and levering it out.

But now he was suddenly aware that darkness had come on. In the young moon objects were dim and shadowy. His mustang nickered in the corral whence came the comfortable crunch of tired beasts' jaws on corn.

A whippoorwill called eerily from the dark shadows of the narrow winding creek. Brill straightened reluctantly. Better get a lantern and continue his explorations by its light.

He felt in his pocket with some idea of wrenching out the stone and exploring the cavity by the aid of matches. Then he stiffened. Was it imagination that he heard a faint sinister rustling, which seemed to come from behind the blocking stone? Snakes! Doubtless they had holes somewhere about the base of the mound and there might be a dozen big diamond-backed rattlers coiled up in that cave-like interior waiting for him to put his hand among them. He shivered slightly at the thought and backed away out of the excavation he had made.

It wouldn't do to go poking about blindly into holes. And for the past few minutes, he realized, he had been aware of a faint foul odor exuding from interstices about the blocking stone – though he admitted that the smell suggested reptiles no more than it did any other menacing scent. It had a charnel-house reek about it – gases formed in the chamber of death, no doubt, and dangerous to the living.

Steve laid down his pick and returned to the house, impatient of the necessary delay. Entering the dark building, he struck a match and located his kerosene lantern hanging on its nail on the wall. Shaking it, he satisfied himself that it was nearly full of coal oil, and lighted it. Then he fared forth again, for his eagerness would not allow him to pause long enough for a bite of food. The mere opening of the mound intrigued him, as it must always intrigue a man of imagination, and the discovery of the Spanish spur whetted his curiosity.

He hurried from his shack, the swinging lantern casting long distorted shadows ahead of him and behind. He chuckled as he visualized Lopez' thoughts and actions when he learned, on the morrow, that the forbidden mound had been pried into. A good thing he opened it that evening, Brill reflected; Lopez might even have tried to prevent him meddling with it, had he known.

In the dreamy hush of the summer night, Brill reached the mound – lifted his lantern – swore bewilderedly. The lantern revealed his excavations, his tools lying carelessly where he had dropped them – and a black gaping aperture! The great blocking stone lay in the bottom of the excavation he had made, as if thrust carelessly inside. Warily he thrust the lantern forward and peered into the small cave-like chamber, expecting to see he knew not what. Nothing met his eyes except the bare rock sides of a long narrow cell, large enough to receive a man's body, which had apparently been built up of roughly hewn square-cut stones, cunningly and strongly joined together.

"Lopez!" exclaimed Steve furiously. "The dirty coyote! He's been watchin' me work – and when I went after the lantern, he snuck up and pried the rock out – and grabbed whatever was in there, I reckon. Blast his greasy hide, I'll fix him!"

Savagely he extinguished the lantern and glared across the shallow, brush-grown valley. And as he looked he stiffened. Over the corner of the hill, on the other side of which the shack of Lopez stood, a shadow moved. The slender moon was setting, the light dim and the play of the shadows baffling. But Steve's eyes were sharpened by the sun and winds of the wastelands, and he knew that it was some two-legged creature that was disappearing over the low shoulder of the mesquite-grown hill.

"Beatin' it to his shack," snarled Brill. "He's shore got somethin' or he wouldn't be travelin' at that speed."

Brill swallowed, wondering why a peculiar trembling had suddenly taken hold of him. What was there unusual about a thieving old Greaser running home with his loot? Brill tried to drown the feeling that there was something peculiar about the gait of the dim shadow, which had seemed to move at a sort of slinking lope. There must have been need for swiftness when stocky old Juan Lopez elected to travel at such a strange pace.

"Whatever he found is as much mine as his," swore Brill, trying to get his mind of the abnormal aspect of the figure's flight. "I got this land leased and I done all the work diggin'. A curse, heck! No wonder he told me that stuff. Wanted me to leave it alone so he could get it hisself. It's a wonder he ain't dug it up long before this. But you can't never tell about them Spigs."

Brill, as he meditated thus, was striding down the gentle slope of the pasture which led down to the creek-bed. He passed into the shadows of the trees and dense underbrush and walked across the dry creek-bed, noting absently that neither whippoorwill nor hoot-owl called in the darkness. There was a waiting, listening tenseness in the night that he did not like. The shadows in the creek bed seemed too thick, too breathless. He wished he had not blown out the lantern, which he still carried, and was glad he had brought the pick, gripped like a battle-ax in his right hand. He had an impulse to whistle, just to break the silence, then swore and dismissed the thought. Yet he was glad when he climbed up the low opposite bank and emerged into the starlight.

He walked up the slope and onto the hill, and looked down on the mesquite flat wherein stood Lopez's squalid hut. A light showed at the one window.

"Packin' his things for a getaway, I reckon," grunted Steve. "Ow, what the – "

He staggered as from a physical impact as a frightful scream knifed the stillness. He wanted to clap his hands over his ears to shut out the horror of that cry, which rose unbearably and then broke in an abhorrent gurgle.

"Good God!" Steve felt the cold sweat spring out upon him. "Lopez – or somebody – "

Even as he gasped the words he was running down the hill as fast as his long legs could carry him. Some unspeakable horror was taking place in that lonely, but he was going to investigate if it meant facing the Devil himself. He tightened his grip on his pick-handle as he ran. Wandering prowlers, murdering old Lopez for the loot he had taken from the mound, Steve thought, and forgot his wrath. It would go hard for any one he caught molesting the old scoundrel, thief though he might be.

He hit the flat, running hard. And then the light in the hut went out and Steve staggered in full flight, bringing up against a mesquite tree with an impact that jolted a grunt out of him and tore his hands on the thorns. Rebounding with a sobbed curse, he rushed for the shack, nerving himself for what he might see – his hair still standing on end at what he had already seen.

Brill tried the one door of the hut and found it bolted. He shouted to Lopez and received no answer. Yet utter silence did not reign. From within came a curious muffled worrying sound, that ceased as Brill swung his pick crashing against the door. The flimsy portal splintered and Brill leaped into the dark hut, eyes blazing, pick swung high for a desperate onslaught. But no sound ruffled the grisly silence, and in the darkness nothing stirred, though Brill's chaotic imagination peopled the shadowed corners of the hut with shapes of horror.

With a hand damp with perspiration he found a match and struck it. Besides himself only old Lopez occupied the hut – old Lopez, stark dead on the dirt floor, arms spread wide like a crucifix, mouth sagging open in a semblance of idiocy, eyes wide and staring with a horror Brill found intolerable. The one window gaped open, showing the method of the slayer's exit – possibly his entrance as well. Brill went to that window and gazed out warily. He saw only the sloping hillside on one hand and the mesquite flat on the other. He started – was that a hint of movement among the stunted shadows of the mesquites and chaparral – or had he but imagined he glimpsed a dim loping figure among the trees?

He turned back, as the match burned down to his fingers. He lit the old coal oil lamp on the rude table, cursing as he burned his hand. The globe of the lamp was very hot, as if it had been burning for hours.

Reluctantly he turned to the corpse on the floor. Whatever sort of death had come to Lopez, it had been horrible, but Brill, gingerly examining the dead man, found no wound – no mark of knife or bludgeon on him. Wait! There was a thin smear of blood on Brill's questing hand. Searching, he found the source – three or four tiny punctures in Lopez's throat, from which blood had oozed sluggishly. At first he thought they had been inflicted with a stiletto – a thin round edgeless dagger – then he shook his head. He had seen stiletto wounds – he had a scar of one on his own body. These wounds more resembled the bite of some animal – they looked like the marks of pointed fangs.

Yet Brill did not believe they were deep enough to have caused death, nor had much blood flowed from them. A belief, abhorrent with grisly speculations, rose up in the dark corners of his mind – that Lopez had died of fright, and that the wounds had been inflicted either simultaneously with his death, or an instant afterward.

And Steve noticed something else; scattered about on the floor lay a number of dingy leaves of paper, scrawled in the old Mexican's crude hand – he would write of the curse on the mound, he had said. There were the sheets on which he had written, there was the stump of a pencil on the floor, there was the hot lamp globe, all mute witnesses that the old Mexican had been seated at the rough-hewn table writing for hours. Then it was not he who opened the mound-chamber and stole the contents – but who was it, in God's name? And who or what was it that Brill had glimpsed loping over the shoulder of the hill?

Well, there was but one thing to do – saddle his mustang and ride the ten miles to Coyote Wells, the nearest town, and inform the sheriff of the murder.

Brill gathered up the papers. The last was crumpled in the old man's clutching hand and Brill secured it with some difficulty. Then as he turned to extinguish the light, he hesitated, and cursed himself for the crawling fear that lurked at the back of his mind – fear of the shadowy thing he had seen cross the window just before the light was extinguished in the hut. The long arm of the murderer, he thought, reaching for the lamp to put it out, no doubt. What had there been abnormal of inhuman about that vision, distorted though it must have been in the dim lamplight and shadow? As a man strives to remember the details of a nightmare dream, Steve tried to define in his mind some clear reason that would explain why that flying glimpse had unnerved him to the extent of blundering headlong into a tree, and why the mere vague remembrance of it now caused cold sweat to break out on him.

Cursing himself to keep up his courage, he lighted his lantern, blew out the lamp on the rough table, and resolutely set forth, grasping his pick like a weapon. After all, why should certain seemingly abnormal aspects about a sordid murder upset him? Such crimes were abhorrent, but common enough, especially among Mexicans, who cherished unguessed feuds.

Then as he stepped into the silent starflecked night he brought up short. From across the creek sounded the sudden soul-shaking scream of a horse in deadly terror – then a mad drumming of hoofs that receded in the distance. And Brill swore in rage and dismay. Was it a panther lurking in the hills – had a monster cat slain old Lopez? Then why was not the victim marked with the scars of fierce hooked talons? *And who extinguished the light in the hut?*

As he wondered, Brill was running swiftly toward the dark creek. Not lightly does a cowpuncher regard the stampeding of his stock. As he passed into the darkness of the brush along the dry creek, Brill found his tongue strangely dry. He kept swallowing, and he held the lantern high. It made but faint impression in the gloom, but seemed to accentuate the blackness of the crowding shadows. For some strange reason, the thought entered Brill's chaotic mind that though the land was new to the Anglo-Saxon, it was in reality very old. That broken and desecrated tomb was mute evidence that the land was ancient to man, and suddenly the night and the hills and the shadows bore on Brill with a sense of hideous antiquity. Here had long generations of men lived and died before Brill's ancestors ever heard of the land. In the night, in the shadows of this very creek, men had no doubt given up their ghosts in grisly ways. With these reflections Brill hurried through the shadows of the thick trees.

He breathed deeply in relief when he emerged from the trees on his own side. Hurrying up the gentle slope to the railed corral, he held up his lantern, investigating. The corral was empty; not even the placid cow was in sight. And the bars were down. That pointed to human agency, and the affair took on a newly sinister aspect. Some one did not intend that Brill should ride to Coyote Wells that night. It meant that the murderer intended making his getaway and wanted a good start on the law, or else – Brill grinned wryly. Far away across a mesquite flat he believed he could still catch the faint and far-away noise of running horses. What in god's name had given them such a fright? A cold finger of fear played shudderingly on Brill's spine.

Steve headed for the house. He did not enter boldly. He crept clear around the shack, peering shudderingly into the dark windows, listening with painful intensity for some sound to betray the presence of the lurking killer. At last he ventured to open a door and step in. He threw the door back against the wall to find if any one were hiding behind it, lifted the lantern high and stepped in, heart pounding, pick gripped fiercely, his feelings a mixture of fear and red rage. But no hidden assassin leaped upon him, and a wary exploration of the shack revealed nothing.

With a sigh of relief Brill locked the doors, made fast the windows and lighted his old coal oil lamp. The thought of old Lopez lying, a glassy-eyed corpse alone in the hut across the creek, made him wince and shiver, but he did not intend to start for town on foot in the night.

He drew from its hiding-place his reliable old Colt .45, spun the blue steel cylinder and grinned mirthlessly. Maybe the killer did not intend to leave any witnesses to his crime alive. Well, let him come! He – or they – would find a young cowpuncher with a six-shooter less easy prey than an old unarmed Mexican. And that reminded Brill of the papers he had brought from the hut. Taking care that he was not in line with a window through which a sudden bullet might come, he settled himself to read, with one ear alert for stealing sounds.

And as he read the crude laborious script, a slow cold horror grew in his soul. It was a tale of fear that the old Mexican had scrawled – a tale handed down from generation to generation – a tale of ancient times.

And Brill read of the wanderings of the caballero Hernando de Estrada and his armored pikemen, who dared the deserts of the Southwest when all was strange and unknown. There were some forty-odd soldiers, servants, and masters, at the beginning, the manuscript ran. There was the captain, de Estrada, and the priest, and young Juan Zavilla, and Don Santiago de Valdez – a mysterious nobleman who had been taken off a helplessly floating ship in the Caribbean Sea – all the others of the crew and passengers had died of plague, he had said, and he had cast their bodies overboard. So de Estrada had taken him aboard the ship that was bearing the expedition from Spain, and de Valdez joined them in their explorations.

Brill read something of their wanderings, told in the crude style of old Lopez, as the old Mexican's ancestors had handed down the tale for over three hundred years. The bare written words dimly reflected the terrific hardships the explorers had encountered – drouth, thirst, floods, the desert sandstorms, the spears of hostile redskins. But it was another peril that old Lopez told – a grisly lurking horror that fell upon the lonely caravan wandering through the immensity of the wild. Man by man they fell and no man knew the slayer. Fear and black suspicion ate at the heart of the expedition like a canker, and their leader knew not where to turn. This they all knew: among them was a fiend in human form.

Men began to draw apart from each other, to scatter along the line of march, and this mutual suspicion, that sought security in solitude, made it easier for the fiend. The skeleton of the expedition staggered through the wilderness, lost, dazed and helpless, and still the unseen horror hung on their flanks, dragging down the stragglers, preying on drowsing sentries and sleeping men. And on the throat of each was found the wounds of pointed fangs that bled the victim white; so that the living knew with what manner of evil they had to deal. Men reeled through the wild, calling on the saints, or blaspheming in their terror, fighting frenziedly against sleep, until they fell with exhaustion and sleep stole on them with horror and death.

Suspicion centered on a great black man, a cannibal slave from Calabar. And they put him in chains. But young Juan Zavilla went the way of the rest, and then the priest was taken. But the priest fought off his fiendish assailant and lived long enough to gasp the demon's name to de Estrada. And Brill, shuddering and wide-eyed, read:

" . . . And now it was evident to de Estrada that the good priest had spoken the truth, and the slayer was Don Santiago de Valdez, who was a vampire, an undead fiend, subsisting on the blood of the living. And de Estrada called to mind a certain foul nobleman who had lurked in the mountains of Castile since the days of the Moors, feeding off the blood of helpless victims which lent him a ghastly immortality. This nobleman had been driven forth; none knew where he had fled but it was evident that he and Don Santiago were the same man. He had fled Spain by ship, and de Estrada knew that the people of that ship had died, not by plague as the fiend had represented, but by the fangs of the vampire.

"De Estrada and the black man and the few soldiers who still lived went searching for him and found him stretched in bestial sleep in a clump of chaparral; full-gorged he was with human blood from his last victim. Now it is well known that a vampire, like a great serpent, when well gorged, falls into a deep sleep and may be taken without peril. But de Estrada was at a loss as to how to dispose of the monster, for how may the dead be slain? For a vampire is a man who has died long ago, yet is quick with a certain foul unlife.

"The men urged that the Caballero drive a stake through the fiend's heart and cut off his head, uttering the holy words that would crumple the long-dead body into dust, but the priest was dead and de Estrada feared that in the act the monster might waken.

"So they took Don Santiago, lifting him softly, and bore him to an old Indian mound near by. This they opened, taking forth the bones they found there, and they placed the vampire within and sealed up the mound – Dios grant until Judgment Day.

"It is a place accursed, and I wish I had starved elsewhere before I came into this part of the country seeking work – for I have known of the land and the creek and the mound with its terrible secret, ever since childhood;

do you see, Señor Brill, why you must not open the mound and wake the fiend – "

There the manuscript ended with an erratic scratch of the pencil that tore the crumpled leaf.

Brill rose, his heart pounding wildly, his face bloodless, his tongue cleaving to his palate. He gagged and found words.

"That's why the spur was in the mound – one of them Spaniards dropped it while they was diggin' – and I mighta knowed it's been dug into before, the way the charcoal was scattered out – but, good God – "

Aghast he shrank from the black visions – an undead monster stirring in the gloom of his tomb, thrusting from within to push aside the stone loosened by the pick of ignorance – a shadowy shape loping over the hill toward a light that betokened a human prey – a frightful long arm that crossed a dim-lighted window. . . .

"It's madness!" he gasped. "Lopez was plump loco! They ain't no such things as vampires! If they is, why didn't he get me first, instead of Lopez – unless he was scoutin' around, makin' sure of everything before he pounced? Aw, hell! It's all a pipe-dream – "

The words froze in his throat. At the window a face glared and gibbered soundlessly at him. Two icy eyes pierced his very soul. A shriek burst from his throat and that ghastly visage vanished. But the very air was permeated by the foul scent that had hung about the ancient mound. And now the door creaked – bent slowly inward. Brill backed up against the wall, his gun shaking in his hand. It did not occur to him to fire through the door; in his chaotic brain he had but one thought – that only that thin portal or wood separated him from some horror born out of the womb of night and gloom and the black past. His eyes were distended as he saw the door give, as he heard the staples of the bolt groan.

The door burst inward. Brill did not scream. His tongue was frozen to the roof of his mouth. His fear-glazed eyes took in the tall, vulture-like form – the icy eyes, the long black finger nails – the moldering garb, hideously ancient – the long spurred boot – the slouch hat with its crumbling feather – the flowing cloak that was falling to slow shreds. Framed in the black doorway crouched that abhorrent shape out of the past, and Brill's brain reeled. A savage cold radiated from the figure – the scent of moldering clay and charnel-house refuse. And then the undead came at the living like a swooping vulture.

Brill fired point-blank and saw a shred of rotten cloth fly from the Thing's breast. The vampire reeled beneath the impact of the heavy ball, then righted himself and came on with frightful speed. Brill reeled back against the wall with a choking cry, the gun falling from his nerveless hand. The black legends were true then – human weapons were powerless – for may a man kill one already dead for long centuries, as mortals die?

Then the claw-like hands at his throat roused the young cowpuncher to a frenzy of madness. As his pioneer ancestors fought hand to hand against brain-shattering odds, Steve Brill fought the cold dead crawling thing that sought his life and soul.

Of that ghastly battle Brill never remembered much. It was a blind chaos in which he scrambled beast-like, tore and slugged and hammered, where long black nails like the talons of a panther tore at him, and pointed teeth snapped again and again at his throat. Rolling and tumbling about the room, both half enveloped by the musty folds of that ancient rotting cloak, they smote and tore at each other among the ruins of the shattered furniture, and the fury of the vampire was not more terrible than the fear-crazed desperation of his victim.

They crashed headlong into the table, knocking it down upon its side, and the coal lamp splintered on the floor, spraying the walls with sudden flame. Brill felt the bite of the burning oil that spattered him, but in the red frenzy of the fight he gave no heed. The black talons were tearing at him, the inhuman eyes burning icily into his soul; between his frantic fingers the withered flesh of the monster was hard as dry wood. And wave after wave of blind madness swept over Steve Brill. Like a man battling a nightmare he screamed and smote, while all about them the fire leaped up and caught at the walls and roof.

Through darting jets and licking tongues of flame they reeled and rolled like a demon and a mortal warring on the fire-lanced floors of hell. And in the growing tumult of the flames, Brill gathered himself for one last volcanic burst of frenzied strength. Breaking away and staggering up, gasping and bloody, he lunged blindly at the foul shape and caught it in a grip not even the vampire could break. And whirling his fiendish assailant bodily on high, he dashed him down across the uptilted edge of the fallen table as a man might break a stick of wood across his knee. Something cracked like a snapping branch and the vampire fell from Brill's grasp to writhe in a strange broken posture on the burning floor. Yet it was not dead, for its flaming eyes still burned on Brill with a ghastly hunger, and it strove to crawl toward him with its broken spine, as a dying snake crawls.

Brill, reeling and gasping, shook the blood from his eyes, and staggered blindly through the broken door. And as a man runs from the portals of hell, he ran stumblingly through the mesquite and chaparral until he fell from utter exhaustion. Looking back he saw the flame of the burning house and thanked God that it would burn until the very bones of Don Santiago de Valdez were utterly consumed and destroyed from the knowledge of men.

The Thunder-Rider

Once I was Iron Heart, the Comanche war-hawk.

This is no fantasy that I speak, nor do I suffer from hallucination; I speak with sure knowledge, of the medicine memory, the only heritage left me by the race which conquered my ancestors.

This is no dream. I sit here in my efficiently-appointed office fifteen stories above the street that thunders and roars with the traffic of the most highly artificialized civilization the planet has ever known. Looking through the nearest window I see the blue sky only between the pinnacles of the towers that rear above this latest Babylon. If I look down I will see only stripes of concrete, over which pour an incessant stream of jostling humanity and wheeled machines. Here are no ocean-like expanses of naked brown prairie beneath a naked blue sky, here no dry grass waving before the invisible feet of the unseen people of the wastes, here no solitude and vastness and mystery to veil the mind with all-seeing blindness and to build dreams and visions and prophesy. Here all is matter reduced to its most mechanical tangibility – power that can be seen and touched and heard, force and energy that crushes all dreams and turns men and women into whimpering automatons.

Yet, I sit here in the midst of this new wilderness of steel and stone and electricity and repeat the inexplicable: I was Iron Heart, the Scalp-Taker, the Avenger, the Thunder-Rider.

I am no darker than many of my customers and patrons. I wear the clothes of civilization with as great ease as any of them. Why should I not? My father wore blanket, war-bonnet, and breech-clout in his youth, but I never wore any garments except those of the white men. I speak English – and French, Spanish, and German too – without an accent, save for a slight Southwestern idiom such as you will find in any white Oklahoman or Texan. Behind me lie years of college life – Carlisle, the University of Texas-Princeton. I am reasonably successful in my profession. I am accepted without question in my chosen social circle – a society made up of men and women of pure Anglo-Saxon descent. My associates scarcely think of me as an Indian. Apparently I have become a white man, and yet –

One heritage remains. A memory. There is nothing vague or hazy or illusive about it. As I remember my yesterdays as John Garfield, so I re-member as more distant yesterdays, the life and deeds of Iron Heart. As I sit here and stare out upon the new wasteland of steel and concrete and wheels, it all seems suddenly as tenuous and unreal as the fog that rises from the shores of Red River in the early morning. I see through it and beyond, back to the drab, brown Wichita Mountains where I was born; I see the dry grass waving under the southwest wind, and the tall white house of Quanah Parker looming against the steel-blue sky. I see the cabin where I was born, and the lean horses and scrubby cows grazing in the sun-scorched pasture, the dry, straggling rows of corn in the little field near-by – but I see beyond that, too. I see a sweep of prairie, brown and dry and breath-takingly vast, where there is no tall white horse, or cabin, or corn-field, only the brown grass waving, and buffalo-hide tipis, and a bronzed, naked warrior with plumes trailing like the train of a blazing meteor riding like the wind in the mad gladness of savage exultation.

I was born in a white-man cabin. I never wore war-paint nor rode the war-path, nor danced the scalp-dance. I can not wield a lance or drive a flint-headed arrow through the bulk of a snorting buffalo. Any Oklahoma farm-boy can surpass me in horsemanship. I am, in short, a civilized man, and yet –

Early in my youth I was aware of a gnawing restlessness, an uneasy and sullen dissatisfaction with my existence. I read the books, I studied, I applied myself to the things the white men valued with a zeal which gratified my white teachers. They pointed me out with pride. They told me, and thought they were complimenting me when they did it, that I was a white man in mind as well as habit.

But the unrest grew, though none suspected it, for I hid it behind the mask of an Indian's face, as my ancestors, bound to an Apache stake, hid their agony from the gaze of their gloating enemies.

But it was there. It lurked at the back of my mind in the class-room when I listened, hiding my innate scorn for the learning I sought in order to advance my material prosperity. It colored my dreams. And these dreams, dim in my childhood, grew more vivid and distinct as I grew older – always a bronzed, naked warrior against a background of storm and cloud and fire and thunder, riding like a centaur, with war-bonnet streaming and the lurid light flashing on the point of a lifted lance.

Racial instincts and superstitions began to stir in me at this repeated visitation. My dreams began to color my waking life, for dreams always played a great part in the lives of the Indians. My mind began turning red. I began to lose my grasp on the white man's existence I had chosen for myself. The shadow of a dripping tomahawk began to take shape, to hover over me. There was a need in my mind, a lawless, untamed urge towards violent action, a restlessness I began to fear only blood would quench. I tossed on my bed at night, fearing to go to sleep, fearing that I would be engulfed by this inexorable tide from the murky, fathomless reservoirs of racial subconsciousness. If this happened I knew I would kill, suddenly, savagely, and, according to the white man's understanding, reasonlessly.

I did not wish to kill men who had never harmed me, and to hang thereafter. Though I despised – as I still despise – the white man's philosophy and code, I find – and found – the material things of his civilization desirable, since the life of my ancestors is denied to me.

I tried to work off this primitive, murderous urge in sports. But I found that football, boxing, and wrestling only increased the feeling. The more fiercely I hurled my hard-muscled body into conflict, the less satisfaction I derived from this artificial conflict, the more I yearned for something I knew not what.

At last I sought aid. I did not go to a white physician or psychologist. I went back to the region of my birth, and sought out old Eagle Feather, a medicine man who dwelt alone among the hills, scorning the white man's ways with a bitter scorn. In my white man's garments I sat cross-legged in his tipi of ancient buffalo hides, and as I talked I dipped my hand into the pot of stewed beef that sat between us. He was old – how old I do not know. His moccasins were frayed and worn, his blanket dingy and patched. He was with that band whom General MacKenzie caught in the Palo Duro, and when the general shot all their horses he beggared old Eagle Feather, for the medicine man's wealth lay in horse-flesh, like that of all the tribe.

He heard me through without speaking and for a long time thereafter he sat unmoving, his head bent on his breast, his withered chin almost touching his bracelet of Pawnee teeth. In the silence I heard the night wind sighing through the lodge-poles, and an owl hooted ghostily deep in the woods. At last he lifted his head and spoke:

"There is a medicine memory which troubles you. This warrior you see is the man you once were. He does not come to urge you to strike an axe into the heads of the white men. He comes in answer to a wildness in your own soul. You come of a long line of warriors. Your grandfather rode with Lone Wolf, and with Peta Nocona. He took many scalps. The white men's books can not content you. Unless you find an outlet, your mind will turn red and the spirits of your ancestors will sing in your ears. Then you will slay, like a man in a dream, without knowing why, and the white men will hang you. It is not well for a Comanche to be choked to death in a noose. He can not sing his death song and his soul can not leave his body, and must dwell for ever underground with his rotting bones.

"You can not be a fighting man. That day is past. But there is a way to escape the bad workings of your medicine. If you could remember – a Comanche, when he dies, goes for a space to the Happy Hunting Ground to rest and hunt the white buffalo. Then, a hundred years later, he is reborn into a tribe unless his spirit has been destroyed by the loss of his scalp. He does not remember – or if at all, but a little, like figures moving in a mist. But there is a medicine to make him remember – a mighty medicine, and a terrible one, which no weakling can survive. I remember. I remember the men whose bodies my soul inhabited in past ages. I can wander in the mist and speak with great ones whose spirits have not yet been reborn – with Quanah Parker, and with Peta Nocona, his father, and with Iron Shirt, his father – with Satanta, the Kiowa, and Sitting Bull, the Ogalalla, and many another great one.

"If you are brave, you may remember, and live over your ancient lives, and be content, knowing your valor and prowess in the past."

He was offering me a solution – a substitute for a violent life in my present existence – a safety valve for the innate ferocity that lurks at the bottom of my soul.

Shall I tell you of the medicine ritual by which I gained full memory of my yesterdays? Alone in the hills, with only old Eagle Feather to see, I fought out my lone fight against such agony as white men only dream of in nightmares. It is an ancient, ancient medicine, a secret medicine, not even guessed by the omniscient anthropologists. It was always Comanche; from it the Sioux borrowed the rituals of their Sun-Dance, and from the Sioux the Arikaras appropriated part of it for their Rain-Dance. But it was always a secret rite, with only a medicine man to look on–no dancing, cheering throngs of women and braves to inspire a man, to stiffen his resolution by listening to his war-songs and his boastings – only the stark silent strength of his endurance, there in the windy darkness under the ancient stars.

Eagle Feather cut deep slits in the muscles of my back. The scars are there to this day; a man can put his clenched fists in the hollows. He cut deep into the muscles and drawing rawhide thongs through the slits, bound them fast. Then he threw the thongs over an oak limb and, with a strength that only a medicine man could explain, he drew me up until my feet hung high above the grassy earth. He made the thongs fast and left me hanging there. He squatted before me and began beating a drum whose head was the skin from the belly of a Lipan chief. Slowly and incessantly he smote it, so that its soft, sinister rumbling played an incessant undertone throughout my agony, mingling with the night wind in the trees.

The night dragged on, the stars changed, the wind died and sprang up and died again. On and on droned the drum until the sound became changed strangely at times, and was a drum no longer but the thunder of unshod horses' hoofs beating the drum of the prairie. The hoot of the owl was a hoot no longer, but the death-yell of forgotten warriors. And the flame of agony before my misted eyes was a roaring fire around which black figures leaped and chanted. No longer I swung on bloody thongs from an oak limb, but I stood upright against a stake, with flames lapping my feet, and sang my death-song in defiance of my enemies. Past and present merged and blended fantastically and terribly, and a hundred personalities struggled within me, until time was not, nor space, nor form nor shape, only a writhing, twisting, whirling chaos of men and things and events and spirits, until all were dashed triumphantly into nothingness by a bronzed, painted, exultant rider on a painted horse whose hoofs struck fire from the prairie. Across a lurid sunset curtain of dusky flame they swept, in barbaric exultation, horse and rider, black against the glow, and with their passing my tormented brain gave way and I knew no more.

In the grey dawn, as I hung limp and senseless, Eagle Feather bound long-treasured buffalo skulls to my feet and their weight tore away flesh and sinew, so that I fell to the grass at the foot of the ancient oak. The sting of that fresh hurt revived me, but the nameless agony of mangled and lacerated flesh was nothing beside the great realization of power that swept over me. In that dark hour before dawn when the drum merged past and present and the material consciousness that always fights the more obscure senses had succumbed, the knowledge I sought had been made mine. Pain was necessary – great pain, to conquer the conscious part of the spirit that rules the material body. There had been an awakening and joining together of senses and sensibilities, and memory remained, call it psychology, magic, what you will. No more would I be tormented by a lack of something, an urge to violence, which was but implanted instinct created by a thousand years of roaming, hunting, and fighting. In my memories I could find relief by living over again the wild days of my yesterdays. So I remember many past lives, lives that stretch back and back into an antiquity that would amaze the historians. This I found – that no hundred years separated the lives of a Comanche. Sometimes rebirth was almost instantaneous – sometimes a stretch of years lay between, for what inscrutable reason I do not know.

I do know that the ego now inhabiting the body of the American citizen now called John Garfield, animated many a wild, painted figure in the past – and not so distant past, either. For instance in my last appearance as a warrior on the stage of the great Southwest I was one Esatema, who rode with Quanah Parker and Satanta the Kiowa, and was killed at the battle of Adobe Walls, in the summer of 1874. There was an interlude between Esatema and John Garfield, in the shape of a weakly, deformed infant who was born during the flight of the tribe from the reservation in 1878 and being unfit, was left to die somewhere on the Staked Plains. I was – but why seek to enumerate all the lives and bodies that have been mine in the past? It is an endless chain of painted, feathered, naked figures stretching back and back into an immemorial past – a past so distant and unthinkable that I myself hesitate before its threshold.

Certainly, my white reader, I shall not seek to carry you with me. For my race is a very old race; it was old when we dwelt in the mountains north of the Yellowstone and traveled on foot, with our scanty goods loaded on the backs of dogs. The researches of the white men stop there, and well for their peace of mind and their beautifully ordered theories of mankind's past that they do; but I could tell you things that would shock you out of the amused tolerance with which you are reading this narrative of a race your ancestors crushed. I could tell you of long wanderings over a continent still teeming with prehuman terrors – but enough.

I will tell you of Iron Heart, the Scalp-Taker. Of all the bodies that have been mine, that of Iron Heart seems somehow more closely linked with that of John Garfield of the Twentieth Century. It was Iron Heart whom I saw in my dreams; it was the memories of Iron Heart, dim and uninterpreted, which haunted me in my childhood and youth. Yet as I speak to you of Iron Heart, I must speak as, and through, the lips of John Garfield, else the telling will be but an incoherent raving, meaning nothing to you. I, John Garfield, am a man of two worlds, with a mind that is neither wholly red nor wholly white, yet with a muddled grasp on each. Let me interpret to you the tale of Iron Heart – not as Iron Heart himself would have told it, but as John Garfield must tell it, so that you may understand it.

Remember, there is much I will not tell. There are cruelties and savageries which I, John Garfield, understand as natural products of the life Iron Heart lived, but which you would not, could not understand, and from which you would turn in horror. There are other things I will slur in the telling. Barbarism has its vices, its sophistries, no less than civilization. Your cynicisms and sophistications are weak and childish beside the elemental cynicism, the vital sophistication of what you call savagery. If our virtues were unspoiled as a new-born panther cub, our sins were older than Nineveh. If – but enough. I will tell you of Iron Heart and the Horror he met, a Horror out of a Time older than the forgotten ruins that lie hidden in the jungles of Yucatan.

Iron Heart lived in the latter part of the Sixteenth Century. The events I shall describe must have taken place somewhere about 1575. Already we were a horse-riding tribe. More than a century before we had drifted down out of the Shoshone Mountains to become plainsmen and buffalo hunters, following the herds on foot, from the Great Slave Lake to the Gulf, bickering eternally with the Crows, the Kiowas, and the Pawnees and Apaches. It was a long, wearisome trek. But the coming of the horse changed all that – changed us, within a short span of years, from a poverty-stricken race of shiftless wanderers to a nation of invincible warriors, sweeping a red trail of conquest from the Blackfoot villages on the Bighorn to the Spanish settlements of Chihuahua.

Historians say the Comanches were mounted by 1714. By that time we had been riding horses for more than a century. When Coronado came in 1541, seeking the fabled Cities of Cibolo, we were already a race of horsemen. Children were taught to ride before they were taught to walk. When I, Iron Heart, was four years old, I was riding my own pony and watching a herd of horses.

Iron Heart was a powerful man, of medium height, stocky and muscular, like most of his race. I will tell you how I got the name. I had a brother a little older than myself, whose name was Red Knife. Affection between brothers is not very common among the Indians, but I felt for him the keen and ardent admiration and worship of a youth for an older brother.

It was an age of racial drift. We had not yet settled upon the great Palo Duro Canyon as the cradle-land of our race. Our northern range still extended north of the Platte, though more and more we were encroaching upon the Staked Plains of the South, driving the Apaches before us in a series of whirlwind battles. A hundred and twenty-five years later we broke their power forever in a seven-day battle on the Wichita River and hurled them broken and beaten westward into the mountains of New Mexico. But in Iron Heart's day they still claimed the South Plains as their domain, and more of our wars were with the Sioux than with the Apaches.

It was the Sioux who killed Red Knife.

They caught us near the shore of the Platte, about a mile from a steep knob crowned with stunted growth. For that knob we raced, with one thought between us. For this was no ordinary raid; it was an attack in force; three thousand warriors rode there, Tetons, Brules, and Yanktons. They meant to sweep on to the Comanche encampment, miles to the south. Unless the tribe was warned it would be caught and crushed by the Sioux. I reached the knob, but Red Knife's horse fell with him and the Sioux took him. They brought him to the foot of the knob, on the crest of which, hidden from their arrows, I was already making ready to send up a signal smoke. The Sioux did not try to climb the knob in the teeth of my lance and arrows, where only one man could come at a time. But they shouted up to me that if I would refrain from sending the signal, they would give Red Knife a quick death and ride on without molesting me.

Red Knife shouted to me: "Light the fire! Warn our people! Death to the Sioux!"

And so they fell to torturing him – but I gave no heed, though the prairie swam in a sea of red about me. They cut him to pieces slowly, member by member, while he laughed at them and sang his death song until his own blood choked him. He lived much longer than it would seem possible for a man to live, sliced as he was sliced. But I gave no heed and the smoke rolling up to the sky warned our people far away.

Then the Sioux knew they had lost and they mounted and rode away, even before the first cloud of dust to the south marked the coming of my brother warriors. With my brother's life I had bought the life of the tribe, and thereafter I had a new name, and it was Iron Heart. And the purpose of my life thereafter was to pay the Sioux the debt I owed them, and again and again I paid it, in singing arrows, and thrusting lance, aye, and in fire, and little, slicing knives – I was Iron Heart, the Scalp-Taker, the Vengeance-Maker, the Thunder-Rider. For when the rolling of the thunder across the echoing prairies made the bravest chiefs hide their heads, then I was wont to ride at a gallop, shaking my lance and chanting of my deeds, heedless of gods or men. For fear died in my heart, there on the knoll when I watched my brother die under the Teton knives, and only once again in all my life did it awaken for a space. And it is of that awakening that I would tell you.

In the autumn, that year of 1575 – as I now calculate it – forty of us rode southward to strike the Spanish settlements. It was September, later to be called the Mexican Moon, when the warriors rode southward for horses, scalps, and women. Aye, it was an ancient trail in Esatema's day, and many a time have I ridden it, in one body or another, but in Iron Heart's day it was less than forty years old.

We were after horses, but this particular raid never reached the Rio Grande. We turned aside to strike the Lipans on the river now called the San Saba, and that was unwise. But we were young warriors, eager to count coupes on our ancient enemies, and we had not yet learned that horses were more important than women, and women more important than scalps. We caught the Lipans off-guard and made a magnificent butchery among them, but we did not know that there was truce between

328

them and the cannibal Tonkewas, always implacable foes of the Comanches, until we settled that score once and for all in the winter of 1864 when
we wiped them out on their reservation on the Clear Fork of the Brazos.
Esatema was in that fight, and he – I! – dipped his hands in blood with an
ardor that had its roots in a dim and forgotten past.

But that autumn of 1575 was a long, long time removed from the butchery on the Brazos. Following the broken, headlong fleeing Lipans, we ran
full into a horde of Tonkewas and their Wichita allies.

With the Lipans, there were about five hundred warriors confronting us
– too great odds even for Comanches. Besides we were fighting in a comparatively wooded country, and there we were at a disadvantage, because
we were plains-born and bred, and preferred to do our fighting in the open
where there was room for our primitive cavalry manoeuvres.

When we broke free of the thickets and fled northward, there were only
fifteen of us left to flee, and the Tonkewas hounded us for nearly a hundred
miles, even after the Lipans had given up the chase. How they hated us!
And then, each was eager to fill his belly with the flesh of a Comanche,
properly roasted, for they believed that transferred the fighting spirit of the
Comanche to that of his devourer; we believed that too, and that is why, in
addition to our natural loathing of cannibalism, we hated the Tonkewas as
viciously as they hated us.

It was near the Double Mountain Fork of the Brazos that we met the
Apaches. We had struck them on our road south and sent them howling to
lick their wounds in the chaparral, and they were eager for revenge. They
got it. It was a running fight on tired horses, and of the forty braves who
rode south so proudly, only five of us lived to cross the Caprock – that
ragged irregular rampart that lies like a giant stairstep across the plains,
mounting to a higher level.

I could tell you how the Plains Indians fought. No such fighting was ever
seen on this planet before, or ever will be again, for the conditions which
produced it have passed forever. From Milk River to the Gulf we fought
alike – on horseback, wheeling, darting like hornets with deadly stings,
raining showers of flint-headed dogwood arrows, charging, circling, retreating, illusive as wasps and dangerous as cobras. But this meeting below the Caprock was no fight in such a sense. We were fifteen Comanches
against a hundred Apaches and we fled, turning to drive arrow or thrust

with lance only when we could no longer elude them. It was nearly sundown when they started us, otherwise the saga of Iron Heart had ended there, and his scalp gone to smoke in an Apache tipi with the other ten the Tigers of the Prairie took that day.

But somehow, when night fell we scattered and eluded them, and came together again above the Caprock – weary, hungry, with empty quivers, on exhausted horses. Sometimes we walked and led them, which shows in what state they were, for a Comanche never walked unless the need was most desperate. But we stumbled on, feeling that we were doomed already, groping our way northward, swinging further to the west than any of us had ever gone before, in the hopes of avoiding our implacable enemies. We were in the heart of the Apache country and none of us had any hope of ever reaching our camp on the Cimarron alive. But we struggled on, through a vast and waterless waste, where not even cacti grew, and on which not even the unshod hoof of a horse left any impression on the iron-hard soil.

It must have been towards dawn that we crossed the Line. More I cannot say. There was no actual line there, and yet at one stride we all felt – we *knew* – that we had come into a different country. There was a sort of vague shock, felt by both horses and men. We were all walking and leading the horses and we all fell to our knees, as if thrown by an earthquake shock. The horses snorted, reared, and would have torn free and bolted if they had not been too weak.

Without comment – we were too far gone to care for anything – we rose and struggled on, noting that apparently clouds had formed in the sky, for the stars were dim, almost obscured. Moreover the wind, which blows almost incessantly across that vast plateau, had subsided suddenly, so it was in a strange silence that we staggered across the plain, stumbling ever northward, until dawn came slowly, sullenly and dimly, and we halted and stared haggardly at each other, like ghosts in the morn after the destruction of the world.

We knew now that we were in a haunted country. Somehow, some time in the night we had crossed a line that separated this strange, haunted, forgotten region from the rest of the natural world. Like the rest of the plain, it stretched drearily, flat and monotonous from horizon to horizon. But a strange dimness hung over it, a sort of dusky mist that was less mist than a lessening of the light of the sun. When it rose it looked pale and watery, more like the moon than the sun. Truly, we had come into the Darkening Land, the dread country still whispered of in Cherokee mythology, though how they came to know of it, I do not know.

We could not see beyond its confines, but we could see, ahead of us, a cluster of conical tipis on the plain. We mounted our tired horses and rode slowly toward them. We knew instinctively there was no life in them. We looked upon an encampment of the dead. We sat our horses in silence, under the leaden sky, with the drab, darkened waste stretching away from us. It was like looking through a smoked glass. Away to the west of us loomed a more solid mass of mist our sight could not penetrate.

Cotopah shuddered and averted his eyes, covering his mouth with his hand. "This is a medicine place," said he. "It is not good to be here." And he made an involuntary movement to pull about his shoulders the blanket lost in the long flight before the Tonkewas.

But I was Iron Heart, and fear was dead in me. I reined my terrified horse to the nearest tipi – and all were of the skins of white buffalo – and drew aside the flap. Then, though I was not afraid, my flesh crawled curiously, for I saw the inmate of that tent.

There was an old, old legend, which had been forgotten for more than a hundred years. In Iron Heart's life it was already dim and vague and distorted. But it told how long, long ago, before the tribes had taken shape as men know them now, a strange and terrible people came out of the North which then was populated by many wild and fearful tribes. They passed southward, slaying and destroying all in their path, until they vanished on the great high plains to the south. The old men said they walked into a mist and vanished. And that was long ago, so long ago, even before the ancestors of the Comanches came into the Valley of the Yellowstone. Yet here before my eyes lay one of the Terrible People.

He was a giant, he who sprawled on the bearskin within the tipi; erect he must have stood fully seven feet in height, and his mighty shoulders and huge limbs were knotted with great muscles. His face was that of a brute, thin lipped, jutting jawed, sloping brow, with a tangled mop of shaggy hair. Beside him lay an axe, a keen-edged blade of what I now know to be green jade, set in the cleft of a shaft of a strange, hard wood which once grew in the far north, and which took a polish like mahogany. At the sight

I desired to possess it, though it was too long-hafted and heavy for easy use on horseback.

I thrust my lance through the door of the lodge and drew the thing out, laughing at the protests of my companions.

"I commit no sacrilege!" I maintained. "This is no death-lodge, where warriors laid the corpse of a great chief. This man died in his sleep, as they all died. Why he has lain here so many ages without being devoured by wolves or buzzards, or his flesh rotting I do not know, but this whole land is a medicine land. But I will take this axe."

It was just as I was about to dismount and secure it, having drawn it outside the lodge, that a sudden cry brought us wheeling about – to face a dozen Pawnees in full war-paint! And one was a woman! She bestrode her horse like a warrior, and waved a flint-headed war-axe.

Warrior-women were rare among the plains tribes, but they did occur now and then. We knew her, instantly, Conchita, the warrior-girl of the southern Pawnees. She was a war-bird, in truth, leading a band of picked fighting men in reckless forays all over the Southwest.

Vividly burns in my memory even now the picture she presented as I whirled and saw her, a slim, supple, arrogant figure, vibrant with life and menace, barbarically magnificent as she sat her rearing charger, with the fierce painted faces of her braves crowding close behind her. She was naked save for a short beaded skirt that lacked something of reaching midthigh. Her girdle was likewise beaded and supported a knife in a beaded sheath. Moccasins were on her slender feet, and her black hair, done up in two thick glossy braids hung down her supple back. Her dark eyes flashed, her red lips parted in a cry of mockery as she brandished her axe at us, managing her bridleless, saddleless steed with a horsemanship that was breath-taking in its negligent grace. And she was a full-blooded Spanish woman, daughter of a captain of Cortez, stolen from below the Rio Grande by the Apaches when a baby and from them stolen in turn by the southern Pawnees, to be raised as an Indian.

All this I saw and knew in the brief glance as I turned, for with a shrill cry she hurled herself at us and her braves swept in behind her. I say hurled, for that is the word. Horse and rider seemed to lunge at us rather than gallop, so swiftly did she come to the attack.

The fight was short. How could it be otherwise? They were twelve men,

on comparatively fresh horses. We were five weary Comanches on foundered steeds. The tall chief with the scarred face came at me with a rush. In
the fog they had not seen us, nor we them, until we were almost together.
Seeing our empty quivers they came in to finish us with their lances and
war-clubs. The tall chief thrust at me, and I wheeled my horse who responded to the nudge of my knee with his last strength. No Pawnee could
ever equal a Comanche in open battle, not even a southern Pawnee. The
lance swished past my breast, and as the horse and rider plunged past
me, carried by their own momentum, I drove my own lance through the
Pawnee's back, so the point came out from his breast.

Even as I did so I was aware of another brave charging down on me from
the left, and I sought to wheel my steed again, as I dragged the lance free.
But the horse was foredone. He rolled like a foundered canoe in the swift
tide of the Missouri, and the club in the Pawnee's hand smashed down. I
threw myself sidewise and saved my skull from crushing like an egg, but
the club fell stunningly on my shoulder, knocking me from my horse. Cat-
like I hit on my feet, drawing my knife, but then the shoulder of a horse hit
me and knocked me sprawling. It was Conchita who had ridden me down
and now as I struggled slowly to my knees, half-stunned, she leaped lightly
down and swung up her flint-headed axe above my head.

I saw the dull glint of the edge, knew in a slow, stunned way that I could
not avoid the downward swing – and then she froze, axe lifted, staring
wide-eyed over my head towards something beyond me. Impelled beyond
my will, I turned my dizzy head and looked.

The other Comanches were down, and five of the Pawnees. All the living
froze, just as Conchita had frozen. One who knelt on dead Cotopah's back,
wrenching at the scalp, his knife between his teeth, crouched there like one
suddenly petrified, staring in the direction towards which all heads were
turned.

For the fog to the west was lifting, and into view floated the walls and flat
roofs of a strange structure. It was like, yet strangely unlike, the pueblos of
the corn-raising Indians far to the west. Like them it was made of adobe,
and the architecture was something similar, and yet there was a strange
unlikeness.

And from it came a train of strange figures – short brown men, clad in
garments of brightly-dyed feathers, men who looked somewhat like the

pueblo Indians. They were weaponless and carried only ropes of rawhide and whips in their hands. Only the foremost, a taller, gaunter Indian, bore a strange shield-shaped disk of gleaming metal in his left hand and a copper mallet in his right.

The curious parade halted before us, and we stared – the warrior-girl, with her axe still poised; the Pawnees, afoot or a-horse wounded or whole; I, crouching on one knee and shaking my fast-clearing head. Then Conchita, sensing sudden peril, cried out a shrill, desperate command and sprang, lifting her axe – and as the warriors tensed for the onslaught, the man with the vulture feathers in his hair smote the gong with the mallet, and a terrible crash of sound leaped at us like an invisible panther. It was like the impact of a thunderbolt, that awful crash of sound, a thing so terrible it was almost tangible. Conchita and the Pawnees went down as if struck by lightning, and the horses reared in agony and bolted. Conchita rolled on the ground, crying out in agony, and clutching her ears. But I was Iron Heart, the Comanche, and fear slept in me.

I came up from the ground in a leap, knife in hand, though my skull seemed bursting from that awful blast of sound. Straight at the throat of Vulture-Crest I sprang. But my knife never sheathed itself in that brown flesh. Again the awful gong clanged and yet again, smiting me in mid-leap like a tangible force, hurling me back and back. And again and yet again the mallet crashed against the gong, so that earth and sky seemed split asunder by its deafening reverberation. Down I went like a man beaten to the ground by a war-club.

When I could see, hear, and think again, I found my hands were bound behind me, a rawhide thong about my neck. I was dragged to my feet and our captors began marching us toward the city. I call it that, though it was more like a castle. Conchita and her Pawnees were served in like manner, except one who was badly wounded. Him they slew, cutting his throat with his own knife, and left him lying among the others. One took up the axe I had dragged from the tipi, looked at it curiously, and then swung it over his shoulder. He must take both hands to manage it.

So we stumbled on towards the castle, half-strangled by the thongs about our necks, and occasionally encouraged by the bite of a rawhide lash across our shoulders. Only Conchita was not so treated, though her captor jerked brutally on her rope when she lagged. Her warriors looked haggard. They were the most warlike of the Pawnee nation – a branch which lived on the headwaters of the Cimarron, and which differed in many ways and customs from their northern brothers. They were more typical of a plains culture than their tribal relatives, and never came in contact with the English-speaking invaders, for smallpox exterminated them about 1641. They wore their hair in long braids that swept the ground, like the Crows and Minnetarees, and loaded the braids with silver ornaments.

The castle – I call it that in the language of John Garfield and in your own language; Iron Heart would have spoken of it as a lodge – the castle stood on the crest of a low rise, not worthy of the name of hill, which broke the flat monotony of the plain. There was a wall around it and a gate in the wall. On one of the flat stages of the roof we saw a tall figure standing, wrapped in a shining mantle of feathers that glistened even in the subdued light. A lifted arm made an imperious gesture and the figure moved majestically through a doorway and vanished.

The gate-posts were of bronze, carved with the feathered serpent, and at the sight the Pawnees shuddered and averted their eyes. Like all the plains Indians, they remembered that abomination from the days of old, when the great and terrible kingdoms of the far South warred with those of the far North.

They led us across a courtyard, up a short flight of bronze steps, and into a corridor, and once within all resemblance to the pueblos ceased. But we knew that once houses like this had risen in mighty cities far in the serpent-haunted jungles of the dim South, for in our souls stirred the echoes of ancient legends.

We came into a broad circular room through which the dim light streamed from an open dome. A black stone altar rose in the centre of the room, with darkly stained channels along the rims. Facing it, on a raised dais, on an ivory throne heaped with sea-otter furs, there lounged the figure we had seen on the roof. He was a tall man, slender and wiry, with a high forehead and a narrow, keen, hawk-like face. There was no mercy in that face, only a cruel arrogance, a mocking cynicism. It was the face of a man who felt himself above the human passions of anger or mercy or love.

With a cruel amusement he swept his eyes over us, and the Pawnees lowered their gaze. Even Conchita, after boldly meeting his stare for a moment, winced and dropped her eyes. But I was Iron Heart, the Comanche, and fear slept in me. I met that piercing stare with my black eyes unwinking. He looked long at me, and presently spoke in the language of the pueblo Indians which in those days was the commercial language of the prairies and understood by most of the horse-riding Indians.

"You are like a wild beast. There is the fire of killing in your eyes. Are you not afraid?"

"Iron Heart is a Comanche," I answered scornfully. "Ask the Sioux if there is anything he fears! His axe is still sticking in their heads. Ask the Apaches, the Kiowas, the Cheyennes, the Lipans, the Crows, the Pawnees! If he were flayed alive and his skin cut into pieces no larger than a man's palm, and each piece used to cover a dead warrior he has slain, the dead uncovered would still be more than the covered ones!"

Even in their fear the eyes of the Pawnees smoldered murderously at this boasting. The man on the throne laughed without mirth.

"He is tough, he is strong, he is nerved by his vanity," he said to the gaunt man with the gong. "He will endure much, Xototl. Place him in the last cell."

"And the woman, lord Tezcatlipoca?" quoth Xototl, bowing low, and Conchita started and stared wide-eyed at the fantastic figure on the throne. She knew the Aztec legends, and the name was the name of one of the sun's incarnations – taken, no doubt, in a spirit of blasphemy by the ruler of this evil castle.

"Place her in the Room of Gold," said Tezcatlipoca, whom they called the Lord of the Mist. Curiously he glanced at the jade axe which had been placed on the altar.

"Why, it is the axe of Guar, the chief of the Northerners!' quoth he. 'He swore that the axe he wore would some day split my skull! But Guar and all his tribe have been dead in their caribou hide tents for more centuries than even I like to remember, and my skull still holds the magic of the ancients! Leave the axe there and take them away! I will talk to the girl presently, and then there shall be sport, as it was in the days of the Golden Kings!"

They led us out of the circular chamber and across a series of broad rooms, where cat-footed brown women, beautiful with a sinister beauty and naked but for their golden ornaments, crowded close, to stare at the prisoners, and especially the warrior-girl of the Pawnees. And they laughed at her, sweet, soft, evil laughter, venomous as poisoned honey.

We came into a long corridor, with heavy doors opening into it, and into each cell as we passed it, a warrior was thrust. I was the last and as I was dragged inside I saw terror bare in Conchita's lovely eyes as she was led away. Within the cell I was thrown roughly to the floor, and my legs were bound with rawhide. Neither food nor water was given to me.

Presently the door opened and I looked up to see the Lord of the Mist looking down at me.

"Poor fool!" he murmured. "I could almost pity you! Bloodthirsty beast of the prairies, with your swaggerings and boastings, your tale of scalps and slayings. Fool! Soon you will howl for death!"

"A Comanche does not cry out at the stake," I answered, my eyes burning red with the murder-lust. My thews swelled and knotted until the rawhide cut into the flesh. But the thongs held. He laughed and silently left my cell, closing the door behind him. Outside a bolt dashed into place.

What happened next I did not see, nor did I learn until long afterward. But Xototl took Conchita up a flight of stairs and into a chamber where the walls, ceiling, and floor were of gold. The doors were of gold and there were gold bars on the windows. There was a golden couch heaped with sea-otter fur. Xototl unbound her and stood gazing at her for a moment with hot desire in his eyes. Then, sullenly and grudgingly, he turned away and locked the door behind her, leaving her alone. Presently to her came the Lord of the Mist, tall, striding like a god, with his strange mantle of rich-hued feathers about hips and about his black mane a band in the form of a golden serpent with head upreared above his forehead.

He told her he was a magician of an ancient, ancient kingdom which was declining even before the barbaric Toltecs wandered into it. For his own reasons he had come far to the north and established his kingdom on that bleak plain, casting about it a mist of enchantment. He had found a tribe of pueblo Indians besieged by the invaders from the North, and they had appealed to him for aid, giving themselves fully into his hands. He had made magic and brought death to the Northerners. But he left them in their tents, and told the pueblo people that he could bring them to life whenever he wished. Beneath his cruel hands the people dwindled away until now not more than a hundred lived to do his bidding. He had come from the south more than a thousand years before. He was not immortal, but almost so.

Then he left her; and as he went the great serpent which did his bidding slithered silently and evilly through the corridors after him; this serpent had devoured many of the subjects of the Lord of the Mist.

Meanwhile, I lay in my cell and heard them drag forth a Pawnee and haul him along the corridor. After a long while I heard a fearful, animal-like scream of agony, and wondered what torment could wring a cry from the throat of a southern Pawnee. I had heard them laugh under the knives of the flayers. Then for the first time fear awoke in me – not physical fear so much as the fear that under the unknown torment I would cry out and so bring shame to the Comanche nation. I lay there and listened to the end of the Pawnees. Each warrior cried out but once.

Meanwhile Xototl had glided into Conchita's chamber, his eyes red with lust. "You are soft, you are white," he mumbled. "I am weary of brown women." He seized her in his arms and forced her back on the golden couch. She did not resist. But suddenly the dagger that had been in his girdle was in her hand. She sank it into his back, swiftly and deadly. Before he could voice the cry that welled to his lips, she choked it in his throat and, falling with him to the floor, stabbed at him again and again until he lay still. Then, rising like a cat, she hurried through the door, snatching up a bow, a knife, and a handful of arrows as she went.

In an instant she was in my cell, bending over me, her wide eyes blazing. "Quickly!" she hissed. "He is slaying the last of the warriors! Prove that you are a man!"

The knife was keen, but the blade was slender and the rawhide tough. She kept at it persistently, finally sawing through. Then I was on my feet, knife in my girdle, bow and arrows in my hand.

We stole from the cell and moved cautiously down the corridor, to come face to face with a surprised guard. Dropping my weapons I had him by the throat before he could cry out, and bearing him to the floor, I broke his neck with my bare hands before he could release his spear and bring his knife into play.

Rising, we stole down the corridor toward the circular room of the open dome. Before it was the gigantic serpent which coiled menacingly at our approach. Quickly and silently I moved forward and placed a single arrow deep in the reptile's eye, and we moved cautiously past its fearsome death throes.

We slipped into the domed room and saw the last Pawnee die in a strange and hideous torment. As the Lord of the Mist turned to face us, I drove an arrow straight at his breast. It glanced harmlessly away. I was paralyzed with surprise when a second arrow behaved similarly.

Casting aside my bow I leaped at him with knife in hand, and we rolled about the chamber seeking a death grip. He was alone; his retainers had been dispatched to another part of the castle while he worked his evil.

My knife would not bite through the strange, close-fitting garment that he wore beneath his feather-mantle, and, try as I would, I could not reach his throat or face. Finally he cast me aside and made ready to invoke his magic when Conchita stopped him with a cry: "The dead men rise from the tents of the Northerners. They march towards the pueblo!"

"A lie!" he cried, going ashy. "They are dead! They can not rise!"

"Nevertheless, they come!" she cried with a wild laugh.

He faltered, turned toward a window, then wheeled back in realization of the trick. Nearby lay the axe of Guar the Northerner, a mighty weapon out of another age. In the instant of his hesitation, I seized it, and, swinging it high, leaped forward. As he turned back to me, fear leaped into his eyes as the axe crashed through his skull, spilling his brains on the floor.

Thunder crashed and rolled, and balls of fire swept over the plains; the pueblo rocked. Conchita and I raced for safety, the screams of the trapped echoing in our ears. And when dawn rose upon the plains, no mist showed. There was only a rare, sun-drenched expanse on which a few bones lay moldering.

"Now we will go to my people," I said, taking her wrist. "There are some horses which did not run away."

But she tried to wrench away from me, crying disdainfully: "Comanche dog! You live only because of my aid! Go your way! You are fit only to be the slave of a Pawnee!"

Rarely a Comanche struck a woman; not because of any particular chivalry, but because we felt a woman was too low in the scale by which we judged mankind for a warrior to demean himself by striking. But I saw this was a special case, and there was no degradation in connection with coercing this spit-fire. So I took her by her glossy braids and flung her face down to the ground, and then I set a foot between her writhing shoulders and belabored her naked hips and thighs with my bow, without anger and without mercy, until she screamed for mercy and sobbingly acquiesced to whatever I might desire. Then I yanked her to her feet and bade her follow me to capture the horses, which she did, weeping and rubbing various smarting bruises. So then we were riding northward, towards the camp on the Canadian, and my beauty seemed quite content, now that she was on horseback. And I knew that I had found a woman worthy even of Iron Heart, the Thunder-Rider.

"The Classic Tale of the Southwest"

From a Letter to August Derleth, circa January 1933

The Indians of Texas were: the Cenis, who lived in the vicinity of the Neches and the Trinity Rivers, and were first encountered by La Salle in 1686 – they soon became extinct; the Adaes, who lived near what is now San Augustine, and who disappeared about 1820; the Carankaways, who lived adjacent to Galveston Bay – a ferocious, cannibalistic race, akin to the Caribs, they were destroyed in a great battle with the Spaniards in 1744; the Jaranamas, Tamiquez, and Anaquas, small clans living on the lower reaches of the San Antonio River; the Coushattis, a branch of the Muskogees, living in the lower valley of the Trinity – they were broken in the battle of Medina; the Alabamas, who lived along the Neches; the Seminoles, who came to Florida with the Cherokees – others later migrated from Florida, and took up their abode near the Border; the Tonkaways, who lived along the Brazos whence they spread to the Guadalupe – they were destroyed on their reservation by the Comanches in 1864; the Lipans, who were a strong and important tribe, in and about Bandera County, until dealt a terrific defeat by Bigfoot Wallace and his rangers, after which the survivors migrated to Mexico; the Apaches, who need no advertisement – I doubt their assumed kinship with the Lipans; the Carrizos, who were of the Pueblo stock, living along the Rio Grande – they were absorbed by the Mexicans; the Tiguas, Pueblos, living near what is now El Paso; the Caddos, who lived mainly in the eastern part of the state – they included the Keechies, Ionies, Wacos, Nacogdoches, Ayish, Tawakana, Towash, Wichitas, Cachatas, Tejas, and Anadarkos; the Kickapoos, who were driven westward by the white drift – many crossed into Mexico; the Cherokees, who emigrated to Texas between 1822 and 1829, were broken in the war of 1839, and moved to reservations in Oklahoma, later; the Delawares, immigrants from the eastern states, and friendly to the white men; the Comanches, the strongest tribe in Texas, and the lords of the western plains – a more ferocious race never trod this continent.

Authorities class the Comanches as members of the Shoshonean race, which also includes the Shoshones, Utes, and Pawnees. But I wouldn't have cared to tell an old-time Comanche that he was of the same blood as the Utes; a knife in the guts would have been the probable retort. Their legends made them blood-kin with the Apaches, whom ethnologists name Athabascans, along with the Navajoes. Yet the Comanches and Apaches seem to have had many points in common, though much intermarrying might explain that. At any rate the Comanches were the most skillful horse-thieves on the continent, not even excepting the white rustlers that worked between El Paso and New Orleans back in the '70s.

It would take a large volume to tell the full story of Quanah Parker, and of Cynthia Anne Parker, yes, and of Peta Nocona, the last war-chief of the Comanches. It is the classic tale of the Southwest, which has been rewritten scores of times, fictionized and dramatized. I will tell it as briefly as possible.

In the year of 1833 a band of settlers, about thirty-four in number, headed by John Parker, came from Illinois and formed a colony on the Navasota River, in Limestone County, Texas – then, of course, part of Mexico. In 1836, when the Texans were fighting for their freedom, the Comanches were particularly bold in raiding the scattered settlements, and it was in one of those raids that Fort Parker fell. Seven hundred Comanches and Kiowas literally wiped it off the earth, with most of its inhabitants. A handful escaped, through the heart-shaking valor of Falkenberry and his son Evan, both of whom fell a year afterward on the shores of the Trinity in a battle so savage and bloody that the Comanches who survived it retold it as long as they lived. But there Fort Parker passed into oblivion, and among the women and children taken captive were Cynthia Anne Parker, nine years old, and her brother John, a child of six.

They were not held by the same clans. John came to manhood as an Indian, but he never forgot his white blood. The sight of a young Mexican girl, Donna Juana Espinosa, in captivity among the red men, wakened the slumbering heritage of his blood. He escaped from the tribe, carrying her with him, and they were married. He took up his life again with the people of his own race, joined General Bee's command, fought with characteristic valor through the Civil War, and afterwards became a well-to-do Texas ranchman.

For Cynthia Anne a different fate was reserved. In 1840 a group of traders found her on the Canadian River with Pahauka's Comanches. They tried to ransom her, but the Indians refused; and then she was seen no more by white men until about 1851. Meanwhile she had grown to womanhood; there were various suitors for her hand, among them Eckitoacup, of whom more later. He was a shrewd fellow, more given to intrigue than to war. But Cynthia Anne became the mate of Peta Nocona, whose fame hung gorily at his scalp-belt, and whose diplomacy was the stroke of a tomahawk. She bore him children, among them a son, Quanah, which means something similar to sweet fragrance. When white men next came into the Comanche camp where Cynthia Anne dwelt, they strove to persuade her to accompany them back to her white relatives. She refused; she had almost forgotten that other life, as she had forgotten her native tongue. Then, in 1860, her Indian life was ended, bloodily, violently, just as her white man's life had ended.

Peta Nocona, apparently kind to her in his way, and possessing all the finer qualities of the red man, was, nevertheless, an unbridled devil along the frontier. His trail was a red one, and many a settler's cabin went up in flames, and many a frontiersman went into the long dark scalpless because of him. When retribution came, it was merciless. On the Pease River his Nemesis overtook him, in the shape of Sul Russ, later governor of the State, and his Rangers. The surprize favored the white men. They were among the tipis shooting and slashing before the Comanches realized what was occurring. They broke and scattered, every man for himself.

Peta Nocona caught up his daughter, a girl of fifteen, and rode away with her. Ross was in full pursuit, knowing his prey. The girl was riding behind her father, and Ross's first shot killed her, and glanced from the shield that hung on Peta Nocona's back. As she fell she pulled the red man off his horse, but he hit on his feet, cat-like, and drove an arrow into the body of Ross's horse. The wounded beast began plunging and Peta Nocona began winging his arrows at the rider in blinding speed. Undoubtedly the erratic motions of the wounded horse caused him to miss his first few shafts, and Ross, firing desperately even while fighting for his seat, struck and shattered the Indian's elbow. Peta Nocona staggered and dropped his bow, and Ross, jerking the trembling horse to a standstill, took good aim and shot his enemy through the body; the Comanche stood as if dazed, then, as another bullet from Ross's pistol tore through his torso, he reeled to a tree near-by, and grasping it for support, began to chant his death-song. Ross approached him, and ordered him to surrender, but his only reply was a ferocious thrust of his lance, which Ross narrowly avoided. Ross shrugged his shoulders, and turned away, making a gesture to his Mexican servant. The crash of a shotgun marked the finish of the last great warchief of the Comanches.

Meanwhile, Lieutenant Kelliheir had ridden down a squaw who was trying to escape on a pony with her papoose. His pistol was cocked and leveled when he saw that she was a white woman. And so Cynthia Anne Parker came again into the lands of her people. The rest is history too obvious to reiterate. She lived with her people, her brother, Colonel Parker, a member of the Legislature, but she was never happy, always mourning for her red mate and children, always seeking to escape back to that wilder life from which she had been brutally torn. In 1864 both she and her baby went into the long dark. And one might question, whether into the Christian Paradise, or the Indian's Happy Hunting Grounds.

It's a grim tale, a terrible, pathetic tale. It did not make for mercy on either side. The story of Quanah Parker is brighter, as the story of man must nearly always be less fraught with tragedy than that of woman. Quanah escaped that slaughter on the Pease River, a lad of about twelve years of age. His life at first was bitter hard, for he lived only by his own skill and cunning; and it was this fierce training as well as his white blood, that made him superior in physique and craft to his red kinsmen. One doubts if he ever gave his white heritage any thought. Indeed, his portraits give no hint of any but Indian blood.

Doubtless his youth was much like that of all other young Comanches; he fished, hunted, stole horses, pillaged the frontiers of his white kinsmen, indulged in tribal warfare and the brutal "smoking horses" and tortured and took the scalps of his enemies when he could. When he came into young man-hood he loved Weckeah, the daughter of old Yellow Bear. But she had another suitor – Tannap, son of that old Eckitoacup, who had rivaled Peta Nocona in his youth. Eckitoacup was crafty and far-sighted, a red-skinned business man, really, and he was very wealthy. The Comanches measured their wealth by the number of their horses; Eckitoacup possessed no less than a hundred ponies. Quanah had exactly one horse. But he had an advantage no other Comanche possessed; he was half-white, and the great-grandson of grim old John Parker who died in the smoking ruins of his fort among a red heap of Comanche corpses. Quanah went to his friends, wild young braves like himself, and they gave him their ponies. The significance of this can easily be under-rated. They were poor young braves; they owned only one horse apiece. When they gave their mounts to Quanah, it was as if they had freely tendered him their whole fortune, all their worldly goods and hope of future advancement. It was more; a Comanche's horse was more to him than his bank account is to the average man. His horse meant the difference between life and death. When he gave it up or lost it, there was only one way to get another, and that was to steal it. And to steal meant that first he must borrow, in the savage ritual of "smoking horses" and carry the terrible scars of a raw-hide whip on his back for the rest of his life. For he could not raid the remudas of the settlers or the rival tribes on foot.

So Quanah brought ten horses to Yellow Bear's wickiup – only to find that Eckitoacup had offered twenty horses to purchase his son a wife. There may be seen less a desire to pamper his worthless son than to avenge on Quanah the defeat he had met at the hands of the young brave's father. Weckeah was prepared for the bridal party.

But, as has been reiterated, Quanah was half a white man. None of the Indian fatalism was his. In his veins burned the hot blood of those unconquerable white-skinned wanderers who have never known any gods but their own desires. Twenty-one young braves listened to Quanah's words in amazement, and fell in with his desires. When night fell, shadowy figures stole to Weckeah's tipi. There was a low rustling of whispering, then she glided from the tent and became herself a shadow among the hurrying shadows. When dawn rose, a fierce yell went up from the camp on the Canadian. Quanah was gone, and with him Weckeah and twenty-one of the most stalwart young braves.

They rode southward, into the mountain country of West Texas. There they pitched their camp and began raiding the ranches of the whites – a dangerous game, a breath-taking, touch-and-go game. But they prospered, and soon owned a great number of mounts. To the outlaw band came other discontented young braves, and the young men slipped back to the main tribe to steal women for themselves. After perhaps a year, the clan had grown from a score-odd to several hundred. A new tribe had come into existence; a new star flashed redly across the frontier; a new chief brandished his scalp-tufted lance and sent his war-whoop shivering across the river-lands.

Then came old Eckitoacup, thirsting for vengeance, with a horde of lean naked riders, painted for war, their lances glimmering in the dust cloud their horses' hoofs lifted along the horizon. It has been said that Eckitoacup was a business man. His lust for vengeance did not exceed his caution, his concern for his own painted hide. He found Quanah's clan ready and more than willing to join battle. And he backed down. There was a parley, the pipe of peace was smoked, and Eckitoacup's injured feelings were soothed with a gift of nineteen fine horses from Quanah's now enormous herds.

But though Quanah's red brothers were no match for him in force or craft, he could not for ever compete on equal terms with his white kin. His continual raids on the horse-herds had the Texans fighting mad. And in those days, when Texans lost their temper, blood was spilt in appalling quantities. The soldiers stationed along the frontier were more or less useless, but the Rangers were riding, and the settlers were notching their sights on their own hook. The crack of the rifle answered the twang of the bow-string, the bowie knife dipped as deeply in red paint as the tomahawk; raid was met by fierce counter-raid, and the white men, who in early days had barely held their own in their tenacious grasp on the land, were moving like a juggernaut westward, crushing all in their path.

Quanah pulled up stakes and drifted back up the long trail to the Canadian River again. Of his desperate defensive wars and eventual and inevitable defeat, there is little point in telling. He came at last to live in a valley of the Wichita Mountains, in a two-storied frame house, "the White House of the Comanches," with thirty rooms and all the comforts of civilization. Of his thousands of acres of land, some two hundred and fifty were put into cultivation; his horses numbered a hundred, and of "whoa-haws" he had a thousand – nor is it recorded that his more needy kinsmen ever lacked for beef. He was one of the six chiefs in the parade at the inauguration of Theodore Roosevelt – the others were Little Plume, the

Blackfoot, American Horse and Hollow Horn Bear, both Sioux, Geronimo, the Apache, and Buckskin Charlie, the Ute. He was a personal friend of Teddy's. He educated his children at Chilocco and at Carlisle. Among the Indians he wore moccasins and buckskins, among the whites he wore the most genteel garments of civilization – so-called. When he died, I do not know, but in 1905 he was living in his big white man's house, in the Wichita valley, with his wives Weckeah, To-ah nook, Too-pay, and Too-ni-ce. And many a swashbuckler of the middle ages has enjoyed a reputation for a dramatic career with less reason than Quanah Parker might boast.

The Parker family played an important part in the settlement and developing of Texas. Colonel Isaac Parker, in particular, Cynthia Anne's uncle, was prominent in the politics of the Republic, and later a Senator when the State carried out its folly of coming into the Union. Parker County, in which I was born, was named for him, in memory of the times he spent in that then wild country, searching for his kidnapped niece. Nor is Quanah forgotten; the county-seat of Hardeman County is named for him.

Such cross-breeds between whites and Comanches were comparatively rare, owing to the savage feud which existed between the races until the eventual defeat of the latter. The lad who delivers my evening paper has a strong strain of Comanche blood in him, which shows itself in his broad head, and bony, faintly hawk-like features. But such cases are rare. Most of the Indian blood that mixed with the white strain in the Southwest was that of the Cherokees, Creeks, Choctaws, and Chickisaws and Osages. Of these the most dominant by far was the Cherokee, a race noways inferior to any on the continent, white, red or brown. I have relatives in Oklahoma who possess Cherokee blood in plenty.

From a Letter to H. P. Lovecraft, 5 December 1935

The Palo Duro is considered by some historians to have been the cradle of the Comanche race. At least it is certain that it was the homeland of the tribe for some centuries. Others consider that the tribe originated and developed somewhere on the plains of the Middle West, and drifted south to the Palo Duro as late as 1700. This is probably erroneous, for it is pretty certain that Coronado found Comanches living in the Palo Duro in 1541. It is possible that the theory of southward drift in 1700 is a confusion with an eastward and southward movement that did occur about that date, but which originated from the Palo Duro, where the Comanches had been living since drifting down from the north centuries before. There was an expansion movement on the part of the Comanches in the latter part of the eighteenth century. Before that time Apaches had occupied western and central Texas, and these were swept southward and westward, with their Lipan kin, before the onslaught of the conquering Comanches, who were soon destroying Spanish outposts along the San Saba, Concho and Llano Rivers, harrying the outskirts of San Antonio, and raiding deep into Mexico itself. Spanish development of the country north of the Rio Grande was checked and hindered, and there is a possibility that the Latins might eventually have been driven south of the Rio Grande entirely, but for the intervention of the Anglo-Saxon colonists. These drove the Comanches implacably northward and westward, shattering their power in battle after battle, until the last remnant of the once proud and merciless nation was cornered and captured in the ancient cradle of their race, and banished permanently to a reservation in the Territory.

The Grim Land

From Sonora to Del Rio is a hundred barren miles
Where the sotol weave and shimmer in the sun –
Like a horde of rearing serpents swaying down the bare defiles
When the scarlet, silver webs of dawn are spun.

There are little 'dobe ranchoes brooding far along the sky,
On the sullen dreary bosoms of the hills;
Not a wolf to break the quiet, not a desert bird to fly
Where the silence is so utter that it thrills.

With an eery sense of vastness, with a curious sense of age,
And the ghosts of eons gone uprear and glide
Like a horde of drifting shadows gleaming through the wilted sage –
They are riding where of old they used to ride.

Muleteer and caballero, with their plunder and their slaves –
Oh, the clink of ghostly stirrups in the morn!
Oh, the soundless flying clatter of the feathered, painted braves,
Oh, the echo of the spur and hoof and horn.

Maybe, in the heat of evening, comes a wind from Mexico
Laden with the heat of seven hells,
And the rattler in the yucca and the buzzard dark and slow
Hear and understand the grisly tales it tells.

Gaunt and stark and bare and mocking rise the everlasting cliffs
Like a row of sullen giants hewn of stone,
Till the traveler, mazed with silence, thinks to look on hieroglyphs,
Thinks to see a carven Pharaoh on his throne.

The Grim Land

Once these sullen hills were beaches and they saw the ocean flee
In the misty ages never known of men,
And they wait in brooding silence till the everlasting sea
Comes foaming forth to claim her own again.

"The Black Stranger" was finally published as Howard intended in *Echoes of Valor*, edited by Karl Edward Wagner, New York: Tor Books, 1987. The text for the story's appearance in this collection has been taken from Howard's typescript.

"Marchers of Valhalla" was first published in *Marchers of Valhalla*, West Kingston RI: Donald M. Grant, 1972.

"The Gods of Bal-Sagoth" first appeared in *Weird Tales*, October 1931.

"Nekht Semerkeht" was first published as a composite draft completed by Andrew J. Offutt in *Swords Against Darkness*, New York: Zebra, 1977. The text for the story's appearance in this collection has been taken from Howard's typescripts for the first and second drafts.

"Black Vulmea's Vengeance" first appeared in *Golden Fleece*, November 1938.

"The Strange Case of Josiah Wilbarger" first appeared in *The West*, September 1967.

"The Valley of the Lost" was first published as "Secret of Lost Valley" in *Startling Mystery Stories*, Spring 1967. The text for the story in this collection is taken from Howard's typescript.

"Kelly the Conjure-Man" first appeared in *The Howard Collector* #5, Summer 1964.

"Black Canaan" first appeared in *Weird Tales*, June 1936.

"Pigeons from Hell" first appeared in *Weird Tales*, May 1938.

"Old Garfield's Heart" first appeared in *Weird Tales*, December 1933.

"The Horror from the Mound" first appeared in *Weird Tales*, May 1932.

"The Thunder-Rider" was first published in *Marchers of Valhalla*, West Kingston RI: Donald M. Grant, 1972. The text for the story's appearance in this collection was taken from the typescript of Howard's first draft; unfortunately, what was becoming an intriguing second draft breaks off suddenly.

The excerpts presented in this collection as "The Classic Tale of the Southwest" are taken from letters to August Derleth and H. P. Lovecraft.

"The Grim Land" first appeared in *The Grim Land and Others*, Lamoni IA: Stygian Isle Press, 1976.

THE WORKS OF ROBERT E. HOWARD

Boxing Stories
Edited and with an introduction by Chris Gruber

The Black Stranger and Other American Tales
Edited and with an introduction by Steven Tompkins

The End of the Trail: Western Stories
Edited and with an introduction by Rusty Burke

Lord of Samarcand and Other Adventure Tales of the Old Orient
Edited by Rusty Burke
Introduction by Patrice Louinet

The Riot at Bucksnort and Other Western Tales
Edited and with an introduction by David Gentzel